Callisto

Torsten Krol is a writer.
Nothing further is known about him.

Callisto

Torsten Krol

Atlantic Books
LONDON

First published in Australia in 2007 by Picador, an imprint
of Pan Macmillan Australia Pty Limited, Sydney.

First published in trade paperback in Great Britain in 2007
by Atlantic Books, an imprint of Grove Atlantic Ltd.

This paperback edition published in Great Britain in 2008
by Atlantic Books.

1 3 5 7 9 8 6 4 2

A CIP catalogue record for this book is
available from the British Library.

ISBN: 978 1 84354 576 7

Printed in the UK by CPI Bookmarque, Croydon, CR0 4TD

Atlantic Books
An imprint of Grove Atlantic Ltd
Ormond House
26–27 Boswell Street
London
WC1N 3JZ

www.groveatlantic.co.uk

Callisto

ONE

My name is Odell Deefus. I am a white person, not black like you might think from hearing the name and not seeing me. If you did see me, you wouldn't remember me for my face, which isn't the kind to stick in anyone's mind, but you might remember me for being tall. I am six-three, which makes women attracted to me, then they find out I don't talk the kind of talk they like to hear, so there goes the romance before it even started. You have to be able to talk to get anywhere. Me, I have to think awhile before I talk, but in the meantime the conversation has moved on, as they say, so forget that. I have had this difficulty all my life, with bad consequences.

I will be twenty-two years old on November 21, 2007. I will not be here then because I am riding this bus to somewhere else away from here. So far I have not said a single word to any of the other passengers. They are all asleep right now as we go speeding through the night. They most likely think I'm a tall dumb hick but they would be wrong about that. I know this because I have read *The Yearling* sixteen times now, and that is a Pulitzer Prize book which you can't be dumb and be able to read it. I have tried three other books to read but they did not satisfy like *The Yearling*. If you have not read the story, it's about a boy that adopts a fawn after its mother gets shot in the woods, and he raises it to be his pet like a dog, only it all goes bad when the fawn gets to be a year old and is a big nuisance around the place, eating the corn crop and so forth, so in the end it has to be shot, which always wets my eyelashes it's so sad. Which is more proof I am not dumb, because a dumb person would not feel all that emotion.

I am writing this on the bus in a school exercise book with lined paper in it and the Little Mermaid on the cover. I got a bunch of these because I have got a long story to tell. There is the Lion King and the Incredibles, the whole family, and there is Nemo and Friends plus Shrek and his buddy the donkey that talks, also everyone from *Toy Story*. I would've got plain covers but the store only had the cartoon kind. There is a little light bulb over my seat to do the writing by. I have got the urge to write it all down, the things that happened to me, while everyone else is asleep, write it all down before something else happens to me. I will figure out later what to do with the story, maybe send it to the *New York Times*, which is the way true things get told no matter if someone wants the story not to get told. They will not stop me or the *NY Times* either.

Okay then.

A little while back I'm driving across Kansas in a '78 Chevy

Monte Carlo with an engine that sounded like it's driving piles into a riverbed. I was on my way to sign up for the Army now that they want people so bad they don't care all that much if you don't have that high school graduation certificate, which I don't, but not because of stupidity. I was not in the best frame of mind that last year of school, resulting in a bad consequence of not graduating, which was something I didn't care about at the time. But later on I did when the best job I could get was working in a grain elevator. I almost got killed in that job, low paid and dangerous with all that wheat thundering into silos two hundred foot tall. The Army wanted enlistees bad since the war in Iraq made guys quit signing up for enlistment. They even paid a bonus now, I heard, so that was the plan, get enlisted and collect that bonus and try my hardest to be a good soldier against the mad dog Islamites over there exploding everything they could get their hands on including their own people. I am not a blood-thirsty person, but that kind of craziness has got to stop right now. I was not a big success in the world yet, but maybe I would be if I could get some combat medals to show.

There was an enlistment office in Callisto, over there in Callisto County, so that was the direction I went, holding to a steady seventy miles per hour which the Chevy's engine operated best at. I had less than forty miles to go when it started sounding real bad, like it's about to throw a rod or something, so I had to slow down or risk the whole thing going up in smoke. You can't drive slow on the interstate highway, so I got off and went real slow and careful along the back roads, not sure exactly where I was but heading in the right direction for enlistment. Then the engine went all ragged and quit on me, so I had to pull over and shut it down. I sat there awhile watching dust blow past, then I got out and raised the hood. Everything under there was all plugged in, nothing I could see disconnected or out of place, not that I'm a mechanical expert. So the problem was somewhere inside the block, most likely an old-age problem with the odometer reading ninety-eight thousand miles, its second go-round after clocking up that first hundred thou. The engine was ticking like a time bomb, blasting heat and oil stench up at me, so I backed away, thinking maybe if I let it cool down it'll be okay for later on. It was around midafternoon by then and I'd been driving most of the day, so I was ready for a break in any case.

There was nothing around to look at, Callisto County being flat and empty like most of Kansas except over in the east where they have got itty-bitty hills to look at. I leaned against the door and looked at the horizon a long ways off, not letting myself get mad about the engine quitting that way. It never does a bit of good to get mad about stuff like that, it's just a waste of time. You see some guys yelling at their car, even kicking it if they're pissed enough, but it never makes a bit of difference to the problem, so why waste your energy. Besides, this has happened before, so I am used to it. I'm thinking when I get out of the Army the first thing I'll get with my wages is a car with less than fifty thou on it and no problems yet.

It was hot in the sun with hardly no cloud cover at all, so I got in the back seat and opened my suitcase which had pretty near everything I owned in it, which just goes to show the sad state into which my life had fallen thus far. A life should not be able to fit in a single suitcase that way. There was some clothes that needed the attention of a laundromat and a quarter-empty bottle of Captain Morgan which I'm partial to and my copy of *The Yearling*, getting split pretty bad along the binding I had it so long now. I studied the Captain in his pirate outfit for a long time, asking myself if I should take a shot or save it for later, being that I only had about twenty-five dollars in my jeans. They better take me on for the Army or I was screwed, financially speaking. In the end I put the bottle down, feeling strong and sensible about it, and picked up the book instead. I have this philosophy – if you have got the choice between picking up a bottle and picking up a book, pick up the book. It is almost always the correct and sensible thing to do. There are some that live by the bottle or else they smoke dope like they can't get enough, and this behavior is a distraction from real life. That was not my way and never would be. That's why I was confident they would pass me for the physical and not worry overmuch about the high school graduation certificate. What does shooting mad-dog Islamites have to do with anything you learned in school anyway?

I started in to read, passing the time. I was at the scene where the boy, Jody, goes to visit his crippled friend, Fodderwing, to say how-do. I have looked at titty magazines and car and gun magazines and there is no satisfaction in them for a mind that craves a story. You might say that I go through *The Yearling* the way some folk with religion go through the Bible, from front to back and start all over again. There is something new to discover every time, I have found.

One time a person I was acquainted with who was not a friend started in making fun of me for reading that book. He said it was a book for little kids because it had a picture on the front of Jody with the fawn in his arms. I told him it was a Pulitzer Prize book, it said so right there under Jody and the fawn, but he wouldn't let up, kept on making these comments about how you'd have to be retarded to be reading a kid's book like that, probably he never even heard of the Pulitzer Prize, so in the end I had to set the book down and teach him a lesson. I am not often that way, getting violent, I mean, but he asked for it the way he was talking. I am tall like I said, but I am no skinny beanpole to be pushed around. This fool that was poking fun was no small person either, but I got the better of him all right with only a grazed cheekbone and knuckles to show for winning the argument. Sometimes things just have to be settled that way. It is not the way I prefer, but there is sometimes no choice in the matter and you have to stand up and do what's right or else get laughed at.

That happened back at my school, Kit Carson High in Yoder, Wyoming. I was held to blame and had to spend three days in suspension for it even though it was not my fault what happened. This is one reason I did not do well in school, resulting in no certificate and a string of jobs like the one at the grain silo, but the US Army would change all that, I hoped.

So I started to read, but then got so hot even with the windows rolled down I couldn't concentrate and had to put the book aside and napped for a short time, maybe an hour. I woke up feeling thirsty, but not for Captain Morgan, more like an ice-cold Coke. Not one vehicle had gone by in that time, so it looked like rescue was not coming down the road anytime soon. I tried starting the engine. It caught and I got rolling again, only the car sounded no better than before. I kept the speed down and limped along that way exactly thirty-seven minutes and then it died on me same as before, only this time fate was kind and I come to a stop a few yards from someone's front gate, only there was no gate, only fence posts either side of where a gate ought to be and a long curving dirt driveway leading to a farmhouse set way back from the road, the only one in those parts, real isolated.

I started up that driveway on foot. It was in a neglected state with a washout halfway along where the land dipped a little and you could see the spring rains runoff had done damage there. I was expecting a dog or three to come running at me like they always do from a farmhouse yard, but there was no dogs at all. It was a ramshackle place, neglected like the driveway, a two-story clapboard house with a porch on three sides, all badly in need of paint with a flaking propane tank alongside like a midget submarine. You can see places like this all across the plains states, a few big old shade trees overhanging it and liable to cause damage to the roof next time a twister comes through, and a big old barn with a beat-up Dodge pickup parked inside.

I went up some sagging steps to the porch and knocked on the screen door. The front door was open so I could see down the long hallway. There wasn't a sound coming from inside except a steady ticking from an old grandfather clock big as a coffin stood on its end halfway along the hall. I knocked again and called out, "Hello? Anyone home?" Well, there wasn't. I knocked a little louder with no result and Helloed some more, louder than before, only it brought no result still. They were all away someplace else and were the kind that leaves their door open with no fear of thieves. There are still country folk like that, but their numbers are getting dwindled real fast what with criminality being everywhere nowadays like it is.

I was thirstier now than before. Maybe there was a tap in the yard but I couldn't see it. I wanted water, which is a free commodity and not like stealing, even if I had to take it from the kitchen and not from the yard. So I opened the door, calling out again, and stepped through into the house. There was that old farmhouse smell from the cracked linoleum floor and faded wallpaper, all of it needing replacement. The clock ticked away deep and slow, like it was measuring out time from a hundred years ago when everything moved slower than today.

The kitchen was right where I expected it to be. There was mess everywhere along the counters and the sink was crammed with dirty dishes. This was not a proud household. I could smell rotten food somewhere, the old-fashioned pantry maybe, or the trash bin that needed emptying. Someone needed to go through that place with a bucket and mop and a scrub brush too, but that was none of my business how people choose to live. There was a swivel tap over the sink and I already saw glasses standing like troopers on parade on the overhead shelf. That shelf needed cleaning too. I would not have allowed that kind of grime if it was my place. I took down a glass and filled it, then drunk it all in one long swallow, then filled it again for a more leisurely drink.

"Put it down," says a voice behind me. It was not a scared voice, not angry either the way you might expect seeing as I wasn't invited. I turned nice and slow with the glass still in my hand. The guy across the kitchen was a little older than me. His T-shirt said *Bad to the Bone – and Proud of It*. He had a baseball bat in his hands. He hadn't shaved in a day or two and there was a kind of twitchiness about him that didn't appeal. If I was a smaller man than I am I would maybe have been a little bit alarmed by him holding the bat like he was. I thought, At least it isn't a gun.

"Afternoon," I said.

"Put it down."

I put the glass on the counter without taking my eyes off of him. His hair was standing out all wild from his head and his eyes were strange. I waited for him to say something else, but he just kept on staring and holding the bat ready to slug me if I made a move towards him.

"I had car trouble," I said to explain myself. "I'm down at the road. I knocked but nobody come. Thank you for the water. I was thirsty."

He still said nothing.

"I'm Odell Deefus, from Wyoming."

"That's a nigger name."

"I knew a black kid in school called Alan White. You can't tell just from a name."

The clock ticked on while he watched me watching him. Then he lowered the bat.

"You can't be too careful," he said, still not relaxed at all, but not jittery and alarmed like he was up till then.

"I knocked, then I figured there's nobody home. I needed that water."

"Go ahead."

I picked up the glass and drunk it down, keeping my eyes

on him but trying to look casual. He was wearing sneakers, so that's why I didn't hear him coming. I set the glass on the counter. "Thank you. I'll be getting back to my car now."

I had to walk past him on my way out of the kitchen. He stepped back a little to let me by. People do that when you're six-three. If I was five-eight he'd still be giving me grief about the water and maybe threatening to call the police, but he was shorter than me by a good six inches and just wanted me out of his house, which is understandable. He followed me down the hall past the grandfather clock, all the way to the screen door.

When I'm on the other side of it he seemed to find some manners at last and says, "Overheated radiator?"

"The car's a junker. Could be anything."

"I'll take a look. I always fixed my own cars."

"Okay."

He leaned his baseball bat against the wall next to the doorway and come outside. We crossed the porch, went down the rickety steps and across the yard to the driveway.

"Hot day to get car trouble," he says.

"I know it. The engine's been sounding bad for three hundred miles. I'm lucky I got this far."

"Where you headed?"

"Callisto. Signing up with Uncle Sam."

"Huh?"

"The Army. They've got a recruiting office there."

"The Army?" He made it sound like something bad.

"I tried other work. It all goes nowhere."

"The Army'll send you to Iraq. You want to go up against those jihadis?"

"Someone has to."

"It's Iraq's business, not ours. They don't need no outside interference. We should keep our nose out of it."

I heard the exact same line many times before. It's what most people were thinking, and I could see why, but when you need to be making decisions about where to go in your life, that kind of argument doesn't stack up so high against serving the nation and making life better for people outside America.

"You're crazy if you do it," he says.

"I want a regular paycheck and a career. That's what they're offering."

"Someone big as you, you should get on a football team. Are you fast?"

"No."

"I bet you could block pretty good, though."

"I never cared for football that much."

It's true, I never did join the team in school, even when the coach kept on at me to be part of something proud. It's hard to be proud of something when you're from Yoder, Wyoming, population 2774. And my old man, he wanted me to be on the team so he could have something to brag about. Maybe I didn't want to do it because of that. Me and the old man never did see eye to eye about a single thing, which is why I left home after school was all over and done with. He told me good riddance, said those very words to me. It hurt when he told me that, but I never did let it show. I paid him back by leaving without saying another word, just got on a bus down to Colorado and worked there awhile in a Denver car wash with a bunch of drop-outs going nowhere. I have never once sent a letter home to him or called on the phone. If my mother was still alive I would have, but not for him, that washed-up son of a bitch. He had no call to look down on me. All he ever was, after he got busted out of the police force down in Cheyenne for reasons he never disclosed, was come home to Yoder and work at the gas station out on the interstate ringing up change. Some big achievement.

We got to the car and he looked under the hood, then said to turn the ignition. The engine rattled to life, then quit again, then restarted. "Sounds like shit," he said. "Why don't you drive it on up to the barn. I can't work on it out in this sun."

"Okay."

I kept it firing all the way up the driveway to the yard, where it quit again. He come walking up behind me, shaking his head. Together we pushed it inside the barn next to his truck. On the Dodge's door it said *Dean's Lawnmowing* with a telephone number.

"That you?"

"That's me, Dean Lowry. Get the hood up again."

He got a set of tools and started poking around in the engine bay, every now and then telling me to start it up, which it never did. After about twenty minutes he says, "I can't see where the problem is. You might need a complete overhaul on something old as this, engine rebuild, the works. Probably cost you more than the car's worth. What'd you pay for it?"

"Seven hundred."

"Hey, take it to the scrapyard and they'll give you fifty bucks for the parts, that's my advice to you."

"Getting it there's the problem."

I looked at the rear of his truck and saw the towbar. He saw me looking and says, "I'll haul you in tomorrow, it's too late today."

"Thanks, Dean."

When you use someone's name for the first time it changes things between you, breaks the ice. Frankly, I wanted him to like me enough to let me stay overnight. There was nowhere else for me to go with a dead car anyway. We both looked at the Monte Carlo, him with contempt, me with something like shame, both of us wondering where to steer the relationship next. Finally he says, "Nothing more we can do here. Come on in the house. Did you eat today?"

"Pancakes for breakfast at Denny's."

"I hate to cook, but you can help yourself to whatever's in the kitchen."

"I'll do that, thank you."

"Better bring your stuff inside, you aren't going nowhere else today."

A little later I'm breaking eggs and chopping ham with Dean sitting backwards in a chair watching me. "You want some of this?" I offered. "I make a pretty good omelet."

"I don't eat pigmeat. I quit that."

"Just plain then."

He shook his head and put a cigarette in his mouth. "These are the next things to go, and beer. There's a sixpack in the fridge if you want it."

"You on a health diet?"

"You might say that." He flicked a lighter and squinted at me through blown smoke. I concentrated on the pan, flipping the eggs around and feeling hunger clutch at my guts when the smell got to me. When it was done I dished up and sat opposite him at the kitchen table to eat. He watched me wolf it down like I'm a starving man.

"Someone your size, you must need a big food intake."

"Just average." I munched and swallowed and felt bliss rush through me. There is nothing like hunger to make you appreciate being alive to satisfy it. All of a sudden I liked Dean more than before, even if I didn't appreciate him blowing smoke across the table. Me, I have never smoked, never wanted to.

"You live here alone?"

"Yeah, except for my aunt. This is her place."

"She's not around today?"

"Nope, she went visiting."

"Callisto?"

"Florida. She'll be there awhile."

Florida is where *The Yearling* is set, back in the swamp and piney woods. I felt a little bit envious. "Is she taking in the wild woods while she's there?"

"She'd only get her ass bit by gators. She likes the beach when she visits. Fort Lauderdale, Miami, places like that with airconditioning, that's what she likes."

I finished the omelet and wished I'd made a bigger one. The beer sounded good. "Okay for a brew?"

"Help yourself."

I got one out of the fridge and sat down again. He watched me pop the cap and start drinking, then he got up and fetched one himself. So much for the health diet.

"I'll quit tomorrow," he said, winking. I laughed at that. He wasn't such a bad guy. We could get along until I was out of his hair and signed up for the Army. He blew a crooked smoke ring and admired it. "So," he says, "you want to go kill Muslims."

"I just want a steady job. They're not so easy to come by without a graduation certificate."

"You've got to have one of those to get in the Army."

"No, they're desperate for enlistees, so you just have to sit for a simple test, I heard, to show you're not a moron."

"Well, you look the part anyway. They'll make you a recruiter maybe."

"That'd suit me fine."

"So you don't care about the Muslims and all that shit over there?"

"We started it, so now we have to finish the job, that's how I see it."

"But you know we never should've started it."

"Everyone knows that."

"Except Bush."

"I bet he knows it, only he can't say so out loud."

"Somebody should kill that guy," he says, which is treasonous talk nowadays, especially to say to a stranger. "But then we'd get the other guy, the VP with his fingers in the war machine and big oil. Fuck the whole bunch is what I say. Every time they open their mouths another turd flops out. You can't trust a damn thing they say, not anymore."

He was probably right. Me, I've never trusted politicians in the first place, war or no war, but I didn't want to get into any political argument with Dean. I was under his roof, eating his food, and tomorrow his truck would tow my Chevy to the junkyard. I lifted the beer. "Victory in Iraq," I said, sounding kind of dumb but not caring about that with food and beer inside me.

"Whatever," says Dean, kind of sneering.

Keeping a line of conversation open has always been a big problem for me, as indicated previously, but I wanted Dean to keep talking so the rest of the day would pass easy and friendly. That is always preferable to silences and strain when nobody talks.

"You make a good living with the lawnmowing?" I asked.

"I get by. Got customers five days a week wanting my services. Today's Sunday so I got no customers."

Dean took a swig from his bottle. He was watching me close, trying to figure me out the way people do once they get over my tallness and the way my shoulders like to split my shirt sometimes, like when The Hulk gets mad about something and turns big and green. I have actually done that, split my shirt, but only an old shirt that was washed a thousand times and the material was weak. I am not bragging about this, only telling. Dean was trying to make up his mind if I'm dumb or not. People do that so I am used to it.

"Anyway," he said, "it's shut down."

"What is?"

"The recruiting office. They shut it down a year ago when nobody wanted to go over there and die for a bunch of people that don't even want us there."

"No, they're offering a bonus, I saw it on the news."

"Maybe in some other town. They shut the Callisto office down.

"Well, I need to see that for myself. That's bad news if it's true. My car, it won't take me to some other town."

"Take the bus."

That would burn up the fifty I expected to get for the Chevy at the junkyard. I have never minded overmuch about not being rich, so long as there is enough cash in my pocket for what I need right this minute and never mind next week, which will take care of itself when the time comes. I have always got by with this philosophy, what they call a working philosophy. It worked so far, so I put worry from my mind until tomorrow.

Dean got two more beers from the fridge and we popped them. Today had worked out okay after all, despite car trouble and now this about the recruiting office shutting down. Dean was looking more relaxed with the second beer inside of him and making a decision he could tolerate me. You can always feel when this point is reached with someone, it just kind of passes between you by way of invisible words.

I began to like Dean a little. He had more than me, a house to live in with his aunt, who was company for him around the place, and he had his own small business with the lawn-mowing, but I could tell he was not a satisfied person with his lot in life, just something in his eyes and his twitchy way of shifting around on the chair. I could tell he was wondering what it would be like to be me, tall and big across the shoulders and a free bird able to go just about anywhere I pleased, money or no money. He wanted that, I could tell just by looking, and then I saw that he knew I knew, and his face clouded over. I would have to tread careful with this guy because he was more complicated than you might think, but then the same could be said about me, I guess.

"You don't want to be going over there," he said, stabbing a finger at me. Dean was a little bit drunk already, being on the smallish side for alcohol consumption per body weight. "They got their own way of looking at things and their own religion. I know because I read some books about it. They got their own Bible called the Koran with a lot of wisdom inside of it. Nobody reads it, though, over here. That's why they don't like us, because we never made the effort to try. You can understand the way they feel. They might even be better people than us, did you ever think about that?"

"Yeah, I thought about it," I said, more to please him than to speak the truth, because I don't believe one bunch is better than another bunch regardless. People are people all over, the same old mishmash of good and bad and smart and dumb etcetera, whatever language they talk, that's my honest opinion. I would still prefer to live in America than any other place, though, so I guess I am a patriot. I wasn't so sure about Dean, though, the way he talked. But that could just be the beer, so I decided to take no offense.

"Anyway," he said, swigging another mouthful, "nobody gives a goddamn what I think or you think or anyone that isn't a powerful rich person thinks. We're just dirt beneath their wheels."

"Got that right," I said, and he did too. The rich and power-ful ones own the planet, but I have never bothered to hate them for it because firstly it is a complete waste of time and emotion to be hating them, because they don't even feel your hatred, it just bounces off of them like raindrops they don't even feel, that's the true fact of the matter. And another thing about why I don't hate them is they don't even know I exist, which is a kind of protection for me. I know who they are because their names and faces and what they think and decide are on the TV for everyone to see, but not me, nossir, I'm not anywhere they can reach me or even know I'm alive, so how can they hurt me? They can't, just like I can't hurt a mouse that's behind the wall because I don't even know it's there living its little mousey life regardless.

We drank our way through those second beers, then Dean got a troubled look on his face. "There's one more apiece, only it's the last liquor I got in the house."

"No problem, there's a three-quarters bottle of rum in my car."

I said bottle, but really it's one of those big flagons with the glass handle for easy carrying. His eyes lit up and he smiled for the first time since I met him. He had got these crooked teeth, so smiling for Dean was not something that made you think him handsomer for it, but even so it's better to see someone smile than not, because a smiling person is easier to deal with, I have found.

"No shit," he says. "Go get it, man."

So I did that, and pretty soon we're watching the sun slide down the sky from the rocker on the porch with little shot glasses of Captain Morgan in our hands. My glass had gold around the rim and said *Souvenir of Kansas City* on it, and Dean's had *Colorado Springs* on it, so someone in the family had been outside of Callisto County sometime. Dean liked the Captain and I told him it's the special Caribbean spices makes it taste so good, a real pirate's drink I kidded him. By the time it started getting dark across the yard we were trading life experiences and so forth, hard luck stories if you want the truth, with family problems and lousy fathers and that kind of thing, but we weren't pissing and moaning about it, no, we made it all sound funny as hell with all the misfunctional bits the funniest part. By the time it's night and we could see fireflies flitting around under the trees Dean and me were like old buddies that grew up together on the same street almost.

Drinking makes you hungry after a while, so I offered to make us more omelets or maybe French toast because I saw he's got a loaf of sliced bread in the kitchen, but Dean says forget that, he's got a whole freezer down in the basement full of frozen dinners which he says Aunt Bree buys by the trolleyload whenever they're on special for the discount prices. He went down and got us a couple TV dinners with roast beef and potato croquettes and peas and gravy, a complete meal and easy made in the microwave or oven, either one, but he's got no microwave so it took a little longer waiting for them to cook. Those TV dinners were the best, Dean said, and the best part was you don't even have to eat them watching TV to appreciate the taste. That got us both laughing like maniacs ho ho ho, pretty drunk by then I have to admit, but that is no crime except when driving a vehicle.

We were drinking five or six hours before the Captain Morgan bottle stood empty on the kitchen table, both of us very snookered by then, especially Dean with his smaller weight affecting the outcome. He says to me, "Okay, thassit, bro, I'm headin' for the barn..." Only that wasn't where he's headed, of course, being a figurine of speech, no, he's headed for bed, which he forgot to tell me where mine is, and I had to snoop around upstairs to locate another one. But there's only a second bed in a room that's obviously a woman's room with lacy bedcovers and whatnot and feminine things on the dresser so it's his Aunt Bree's room where

I had no right to be. Back downstairs I went, almost tumbling over my legs doing it, craving sleep now like a drug, and dived onto the living room sofa which was plenty soft enough for me, believe it.

T W O

It has been said that youth suffers less the morning after a bout of drinking, but this is a lie. I woke up with an axe buried between my ears and for a minute did not even know where I am. Then the old-fashioned high ceiling swum into view and I recollected it's Dean's place where I am at. I sat upright and moaned out loud, that's how bad I'm feeling, and only after I thought about it a long time could I get on my feet and go through to the kitchen for a glass of water followed by two more of the same, which gave some small relief from all that pounding inside my skull.

The TV dinner trays were on the table like giant scrunched-up silver cockroaches. Just thinking about food made me feel sick so I turned away and went outside, which was a mistake because of the early morning brightness waiting out there. I tolerated it long enough to take an everlasting evil yellow piss in the yard, then I felt my way back inside to the sofa and lay down on it again, regretting I ever left it in the first place.

That was my first awakening. The second one happened a few hours later and was not so painful. What woke me this time was the sound of Dean clumping downstairs one slow step at a time he's so hung over. He eased himself into the kitchen and sat down at the table, then let his head fall into his hands while he moaned. I got him a glass of water and set it down in front of him but he took no notice, just kept right on moaning and groaning, truly pitiful. "You should drink that, Dean," I told him, but he couldn't speak back to me at all, no way. After awhile I noticed the grandfather clock striking the hour, but I couldn't keep a straight count so I had to go over and stare at it close up to read the time. Then I said, "Dean, it's nine o'clock. Didn't you say you had business to do today, lawns to mow, huh?"

"Fuck it..." he croaks. He still hadn't touched the water. He looked bad, his face all shriveled up like an old man at death's door. I saw for the first time that he was already starting to lose his hair on top, the way he was slumped over the table. I felt sorry for him. It was my booze that did this so I am partway responsible for his terrible condition, so you could say that it was guilt and nothing more that made me offer to mow his lawns that day while he rested up and pulled himself together. I had to make the offer twice before he understood, and it was not till after I made coffee for us both that he said okay, go do it if I wanted, the schedule was on the dashboard and there's a Callisto street map in the glove box. I hadn't really been expecting him to take up the offer, frankly, but that's okay because I needed distraction from my own head, still thudding along nicely like a pile-driver.

"Keys are on the hook..." he says, pointing to the wall. I took them down. The tag had a skull and crossbones sunk in clear plastic. I went out to the barn. There's two lawnmowers in the back of the truck already, with mulching or non-mulching abilities, plus cans of gas and a weed whacker so I'm all set, apart from the pounding head. I got in the cab and started her up. Dean is the kind of driver that never cleans the cab out so there's all kinds of trash in there, most of it fast-food containers and cups and so forth all drifting around on the floor, so much of it you couldn't hardly see the rubber mats. The Dodge was an older model but the engine sounded good. I backed out and headed down the drive in low gear. There was a pair of fancy teardrop sunglasses on the dash so I put them on to ease my pain. Out on the road I turned left and headed for Callisto.

Along the way I stopped at International House of Pancakes for a breakfast I knew I'd appreciate later in the morning even if I had to shove it down myself right now. I had the blueberry waffles with cream and an orange juice. The food started making me feel better directly. I had brung in Dean's schedule and map from the truck and soon figured out it's a week by week setup, meaning most of his regular customers had him stop by and cut their lawns every other week or else just once a month. I pretty soon worked out which job was where, with the first one starting at ten, so I had to finish eating and get moving again, feeling much better now on account of eating a healthy breakfast.

1123 Tarrant Street, that was the first job. I found it and

parked and wrestled one of the mowers down. The lawn looked okay to me, not what I would have bothered mowing if it was mine, but people with money want their lawn looking just right all the time and are prepared to pay for it if they can't do it themselves because of old age or bad health or whatever. It was no surprise when a silver-haired old lady very nicely dressed come out and wanted to know where's Dean. I told her he was sick today and I'm taking his place and did she want me to start on the back or the front lawn. She didn't care so I started at the front and worked my way around to the rear, which took about an hour. The schedule had the prices for each customer marked next to the address, usually forty or fifty dollars depending on the lawn size, so when I was done and the mower loaded back onto the truck I knew how much to expect when I knocked at the door. The silver-haired lady come out and paid me forty dollars and said she hopes Dean gets better soon, which I said I would pass it on.

That first job pretty much set the tone for the five other jobs listed for Monday. It said in the schedule if each customer wanted the clippings blasted directly back into the lawn or collected in the grasscatcher for taking away in the big plastic bags Dean kept stored in the truck. The day went like clockwork, pretty much all walking in squares and curves for the amount of time it took. And then the payment, most of it in cash but one old fart says he only pays by check because you can't be sure "unscrupulous types" aren't under-reporting their income to the taxman, which is bad for the democratic system we have got here in the USA. He practically called me a conman, but the strange part is he never asked like the others did about where's Dean, just handed me the check like it's printed on gold leaf or something.

I stopped for lunch at McDonald's and had two burgers because I'm truly hungry by then from all that walking around behind the mower under a hot sun. My head got hot, and the back of my neck started to burn from all that sunlight pouring down from above. There was an old baseball cap of Dean's in the truck but it was filthy dirty and I have never wanted to wear someone else's cap nor their underpants neither. And I was not prepared in the clothing department for lawnmowing and got very hot and sweaty in jeans and shirt that I already wore all day yesterday and last night. It's a good thing lawnmowing is outdoor work because I stunk very bad by the end of the afternoon and was headed back to Dean's with takeout Chinese for us both, which I bet he didn't have in the basement freezer.

I had over three hundred dollars and a check in my pocket, and a feeling I had done a good job that day. This feeling was not there at the end of a working day at those other shit jobs like the grain elevator, so this was a new feeling. Maybe it wasn't so much the job itself, I mean how can mowing lawns all day be interesting, but the fact that I did it to help out a friend. That's how I was thinking about Dean, in terms of friendship even if we only knew each other for a single afternoon and night and a few minutes this morning. So that was a different feeling also.

Dean was on the porch rocker smoking a cigarette when I drove up and parked in the barn. He looked worn out and dirty like he'd been the one hard at work all day and not me. He still looked kind of sick too, so I asked if he's okay. "I'm fine," he says, not sounding too friendly. I showed him the takeouts and his face brightened. I sat next to him on the rocker and we ate them up right then and there. The food worked on him the way I hoped and he thanked me for helping out with the mowing. He counted the cash and peeled off a hundred for me.

"No charge," I told him. "Room and board all accounted for."

"Bullshit, you're taking it."

Which I did, not wanting to provoke an argument between friends. He lit a fresh smoke and we sat without talking for awhile. It was not like last night when the both of us were liquored up and talkative. Now he was quiet and played out. I told him about the old fart tax freak. "The others were okay, just handed over the cash."

"Yeah, they even give me a tip sometimes. Did anyone do that?"

"Nope."

He gave me a long look, like he's doubting me. This made me uncomfortable but I did not show it, and he looked away. Just his doing that made me remember I'll be leaving tomorrow. Dean would tow my car to the junkyard and that would be that. I hadn't had time today to check if the enlistment office was still there in town or not, but there would be time enough for that tomorrow after the Monte Carlo got disposed of. I was determined to overlook Dean's character shortcomings so the rest of the evening would proceed smooth, even if we had no liquor now to do the smoothing. The friendship was already over if you cared to think about it that way.

"I've got five bags of lawn clippings. Where do I dump them, around back?"

"No! Stay out of there. Dump it over that way," he says, pointing. "You'll see the pile. Mostly it blows away after awhile. Don't take any of it around back."

"Okay, I'm only asking."

"I saw a rattlesnake back there today. You don't want to mess with those fuckers."

"Got it."

I went to drag the bags away from the Dodge and empty them where he said. The job could have waited, but it was already late in the day and also I felt uncomfortable being near Dean now. He had gone all twitchy on me again. He didn't offer to help with the dumping, just stayed on the porch smoking another cigarette.

When it was done I went back to the house. He had already went inside and was staring at the clock tick-tocking all solemn and serene in the hall, watching it like he's waiting for a cuckoo to pop out, but it isn't that kind of clock. I went upstairs to the bathroom to take a shower and got into the last of my clean clothes from the suitcase then come down again where Dean is sat in front of the TV watching after-school cartoon shows before the news starts. He sat there so quiet and distracted I wondered if maybe he's on drugs, which would be bad news because most of those drugtaker types are creepy to be around unless you're a doper too, which I have already said I am not. So the evening was not shaping up too good.

When the news come on Dean tried to find more cartoons, but they're all finished so now he had to choose

between news and game shows with lots of screaming con-
testants peeing their pants over the dishwasher and TV and
brand new coupe. He settled for news. The lead item was the
election next year and who all will be running against who.
Bush is a second-term lame duck that won't be running again
and the Veep is bowing out on medical grounds after more
heart trouble plus there was that quail-shooting thing that
happened, so now the big contender for the Republicans is
looking like it'll be Senator Ketchum. He's one of those guys
born to be a politician, rich man son of a rich man that
jumped into the Washington pool young and never left it.
He's got a full head of graying hair that makes him look like a
judge or something noble and wise, plus this profile like they
have on old statues, all nose and jutting chin. He looks like a
leader is what he looks like, which is already half the game
won. His voice was a big asset too, very deep and friendly
sounding. The senator is running on a ticket torn from Bush's
game plan, keeping up the tight security we have got every-
place now and not dropping the ball so Al Kayda could do
another sneak attack and destroy American lives. When
Senator Ketchum spoke about guarding our shores and making the world safer for Freedom and Democracy it sounded
more true than some other guy could make it.

"Someone oughta shoot that prick," says Dean.

"Why?"

"So he'd be dead and I wouldn't have to watch him spout
bullshit from now till November next year."

"He's no worse than the rest."

"You think so? What's that say about the rest of 'em?"

I shrugged. "Beats me."

"You're some deep thinker, Odell."

"I don't much care for politics."

"That's good, because you don't know what's going on. You're in the dark, my friend. That's where most people are, in the dark. They got that way by sticking their heads so far up their asses they think it's midnight."

"I don't think most folks are like that."

"Shit, you're exactly perfect to go vote then."

"How do you mean?"

"I mean...Aah, forget it."

That kind of sarcastic talk is a real irritation to me. I hate it when someone like Dean talks to me like I'm a fool that can't understand the meaning of what he's saying, especially when the one doing the talking isn't one bit smarter than me, which I could tell Dean was not, no way. But saying nothing is better than getting into a big stupid argument over something so dumb as politics, so I let it go.

There was discomfort in the room now on account of Dean's bad behavior, which got covered over by noise and light spilling from the TV. I said to Dean in the commercial break, "Okay if I wash some clothes in the machine?"

"Help yourself."

I brung my dirty duds down to the laundry and put them in the tub on top of a shirt and pants Dean already put in there but forgot to wash. They were real dirty like he'd been doing yard work or something, only the house yard showed he wasn't the home and garden kind, more like the kind that does diddly to keep things spick and span outdoors for the sake of appearances and real estate value. Dean was a lazy guy, I'd already made my decision on that, and it was one more reason not to have regret over the friendship going nowhere. I added soap powder and shut the lid, then had to figure out the buttons. That didn't take long and soon there's water rushing into the machine.

The laundry was at the back of the house, with its own door to the back yard where the clothesline was. I already had enough of sitting with Dean in front of the TV so I went out that door just to see the sun starting to go down and get some air that didn't have cigarette smoke mixed all through it. The clothesline was the rotatory kind, sagging to the left a little but you could still use it. I wandered over and gave it a twirl that made the central column squeak and complain.

That was interesting for about five seconds, then I moved on to the chicken coop. It was the kind without a floor that you can pick up with two people and move someplace else so you could fertilize different patches of the yard. Most folk don't have chickens nowadays, they just get their eggs and drumsticks too from the supermarket. There was maybe nine or ten chickens scratching around on the loose and a couple more inside the coop where I guess they headed when the sun got low.

Then I saw there's a mound of dirt behind the coop and walked around to look at it, thinking this must be what Dean got his clothes all dirty shoveling. It was a fair-sized pile and next to it there's a hole. Not a round hole and not a square hole neither. A long hole, like for a coffin burial. I had to look inside, like anyone would, but there's no corpse or coffin inside, just a long deep empty hole ready and waiting for a body. It couldn't be for anything else, not that shape, that deep. A graveyard hole, that's what Dean dug today, only who was it for? He didn't want me coming back there, said it was dangerous because he saw a rattler, but he never did see any such thing, no, he wanted me not to see this hole is the reason.

Now I am not a cowardly person, very few men that's six-three is that kind, but I will admit that standing over the graveyard hole I felt a kind of shiver all over. It puckered up my skin even if the air's still warm. Dean, he never wanted me to see that hole because he's got the intention of putting me inside of it. It was plain to see that was his plan, only not so easy to figure out why. What did I do to him that he needed to plan my death and burying this way? He was not a big man so he used all day to dig that hole while I'm out there mowing lawns and keeping his customers happy. No wonder he gave me a hundred bucks, he's only going to take it back out of my pocket after he murders me.

That made me good and mad I don't mind admitting. The two-faced way he did things was a lesson in human nature, which is unpredictable at the best of times. That did not stop me trying to figure out why he would make preparations this way for taking me down without a single good reason for it that I could see. And I bet he intended putting the chicken coop over the hole once it was filled in again so's no one would notice the fresh-turned dirt if they come snooping around. But no one would come snooping around because nobody even knew I was here, so how would they miss me when I'm dead and buried under a chicken coop? It was a clever and deviant plan he had all right, but I know about it now, which is the best way not to let a plan like that happen. It was a lucky break for me, coming out into the yard like this before the sun went down.

I backed away from the hole and went inside the house through the laundry door, then back into the living room where Dean is still sat in front of the TV, which is giving the stock report. He says to me, "You pick up any more beer in town?"

"You never said to."

"Well, don't you do things that nobody told you to?"

"Sure."

"Only not today, huh?"

"I got the clothes in the wash."

"That's fine, Odell. You'd find time goes by quicker while you wait for the wash cycle if you got a Coors in your hand, but it makes no difference to me."

"Okay."

He wasn't talking sense, but even if he was I only would've heard half of it, my mind was all aswirl with trying to figure out what's happening here. He didn't look crazy, even if he got twitchy now and then, so what was the motive behind this plan? I never did a thing to hurt him for motivation to murder. Maybe he is one of them crazy killers that does it for no reason except the insane part of his brain telling him he has to. They always say the craziest axe murderers and serial killers and cannibals etcetera look just like you and me. They don't drool and giggle crazy and roll their eyes, nothing like that, no, they drive to the store and bring home the groceries and pay their bills and stop at the stoplights. Until that switch in their head gets flipped and then they're someone else, only still disguised as theirself if you see what I mean. So that must be the kind Dean was right now watching the TV like he didn't have murder on his mind, just beer.

"I won't need to be staying here tonight again, Dean, not if there's the inconvenience of it."

"Huh?"

"I'm saying I can go some other place."

"Driving what? Your wheels are dead, dude."

"I could walk."

"You're talking shit now. Siddown and watch TV. And use the clothes dryer."

"Pardon me?"

"Use the clothes dryer to dry the clothes. Don't go out in the yard using the clothesline, not with that fuckin' snake out there. Snakes get active at night. I don't want the responsibility of someone getting snakebit on my property and then suing me over it."

"I wouldn't sue anybody for a snakebite. Maybe I'd sue the snake seeing as he's the one that did it."

Dean laughed. It was an evil laugh, not humorous. He was playing with me now, very confident he could murder me and get away with it, leaving his victim under the chicken coop for all time.

I sat down in the armchair again and tried to get things settled in my mind about how not to get murdered. First off, he must be planning to do it while I'm asleep seeing as he must know he can't attack someone my size while I'm awake. That meant I had to stay awake to keep it from happening. Once he saw I wasn't asleep he'd just forget about it, what else could he do? Unless he had a gun. With a gun it makes no difference if the shootist is big or small, the shootee winds up dead anyway.

"Why don't you go shoot it?"

"Huh?"

"Shoot the snake, then everyone's okay."

"Oh sure, like it's gonna be out there all coiled up in a neat pile waiting for me to come out and blast it."

"Have you got a gun to do it?"

"Got a shotgun, ten-gauge. Don't have no shells for it, though."

The liar! Nobody keeps a shotgun with no shells, that's just bullshit, but he said it real casual to make me believe it's true. He was a cool killer all right, sat there watching the weather report like he isn't planning to blow my brains out and bury me deep and put the chicken coop over me instead of a tombstone. There is no dignity in finishing that way.

"Hey, Dean?"

"What?"

"Those eggs yesterday, were those supermarket eggs?"

"They come in a supermarket egg package, didn't they?"

"Well, yeah, but people that run their own chickens, they use those egg cartons for the convenience, so they don't break. I noticed you got chickens here."

"Aunt Bree, she's got some running around. Stupid fuckers lay their eggs where you never can find them because she lets 'em run wild. It's those goddamn chickens brung the snake. There's nothing a snake likes more than eggs."

"So she doesn't collect the eggs?"

"Listen, Bree's a crazy old lady that doesn't even live in the same world as regular people. She acts like those chickens are pets. I mean...she *talks* to them."

"That's pretty crazy."

"You bet it is. If I didn't know she'd throw a shitfit about it

I'd chop their goddamn heads off and be done with it. I can't stand that racket they make, you know?"

"You could tell her when she comes back the snake ate them."

"Good plan, Odell. How big of a snake you figure can eat a dozen chickens, huh? Maybe one of those jungle pythons fifteen foot long, but you know what? We don't have that kind around here."

"Okay."

He looks over at me, still smiling that evil smile. "Anyone ever tell you you're weird, Odell?"

"No, they never did."

Which is a big lie. Back at Kit Carson High School in Yoder there was this girl, Feenie Myers, the only person I know that graduated with honors and went on down to college in Durango, Colorado, she told me I'm weird. See, in Kit Carson High there's three kinds of kid. There's the Jocks that play football, there's the Skaters that wear baseball caps backwards and baggy clothes and ride around on their boards, and then there's the Ropers, which means guys that wear jeans and boots and cowboy hats. I never had a cowboy hat but got called a Roper anyway. You have got to be one of these three. Anyway, this Feenie Myers, she says I'm a Roper with Geek characteristics. That's another thing you can be, a Geek, but it's almost as rare as being a Nerd. There has never been a Nerd at Kit Carson High except maybe for Feenie Myers. They are very rare in Wyoming, I believe. They are in Yoder anyway.

We watched more TV. There is only four kinds of shows they make. Cop shows, Lawyer shows, Doctor shows and Teen shows. We watched a Teen show that has got these smart-talking teens like nobody ever met outside of Hollywood. These guys, they only ever say stuff that's smart and cutting and they never have acne or do stupid stuff that's embarrassing. Back at Kit Carson High these characters would have ruled the school if they were real, which everyone knows they are not. This is the reason I am not a fan of TV, the falsity of it. I am no genius but I can figure out that much. This is what made me discover *The Yearling*, which has got real people in it and no glamorousness to make it false and not believable. I was glad to get away from the TV after awhile and put the clothes in the dryer like Dean said.

After the Teen show we watched a Lawyer show and then a Doctor show, then along about ten o'clock Dean gets up and switches off the tube without asking if maybe I'd like to keep watching, which I didn't so that's okay, and he says, "Gotta get up early tomorrow if we're gonna drop off your car at the junkyard."

"Yeah."

He went clomping off upstairs without even saying Goodnight or Pleasant dreams or anything polite like that. You might think that even an axe murderer could be a little bit polite, but not Dean, he just couldn't be bothered it seemed like. I snuck along the hall to the front door where Dean's baseball bat was still propped against the wall and brung it back to the sofa and laid it alongside where I can reach for it in a hurry. Then I turned out the lights and lay down on the sofa same as last night without even a blanket, which Dean never did make the offer of, and stared at the ceiling far away, wondering when he'd come sneaking down to do what he had the intention of – murdering.

The grandpa clock bonged soft and mellow on the quarter and half and three quarter hours while I kept on waiting. I guess it sounds crazy, me waiting around to get killed, but there's a part of me still didn't believe it'll actually happen in reality, one side of my brain saying to the other side, You have got it All Wrong and the hole in the yard is for locating a leaky septic system pipe that needs replacing. Why the hell would Dean be wanting to murder a complete stranger that never did him harm? And I could leave anytime, so why lay there waiting for the blow to fall, a shotgun blast to come blazing from the darkness?

But that is exactly what I did, telling myself if he come tiptoeing downstairs with the shotgun I'd hear him coming. And he never would've blasted me right there on the sofa, tearing it up and splattering blood everywhere in his own living room. Dean was not houseproud but he wouldn't have wanted a mess like that. He would do what they do in wartime, which is take the victim at gunpoint to his grave and make him stand over it, then blast him from behind so he goes toppling down into the hole without making a big mess to clean up later. I would have to get the better of him between the time he roused me by poking the shotgun barrel in the side of my neck to wake me and the time he stood me alongside the grave hole.

Bong bong bong etcetera. Eleven o'clock and he still didn't show. Because he wasn't going to, I finally told myself, it's all just bullshit in my brain, which was a big relief. What a big idiot I was to think all that about Dean, which even if he wasn't the greatest guy in the world was definitely not some cold-blooded psycho killer. I got that settled in my mind by the quarter hour and felt myself drifting off into dreamland. That sofa was not the cleanest I ever lay on, but it was plenty soft and the cushion under my head fit just right. I felt myself sliding into darkness the way you do when sleep is coming, like sliding down a velvet chute into a deep pool filled with stillness and calm...

"Odell?"

Dean was drifting alongside me in the pool. How did he get there?

"Odell?"

I woke up. Dean was squatting right by my head, whispering in my ear!

My arm had fallen down from the sofa and lay with my fingertips just barely touching the baseball bat. They wrapped theirselves around it by pure instinct for survival and begun lifting it, and at the same time I'm rearing up in slow motion with alarm bells and sirens screaming in my head and this voice saying over and over *Get him get him get him* ... and Dean is looking at me strange in the darkness, just this little bit of light from the windows coming through... *And why the fuck is he right beside the sofa on his haunches that way, practically whispering in my ear?* ... that was the scariest part, not the shotgun, which was beside him on the floor, not in his hand, which gave me the advantage while I'm rearing up and he's saying, "I thought I heard something..." The bat was raised high to shut out that little-boy voice he's using, pretending to be all helpless because he heard the boogeyman prowling around downstairs, which is the lamest kind of deceiving...

The bat come down like a lightning bolt from above and made this awful *thonk* sound as it bashed the top of his head.

His face was upraised to look at me – I'm on my feet now – and there's this expression of total surprise on it because he wasn't expecting me to be prearmed with the bat like I am, and now he recognizes it's too late for a surprise attack because he made the mistake of whispering my name when what he should've done is poke me awake with the gun barrel like I predicted. Well, it was too late now for him to succeed in his criminal intent because he's falling backwards away from me with his eyes wide open still...and hits the floor with a thud.

I stood over him with the bat raised again. There's blood hammering through my head and my heart going *budumbudumbudum* so fast I thought it might bust out of my chest. Dean didn't move, so I must have whanged him good. He looked dead, he's so still. He only had pajama pants on without the jacket, so I could see his scrawny chest heaving the breath in and out of him so he's okay, only unconscious, which made sense because I only hit him the one time and not all that hard neither because I was rising up from the sofa at the same time I whanged him, not the best position to swing a baseball bat. The shotgun was next to him. I picked it up and opened it up. No shell inside. Now why the fuck would he come downstairs to kill me with no shell in the gun? He said, just before I hit him, he thought he heard something, meaning a prowler, I guess, but again, how would an empty gun be useful as a threat against intruders, unless he was only going to bluff them with it? Or bluff me into going out to the hole to await execution. With what, though? None of it was making any sense.

I listened to him breathing kind of ragged for awhile,

waiting for him to come around so I can ask him what's going on here. After a time my heart slowed and I started thinking I must have hit him too hard even if I didn't have a good swing for maximum impact. I was even starting to feel a little sorry for having hit him at all, but I mean, what else did he expect, whispering in my ear like that and a shotgun beside him? It was the dumbest way to wake someone up you can think of, so it's all his own fault, that's how I saw it. There was no way I could go back to sleep, not with Dean lying next to the sofa that way with air whistling through his nose, so I went and had a glass of water and come back. Here's a strange thing – I almost felt like crying, I really did. I had never before hit anyone with nothing but my fist and only when they asked for it by needling me about this or that. I had hit someone now with a baseball bat, which is a truly awful thing to do when you think about it, not so bad as hacking at them with a machete or shooting a bullet into them, but plenty bad enough.

Listening to him was more than I could take, so I lifted him and carried him upstairs to his room and put him on the bed in a nice comfortable position, then I turned out the light and left. All kinds of thoughts kept galloping through my head and I knew sleep was not going to come back again to comfort me. I tried a few pages of *The Yearling* but the words kept switching around and making no sense so I quit and went outside to sit on the porch rocker and listen to the night.

THREE

It was a chicken that woke me. I was on the rocker fast asleep and the stupid bird flapped up onto my chest and pretty near gave me a heart attack. I jumped up so fast it squawked and went running away down the porch steps. I waited a minute to calm down then went inside just as the clock is striking five.

Up the stairs and into Dean's room, where I found him still unconscious or maybe just asleep, it's hard to tell. He had gone and urinated in the crotch of his pajamas but I wasn't about to peel them off and put on another pair in case he woke up while I'm doing it and figures I'm doing weird homo stuff with him while he's helpless. So I left him like he was and looked at his head, then felt it. There's a good-sized lump there on top where the bat connected but no bleeding, a good sign I didn't hit him all that hard. I felt better knowing that and went to fix breakfast for myself. I was fully prepared to forgive Dean for his dumbass stunt in the middle of the night and fix breakfast for him too, just as soon as he's ready.

With food inside me everything seemed brighter. Bacon and eggs plus toast, what could be better? Bacon and ham, those are what Dean had called "pigmeat" which he didn't eat, so they must have been for Aunt Bree. I wondered when she was coming home from Florida. Dean hadn't said. Maybe she'd be home today! That got me thinking hard about what to do next. I went upstairs to see if Dean was awake and ready to eat but he wasn't, not yet awhile, so I went out to the porch again and considered the situation.

According to the lawnmowing schedule Dean has got four customers today, but it was clear he wasn't going to be ready to take care of things in that department any better than yesterday. Dean, he kept having these head problems that kept him from his work, and in a way I was the cause for both times, so I had an obligation to take care of business again today. That was the least I could do to make amends for slugging him, even if he asked for it with his dumb behavior, that's the way I saw it, so after tidying up the kitchen I got in the Dodge and drove away to mow some more lawns. I left a note for Dean on the kitchen table explaining things for when he woke up and wondered what the hell is going on.

Halfway through the morning I stopped at Wal-Mart and got myself a straw hat like they wear in Hawaii to protect my head from the sun and some shorts to keep my legs cool while I mowed, plus cheap sneakers because cowboy boots look ridiculous with short pants unless you happen to be a topless model wearing micro-shorts. Total outlay come to less than forty dollars. I zoomed through the work with time out for lunch at McDonald's again, and then I got hold of a phone book at a public call box and looked up the address of the recruiting center, which is on Lincoln Avenue.

I went there directly, but the store front had windows that are painted over with whitewash on the inside, so it looks like Dean was right about that, which means the phone book was outdated and should've been replaced but they never do that in a phone booth like they should. Just to be sure I went in the store next door which is a hardware place and asked about it. The guy there, he says the recruiting center was dislocated to Manhattan, which is a much bigger town than Callisto. Manhattan, Kansas, not New York. So that was a big pain I hadn't counted on with my plan for military work. Still, if Dean let me work a few more days, I could buy a ticket and ride the bus to Manhattan and sign up anyway.

Driving along on the road home I got overtaken by a beige Cadillac going way over the limit. I had to wind the window up to keep his dust from coming inside. I didn't think any more about that Caddy until I pulled in off the road at Dean's place and there it is parked in the front yard and some guy standing on the porch by the front door. I pulled up inside the barn and took my time getting out, thinking Dean would be talking to the guy by now, but he wasn't. The guy's turned around and he's looking over at me. Where was Dean? He should've been up and about by now, or maybe he was just in a bad mood over what happened last night and didn't want to talk to anyone so he's ignoring the doorbell.

I went on over to the porch and the guy meets me at the steps. "Mr Lowry?" he says. I considered what to say. This is one of those times I mentioned about being slow with a conversational response, only this time there's a reason for it, namely not knowing how bad Dean is, maybe still unconscious, which would be a bad thing, and not wanting to explain about last night's weirdness to this guy who might have been selling insurance for all I knew. So I just kept looking at him while my brain whizzed and sputtered, then I said to him, "What can I do for you?" That was the correct response to his question under the circumstances, because it showed politeness without me admitting I'm not Dean like he thinks I am.

He put out his hand which I had to reach up to take hold of because he's at the top of the steps and I'm at the bottom. He's an old guy, way past sixty with gray hair that's still thick and neatly barbered. He's wearing a suit and tie and there's a little neat mustache on his lip. I could smell the aftershave on him, which reminded me I hadn't shaved in a couple days plus I'm stinking with sweat after a long day pushing lawnmowers in the sun. "Chet Marchand," he says. "Thought it might be you I passed on the road. Saw the sign on the truck door. How's business this fine day?"

"Okay, I guess."

I come on up the steps and opened the door, still hoping maybe Dean's going to come out yawning and take care of this, but that didn't happen, so I had to step aside polite and let this guy into the house. I led him on through the kitchen, glad I tidied it up this morning, and invited him to take a seat, then thought maybe I should've taken him through to the living room instead, but it's too late now. The living room was kind of a mess anyway, so this way is better. I sat down too, thinking maybe I should offer him a glass of water, which I wanted one of myself but it could wait. Obviously this guy Chet was nobody Dean knew, so the visit couldn't be important and wouldn't take long to finish off. I was still thinking it's insurance he's selling. The note I left for Dean was still on the table so I scrunched it up good.

Chet gave me a smile, very friendly and says, "Is Mrs Wayne at home today?"

Who the fuck is that, I'm thinking, then it strikes me Mrs Wayne must be Aunt Bree. Where the hell was Dean who should be answering this family stuff?

"She's in Florida on vacation."

"Florida on vacation," he says. "That's a fine state to visit and see the natural wonders."

"I'm going there someday myself. *The Yearling*, that's a Pulitzer Prize book, it happens there in Florida, only a long time ago."

"That's a fine book. I remember reading it when I was young."

He was starting to make me nervous. What did he want?

"Well," he says, getting down to business, "I must say I'm a little bit surprised Mrs Wayne isn't here, but no matter, we can discuss matters just between the two of us. Okay if I call you Dean?"

"Sure." He could call me Donald Duck, but that didn't make it so.

"Please call me Chet. Now about my little trip out here, Dean, has your aunt given you any indication what this might be about?"

I looked up at the ceiling like I'm thinking hard about it. "No."

"Oh, well, I'm surprised about that, but that's okay. Given

the nature of the correspondence between us, I assumed there'd be discussion between the two of you concerning the matter."

"Nope, she never mentioned a word about it, not to me." That was a true statement. I was finding it's possible to tell people lies without actually lying. This was something I never thought of before and was a big surprise.

"Well, then," he says, "maybe I should start at the beginning, as they say."

"Okay."

"Mrs Wayne is concerned about you, Dean. I might have said worried, I might even have said distraught, but the word I've chosen, just to keep things in perspective, is concerned. This good Christian woman is concerned for your future, Dean, and I apologize for the dramatic nature of what I'm going to say next, but she's concerned for your very soul."

"Uhuh."

"Mrs Wayne has been in touch with our ministry and expressed her deep concern about you, Dean, concerning recent developments in your life. Maybe I should say your interior life, by which I mean in your heart and your soul, Dean. I'm sure you know what I'm referring to."

I shook my head. Dean never said a word to me about his heart or his soul. What he talked about mainly while we were drinking down my bottle of Captain Morgan was how lousy our dads were and it's a shame our moms had died young in my case and run off with another guy, that's what happened to Dean's mom and he never heard from her again. Even her sister, that's Aunt Bree, she never heard either, which is a shame when family breaks apart that way.

"You can't guess what I'm referring to, Dean?"

"Nossir, he never mentioned it. She, I mean."

"Then I'll spell it out loud and clear. Your aunt has expressed deep concern to us at the ministry...you're familiar with our organization, the Born Again Foundation?"

That had a familiar ring to it, then I remembered it's something on TV late at night when it's mainly religious shows and infomercials about skin care products. Once or twice I have seen that show with the old guy with the slicked-back hair and the stabbing fingers when he gets all worked up preaching...what was his name again?

"Preacher Bob," I said, remembering.

"That's what folks like to call him," says Chet. "Of course, around the office, if I might use that term, we call him just plain Bob, that's how he likes it, informal and without pretension. Robert Jerome Ministries is the official title of our overall organization, but we don't need to get into that kind of detail today, Dean. What we're here to discuss is you."

"Why?" I really wanted to know why a big name TV personality with his own Bible college near Topeka and his own network show that millions of people watched, I bet, what he wanted with me. With Dean, that is. It was a real mystery.

"Now, Dean, you must have some notion of what it is I'm referring to. I think maybe you're being just a little bit disingenuous here."

Nobody ever called me a genius before, and it made me suspicious that he's trying to pump up my self-esteem so's he can sell me something. I know for a fact I am not a genius, so now I'm suspicious as hell, even if he's still smiling at me. I didn't say a thing, just smiled back, waiting for him to say why he thinks I'm so smart. Thinks Dean is so smart, I mean, which Dean never struck me as being even very clever, never mind at the genius level.

"Dean, I'll speak directly to the problem. Mrs Wayne has written to us about your decision to reject the faith of your fathers and embrace...the religion of Islam."

I stared at him. What was he talking about? Dean never spoke a word to me about being an Islamite. They don't look anything like Dean, with his *Bad to the Bone* T-shirt, and they don't drink liquor either, everyone knows that, but Dean did and I don't mean sipping. It made no sense at all. I couldn't think what to say, it's so ridiculous, but Chet was watching my face, waiting for a response. After he left I was going to wake Dean up and question him big time about all this.

"Are you still considering this radical and dangerous act, Dean? I can think of nothing more certain to condemn your soul, your *immortal soul*, Dean, to punishment so extreme it pains me to think about it happening to a young man like yourself with so much of life before you. Think carefully now."

I was doing that, thinking at top speed, and it come back to me how Dean said he didn't eat pigmeat, which is something everyone knows the Islamites do because pigs are unholy creatures or something religious like that. So it was true what Chet was saying!

"Yeah," I said.

Chet's face fell, I mean he really did look upset, like I'd just told him I drowned a sack of puppies. I felt bad about upsetting him that way, especially since it wasn't me that's going Islamite, it's the guy upstairs giving grief to his aunt and

Preacher Bob and Chet too. I was going to have strong words with Dean about this because it's so dumb to be a Muslim when you aren't even Arabian. Americans are Christians, everyone knows that. Now I have never been a churchgoer and my dad wasn't either, so you might say there was a bad influence in my life that kept me away from getting churchified like some do, but even so I could tell straight off that Dean was doing something dumb here with this religious conversioning intention he had. No wonder Chet was upset like this.

"Are you thinking hard, Dean?"

"Yessir, I am."

"Take into consideration the feelings of others in this crucial decision. We're not just talking about the fate of your soul, we're talking here about the effect this will have on your loved ones like Mrs Wayne, who I believe has taken care of you ever since your mother departed. Consider the pain a decision like this will inflict on a generous and good woman. You don't want the responsibility of causing that type of person pain, do you, Dean? I know it causes me pain just to think about the rashness of what you're contemplating, and Bob too, he sent me out here personally to see if there isn't something we can do to help you change your mind and step back from this terrible mistake you're about to make. Or have you already made it? Have you received instruction in Muslim doctrine yet? I would imagine that's hard to come by in this area. Am I right about that, Dean?"

"It's rare out here," I agreed, saying something truthful to make myself feel better. I saw now it was a mistake not to tell Chet straight off I'm not Dean, but there's no way I can go back now and change the situation.

"Can you tell me what it is, Dean, that makes you think Islam can offer you something that Christianity can't. What's the appeal?"

I couldn't answer that. Still no sound from upstairs, so I'm thinking Dean must have gone off somewhere. He couldn't still be asleep since this morning. Then again, how would he go anyplace without wheels?

"Mrs Wayne has hinted at a troubled upbringing, Dean, so I'm thinking this thing you're considering doing is maybe a reaction to personal difficulties that never got resolved. She says you started refusing to accompany her to church a long time ago and have been verbally abusive toward her about her own faith which has never wavered. Is it a personal issue, Dean? Talking to the right person can very often resolve those intensely painful inner turmoils people are prone to without guidance from the Lord. Is that the case here? You may think I've gotten very personal all of a sudden, and I won't blame you for that, there's nothing so personal as inner feelings, but there's a connection here, Dean, or maybe I mean a disconnection. You've gone and been disconnected from the natural and everlasting faith we know is true. Now I have respect for the lesser faiths, and I respect the right of people in other cultures to believe those things they choose to believe, but this is America we're living in, and this nation was founded on Christian principles. Any turning away from hundreds of years of history – *thousands* of years – is a mistake of the first magnitude, Dean. Can you see what I mean, son?"

"Uhuh."

"Then I'm asking you to consider very carefully this whole business."

I had a picture flash into my mind right then, and this is the picture – Dean has gone and fallen in the hole in the yard while he's still dizzy from the whack on the head he got. He went all dizzy out the back door and fell into the hole, which is the reason he's not sat at the table right now talking with Chet about all this crap. Why didn't I think of this before? Dean needed assistance right now because he hit his head again when he fell in the hole, I bet.

"Excuse me..."

I got up and hurried through the house to the back door and went outside. Over to the hole. The hole is empty. Okay then, big relief he isn't there like I thought. Only where is he? Back into the house and up the stairs. Dean is lying on his bed like I left him this morning, exactly the same. I went over and poked him on the shoulder, and the way he didn't wake up or grunt or anything made me know the truth, which I did not want to believe, so I bent low and listened close to his mouth to that awful sound of nothing at all. Dean was dead, had most likely died after I left and been laying there all day waiting for me to come back and discover him no longer among the living.

Jesus Christ! What was I going to do now? I walked in circles around the room. I kept flinging my arms out and back, out and back, don't ask me why, and bobbing my body up and down, I think, it's hard to remember this part, what I was doing and what I was thinking as the full impact of this bad consequence of my actions with the baseball bat rose up to hit me from yesterday.

I don't know how long I walked in circles before I remembered Chet downstairs waiting for answers from poor dead Dean, who at least had died a Christian still without changing over to being a Muslim person, so if it's true what they say about the soul going to heaven then he went there instead of wherever Muslim folk go to, which I have heard has got virgin girls there, a whole bunch for every man. So maybe he would have wanted to go there instead, but it's too late now, he's gone and died a Christian. Been *murdered* like a Christian I would have said if I wanted to look at it clear and plain, which I did not, I wanted it all to go away and never have happened, every part of it from the time my Chevy died on me till right now.

I heard Chet's chair scrape on the kitchen floor. He couldn't come up here, couldn't see Dean lying there with no breath of life inside him. Murdered. Chet couldn't see that, so I went down the stairs real slow, gathering my thoughts as they say, but it was a very small bunch of thinking, mainly just one thing – I couldn't back away from being Dean now. I hadn't told any lies as such, but from here on in it was all lying even if I didn't say another word, that's what I was thinking.

I saw him standing in front of the grandaddy clock in the hall. "That's a fine old piece," he said, his face up close against the dial to see the scrollwork clear. "How long has it been in the family?"

"Oh, around fifty or eighty years, I guess."

Lie number one. It had started. Everything in my entire life would be different now that I had a Dark Secret to hide. It must have been affecting my mind, the sudden shock etcetera, because I had this picture of me murdering Chet and burying him in the hole in the yard, which made not one bit of sense seeing as he never knew about the Secret, so what threat is he to me? None at all, so I did not follow through and murder Chet. I wanted him gone, though, and fast, before he sees there's something changed about me, like there's a sign hung around my neck that says *Murderer* or maybe something crazy in my eyes that he'll see.

"Is everything all right, Dean?"

"Yup, no problem."

"The way you rushed out, I thought maybe there's something wrong."

"Nah, no way."

"Well, how about we get back to discussing the matter that brought me here?"

"Okay."

We stared at each other for a little while, then Chet says, "Should we go back to the kitchen, or would you be more comfortable in the living room?"

"I don't care, whichever."

We went and sat on the sofa together, which was a mistake. I should've sat in the armchair so he's not so close. I knew sooner or later he's going to reach out and touch my arm all fatherly and concerned for my soul, and I didn't want that, I wanted him gone gone gone.

"Now, Dean," he says, "I want you to tell me honest and true what's on your mind with regard to this crisis in your life. I suspect there's a whole separate agenda going on here that has got nothing to do with choosing another religion on a ... what you might call a philosophical basis. I suspect, and Bob does too, that your dereliction of duty to the faith you were raised in has got its basis in something purely emotional. Might that be the case here, Dean, do you think? Maybe some personal problem? Are relationships an issue with you at this time, Dean? Women trouble, you know. Any difficulties in that area you'd care to discuss?"

"Hell no."

His face hardened a little when I said that, like I said Fuck or something. The religious kind like Chet are very easy offended about shit like that, so I would have to watch my tongue and be polite. "I don't have a girlfriend right now, so that's not a problem," I said, wanting to be cooperating with him.

"Nobody at all? You're a well setup young man, Dean, so I'm surprised to learn there are no romantic entanglements in your life. There have been girlfriends in the past, am I assuming correctly about that?"

"Oh sure, I'm not gay or anything."

"That's good to hear. Homosexuality is an abomination, as I'm sure you've been taught. I'm going to be direct here, maybe downright intrusive, and I make no apology for it." He kind of gathered himself up and looked me directly in the eye. "Dean," he says, "what ails you, boy?"

It was a good question, and one that I asked myself more than once. I mean, there has to be something to account for the fact that I don't feel like I fit in anywhere. What guy six-three is going to get respect by saying he still feels like a little boy? No guy, that's who. So I said nothing. The conversation was over.

"Dean?"

"Uhuh?"

"Do you have anything to say to me?"

"This conversation is over."

He looked troubled, even a little bit annoyed. "What do you mean by that?"

"I have to take a shower. I stink."

"Well, of course, you've been hard at work all day. Mrs Wayne has always been proud of the way you made an effort with the lawnmowing after she bought you the truck and the mowers. No question about that, you've been a credit to her, working hard that way —"

"And you have to go."

That made his face go hard but he tried not to show it. We looked at each other while nothing happened, then he got up and I did too, relieved that he's leaving so I could sit down and think my way through this real bad situation that sprung up out of nowhere. But he didn't head for the front door like I wanted, which started making me mad. He had to get out of there because there was no room in the house for nobody except me and the dead man upstairs, who being dead occupied more space than his living body had. Being a murder victim makes you ten times bigger than you were and a hundred times more of a problem. I had got a giant upstairs and Chet had to go.

"Dean, maybe I approached you the wrong way. I was expecting to find Mrs Wayne here. This has not gone the way I intended and I blame myself for that. I can see you need to be alone and clean up after an honest day's work, and I'm going now, but I'll ask this of you, Dean – don't say to me that I can't come back at least one more time to chat with you about the consequences of your choice."

"Okay."

I said that to shut him up and move him along in the direction of the door. If he stayed there one more minute I swear I would've blabbed the whole truth to him and most likely burst out in tears or something creepy and little-boyish.

At the door he stops and puts out his mitt. "This is the hand of a friend, Dean. I know you don't think so right now, but it's an absolute fact. Everybody in this world needs friends, and next to Jesus I want you to think of me as your greatest friend. That may sound presumptuous, but it's true, Dean, and that's the thought I want to leave you with today. Thank you for your hospitality."

He pumped my hand one or two times and then he's out the door and crossing the porch to the steps. I watched him through the screen while he got in his Cadillac and drove away. Pretty soon the sound of the car and the dust his tires kicked up have all gone away and I'm on my own again, except for Dean upstairs. I should have gone back up there but was too cowardly to face him again. I tried telling myself that Dean was a very fucked-up person and I had solved all his problems, but that didn't sound right at all and was just a lame excuse for the guiltiness I felt crowding inside me.

I couldn't think straight anymore. I wanted a drink to smooth away the thorns growing inside my skull. So I got in the truck and drove away to town. Halfway there I remembered I forgot to lock the front door, or even close it behind me. That's how rattled I was about everything.

I knew there was a store called Freedom Liquor in the shopping strip nearest to Dean's side of town, so that's where I went, only when I got there what do I see but Chet's beige Cadillac parked next to the Fancy-Free Boutique. He's got a cell phone up to his face and he's gabbing into it. He didn't see me and I didn't want him to, so I drove around the other side of the strip to the parking lot there and went into Freedom Liquor by the back door. I come out again a few minutes later with two flagons of Captain Morgan and a six-pack of Coors. Then me and the Captain went home to discuss the situation man to man.

FOUR

I laid it out for myself plain and clear. Dean was dead and could not be brung back. I did it even if it was accidental and partly his own fault. I had to get on over to Manhattan to enlist but my car was dead as Dean. Aunt Bree was due home sometime soon, and Chet would be back for more sermonizing. I had a bunch of Dean's money, but I figured I could call it mine because I'm the one that pushed those mowers around. And Dean was already starting to smell bad.

The Captain and me made a plan, and this is it – I would use Dean's truck to tow my Monte Carlo away from his place and dump it somewhere and remove the license plates and Vehicle Identity Number from the dash so it can't be traced to me, not that anyone would bother anyway with an old junker like that. I would take Dean's truck back and park it in the barn like before, then write a note and leave it on the front door for Chet saying I will stay Christian after all and thank you for stopping by. Then I would walk away from Dean's place and hitchhike into Callisto to get the bus to Manhattan, and my problems would be over. I liked the plan because it was simple. It was a shame about the terrible shock Aunt Bree would get when she come home and found Dean stinking the place out, but there was nothing I could do about that.

And there was still the big mystery of why Dean went and dug that hole in the yard. Looking for answers to that, I went through his dresser and found some books about Muslims, *Under the Banner of the Prophet* and *Sword of Islam*, and a Koran with a green leather cover with fancy gold patterns on it, so it was true what Aunt Bree had wrote to Preacher Bob about, Dean really was going to be a convertible. I shook my head over that, but it was none of my business what religion he wanted to be, so I put those books back where I found them.

It was way into the night by then, and after all that drinking and no meal after working all day I was real hungry. The fridge had been ate out pretty good so I went downstairs to the basement for another one of those good TV dinners we had the first night. I had trouble finding the light switch but it's on the side of the staircase and I went on down. There was plenty of junk down there, typical basement crap, and over in the corner there's a good-sized freezer, the kind with the lift-up top. Inside it was crammed with TV dinners and bags of vegetables and pizzas etcetera, a real good selection to choose from, so I started digging in, lifting aside pizza boxes and frozen peas to see what's underneath, and that's when I saw the hair.

I thought maybe Dean or more likely Aunt Bree had a wig or hairpiece they kept in the freezer so the moths can't get to it, but nobody has a gray wig like that, they have a dark wig to hide gray hair if it's a woman that owns it. I took hold of it to lift it up for examining but it wouldn't come, because it's attached there, I thought, maybe froze to something else, so I yanked a little harder but it still wouldn't come, so I lifted aside some packets of baby corn and saw the reason for it. The wig was attached to a head, which means it wasn't a wig at all, it's real hair. Somehow that drove me over to the other side of the basement, then I found my manhood and went back for another look.

No doubt about it, there's a woman in the freezer. I dug out all the frozen goods from around her and there she is, a small-ish woman in her nightgown, all folded down on herself like she was praying by the bedside and then just collapsed. It was pretty clear Aunt Bree had not gone to Florida after all but had ended up in a cooler place. I gritted my teeth and lifted her out, which was easy she's so small, and then I saw why she's been folded over that way. The front of her, the stomach hid away behind her folded-up legs, was all bloody and blasted open, near as I could tell, so then the whole truth revealed itself to me and this is it – Dean has gone and shot his Aunt Bree in the stomach, most likely with the last shell for his ten-gauge, and has hid her down here while he figures what to do with her, and he decided to dig a hole in the yard and bury her under the chicken coop. Most likely he killed her just a little while before I come strolling up the driveway looking for help. No wonder he looked kind of crazy at first.

Why did he kill her? I would never know that now, but I could guess that he got mad when she told him she wrote to Preacher Bob about his Muslim converting plan.

I have to admit I felt less bad about whacking Dean with

the baseball bat now, knowing that he's a murderer like he was, but it put me in a peculiar situation with regard to that event. The plan I already made come unglued the minute I found Bree down there in the basement. It's two dead bodies not just one, so now what was I supposed to do? I put Bree back in the freezer and arranged all the frozen food around her like before, holding back one large Cheese Supreme pizza for dinner. I took that back upstairs and put it in the oven, not caring that it would take awhile to cook straight from the freezer like it was, because I had lost part of my appetite over the Big Discovery down there and needed time anyway to come up with an entirely different plan to suit the new situation I'm in. If only my car had kept on going another few miles before quitting, none of this would've happened to me. It was spooky the way the engine died right next to Dean's driveway like it did. That was the Hand of Fate working hard to Fuck Me Up Big Time.

But there was no use weeping and moaning about that now. What was done could not be undone, so I had to make another plan and move on. It seemed like the best thing was to leave Bree and Dean right where they were. That way, when they got discovered by a neighbor or the guy that comes to read the electric meter or whoever, it'll look like Dean killed Bree and put her in the freezer, then dug a hole to bury her in. Only he never did get that far with his scheme because the whack that Bree was able to give him on the head before he shot her took its toll a little later with a brain concussion that turned into a hemmeridge like what happens sometimes in the Doctor shows. That sounded believable to me, so long as I'm a long ways off when they get discovered. I didn't want

Chet to be the one that discovered them, because he'll tell the cops about the six-three guy pretending to be Dean, which will trigger a manhunt. So the idea to leave a note for Chet on the door that'll make him go back to Topeka happy that him and Preacher Bob saved my soul is still good to go.

The kitchen started filling with that fine pizza smell and my stomach did flips, but according to the cooking instructions there's still another ten minutes to go if you're cooking a frozen pizza not thawed, which is what the situation was. To pass the time I went upstairs to Dean's room and opened the windows wide, then went over to the west side of the house and opened up all the windows there, because the wind almost always comes from the west in Kansas and this way it'll blow through the upper floor and clean out the bad smell Dean was giving off. I didn't want to have to live with that overnight. He looked peaceful and serene apart from his mouth which had come open some and would not close again no matter how many times I pushed his chin up, so I left him that way. I could feel the night breeze coming through from the west side and was pretty sure the smell was already easing, but it's hard to say because the pizza smell was coming up from downstairs by now.

I turned out the light in Dean's room and was just about to go down to the kitchen when I heard a car coming up the drive. That froze my blood for maybe five seconds, then I sprinted for the window to see who it is, maybe Chet come back again already to do more of God's good work, but it isn't a Caddy it's a little car, I can't tell what kind in the dark. It pulled into the yard and the engine shut off. I could have panicked and maybe most guys would, but so much happened already that day I was already primed for surprises, and so instead of running around like a chicken with its head cut off I did the right thing immediate and without hesitation, which is to scoop Dean up off the bed, set him on the floor beside the bed, lift the mattress drapes and shove him under, then let those drapes fall again nice and natural. I did not even stop for a second after this sensible precaution against discovery because who knows what might happen next. I stood up and told my heart to quit hammering that way just as there comes a knocking on the screen door which I went down to answer without hesitating like an innocent man would.

There's a woman standing there, a policewoman or highway patrol, some kind of police uniform except no hat, that's all I could make out by the light spilling out onto the porch from the hallway. When I got to the door she's looking right at me with suspicion in her eyes it seemed to me, but that might be my guilty conscience working. I turned on the porch light and said, "Can I help you?" without my voice cracking, so I'm on top of the situation all right.

"Who're you?" she says. She's a good-sized woman, not some skin and bony type, maybe thirty or so with her hair pinned back mannish like policewomen have to look if they want the job. She didn't give me no Good evening, sir, I wonder if you might help me out with my inquiry, nothing polite like most police are despite what people say.

"Huh?"

"Who the hell are you and what are you doing in my brother's house?"

It's a good thing she said that, about the brother I mean, because otherwise I might have said I'm Dean. She wouldn't

have fallen for that like Chet did, being related. I thought fast
and come up with the only name that'll work, because being
a cop she might want to see some ID and the only kind I've
got is my own.

"Odell," I said, kind of pushing it past my lips. This is not
what I expected or wanted, Dean having a sister that's a cop. I
looked but she wasn't wearing a gunbelt, so maybe she's off
duty this late, which made no difference really, it's still a cop,
the last kind of person I wanted around the place right then.

"Say what?"

"Odell Deefus."

She took that in, then says, "Where's Dean?"

I wasn't prepared for that, who could be? I tracked her face
with my eyes, wondering how smart she might be, or how
good of a nose she had for bullshit. She looked smart enough,
kind of attractive too, with a lot of solid womanliness despite
the uniform, or maybe because of it, it fit so tight everywhere.
It's not a cop's uniform, though, because the color's wrong,
and it's a shade darker than the highway patrol.

"He's not here," I said, stalling.

"Well, where's Bree?"

"Florida, on vacation, Dean said."

"Step aside there."

She said it with a tone that made you want to do it even if
there's a pile of dogshit next to you that you're going to tromp
in. This woman was no Shrinking Violet. I opened up the
screen door and she come on in, still looking at me suspicious. If I was a smaller man I might have found that direct
staring way she had about her unsettling, but I had myself
under control, still impressed by the way I stashed Dean

under the bed almost by instinct like I did, and that was some lucky break considering who this coplady was. No doubt in my mind she would go over the place like a vacuum cleaner with her Crime Radar scanning at full sweep.

She went ahead of me down the hall to the kitchen, which gave me the opportunity to admire her big ass that looked less big than it truly was because above it there's a waistline cinched nice and tight for contrast. She looks around the kitchen and smells the pizza. "That's ready to come out," she says, so I got it out with the oven mitts, feeling a little foolish about having those big pink padded things on my hands like a woman. The pizza got set on the counter to cool a little, the cheese still sizzling too hot to eat yet. I took off the mitts and tossed them onto the table.

"Okay," she says, "what's the story here?"

"Story?"

"Where's Dean, you didn't tell me yet."

"He left yesterday, but he didn't say where he's going."

"How could he leave when his truck's out there?"

"He went with another guy in the guy's car."

"Was it a green Pontiac?"

I took a chance. "I believe so."

That seemed to work. "What's your name again?" she says.

"Odell Deefus, from Wyoming."

"And you know Dean how exactly?"

Honesty was probably the best policy for this part, since there are bits of it she can check out police-style and see I'm not lying. "I had car trouble and asked Dean for help. He says park it in the barn, only we couldn't get it fixed up right, so he let me stay over seeing as I'm stuck anyway. He's real friendly, Dean, even fed me and we got to be friends, kind of. Then this guy comes to collect him, and before he left, Dean says can I go mow his lawns while he's gone and there's five hundred bucks in it for me if I do, then he went away. I believe he said it'll be a few days, but he'll be back by the end of the week, definitely."

"He better be," she says, very firm, and I almost felt sorry for Dean if he's not back by then, then I remembered he's dead, so it was an empty threat.

"So he lets you stay in his house and run his business even though he only just met you." The way she said it, the story sounds about as lame as a one-legged cat.

"I was surprised about that myself, but Dean, he's a trusting kind of guy, I guess."

"Bullshit. He's paranoid and mean and a little crazy besides. You didn't get that?"

"Uh, no, he struck me as a totally decent guy, the way he tried to get my car started, only it's in so bad of a shape he couldn't. I'll get it fixed up with the five hundred and be on my way."

"I rung him up earlier," she says. "No answer, so I came on out."

She must've called when I was out getting liquor because I haven't heard the phone ring since I got here. I said nothing, hoping she's losing a little of her suspicion even if the story doesn't make complete sense. But my feeling is it does make sense, kind of, because Dean the way she describes him is the kind of guy that does crazy unplanned stuff that most people wouldn't, so it all kind of fits together even if there's gaps you could drive a tank through if you wanted to.

She says, "I got a call today from someone who says he saw a stranger driving around in Dean's truck. That got me worried."

"Yeah, it would."

"So did he leave anything for me? I'm Lorraine, by the way."

"Like a message, you mean?"

"Or a package. He leave anything like that?"

"No, all he said is maybe his sister might come around. Didn't even tell me what name to call you. He was in kind of a hurry."

"Describe the guy in the Pontiac."

"I didn't see him, he never come in the house, just pulled up outside and Dean went out and talked with him awhile and then comes back and tells me what I said. This was last night."

"And you've been here how long?"

"Oh, a couple days before that. We got along pretty good, Dean and me."

"That's nice. Usually people don't take to him. You cook that pizza to eat or just smell it?"

"I guess it's ready. You want some ... Lorraine?"

"I wasn't asking just to make conversation."

She went to the cupboard and fetched out two plates, then to the drawer to get a pizza cutter, like she knows where everything is, which is understandable in your own brother's place. Pretty soon we're chomping away like this is a regular thing.

"What line of work are you in, Adele?"

"*Odell*. Adele is a woman's name."

"Well, excuse me all to pieces, *Odell*."

"I'm enlisting soon as I get my car running again."

"Enlisting in what?"

"The Army."

"What? Are you crazy? What kind of a thing is that to do?"

"Well, they need men bad on account of the war ..."

"So who says it has to be you that signs up and gets his head blown off? Do something else is what I'd advise."

"I didn't make the cut come graduation day," I said, "so I've got limited options."

"You've got the option of staying in one piece or getting your head blown off. I'd call that options."

"I guess you're entitled to your opinion."

"I guess you're right about that. Did your mother say it's okay?"

"It's got nothing to do with her. I'm over twenty-one, and anyway she's dead."

"Oh, excuse me. Look, sometimes I talk in a straight line when by rights I should go a roundabout route, it's just my nature, okay, but no harm intended."

"That's okay."

"This is good pizza."

"Dean's got a lot of it down in the freezer."

I shouldn't have said that, even though it's a simple statement of fact. I was letting my guard down, and I knew the reason why. It's her – Lorraine. I liked her even if she's treating me like some kind of a fool, but like she said it's just her way, so I decided to overlook it. If she was not so good-looking I might have felt different about it, but that's what happens when you bump into someone you like the look of, it makes you do stupid things. It does to me anyhow. I chewed more pizza to keep from saying anything more about anything that might get me in trouble.

"When's Bree coming home?" she asked.

"I don't know, Dean never said."

"Well, you'll have to be gone by then. She won't want strangers around the place. Bree's a little strange herself and doesn't like it when things get changed around. She likes everything a particular way and that's that. You won't fit in even if you're Dean's friend like you say you are."

She made it sound like she doesn't believe that part, which is my warning not to let my guard down yet because she's still suspicious. Then she says, "Where in Florida?"

"I don't know. Dean said Miami and Fort Lauderdale, but which one it is he didn't say. He left straight after in a big rush."

"Bree's got some old high school friend in Fort Lauderdale, and she just loves to visit all the tourist places. I got some postcards from her before, Disney World, Epcot Center, places like that. SeaWorld she likes."

"Uhuh."

"So don't get comfortable here."

"Okay."

"You're sure he didn't leave a package or a message?"

"Nope."

"The thing about Dean, he's sometimes reliable and some-times not. You don't ever know where you stand with him from one week to the next. He has got mood swings. You didn't get into any argument with him?"

"No, we got along just fine."

"Maybe you're a good influence then. Dean, he's not one for making friends and sticking with them. Whenever he's close to making a friend the mood swings mess it all up. I expect you'll see all that if you stick around. Not that you'll be doing that with Bree coming home again." She took another slice of pizza. Lorraine had a real good appetite. "It's a shame," she says. "Dean needs a friend. So far I'm the only one he's got, and we don't see things the same way every day of the week. I don't know why I'm telling you this seeing as you won't be staying here long. It's family. You've got obligations to family that you wouldn't spend five minutes doing with someone else. But with family you're obligated. How many in your family?"

"Just me and my dad. We don't get along."

"That's a shame," she says, but not really meaning it, just being polite. "How tall are you, Odell?"

"Six-three."

"How much do you weigh?"

"I don't know, two hundred something."

"I'd say two-ten, two-fifteen. I'm good at guessing weight."

"I'm good at guessing how many marbles is in a jar. One time they had this contest to guess how many marbles in this jar, and mine was the closest one. I won a prize for that."

"What kind of a prize?"

"Oh, just a basket of stuff from the store. It was for the New Orleans cleanup fund after the hurricane. You had to pay ten cents to enter, so I did."

"Had much education?"

"I didn't graduate, I said that."

"Well, it's just ridiculous you going off to join the Army. There's other work you can get without a graduation certificate if you know where to look."

"I'm not picking no crops," I told her, "that's for Mexicans and they don't even want you to try, I found that out. They like to keep all that kind of work theirself, which you can't blame them. And the farmers too, because they can pay them less, so they like it that way. There's no point even asking, I found out."

"So you looked in the wrong place. I'm saying there's other kinds of jobs."

"Like what, pumping gas?"

"Prison guard. We've got this big prison now out the other side of town, Callisto State Penitentiary. Only opened for business eighteen months ago, brand-new facility, state-of-the-art lockdown, closed-circuit TV spycams, you name it. How does that sound?"

"I never thought about something like that," I said, which is true.

"They like big guys for the job. They look the part. Those are tough cookies, those inmates. They'll stare you down and give no respect unless you earn it. You have to be a hardass like them, it's the only way. Small guys, they just can't carry it off. Now, you, they'd look at you coming along the corridor and think Whoa, that is one big guy I don't feel like messing with. It's a built-in advantage for the position. I could talk to my supervisor. You can read and write okay?"

"I like to read," I said.

"Okay then, you want me to put in a word for you? You don't have any kind of a criminal record, do you?"

"No, I'm law-abiding."

"Good. Now it's not top wages to begin with, but if you prove yourself the pay goes up. I already moved up a level myself since I got started there. Before that I was at the Safeway. You can stick that job where the sun don't shine." She laughed when she said that, so now I'm thinking she likes me, you don't try and get someone a job just like that if you don't like them.

"Thank you."

"Don't thank me yet, you haven't got the job. You want the job?"

"Sure," I said, which I would if I could stay around Callisto, which obviously I can't with two dead bodies in the house and I killed one of them. But it was real nice of her to do that for me, and we only just now met, so I'm making the right impression as they say. I was proud of myself for not giving off a nervous sweat like you might expect me to with the situation the way it is, bodies etcetera, but no, I'm winging it good and surprising myself with how cool I am. And another thing I noticed – Lorraine, she likes me, I can tell, and here's the reason. Mostly when I talk to a girl I don't have a damn thing to say for myself and they get impatient waiting for the conversation to flow, which with me it never does. But with Lorraine she's a talker herself, kind of leading the conversation this way and that, so all I have to do is listen polite and answer the questions she puts to me direct, policewoman style, which I have got the answers ready because I'm just saying the truth most of the time, and even the lies have been coming out quick and clean, very impressing if you weren't that way before. So you could say I was feeling confident about things, which should have been another warning sign when that happens, only my mouth is full of pizza and my eyes are full of Lorraine, if you know what I mean.

She stood up and I got the full effect of that tight uniform again, and she says, "I'll just go upstairs and see if Dean left anything for me. He was supposed to, but with him you can't depend on it. You finish up that pizza, Odell."

And away she went up the stairs and I could hear her moving around in Dean's room, opening drawers and shutting them, then the big old-fashioned wardrobe he's got in there, so it's a good thing that's not where I stashed him, I'm thinking, but I've quit chewing I'm so wound up about her stomping around up there with her brother right under the bed, which is a place you sometimes look if you're looking for something hid away like an Easter egg hunt or something, so I can't swallow my pizza until she's all done and coming down the stairs again. She's a big woman like I said, and you can hear where she is and when she's coming, especially in a house so old it's got creaking floorboards and so forth. Then she's back in the kitchen and she doesn't look real pleased over what she didn't find.

"You tell him to call me the minute he gets back, okay? This is important and he hasn't followed through – again. You tell him I said if he doesn't fix this he's out of the loop, he'll know what that means. You can't do business with someone like that even if he's my own brother, you tell him I said so."

"Okay."

She looked me directly in the eye. "Have you told me everything, Odell? Because it's a little weird to find someone you never met before in your aunt's house when she's away. Are you being straight with me?"

"Sure."

"People that are straight with me, they don't regret it, but people that mess me around, I make sure they don't do it again, hear what I'm saying, Odell?"

"I sure do, and thank you about the job, Lorraine."

She lost a little of the hard look she's giving me and hitches at her belt to settle things, which I noticed she sees that I'm watching her waist, probably with a look on my face that says I like what I see. There is no hiding that stuff. I was thinking to myself how it'd be if she's wearing a gunbelt, and then before you know it I'm thinking about her wearing nothing *but* a gunbelt, which got me hard in about three seconds.

"Okay then, you going to be a gentleman and see me to the door?"

I didn't want to stand up with my dick like a police baton in my pants that way, but it would've been not polite to stay sat at the table like I am, so I got up kind of hunched over a little bit with my hands on the table to shield things from view, but then I had to step away from the table to get started towards the hall, and I could see right off she noticed what happened to me. She says, "Those are cute shorts."

"I got them special for the lawnmowing," I said, feeling the blush shoot up my neck like a flame.

"Well, they suit you. They don't suit every guy."

"Uhuh."

She had this tiny smirk on her face which got me blushing even more, then she says, "Think you can walk me as far as the door without tripping over?" That was a joke, I think.

"Sure."

We went to the door and she turned to me and says, "Nice to meet you, Odell."

"Nice to meet you too, Lorraine."

"So I guess I'll see you around. You get Dean to call me pronto."

"I will."

She opened the screen door and I got set to follow her out, then she stops all of a sudden to say something else, and I kind of banged into her by accident, which because she's turning to speak, I banged into her front, which was like getting an electric shock right through me from those breasts she has got, and she knew it too. "It's a big old house, Odell, no need to stand so close."

"I didn't mean to."

"I was going to say, my number's on the wall next to the phone if you need to reach me."

"Okay."

"No need to walk me to the car, you might break something."

"Okay."

"You're a man of few words, Odell."

"Yeah."

She made this noise in her throat like she's choking off a laugh, which made me feel like a fool about what happened. If only she hadn't hitched at her belt and got me thinking about other things I would not have suffered this embarrassment that I did, but I can't do a thing about it now.

Lorraine got moving across the porch and down the steps to her car. She gave a look back at me before she got in but didn't wave, so I didn't either. Then she started it up and drove on out of there and I went back in the kitchen. With Lorraine gone it's like I can think clear again, and the situation has gotten even worse than before, because here's this woman that I wasn't expecting to show up but she did, and now what am I going to do?

Then I got this idea, which is to get Bree and Dean and take them somewhere and hide them both away so nobody can find them and start accusing me of something, and that way I'll have some breathing room to figure things out, it's just too nervewracking with corpses around the place. Only where to put them? Well, the obvious place is in the hole that Dean already dug convenient for the job, only there'll be a heap of dirt left over but that's okay, I can put it here and there around the place, distributing the dirt so there's nothing left and then put the chicken coop over the mound like Dean planned. If I had've been more familiar with the Callisto area, maybe I could think of a better place, but I wasn't from around here so the first plan was the best.

I went upstairs to fetch Dean down for taking out to the hole in the yard. I could just as easy have brung Bree up from the basement but I wanted to get Dean first, working my way from the top down, I guess, or maybe I wanted him buried first on account of the guilty feelings I have got concerning the baseball bat and what happened there, I don't know. Anyway, I went upstairs to his room, which has definitely aired out pretty good so Lorraine never did mention a bad smell, thank goodness, and I got down next to the bed to drag him out.

Now here's where things took a whole different turn in the road, because when I lifted up the bed drapes to grab ahold of him I see this envelope sticking out of a cowboy boot right next to his head which I didn't see when I put him there I'm in such a godawful rush to get him hid when Lorraine drove up. I looked at the envelope, thinking why would that be there, then I did what anyone would and took it out and opened her up, and guess what – there's money inside, a lot of cash money, the folding kind. I counted it and there's exactly two thousand dollars legal tender in that envelope. Okay, straight off it struck me this is what Lorraine was looking to find, but what's the money for?

I'm sitting there next to the bed wondering about this and forgetting entirely about redisposing Dean elsewhere and then, like dayjar-voo on rewind, I hear this car coming up the drive and figure it's Lorraine come back because of something she forgot maybe, so I shoved the money back in the boot and the bed drapes got dropped into place like before. Then downstairs I went again, rearranging my face to be peaceful and calm which I was not feeling inside, no way.

I went to the front door and already knew it isn't Lorraine because the engine sounds different, a big American engine. I turned on the porch light right about the time the car stops in the yard, and my heart give a tiny kick when I saw it's a green Pontiac like Lorraine asked if that's the kind Dean went away in, and here it is. The driver got out and come on over, only he stops at the bottom of the steps when he saw me waiting in the doorway, someone he wasn't expecting, someone not Dean. Then he kept on coming and he's at the door, a skinny guy maybe thirty-five with his hair short all over except at the back where it hangs over his collar. He looked at me suspicious for a couple heartbeats then says, like Lorraine did, exactly the same, "Who're you?"

"Odell," I told him.

"Where's Dean?"

"He's not here right now."

He looked at me, then behind me down the hall, like he's

expecting Dean to appear and make me a big liar. "Well, where is he?"

"Over at his sister's place, I think. He wasn't real clear."

"So who're you?"

"Odell."

"No, man, that's a nigger name. What's it really?"

"Odell."

"What're you to Dean, related or something?"

"Just a friend."

He wasn't happy about any of this. "He's supposed to be here. He coming back or what?"

"I don't think so, the way he talked. I believe there's a family emergency."

"Like what, his aunt? She have a heart attack?"

"No, Bree's away in Florida on vacation right now."

"Well, shit, he was supposed to be here. Did he leave something? How close of a friend exactly are you?"

"Oh, we're pretty close, Dean and me."

"Well, did he?"

"Did he what?"

"Leave something for me."

He was getting agitated now, and it seemed to me he's the drug-taking kind, with a leather thong around his neck and a silver spider on it. He was shifty-eyed and squirmy too, like Dean was before he passed on, so they are two of a kind, I'm thinking. He would've been a lot more pissed off about Dean not being there if I was a shorter man, I knew that just by looking.

"Like what?" I said.

"Jesus, man ... *payment*, like we arranged."

So he wants the money that Lorraine was looking for. I

thought about what to do with regard to this. I would have rather it went to Lorraine than this guy because I liked her and didn't like him.

"What's your name?" I asked.

"What is this, some kind of a fuckin' test?"

All of a sudden he's afraid, and I knew the reason for it – he's thinking I'm a cop because of the six-three and my hair's kind of short like cops have it, regulation crewcut, which I got in Colorado last week to make myself look more like a soldier so they take me in the Army, and he's thinking the T-shirt and shorts is my undercover disguise.

"He's supposed to be here," he said again, "or call me if there's a problem. If you know Dean then you know what I'm talking about."

It was a challenge to let me know he's suspicious about me. I wanted him gone so I could get on with what I was getting set to do, the burying thing, and it seemed like the best idea was to give this guy what he come for so he goes away, otherwise he'll be back. This was definitely shaping up to be some kind of illegal situation, I'm thinking, but that can't be helped.

"He did leave something," I said.

"Yeah? Well, good, I'm glad about that. You gonna hand it over or what?"

"I have to give it to the right guy."

"Jesus . . . okay, I'm Darko."

"Darko?"

"Donnie, but they call me Darko for the movie."

"What movie?"

"Fuck, man, don't you go to the movies? Donnie fuckin' Darko, okay?"

I could tell he wasn't testing me by using a fake name to see if I really knew who's supposed to collect the money. If he was doing that he would've said his name's John or Frank or something, not Donnie Darko.

"Wait here."

I went upstairs and got the money, then come down again and handed it over. It hurt to do that, even if the money's not mine to begin with, but it seemed like the safest thing to do. He took it and counted it then says, "Back in a minute," and went down to his car, where he opens the trunk and gets out a package and brings it back. It was wrapped in newspaper and taped every which way, about the size of a lunch bucket. He wasn't nervous like before, now that he had the money and was sure I'm no cop.

"Tell Dean next time I want to see him here, not some substitute."

"Okay."

He got in his car and drove away. I sat on the porch rocker for a little while, waiting to see if anyone else might show up unexpected, but nobody did. This is called adapting to circumstances, which I was very fast learning I had the knack of. It was kind of late by then, and I had a long hard day behind me with plenty of surprises that I was not expecting a single one of them, which takes its toll, so I decided to fix up Dean and Bree tomorrow, real early. Then I took a shower and went to bed, I already spent one night on the sofa and one night on the porch rocker, so this time I did the sensible thing and used Bree's bed, even if there's too strong of a perfumey smell in her room like you find with old ladies. They must think they start to smell bad when they get old or something.

FIVE

There is nothing like a good night's rest to make you wake up feeling better about things than they seemed like the night before when they were dark and confusing. You might think I should've had bad dreams over what happened but no, so that means I don't have a guilty conscience like I thought I did. When I looked at everything that happened, I was not a bad person yet. Whanging Dean with the bat was not intended to kill him as it was not done hard enough for that. I don't know what made him die anyway, but it would have had to be something else that happened afterwards, a medical development inside the head I did not make happen. So I was not guilty, that's how I felt, and it was a good feeling. But here's the thing – if I went and buried the both of them, Dean and Bree, then I knew it would make me feel bad and guilty and a very evil person, which I did not want to be, who would?

But if I didn't bury them what else could I do with them

that won't get me in trouble? I lay in bed thinking about that, watching sunlight creep across the ceiling slow and peaceful. I have always been early to rise and am a good thinker at that time before getting out of bed to greet the day, only 6.18 so far says Bree's clock by the bedside, so I don't have to get up yet and can keep on thinking like I was.

And it worked, the thinking, because a new plan come to mind and here it is – I won't bury them, either one, I'll tell Lorraine I went down to the freezer to get something for breakfast and when I dug around in there I found Bree, which was a big shock as you might expect, and then I noticed a bad smell and figured it can't be Bree because she's all froze up, so there must be something else down there stinking the place out, and it didn't take me long to find Dean stuffed under the stairs...Only that won't work because I already told Lorraine he went away with the guy in the green Pontiac. So Dean is still a problem, but at least Bree is explained, by which I mean it'll look like Dean killed her, which he did, and then run away in the Pontiac...but I intend handing over the package the Pontiac guy delivered last night to make Lorraine happy that she got what she was looking for, after all – the package, not the money, I finally got that right – so if the Pontiac guy Donnie Darko come by last night with the package, how come he didn't have Dean with him still?...And the smell will let Lorraine know Dean's been dead awhile now...and it wouldn't work, so I had to think again.

I got restless because the problem wasn't solved and got up. While the air is still cool I decided to fill in the hole in the yard before I get tempted to bury Dean in it, which would make me a criminal. It took around fifteen minutes and made

83

a fairly high mound that would take a long time to settle back
level, but that could be hid from view by putting the chicken
coop over it the way I'm sure Dean planned. So I did that, following his wishes, you might say, dragged the coop over and
positioned it over the mound, which got the chickens cluck-
ing angry at me for messing with their house, but it worked
out fine that way, with the mound out of sight inside which
you couldn't see it except if you lifted the coop aside and
looked, and who's going to do that? Nobody, that's who.
There's a square patch of scratched-over dirt piled with
chicken shit left there where the coop stood till now, but
that's a natural thing that won't get anyone interested in it, I'm
thinking.

So that was done, but I still had to figure what I'll do with
Dean, who is the pesky fly in the soup here. I went in his
room and the smell there has gotten a lot worse because
Dean has gone and shit himself, don't ask me how a dead man
can do that but he did, so now his room is just awful to be in.
What I did, I got a spare sheet from the closet and laid it out
on the floor, then drug Dean out from under the bed and
rolled him up in the sheet and carried him downstairs and
out to the barn just to get that smell gone from the house. I
put him up in the hayloft out of harm's way where no one's
likely to catch a whiff of him and smell a rat. It's a good thing
I already filled in the yard hole or I might have been tempted
to put Dean in there just to be rid of that stink he's making,
but there's no way I'm digging that dirt out again, so he can
stay in the barn for just now while I do some more thinking
about how I'm going to fix this.

While I was out in the barn I checked the lawnmowing

schedule for today and there's no job penciled in until eleven, which suits the first part of my plan perfect. I took a shower then and put my clothes in the washing machine because I worked up a sweat filling the hole and carrying Dean out to the barn, then I went and phoned Lorraine. I was real hungry by then but it would not look good when she come over to have the house smelling of breakfast when I'm supposed to be in shock and horror about finding Bree down in the freezer. I got the story fixed in my mind, then I called Lorraine's number right by the phone like she said. The phone rang a few times then her voice says, "Hello?" It's still only 7.20 so I might have woke her up.

"Hey, Lorraine," I said, "it's me."

"Who?"

"Me, Odell."

"Odell?"

"Yeah, how're you?"

"What do you want, Odell?" She sounded grumpy, so I must have woke her.

"Well, I have got good news and bad. Which one do you want first?"

"The bad," she says, which was a surprise. Most people want the good news first to give them something to fall back on when they get hit by the bad, but it takes all kinds.

"Uh, maybe you should hear the good news first."

"Whatever." She still sounded sore.

"Well, this morning I went out on the porch to greet the day and there's a package there waiting, so I thought maybe that's the thing you were looking for last night. You said a package, so I'm thinking maybe this is the one."

"A package?"

"Right outside the door, all taped up."

"Did you open it?" Her voice was awake now, with an edge to it, so I have got her attention, all right.

"No."

"Well, don't. When I get out there I expect to find that package intact. How the hell did it get there?"

"I was thinking about that, and I think someone must've left it in the night. I'm a heavy sleeper so maybe that's when it happened, when I'm asleep, that's all I can think of how it happened."

"You put that package somewhere out of sight and leave it there till I come over. I'm coming over there right now."

"Okay..."

Then she went and hung up on me, which shows how agitated she is about the package, not waiting to hear the bad news even. I hung up the phone, thinking to myself it's clever the way I don't have to explain about finding the money now and talking to Donnie Darko, which would have opened up a whole new can of worms, as they say. Those early morning plans are generally the best kind.

In around twenty minutes she showed up, wearing her uniform same as last night, and without even saying Good morning or anything she says, "Where is it?"

I brung it out of the kitchen cupboard where I had it stashed and the look on her face says she's relieved it isn't opened like she wanted. She turned it over and over a few times, then made me tell the story again about finding it on the porch right next to the screen door. That part she doesn't like, I could tell, because it's mysterious and unexplained, which are both things that upset some people. I was not upset because to me there's nothing mysterious and unexplained about it, just a simple fiberoo to smooth things over.

"I need breakfast," she said, setting the package down. "Would you mind?"

"Well, there's a problem about that."

"What problem? You didn't eat your way through all the food, did you? The freezer's got plenty, you said."

"Well, about that freezer, it's got a problem. That's the bad news I told you about but you hung up the phone so fast I didn't get to tell you about it."

"If it's broken, call an electrician, just keep the lid down to keep the cold in."

"No, it's working fine, but there's something in there that's not frozen food. Okay, it's frozen, but it isn't food ..."

"Odell, you're making my head ache. What's wrong with the damn freezer?"

"It's got Bree in it."

I watched her face. She's thinking, Bree in the freezer ... and then she gets it, only she doesn't want to.

"Bree ...?" her voice was all little and soft like a girl's, which is a side to Lorraine that I did not see till right now, she has got a softer side, which I liked.

"I went down to get something for breakfast," I said, following the script careful, "and I'm digging around to find something besides pizza, which isn't right for breakfast, only lunch and dinner generally, maybe some breakfast sausages and waffles if there's any there, and that's when I found her. I don't know how to say this ... she's dead. I'm real sorry."

She looked at me like I just told her a flying saucer landed on the roof, then she did something very unexpected, which is slap me right in the face very hard, and she is a big woman like I said, so it hurt.

"Don't you tell me a story like that! Fuck you!"

I didn't hit her back, of course, she's a woman in shock so what she did is excusable, but I got ready to block a second slap if there was another one coming my way, which there wasn't, she just kept on looking at me, reading my eyes to see if it's the truth I'm telling, which it was, mostly. Then she rushed out of the kitchen and down to the basement to investigate the situation there. I stayed where I am, not wanting to intrude on family grief, which is a very private thing restricted to family members only. Then I heard what I kind of expected, namely a scream, but it was short. Then after awhile she come up again and looked me square in the face. "Did you have anything to do with this?" she asked me, very cold, her mouth all tight.

"No, all I did was find her down there," I said, the whole truth this time.

"Then it was Dean," she said, slumping down in a chair and staring at the tabletop. "Oh, God…he went and did it…He went crazy again and did it…" She looked over at me. "When he left, did he have any luggage with him, a suitcase or whatever?"

"No, just the clothes he was wearing, unless he had something in his pockets I couldn't see."

"That'd be right," she says, kind of talking to herself. "He took the money and…then he came back to deliver the package. Oh, Jesus, Dean, why'd you have to go and fuck everything up?"

She was mad at him. I stayed quiet, not knowing which

way to jump. Lorraine's face had gone all pale and her mouth hung open a little, but it wasn't unattractive like Dean's had been.

"Do you still want breakfast?"

"No, I do not want breakfast! Just shut up and let me think!"

"Okay."

I respected her wishes even if my guts were growling by then, just sat quiet on the other side of the table looking at the wall or sometimes the ceiling. Lorraine, she's away somewhere else, thinking hard about all this. Finally she looks me in the eye and says, "You're going to have to help me, Odell."

"Okay."

"There's no way I can keep you out of this. You've been seen driving his truck around town and mowing his lawns, so you can't just disappear. Believe me, that's what I'd prefer, just have you vanish, but that can't happen now. God almighty, Dean went and did it, went crazy all the way and killed her. She never should've let him stay here, the way he was ..."

Lorraine started in on what a crazy guy Dean was, all fucked up from an early age with no friends that stuck with him in school and a bad record with employment, which is why Aunt Bree set him up with his own small business that prospered okay but behind the smiling lawnmower man there's someone else, a crazy person waiting to get out. He was into drugs, she said, all kinds, which didn't help one bit with the crazy part, and him and Bree argued a lot because he wouldn't turn to Jesus to save himself. Bree was very big on the Lord, all the time watching those late night TV shows, which I already figured out because of Chet and Preacher

Bob getting called in to settle the situation, only I couldn't say that to Lorraine, of course. And on top of everything else she says Dean had a problem about "unresolved sexuality" which means he was kind of gay the way she explained it, only he didn't want to admit it even to himself.

"Did he make any moves on you?" she asked.

"No ... except that first night when he woke me up saying he thought he heard someone prowling around, but there was nobody."

"Then what happened?"

"Well ... nothing, he went back to bed, only it was strange the way he woke me up, whispering in my ear. It gave me a fright if you want the honest truth. That's no way to wake someone up unless you want them to get a big surprise, which I did."

"It figures," she said. "You're exactly the kind of guy he was always falling for, big and tall, the exact opposite of Dean. Listen, don't tell anyone about that part, okay? It's got nothing to do with what happened here."

"Okay."

"Pretty soon I'm going to call the Chief of Police. He's a personal friend of mine so he'll go easy, but I'm telling you, Odell, you're going to come under suspicion because of the circumstances, you understand that, don't you?"

"Well, yeah ..."

"So that means you're going to have to trim the truth a little, are you following me?"

"Sure. How do you mean?"

"I mean, as well as leaving out the part about Dean waking you up by whispering in your ear, you've got to leave out the part about Dean going away with the guy in the green Pontiac, and especially about the package getting delivered here. You can't talk to *anyone* about that, okay?"

"Okay. Why not?"

"Because I'm asking you to. Believe me, it'll only make a bad situation worse for everyone, not just Dean, everyone, including you, but mainly it'd make big trouble for me, that's why."

"Why would it do that?"

"Jesus ... it just would. Now, listen up good, Odell. Do you like me?"

"Uhuh."

"That's good, because I like you too, but if you tell anyone at all, especially the Chief of Police, about this package here, it'll most likely mean I end up in jail. Would you want to see me in jail, Odell?"

"No."

"Well, all right then, just keep your lip zipped about the green Pontiac and the package and everything'll go okay, except now Dean is gonna be a wanted man. He won't run far, hasn't got the connections or the smarts. Jesus, Dean ..."

She put her head in her hands and didn't move for awhile. My guts rumbled but I don't think she heard. I really wanted breakfast, but how would it look when the cops come and I'm chowing down on sausages and waffles, with maybe some bacon on the side, plus coffee, when there's a dead frozen woman been discovered down in the basement? It wouldn't look good, that's how it'd look. I had to make the sacrifice, not just for me, for Lorraine too. Seeing her there looking miserable about what happened, it made my heart hurt, so if she wanted me to trim the truth like she described it, then I would.

"Odell," she says, "we've got to get your story set about how Dean went away from here. This is what happened, are you listening close?"

"I'm listening."

"About ten o' clock Monday night you and Dean heard a car horn outside. You went out on the porch and there's a car parked halfway along the driveway, so far away you can't see what kind in the dark. That's important – you can't see what kind or who's in it. But Dean acts like it's nothing strange and goes down to talk to the guy or guys in the car, then he comes back and says he has to go away for a few days and will you take over his lawnmowing schedule till he gets back, which you said you will because he's been pretty good to you even if you only met a little while ago. So Dean goes away with these guys without even packing a bag – remember that detail because they'll look over everything in his room and see his razor's still there and stuff like that, so get that part right, he left with just the clothes he's wearing. It'll sound peculiar but the facts will bear it out … except if they catch Dean and he says something different, which he would … Well, we just have to hope they don't catch him. Maybe they won't. I hate to say it, but Dean is so messed up he might just kill himself over this from remorse or something …"

I waited for more things to remember but she was done. "Can you remember that story, Odell?"

"I sure can, it's simple."

"Okay," she says, standing up, "I'm going to call Chief Webb. Have you got your ducks in a row, Odell?"

"Ducks?"

"Are your thoughts all organized about what happened and didn't happen here, like I explained?"

"Sure thing."

"Because Andy Webb is no fool. He'll try and trip you up, so you better be ready."

"I'm ready."

"Okay then."

And she started tapping the phone with her fingertip. "Chief Webb," she says, then, "Lorraine Lowry. Tell him it's urgent." A few seconds went by then she says, "Andy, I've got a situation here. I'm out at my Aunt Bree's place and...she's dead. It's murder, Andy...She's in the freezer...In the freezer, yes...And Dean's gone missing as of two days back...Right... Andy, I'd be real appreciative if you didn't pass this on to the media till after the coroner's come and gone, is that possible?"

It sounded like it was, because she said Thank you more than once then hung up. Then she picked up the package and waved it under my nose. "You know what this is in my hand?" she asked.

"A package?"

"Wrong. There's nothing at all in my hand, because no package got delivered here, got that straight? There never was any package. If you can just keep that fact uppermost in your mind you and me can continue to be friends."

"I'd like that."

"Well, fine, I'd like that too. Everyone needs friends, especially when there's a tragedy like this. That's what friends are for, to cover for each other and keep the other guy out of trouble with the law. Once you're in trouble with the law, you're toast, I've seen it happen. Dean, he's in the biggest trouble of his life now..."

She sat down again at the table and I thought she's going to cry, but she didn't, just looked at the package in her hand and got straight up again, like she didn't know which way to go or what to do at that exact moment, then she says to me, "I'm taking this out to my car. When this package disappears out of this kitchen it disappears out of your thoughts. Forever. Got that, Odell?"

"Got it."

And away she goes. Soon as she's gone I took a packet of cookies from the pantry and crammed three or four into my mouth I'm so starving hungry by then, and then three or four more, just to take the edge off of my appetite as they say, which had got my stomach churning so bad it's painful, but those cookies kept the wolf from the door until I could eat a true meal later on after the cops came and went.

Lorraine come back in the house just as I'm swallowing the last of the cookies and tossing the empty packet in the trash bin under the sink. Her face was set very grim and determined so I made mine the same way so our stories would match up for Andy Webb. The thing I was thinking is this – if Lorraine and me can bring this off it brings us closer together like they say tragedy does, and from being closer who knows what might happen? I was getting those feelings about her even if she's an older woman, but I could overlook that if we're made for each other the way I'm thinking we are, which Lorraine might not have been, seeing as she's got other things on her mind right now. But not me, I'm thinking hard about her and me, which helps to wipe away any thinking about that package, which I knew good and well was something illegal, which means she's doing something against the law but, hey, nobody's perfect and I could overlook that part too because love is blind.

What I'm saying is, I would put my hands over my eyes deliberate for this woman to bring us happiness. Already I junked my plan to join the Army because she's right, her and Dean, saying it's crazy to risk getting my head blown off in Iraq if Lorraine can get me a good job as a prison guard. That is steady work because there will always be criminals who have to be kept under lock and key for the protection of us all, so it's a job for life being handed to me on a silver plate. I would have to be crazy to say no, and I am not crazy.

Maybe twenty minutes later two cop cars and an ambulance turned off the road and came up the driveway, going slow and with no sirens because there's no emergency here, and the twinkle bars were not flashing either, same reason. They all pulled up in the yard which got it pretty crowded out there, and it was plain from the start which one is Andy Webb. He's a big guy, although not so big as me, around forty-five maybe, and he looks like a police chief should, smart and tough at the same time, and he's got three other cops with him.

I watched from the porch while Lorraine went down to speak a few words. He even gave her a quick hug, which was a surprise, not what you might expect from cops investigating a murder scene, but she did say they're old friends so no big deal. The other cops acted like they didn't even see it. Then they all came up to the house and Lorraine introduced me to the Chief by way of saying I'm an acquaintance of Dean's, which was clever of her because an acquaintance is not so close a thing as a friend, so if I did not have all the answers about Dean there's a reason, namely I'm only an acquaintance, which would be a big help with the questioning.

We all trooped down to the basement and Andy says to me, "Tell me what happened, how you found her."

So I did, and while I'm talking a couple of the cops are taking pictures of Bree in the freezer, and when they had enough Andy says to start pulling out the pizzas and so forth and get her out of there, which they did, setting everything aside neat till you could see Bree exposed which they took more pictures of, then it's time to lift her out, which was done real careful out of respect for the dead. They even put on rubber gloves for this part like in a TV operating theater. When they got her out and saw the way her being folded over has hid the shotgun wound in her stomach they looked at each other like to say officially that it's murder all right and more pictures got took of Bree on the floor next to the freezer with the pizzas and Birds Eye peas beside her. Then the ambulance guys from the coroner set her on a stretcher to take her away and Andy says he wants to talk with me upstairs, so that's where we went.

Andy and another cop took me to the living room and sat me down. "Odell," he says, "this is Detective Sergeant Vine. We need to get your account of what happened from the time you came here till this morning when you went down and found her in the freezer. Take your time and tell it just the way you remember. Don't leave anything out even if you think it's so small of a detail it isn't important, because it might be, you never know."

I must've talked about fifteen minutes telling about my car trouble and how Dean took me in and fed me etcetera only I said it happened late Saturday not late Sunday, which gave us an extra day to get acquainted and would explain why he trusted me enough to ask me would I mow those lawns till he gets back. He would not have done that if we only met that day, I'm thinking, and it all has to sound convincing. While I'm talking I heard the ambulance drive away so Aunt Bree has left the building.

When I was done Andy stared at me a long while then says, "That story won't fly, Odell. After just two days a man trusts you enough to handle his business for him? He leaves without even packing a bag and drives away with someone that you didn't see, not even what kind of car?"

"It struck me as strange at the time," I said, "but that's what happened. I was happy to do the lawnmowing, though. He treated me right, so that was okay by me. I've still got the money they paid me, his customers. I can show you. I didn't spend a dime of it, two days' mowing."

"Two days? I thought he left Monday night, so that's just Tuesday you did the mowing."

I thought fast and decided the truth would sound best. "Well, I mowed those lawns for him Monday too, on account of he was real hungover from drinking Sunday night. He ought not to drink so much for a small guy, but he did anyway. So that's why he trusted me to do the lawns Tuesday when he's gone, because I already showed him I can do the job Monday. I've got the money right here."

"No one's accusing you of anything, Odell, we just want to get the entire story. Did Dean say he didn't like his aunt?"

"Well, he went so far as to say they argued about this and that."

"What kind of this and that?"

"Well...religion mainly."

"Religion?"

"Because he wanted to be a Muslim, he said."

"A Muslim?"

"Dean didn't want to be Christian anymore, so he was thinking about being a Muslim instead. He told me his aunt was a diehard Christian with objections to that, which she thought she had the right to say no because she set him up with the lawnmowing business."

"And did you get to hear any of these arguments?"

"Nossir, Aunt Bree was away in Florida he told me, so I never met the lady until today."

They were not believing me, I could tell, which got me a little bit scared and at the same time a little bit mad, because I'm only telling them around ten percent lies and they're acting like it's ninety percent or something like that. So I trotted out some more truth to set things right. "He's got books in his room, Muslim books. He showed me them and said I ought to think about going over to the Muslims because Christianity has got it all wrong and they're the ones has got it right. He told me America is doomed unless everybody quits being a Christian and goes over to the Islamites like he's doing."

"And what did you say back at him?"

"I said I'm proud to be American and even if I'm not a regular churchgoer it's better to be a Christian than one of those others."

"And what happened then, did he get mad?"

"No, he laughed and says I'm wrong about that entirely, and someday soon I'll see how wrong I am and I'll regret it same as those others will."

"What others?"

"He didn't say, Christians I guess."

"Was he making a threat?"

"Not exactly."

"And during all this religious talk he never once acted like a man that's killed his aunt and put her down in the basement freezer?"

"No, I would've noticed if he acted that way. He was acting normal apart from the Muslim talk. He's got those books in his dresser."

Andy gave the nod to Vine and he went away upstairs.

"Relax, Odell, you're looking kind of anxious."

"I don't want people thinking I did something wrong."

"Nobody's saying you did."

"But those others, in the car, they might think so when they read about this in the papers. They might come back for revenge against me." That sounded good, I thought.

"You said you couldn't see them, or how many there were. Maybe it was only one man out there."

"Okay, but he called them his brothers, which I know from Lorraine he doesn't have, only the one sister."

"Brothers?"

"Yessir, that's what he said when he come back up the driveway and says he has to go right there and then ... because his brothers want him to and he can't say no."

"You didn't say this about the brothers before, and Lorraine never mentioned you saying anything to her about it."

"Well, I...I was embarrassed about what he said, us Christians being wrong and so forth. She wouldn't have wanted to hear about her own brother saying stuff like that."

"So you're saying you think it was a bunch of Muslims out in that car?"

"I don't know who they were except he said they're his brothers and he has to go and could I do the lawnmowing for a few days."

Andy sat looking thoughtful at me and was still doing it when Vine come back down with the Muslim books in his hand and he shows them to Andy. Vine had rubber gloves on but Andy didn't so he doesn't want to touch the books, which are evidence now, I bet. Vine showed him the covers and then put them all in a plastic bag and took them away so it's just Andy and me again.

"Odell," he says, "did you have the impression Dean was a terrorist? You know what that means, don't you?"

"Sure, everybody knows about terrorists. Nine-eleven, that was terrorists."

"Right, and are you saying you think Dean was maybe thinking about joining up with that kind?"

I already told a high percentage of lies about the brothers in the car and making Dean look bad, not that it mattered because he's dead, but Andy doesn't know that so I didn't want it to look like I'm pointing the finger at a man that was friendly to me.

"I wouldn't say that, no. He just said he had to go away with the brothers."

Is telling lies about a dead man who's a murderer okay? I was asking myself this big question because I'm starting to feel guilty. I had to tell myself I'm doing this for Lorraine, along with not mentioning about the package, so we can have a happy life together, and if I was dissing Dean behind his back, it was partway true what I'm saying, and he can't get hurt by it on account of being dead, so where was the guilt coming from? Maybe I only felt bad because I did not have breakfast yet and that has always been an important meal for me, the one that sets you up for the day and without the right kind you run out of energy midmorning and start reaching for snacks between meals which leads directly to overbesity in children and adults alike nowadays.

Andy stood up. "Let's take a look at that car of yours," he said, so I got up too and we went out to the barn, which I wanted very much not to go there because of you-know-who stashed up in the hayloft but stayed calm anyway. Vine come out there too and him and Andy walked around the Monte Carlo. Vine wrote down the plate number in his cop note-book, so you can be sure they'll run it and find if the car's mine, which it is and paid for besides, also registered correct and insured for third party so no problem there. And another good thing was I couldn't smell Dean at all, he's positioned up too high, but that would change when he really started going rotten which is soon, it's summertime after all. I had to think of a place where he can get put and not be found.

"Open it up," says Andy, meaning my car. I did it, then he tells me to turn the ignition. The engine coughed and hacked a couple times and died. He had me get out and Vine got in to try starting her up, but it would not do that. What they're doing is testing my story about car trouble, so now things are looking good because so far there is not a damn thing they can prove I told that's a lie. They poked around inside my car, examining stuff in the glovebox, then they run their noses over Dean's truck, only I can tell they aren't really expecting to find evidence there. We went out in the yard again and Andy told me to hang around out there while he talks with Lorraine, who has been talking with the two other cops meantime.

Andy and Vine went back in the house and I strolled around casual, waiting to see if anyone else went out to the barn but that did not happen. So then I strolled around to the back yard and the two cops that were talking with Lorraine before are back there poking around. One of them is looking at the square of ground where the chicken coop was until early this morning, kind of kicking at it, then he called the other one over and said something I can't hear, maybe because he's talking low on account of they both know I'm there acting natural and unconcerned. Then they both went over to the coop and got on either side of it and started lifting it up! When I saw them do that my heart flipped very alarming and something like a blade run right through me, which I knew was fear, plain and simple.

They moved the coop aside and set it down and there was the mound of fresh-turned dirt looking exactly like what it wasn't – a new grave. I strolled on over like an innocent man would've done and said, "That's been done just recent, you can tell." A guilty man would not have said that, which is my way to lead them off the track without it looking like that's what I'm doing.

"That's how it looks to us too," says one of the cops, then the other one headed for the house. I went up closer to the mound but the first cop stopped me. "Stay back," he says, "that's evidence."

"Evidence?"

"Got a hunch there's something buried under there, and I don't mean chickens."

I come over all thunderstruck, acting so good I should get the Oscar, and said, "I bet...I bet Dean's under there!"

"Think so?"

"I bet he is! Him or someone else, anyway."

"Maybe."

We stood looking at the mound while chickens pecked at the dirt like we aren't even there. Andy and Vine came out with cop number two plus Lorraine, and we all stood over the mound. "That's recent," said Andy. "Take some pictures then dig it up."

The camera cop got busy and then they searched around for a spade to use, which was easy because I left it propped against the side of the house after I finished with it this morning. One of the cops took off his jacket and started spading the dirt out with everyone else watching. And while I was doing my share of the watching I looked up at the rest and they're all looking at me, including Lorraine, and I knew they all thought I did this, dug a grave and put Dean in it and covered it over with the coop. It was just so obvious that they thought that, which was upsetting getting thought about that way, so I said out loud and very firm, "I didn't do it." Even to myself I sounded like a little kid caught standing over a broken lamp.

"No one's saying you did," says Andy, not sounding truthful at all.

I was upset but tried not to show it. All I did was fill in a hole, and there they stood, four cops and Lorraine, all thinking the worst about me. I didn't care about the cops but it hurt to see Lorraine look at me that way. Another cop took over after the first one got tired and pretty soon they got to the bottom of the hole. You could tell it's the bottom of the hole because the dirt wasn't loose and easy to shovel anymore. And of course there's nobody there, which is no surprise to me but it definitely was for the rest of them. They were ignoring me now, like all of a sudden I dropped off their suspect radar, which would be a good thing.

"This is not making sense," Vine said to Andy, who's looking puzzled himself about it all, and Lorraine was avoiding my eye, maybe embarrassed about thinking I buried her brother under the coop.

"Show me your hands, Odell," says Andy, and I did. He looked at the palms and felt them with his fingers, then turned my hands over and looked at the nails, which I cleaned with a nailbrush in the shower that morning before calling Lorraine. There's no sign of calluses on my palms because I used the lawnmowing gloves for all that spadework, then put those back in the truck.

"Fill it up," he said, and the first cop took up the shovel again, only this time he's not so excited as before. Andy says to me, "How recent was that earth spaded up would you say, Odell?"

"About five minutes ago now."

"I mean before we dug it up. There was no chicken poop on it despite the henhouse being put over it to hide the mound."

"Well, those chickens, I've noticed they tend not to go in the coop hardly at all. See how the door's been busted off? They can't be kept inside if they don't want to, and I guess they don't want to. If I was a chicken I'd want to have freedom and use the whole yard, not be locked in a henhouse. Anyway, Dean said I should stay out of the yard because he saw a rattlesnake back here. He even said to use the clothes dryer in the laundry and not the clothesline out here because he doesn't want me getting bit and then I'll sue him for the responsibility of it. Which I wouldn't have done, I'm not that kind."

They were all looking at me like I'm an idiot except for the cop doing the shoveling, and I was telling the truth, so that shows how people can never truly understand each other and know when the truth is being told.

Andy scratched at the side of his head, then says to me, "You're saying it was Dean spaded out this hole and then filled it again?"

"Well, I don't know because I didn't see him do it. I only know it wasn't me, but it was done recent like you said because it wasn't all dried out on top like it would be if it was done some time ago."

You might think I'm putting my neck in a noose talking that way, incriminating talk, but I was doing it because they would not expect someone to say something that puts him in a bad light, so it makes me look even more innocent than I am.

Lorraine said, "With the coop over it keeping the sun off, that dirt'd stay fresh-looking and moist, and if the chickens stayed out of there that explains no chicken poop."

"Okay," says Andy, "but it doesn't explain why the heck someone dug a grave and then decided not to use it."

"Well, maybe it was Dean that dug it to put Bree in, then he changed his mind for some reason and put her in the freezer instead." Lorraine was doing her best to get their attention back on Dean, who's gone missing under Suspicious Circumstances as the saying goes. Andy kept looking at the dirt being shoveled back in the hole very rapid and thinking whatever cops think, most likely thoughts about why it was done and who's the one that did it.

"I'm thinking about turning this over to Homeland," Andy said to Vine.

"Why?"

"This Muslim connection, I don't like it."

"It's a little vague, don't you think?"

"Anyone that can kill his aunt over a religious argument has got it in him to be a terrorist. He hasn't come back from wherever he went, so I'm thinking he's with like-minded people. Homeland will know if there's a cell operating around here."

"Here?" Vine made it sound like Andy thinks there's fairies in Callisto, Kansas.

"Why not."

Now there's Homeland Security involved, and that's a big agency. Dean has started something here all right, and I have gone and watered his garden so to speak with my ten percent lies, but it's too late now to be backing away from all this. I figured it'll look good if I come to Dean's defense, going against the grain of what everyone else is thinking, because once again it makes me sound innocent. "Dean wouldn't be a terrorist," I said, "he's too much of a friendly type guy. Look at how he trusts me to do the lawnmowing without he hardly knows me. That's trusting, not mean. Terrorists are mean."

Andy gave me a look and says, "He was mean enough to kill his aunt. That not mean enough for you, Odell?"

I said, "Maybe it was done by someone else we don't know about yet."

I can tell they think I'm a fool for thinking something like that, but it's okay that they think that about me because it distracts them, which is my plan and they fell into the trap I laid because there was noplace else for the conversation to go after that.

When the hole was filled again the cops started getting ready to leave. They had Dean's shotgun with them in a plastic bag. Andy had a long talk with Lorraine first, then he comes over to me. "Odell, you're a key witness in this investigation, so you'll have to stick around awhile and be available for further questioning. Special agents will take you through it all again pretty soon. In the meantime if there's anything you remember that you didn't tell me already, call me anytime, it could be important."

"How about that chicken coop? Think I should put it back over the dirt mound?"

"No, leave it like it is for now."

There was more talking back and forth among the cops, then they got in their cop cars and drove away. Lorraine and me watched them go, then she turned to me and said, "That was good, Odell. You acted just right. You looked so guilty there I even thought you buried someone myself, then there's nothing in the hole and all you looked like was dumb. Brilliant!"

"I have to get ready for work. There's a lawn to get mowed at eleven."

"You want to keep doing that?"

"When Dean comes back he'll appreciate that I kept the business going, otherwise his customers are gonna hire someone else to do the job and he'll have to start all over again." I figure it's smart to talk about Dean like he's still alive, what you might call verbal camouflage.

"Odell," she says, "that's sweet, but you know as well as I do that Dean won't be coming back here to mow lawns, if he even comes back at all. You do understand that he's the one killed Bree, don't you? I appreciate you standing by him like that, saying those things, but it's clear as day he's the one that did it and now he's on the run with a bunch of terrorists that'll do God knows what. But you keep on mowing those lawns, there's no reason not to, it's cash money that you can keep until I talk to them at the prison about a job. You're still interested in that, aren't you?"

"You bet."

"Because after all this terrible business has blown over there's still real life to get back to for all of us, meaning a job of work that we have to do to pay the rent and put food on the table. That's what you want, right?"

"A steady job, that's all I want."

"Well, maybe I can get that for you." She turned and looked at the house. "This is my place now, Bree let me know awhile back she made out a will that says it's mine and Dean's after she dies, and somehow I don't think Dean's going to be collecting his half share." She sighed this big sigh of sadness that shows what a sympathetic person she is, which are the best kind to know. "Meantime I'd appreciate it if you'd stay on here and look after the place till I can move in. When this gets on the news there'll be people out here busting their necks to check out the murder scene, reporters too, can you handle that?"

"I'll just say No comment."

"That'd be the best thing." She laid a hand on my arm. "I really appreciate this, Odell, about the package and everything else. I'd hate to be going through all this embarrassment and publicity that's going to happen now without someone to help me out like you are."

"No problem, I like to help people."

She took her hand away. "I have to get to work. I'm already late but they'll be okay about it when I tell them what happened. I'm going to tell them about how you're helping me out here, Odell, and that'll stick in their mind like a character witness statement and maybe make it easier for you to get the job, that's what I'm hoping anyway."

"Okay."

"I'll call you tonight," she says, getting in her car.

I watched her drive away, then checked my watch. It's a cheap one, $29.95, but it keeps good time. I still had an hour and eleven minutes till that first lawn needs to get mowed. First thing I did, I washed Dean's baseball bat good with soap and water in case there's forensic evidence stuck to it so small I can't see but which those smart folk at CSI can spot under laser beam light and so forth. Next thing I did, I went in the barn and got those lawnmowing gloves again, then fetched Dean down, smelling real bad now, and carried him around back and set him gentle on the ground. Then I dug out that hole again in record time, the dirt has been shifted around so many times now it's loose as a goose. When it's standing empty again like before, I laid Dean down inside of it. I shoveled that dirt back again till it looked like it did when the cops finished with it, and so am I. I hope I never have to shovel dirt again I am so sick and tired of it now.

All that hard work gave me an appetite seeing as it was done with only half a packet of cookies to give me strength, so I went down to the basement to grab some breakfast. That's when I find the cops have investigated the scene without putting the frozen food back in the freezer, which is still standing with the lid open while the motor's running overtime trying to cope with the situation. How unprofessional is that! I picked what I wanted, blueberry waffles, and flung everything else back in the freezer before it gets even more thawed than it is and slammed the lid. I was so mad about what they did I let it spoil my breakfast enjoyment, but then I put it behind me like you have to when things are not going the way they should.

I had another quick shower and then I'm out the door and on my way to work like a regular citizen going about his job like always. This time I locked the door with the key Dean has got on his skull'n'bones key ring so nobody can get inside. It was a good start to the day.

SIX

There was five jobs that day which I took care of with a smile in my heart and on my face because I am so happy. If I keep doing the lawnmowing it means I'll still be at Dean's when Lorraine moves in there, which means her and me will be there together like we're married almost. I wanted that very much, being in love with her, which I decided between jobs two and three that I definitely am, so things are looking good. It's a tragedy about Dean being a murdering homosexual Muslim terrorist but there's nothing I can do about that. I put in a good word for him with Chief Webb and that's all I can do. I didn't want to think about Dean anymore, only Lorraine. If Dean was a dark cloud then Lorraine, she's the silver lining. I had impressed her this morning with my quick thinking that I displayed and she was grateful, I could tell, plus she told me to stick around. Okay, I'd have to do that anyway because of the investigation, but she wants me to anyway so that counts for plenty.

I collected two hundred and forty bucks for the mowing and drove home (that's how I'm thinking of Dean's place now) still with that smile on the inside and the outside of me, but that went away when I got there and the yard has got a van with *Channel 7* on the door and two people waiting for me. I parked in the barn and got out and they're right in my face with the camera carried by a guy and a mike carried by a woman.

She says, "Sir, what can you tell us about events that occurred here today?".

"No comment."

"Are you the owner of this property? We couldn't help but notice there's a recent grave dug in the back yard. What do you have to say about that?"

"It isn't a grave it's a hole, and the police already dug it up and filled it again because there's nothing there, you can ask them."

"We're asking you, sir."

"If it was a crime scene back there I guess you'd see some yellow police tape like they have, wouldn't you? Well, where is it if it's a crime scene, huh?"

That was a smart thing to say but it didn't stop them.

"We're told that a woman has been murdered here and her body found in a basement freezer. What can you tell us about that?"

"No comment."

I pushed past her and headed for the porch but she kept up with me, trotting sideways to do it and the camera guy kept up too. It was very irritating the way they just wouldn't quit. "Sir, Channel Seven News has learned that a terrorist cell is thought to be operating in this area. Can you comment on a possible connection between that and this incident of murder?"

"Nope, no connection that I know of."

I was at the steps by then and they followed me up, only the camera guy missed his footing halfway up and tripped himself. He made a squawk as he went down, trying to keep the camera from hitting anything and getting busted, and the distraction when she turned to him was enough for me to get inside and close the door on them. They knocked and Helloed but no way was I letting them in to ask more questions. I went to the back and looked out the window but the grave was okay, they hadn't messed with it, but I bet they got plenty of footage for the evening report. Lorraine was not going to be happy about this.

They hung around another twenty minutes, then just as they're getting ready to leave another van comes up the driveway and into the yard. This one was Channel Nine. The two teams talked a few minutes then the Seven people departed the scene and the Niners banged on the door. "Hello? Sir, we're informed you're in there! What can you tell us about what's happened here? Sir?"

"I don't know a goddamn thing!" I yelled through the door.

"What did you tell that other bunch? We have a right to the same information!"

"I'll tell you everything I know for a thousand bucks!"

"Sir, Channel Nine News does not conduct checkbook journalism!"

"That's okay, cash is fine!"

"That isn't how it's done, sir, I'm sure you're aware of that!"

"Fifty bucks!"

I waited, then two tens and a twenty come sliding under the door. I picked it up and opened the door and threw the money out. "Now do you believe I don't know a goddamn thing?"

I slammed the door shut again and locked it. I could hear them talking, then their footsteps went down the steps and I knew where they're headed. I watched through the back window while they aimed their camera at the grave, then at the house, then they got tired of waiting or maybe they wanted to make the early news deadline, anyway they drove off and I could relax at last unless Channel Twelve comes around.

The phone rang. I let it ring, thinking most likely it's the news wanting to know when they can interview me, but a ringing telephone is a powerful irritation so in the end I answered it, only I didn't say anything. If it was the news, they weren't even getting a single word out of me.

"Odell?"

"Hey, Lorraine."

"How's your day been?"

"I mowed all the lawns. Two-hundred forty bucks. Do I give that to you? You probably inherited Dean's lawnmowing business as well as the house ... I mean most likely that'll happen if ... something happens to him, which let's hope it doesn't ..."

"You keep that for spending money, Odell, you earned it."

"Okay."

"Did you have dinner yet?"

"I only just got home." There it is again – Home.

"Well, don't go down to that freezer, that's too spooky. I'm on my way over with burgers, okay? I got two for you because you're my big guy with an appetite to match, I bet."

"Okay."

Her big guy! This is a lovematch for sure happening here.

"Did anyone come out there asking questions yet?"

"Two TV crews but I didn't tell them anything, just No comment."

"That's good. You get cleaned up and I'll see you in a little while."

"Yeah."

She hung up. My ears were burning. Her big guy. This was getting serious very fast, but they do say that's how it happens when it's real love, like a lightning bolt from the blue – *kaboom!* My life is shaping up at last and all because my car quit on me, so it's an ill wind that blows you good as the saying goes, and I was ready to be blown.

I hung out my laundry that I did this morning and then had a shower and put on my best jeans, the tight ones that make your wedding package stand out if you've got one. Lorraine's waiting for a package delivery? Here's your package, honey! I turned on Dean's stereo and danced around on my own awhile to Limp Bizkit and Linkin Park. These bands, they can't spell worth a damn but they make millions, why is that? Looking at myself in the mirror I'm thinking maybe I should've done what the coach and the old man wanted and gone for football. Then I reminded myself it isn't just about size in sport, you have got to have commitment which I had none of, so there goes the two mil per year and the high-seven-figure contract with Nike. But if I was a football star I wouldn't have met Lorraine, which is what they call Destiny. Or maybe it's Fate. Could be both.

When she come up the driveway I'm at the door to meet

her. She's carrying a big brown paper bag with grease soaking through the bottom and my stomach lurched.

"Hey there!" she waves, looking bright and breezy in spite of the uniform.

"Hey."

We went directly through to the kitchen and started chowing down on burgers and fries. I never tasted food so good. Lorraine, she told me about her day at the prison to make a change from talking about Dean and Bree and all that sad mess. What they have at the prison is this closed-circuit TV everywhere pointing in all directions so the inmates can't kill each other without the evidence getting caught on disk, Preventive Detection she calls it. Only there's a few extra cameras that are so small and hidden away the inmates don't know about them, but the guards do and that gives them an advantage to snoop.

What happened today was, one of the toughest guys in the place got seen while he's off by himself in a storeroom where he thinks he's invisible, and he starts sashaying around like a woman, with one hand on his hip and the other one held out crooked sideways. What he's saying, or rather singing, is that old nursery rhyme – "I'm a little teapot short and stout, Here is my handle, Here is my spout" – over and over again, prancing around the room like some show-off little kid on stage at the school show. The guards all fell over from laughing at it on replay it's so funny, and the security specialist there that runs the cameras says he'll make everyone a copy. On the serious side, it means the guards can make this teapot guy cooperate when they want him to from now on just by threatening him with the recording.

"Some badass," says Lorraine. "All we have to do is whisper Teapot and he'll bend over for us. You don't know what a weapon that is for us inside. Hey, I put in a word for you with Connors, he's the hire'n'fire guy. I bet he wants to see you soon because everyone there is sympathetic as hell about what happened. Did those news guys bug you pretty bad?"

"They were kind of pesky but I could handle it. Too bad Chief Webb told them."

"That's his job when something like this happens. He's got to inform the public, doesn't he? That's democracy in action, everyone knowing what's going on and no hidden secrets like they used to have in Russia and places. Anyway they'll get their info from police headquarters from now on, official statements they give out."

"Good, I don't want anyone coming around here."

"What about me? I can come here can't I?"

"Well, sure, it's your place after all now that Dean's ..."

"Go on, you can say it."

"Okay, now that Dean's dead."

"Dead?" She got a little frown between her eyebrows and I knew I'd gone and let my guard down which I had told myself not to do. "I thought you were going to say being hunted down, which they'll do now that Andy brung in the Homeland people. That'll be some circus. Why do you think he's dead?"

"Well, I ... I shouldn't have thought it. I don't know why I did ... excuse me for saying it."

"He may be a grade-A fuckup but he's still my brother. I don't want him gunned down like a dog by the feds."

"Heck no."

"So don't use that word again, please. It's bad enough Bree's … passed on, I can't even think about losing Dean too."

"Maybe they'll catch him and put him in your prison and you could see him every day and kind of take care of him. And I could too if I'm working there. We could take care of him together."

She shook her head. "If he gets caught he knows what's in store for someone like him – solitary, that's what he'll get. Nobody in prison approves of terrorists, and that's the label been stuck on him now. He'd be better off being an ordinary woman-killer, but being a terrorist he'd be dead meat on the block. I can't see Dean being able to survive solitary, he'd go completely nuts after awhile … Why are we talking about this bad shit? I don't want to. No more shit talk, okay?"

"Okay."

She munched on her burger some more then says, "You know what I like about you, Odell?

"No."

It's true, I didn't know, but I bet it was being tall like I am and broad across the shoulders. All the women like that and Lorraine would be the same, I'm thinking.

"The way you don't argue with me. God, that pisses me off, the way men think they're always right and no woman can say something different without her getting a load of horseshit about it. But you don't do that, do you."

"I guess not."

"That's why we'll get along. The guys at work, they're not too bad, but as soon as you sleep with a guy it's like he's got the green light to start telling you what to do."

I'm getting a mixed message here. Is she saying as soon as

she sleeps with me it'll turn bad between us, so she won't take that risk by sleeping with me? Bad news. Or is she saying she'll sleep with me because I'm not that kind before or even after sleeping with her? That would be good news. Or is she saying she slept with the guys at work and after she did they gave her the kind of shit she's talking about? Baddest news yet. I wanted to ask but couldn't, not out loud, you can't do that. I didn't like to think about her and the guys at work. The sooner I got to be one of the guys at work the better.

"Do you carry a gun at work?"

"No way, not while we're on the block, we might have it snatched and used against us. Only the guys on the outside carry guns, the guys in the towers and in the restricted areas. There's an armory for use in a breakout or riot, but basically you can go all day without seeing a gun. It isn't about guns, it's about management of time and individual units. What that means is, you have to keep the inmates from congregating too many in one place. Sometimes when they do that it's what they call critical mass and stuff starts happening maybe for no good reason and you've got a riot and you have to go to lockdown, which nobody wants. You've got to give the inmates just enough freedom to move around in the main areas together so they get to socialize a little bit and don't go stir-crazy, which is what happens if you keep 'em cooped up in their cells too much. That's a bad thing for morale, shutting somebody away like that, and it doesn't serve any purpose, that's what they teach nowadays in Penal Management. It's all about psychology and how to make every son of a bitch feel good about himself."

"Okay."

What I was thinking about was Lorraine and her gun with no uniform on, not even underwear, just the gunbelt, and it's having an effect on me like before.

"You're getting kind of squirmy there, Odell. Like the burgers?"

"They're good. So when they catch Dean he'll go stir-crazy on account of being put in solitary?"

"Dean has gone and made his bed and has to lie in it," she said. "He's been heading for big trouble all his life. Even when he was a kid there's all kinds of shit he got up to that drove Bree nuts, setting fires and stealing and one time she caught him torturing a cat."

"A cat?"

"Then there was the time a neighbor caught him trying to have sex with another boy age eight. That got Dean in a lot of trouble. If he had've been older at the time, fourteen, I think, then he would've had even more trouble from that particular incident, which was the first time he got caught but not the last bad sexual act he did if you take my meaning. You think he was coming on to you with that whispering in the ear thing?"

"Maybe. It made me jump right up off the sofa."

"Well, it would if you aren't expecting it. Whispering in the ear, that's something nice if it's in bed with your loved one and not getting hit on by some gay terrorist."

My hard-on started going down with all that talk about tortured cats and setting fires. Dean was some fucked-up dude all right, and he had some nerve getting me involved in his terrorist lifestyle plus drug smuggling with his pal Donnie Darko.

"What was in it?" The question just popped out of me.

"What was in what? You've just got the strangest way of conversing sometimes."

"The package."

She stopped eating and looked at me very steamed, then she says, "There never was any package, Odell, you and me agreed about that."

"So there won't be no more packages coming this way?"

That made her stop and think before answering. "Well, I was going to talk to you about that as a matter of fact. See, if you're here all the time, kind of like a tenant, you'll need to be taking care of the place, you know, keeping it clean and tidy, also bringing in the mail and regular chores like that. Which will include every Tuesday night there's a delivery from a certain friend of Dean's that you have to receive and pass over some payment for it. That's all you need to do, receive the package and give over the payment. The schedule got upset this week by Dean going away like he did, but the package arrived anyway, which I'm thinking was Dean's way of saying he's going away and it'll be different from now on seeing as he didn't come in, just left it on his own doorstep. If it was Dean and not the other guy."

"Donnie Darko."

She gave me a long look. I had done it again about letting my guard down. I think it's because I am so distracted by this woman sat across the table and this is having a bad effect on my brain.

"Donnie who?"

"Darko."

"That's a movie. Where'd you hear it?"

"I must've gone to the movies."

"That wouldn't make you say the name right here and now. Did Dean tell you who's coming Tuesday night? You told me you didn't see him."

"All I saw was the green Pontiac. Maybe Dean said the name, I don't remember."

She was still looking at me suspicious. "I hope you're not holding things back from me, Odell. We can't be friends if you're going to do that to me. Friendship is based on Trust with a capital T."

"I'm not holding back. I remember now ... Dean said his friend Donnie D is coming and I better not go outside when he does because it's private business needs taking care of. I peeked through the window anyway, that's how come I know what kind of car ... and when he said Donnie D I asked what kind of a name is that and he told me about that movie *Donnie Darko* that this guy must like, I guess."

She started eating again, chewing on a fry. "I guess you can't help but be a little curious."

"No I can't. What's in the package that comes every Tuesday?"

"See, that's what I'm worried about, will it come next Tuesday after all this other shit has come down thanks to Dean? Donnie, he'll hear about it and maybe get cold feet. That package has to come through regular as clockwork or there's people are gonna want to know why."

"So what's in the package?"

That is three times now I asked her. I knew what's in it, all right. There's only one thing it can be.

"Relief," she says. "You've heard of relief packages like

prisoners of war used to get from the Red Cross in World War Two or something? You know, packages from home with coffee and chocolate and stuff the Germans didn't have. Relief."

"So it's coffee and chocolate?"

"Kind of. Stuff people want that gives them relief."

"Like hemmeroyd cream?"

"That's not funny."

"Well, why aren't you telling me what it is if I'm the one that's gonna receive it?"

"Can't you guess?"

"Drugs," I said. It's a bad word that come out easy.

"Okay, there you go, you knew all along."

"And you take it inside the prison."

"Someone has to."

"To give the prisoners relief. What kind?"

"All kinds. Weed, smack, cocaine, you name it, only no acid, not ever, that's too weird what it does and calls attention to itself when some guy does crazy things on it, so that's banned."

"So you and me, we'll be drug smugglers."

That got her mad. "It's not like that at all. Dean and me do a particular service that people want and get paid for it like a simple business transaction. Nobody gets hurt. I'm going way out on a limb telling you shit like this, Odell. You better not betray me now that I made myself vulnlible."

She was upset again, which I did not want. I wanted her smiling and happy, the way things are supposed to be before people that are attracted get down and make love, which is the ultimate aim here for me. Her too, I hope.

"It's a secret," I said. "Our secret."

"That's a good way to put it," she says, cheering up. "When

people share a secret it's like a bond between them that ties them tighter. Is that going to be a problem for you, Odell?"

"Tighter the better."

She laughed. Not too many women have laughed at something I said like that, which is a Sign that she and me are meant to be together, partners in crime. Lorraine is a drug smuggler and me, I'm a murderer although that was accidental. But I am definitely a body hider so cannot stand on my high horse about Lorraine's crime.

"That's all settled then," she said, sounding relieved.

"Yeah. How do you get it inside the place?"

"Inside my bra and panties."

"They don't check for stuff like that?"

"Of course they check. Callisto State Penitentiary is a high-tech containment facility which has got every kind of check and counter-check to make sure nothing happens that isn't supposed to happen. It just so happens that Wednesday morning a certain female guard is on duty for checking out female personnel for smuggling and she doesn't find anything. Then later on I slip her some cash after I get mine from a certain other person, no harm done. You just don't do any of the money handing-over where a camera can see you do it, which we all know where they're located so no problem. It's a good clean system."

"Uhuh."

"You're looking all doubtful. Maybe you don't think it's a good thing."

"I don't know what kind of a thing it is. How many people there are mixed up in it?"

"That's classified till you join up, which you might not even do unless Connors says you can. Maybe all you'll do is mow lawns and be here Tuesday nights to get the package from Donnie D, I just don't know yet. I'm trusting you ahead of time, Odell, because you tried to cover for Dean today even if that's a lost cause. You've got decent instincts in you so that's why I'm telling you."

"Okay."

"And look at it this way – by taking in drugs to keep the inmates happy we spare ourselves and them and their families a lot of grief that might happen if they're not so mellowed-out as they are thanks to what I do, me and others. Think what kind of a place prison would be if all those dopers and crackheads couldn't get what they wanted. It'd be chaos in there with riots happening every other day and plenty of perp-on-perp conflict happening. We couldn't control it, a situation like that, and everyone knows it."

"So looked at that way, it's a good thing."

"I like to think so."

I thought about it and saw that it makes sense the way she puts it. "Okay then."

She looked at her watch. "News time," she says, so we went on through to the living room and she turned on the TV. There was the usual stuff, floods and forest fires made by global warming, plus terrorist bombs going off in all the usual places which got Lorraine mad all over again. "Those people," she says, "they don't care who they kill, even their own Muslim kind, little kids and old ladies, they don't care. That's the one thing I won't forgive Dean about, him getting into that nasty shit. It's one thing to torture a cat, but this killing that they do over there it's just…it's un-American!"

"Got that right."

"I will never, never understand that part of Dean."

"He's a messed-up guy."

"Well, he's gone too far this time. And I was fond of Bree too. What he did to her is unforgivable." She started in sobbing a little bit, which gave me a good reason to slide over next to her on the sofa and put my arm around her shoulder for comfort but not sexual, not yet awhile, I'm thinking, not till she calms down.

Then there's stuff about Senator Ketchum who gave a big speech today about not backing down in the face of terror like some wishy-washy types would have us do, "furl the flag and go home with our tail between our legs," is the way he puts it and it's something only quitters and cowards would ever think of, which means Democrats, I think. And another thing he says is about the terrorist threat right here at home in the USA, invisible terrorists that you can't say who they are because they don't wear that teatowel headgear like over there but we should all be watching out for them because for sure they are out there plotting to commit Terrible Deeds. Lorraine says Amen to what Senator Ketchum's saying. "I'll be voting for him next year."

Next it's some fat lady that won seven million dollars in the lottery and she can't quit smiling about it, but she says it won't change her at all and she'll turn up tomorrow for work at the meat-packing factory like always. "Yeah," says Lorraine, "for five minutes to tell the boss where to cram it, then she'll be down the street to the Mercedes dealership. Look at her, she'll look so stupid behind the wheel of a fancy car, fat like she is."

"What kind of a car's right for fat people?"

"I don't know, some old boat like that one you've got out there."

"Well, thank you. I intend trading up when you get me that job."

"Here it is!"

The newsreader is saying how in Callisto there has been a murder and the police are looking for Dean Leonard Lowry age twenty-seven. There's a mug shot of him with longer hair than he had and Lorraine says, "They got that from his record, I bet. I didn't give them any pictures. Oh, shoot, remind me I have to give Andy a picture of Bree that I've got, he needs it for the police report."

"Okay."

The news went on to say Dean is suspected of being part of a terrorist cell only the police are not commenting if that's related to his crime of murder or not. The way they said it sounds like maybe Dean killed Bree because she found out he's a terrorist, but maybe they didn't mean it that way. It makes no difference to Dean now anyway, only it's a shame he can't put them straight about that. They said he's to be considered armed and dangerous and must not be approached if seen, only reported to the police or FBI if you spot him out there hiding from justice.

Lorraine didn't say anything after the story's over so I kept my mouth shut too so she doesn't get all upset about having a killer-terrorist brother on the news. I wanted her calm and ready for love, which is pushing impatient at the front of my jeans, but you have to wait until the lady is in the mood. I read that in a magazine and it makes sense even if it is a hard thing to do.

"Well, that's that," she said, then starts flipping through the channels till she finds a sitcom with laughter busting out of the can the way they do it to make you think it's hilarious and you must be an idiot if you're not laughing too. "You like this show, Odell?"

"Sure."

"It's my favorite. Have you got anything to drink?"

I got the leftover Coors and Captain Morgan and scrubbed out some shot glasses, thinking Lorraine is most likely a drink-from-the-bottle kind of beer drinker, but you don't do that with hard liquor unless you're some kind of desperate alcoholic person. I set it all up on a tin tray in the kitchen there with blue pelicans on it and brung it back to the living room like a waiter or something and set it down.

"Now that's what I call service," says Lorraine, appreciative, then, "You'll make some lucky soul a real good wife."

Now that got me sore, being what they all say when a man does anything the least bit useful around the place that does not involve a power tool. But I bit my tongue because I don't want to be upsetting the apple cart here with regard to love-making later on, or better yet sooner rather than later. Lorraine picked up a Coors and popped it while I poured us both a shot of the Captain. It went down easy and I reached for a beer, then the phone rang. Lorraine and me both looked at each other, seeing as neither one of us truly lives at Dean's place, so who could the call be for?

"More reporters maybe?" I said.

"I can't handle reporters right now."

"Only it's after hours so it most likely isn't."

"I don't care who it is, my nerves are shot for today."

So I got up and went to the phone. "Hello?"

Silence on the line, but it's open, you can always tell. "Hello?"

"Are you the guy?" says a voice. It's partway familiar but then again not.

"Yeah, I'm a guy."

"The guy I gave the package to, that guy."

"Yeah, that's me."

It's Donnie D on the line.

"Yeah, listen, I just now saw the news, so what's that all about?"

"Dean did a bad thing."

"I guess." Silence for a few seconds, then, "So how does this work from now on?"

"No difference, same as usual, only now it's me, not him."

"You're gonna be the guy there now?"

"That's right."

"The sister, she knows about it?"

"She does."

"So no difference then."

"No difference."

"So why'd he do it?"

"Hey, who knows. Dean was always a little weird."

"Too true. So you're the guy now."

"That's me."

"Okay then, see ya."

He hung up. I went back to the living room.

"Who was it?"

"Donnie D."

"Donnie D?"

"He wants to know what's going down with Dean out of the picture, so I told him it's the same as usual only now it's me not Dean."

"Was he cool with that?"

"Sure, he wants to deal with me, nobody else, to protect himself, he said. Too many links in the chain makes a weak chain, he said."

"That's fine, only what'd he say about Dean?"

"Said he was weird."

"I mean about how Dean went away with him that night. What happened there? Does he know where Dean is right now?"

"Well, not exactly…"

My mind is racing a mile a minute.

"Well, then, what? What happened? That Donnie, he's so paranoid he never gives out even a phone number or I would've asked him already…so what happened?"

"He says Dean asked him to get dropped off downtown after they went and got the package. Donnie didn't have the package with him because he had this sudden fearfulness about a trap or something, so he come out here without it and Dean went with him to get it, then Dean says to drop him off downtown, he's got to meet some people only he didn't say who…and that's what Donnie did and went on home with his two grand, and now tonight he saw the news and he's wondering who those people were that Dean waited downtown for."

"The terrorist guys?"

"I guess. Anyway he's okay about me stepping into Dean's shoes about this, only like I said he doesn't ever want to see anyone else around the place or talk to anyone, only me."

See, I didn't want Donnie and Lorraine talking together or she'll get told a different story than the one I just now made up, which would make her know stuff she doesn't need to know and be a roadblock on the road to romance. It's another big fiberoo that I truly regretted the need for it, but that's how it goes sometimes when life gets complicated like right now.

"So we still don't know where Dean went," says Lorraine, looking upset again.

"Nope, still in the dark about that. Or the Darko."

It was not a good joke and she didn't laugh, just took a big slug of the Captain and followed up with more Coors. She held that bottle neck between two fingers like she was born that way, so I'm right about what kind of a beer drinker she is. When you have been around the block a time or two you get to be a judge of human nature that way. But it isn't looking good for love after that phone call from Donnie, damn his ass, why couldn't he wait till tomorrow, but that's how it goes sometimes like I said before. Maybe if she stayed long enough and drank enough liquor she'd get smoothed over again, only she's looking agitated and unloving so the chances are not so hot.

We watched another sitcom but Lorraine didn't laugh. I started to think maybe I'm getting ahead of myself with this in regard to romance, I mean, she only got told this morning her aunt's been murdered and the one that did it is her psycho brother, who it turns out is also a Muslim terrorist. So I can understand her being upset, especially since Dean was mixed up with her and Donnie D smuggling drugs into the prison etcetera but at least that part has already been worked out okay thanks to me. It's a lot of things to be happening at once, maybe too many to let her relax and think about me more like in a personal sense than just a business partner. Maybe that will take time. It'd be dumb of me to make a move that'll piss her off, so I just sat there drinking and watching these dumb shows she liked and saying nothing, her neither but I could tell she's thinking about all this bad shit that happened all of a sudden.

Then around nine o' clock she said she has to go, it's been a long day and so forth, and I told her I understand about all that. I walked her out to the car hoping for maybe a goodbye kiss but got nothing, only a warning. "Keep your head straight about all this, Odell. You're in it up to your neck, so don't relax. I'm trusting you here and you better earn it."

"Sure will."

"Bye."

And away she went, leaving me a disappointed man but that's okay, there will be another night for making this happen between us. I stood for a long while under the stars just watching them do nothing while the night breeze blew soft and gentle over me. I did truly feel my ducks are standing in a row.

SEVEN

Next day I did six lawns and got paid three hundred and twenty bucks. At three of those jobs I got asked about Dean because those people watched the news last night and recognized his face, so now they want to know what happened with the murder, which I was unable to give them information, I said, because of the Ongoing Investigating into that particular crime and I have been sworn to not talk about it. That's what I told them to shut them up, but a couple of the old ladies kept watching me through their window while I worked like I'm a suspicious character that might start murdering old ladies like Dean did.

On job number five the old guy there at 2358 Willowwood called the cops because of his suspicioning I'm in the murder with Dean and a cop car arrived while I'm halfway through the job. Soon as I explained they understood, because now the whole Callisto PD knows who I am so I was not arrested.

But one of the cops still had to explain about that to the old fool that rung them about me. It is my hope that when I'm old I get run down by a Mack truck before my brain quits being functional like some of these old folk now.

At the end of the day I went home, wondering if maybe Lorraine is going to call around or even just talk on the phone awhile which would be good. But thoughts of Lorraine were pushed out of my head when I saw what's waiting for me in the yard, namely Chet Marchand and his beige Cadillac. I had thought he went back to Topeka when I was just plain rude to him after I found Dean dead upstairs that day. Now I'm in big trouble because I told him I'm Dean, which will be hard to explain in a way that'll make sense. I got out of the truck and he come over, looking very neat and respectable like the other time. I expected him to look mad about being lied to but he looks okay, so maybe he didn't watch the news.

"Hello there," he says, smiling.

"Hey, Chet."

"Glad to see you remembered my name," he says. "But I do believe I may have forgotten yours."

That's his way of letting me know polite that he knows what a big liar I am, so he went and watched the news all right. Now what was I going to do? I felt like an idiot standing there looking at his smile which has got perfect teeth, so good they must not be real. He knew damn well I'm trying to think of something but he let me think on and on like he's got all day and is happy to wait till Hell gets hit by global freezing.

He says, "I think you and I need to have a little talk about things, don't you?"

"Could be."

"How about a cool glass of water to wet our throats?"

"Okay."

I opened up the door and we went through to the kitchen like before. I got two glasses of water and set them down but he didn't pick up his. Me, I drank mine down because it's another scorching Kansas day out there and I worked hard for those dollars.

"Should I keep on calling you Dean?" he asked.

"I guess not."

"What's your real name, friend?"

"Odell, Odell Deefus."

He took that in then says, "And may I ask why it is that you pretended to be Dean Lowry the last time?"

"I was ... doing Dean a favor."

"A favor. What kind of a favor would that be?"

"A personal kind of favor. He wanted me to be him for a couple days, take care of business while he's away somewhere, but he didn't tell me where or why, just asked me the favor, so I did it to help out."

"Kind of playing a role, you might say."

"That's it."

"I see. Well, it looks like the man went and deceived you as well as everyone else that was decent and kind to him, up to and including the woman he murdered. His own aunt, Odell. How did that make you feel?"

"I didn't know about it."

"Of course not, but I meant after you found out."

"It was a big shock."

"I imagine it would be, finding out you've been covering for a murderer."

"Well, it was, I have to say."

"And you're still here, I see."

"She said I could stay on and take care of things."

"Who did?"

"Dean's sister. She's been shook up very bad about this. She said to keep on taking care of things and that's what I'm doing."

He turned his glass of water around and around but still didn't drink. "I guess the police have interviewed you extensively."

"I told them everything. I didn't do anything."

"I'm sure nobody's suggesting you did. You were tricked."

"I was."

"And how do you feel about Dean Lowry now that you know the truth?"

"Bad, I feel bad. He tricked me into doing it."

"A liar and a trickster both, and a murderer besides. I think Mr Lowry must be about the baddest apple in these parts and I bet I'm not the only one with that opinion."

"Probably not."

"What connection might there be, do you think, between his murderous impulse and the fact that he considers the Muslim religion preferable to our kind?"

I shrugged. Chet studied me awhile then said, "No thoughts on the matter?"

"Maybe he was just plain crazy … *is* just plain crazy," I corrected myself, "seeing as he's still out there somewhere hiding from the law."

"You may be right about that, Odell. I've been discussing this with Bob, Reverend Jerome, that is, and we find it mighty interesting how the mind of a killer and his Muslim affiliation are presented in one package here, not so different to the crazy jihadis over there in the Middle East slaying left and right like mad dogs. He's one of their own, even if he's allegedly an American. Now that's a shock, don't you think?"

"Uhuh."

I got myself another glass of water. I was ready to take a shower and raid the freezer for pizza then settle down to read a couple chapters of *The Yearling* while I waited for Lorraine to call, or maybe I'd call her. Chet was looking like a man very interested in his own thoughts and wanting to spout them for approving, which I was prepared to be a good listener, I owed him that for the lies I told, so no pizza just yet awhile.

"I guess you told the police about Dean's Muslim tendencies."

"I sure did. I showed them the books he had in his dresser, Muslim books. They took those away along with the shotgun."

He nods his head, staring at his water glass. Chet wasn't thirsty at all.

"While I was waiting for you, Odell, I took a stroll around to the back yard. They showed that grave on TV. There's no one in it, is there?"

"Nope, the police dug it up and then filled it in again. I told the TV people that but they took pictures of it anyway. I guess they think it'll look interesting on the news even if it's empty."

"And it was Dean who dug that grave?"

"Must've been. It wasn't me. It's like he dug it to put his aunt in but then he changed his mind and filled it in again. It just proves how crazy he was...is."

"That's most likely correct. People unhinged that way, who can understand or explain their actions? Maybe not even them."

"Maybe so."

"And you have no idea where he's gone now?"

I shook my head. Chet had a way of going around and around the subject six times over. For me there's no point in talking about Dean and why he was the way he was and what he did and where he's hiding out from the law. He's a crazy dead guy buried out in the yard, end of story. It would've been nice to tell that to Chet and Andy and Lorraine and the TV news so they'd all quit asking questions and putting out Have You Seen This Man messages on the tube, which is all a big waste of time. But of course I couldn't do that, share my Secret Knowledge about events that happened here. They do say that knowing stuff other people don't know gives you power, but to me it only gave a big pain and I wished I didn't know it, but the burden of knowing is there regardless of how I feel about it.

"I guess you'll be going back to Topeka and report to Preacher Bob," I said.

"I have a cell, Odell."

"Oh, okay."

"The reverend and I are concerned about homegrown terrorist activity. We believe there's a whole lot more of it buried under the appearance of everyday life clear across the country, sleeper cells waiting to be activated. We feel this will happen the closer we get to election day next year. Think about that for a moment. Hundreds, if not thousands, of Dean Lowrys rising up to create mayhem and slaughter on American streets. It can't be allowed to happen."

"I know, I heard Senator Ketchum say that on TV."

"The senator is doing everything he can to wake up the people, make them aware of the threat in our very midst.

There are so many closed eyes and closed minds out there it's scary. Folks just don't want to be aware of how dangerous things have become these last few years. Senator Ketchum's message is the one we all need to be heeding in these days of internal threat and menace."

"Dean wanted to shoot him," I said, and Chet gave me a strange look, like he can't quite believe it even if he was just now talking about danger and so forth.

"Excuse me?"

"Dean and me, we're watching the TV news and Senator Ketchum come on with a speech about what you're saying, and Dean, he said straight out he'd like to kill him. What the exact words were is kind of... 'Someone oughta shoot that prick,' that's pretty much what he said."

"Have you reported this to the police?"

"Uh, no, I believe it slipped my mind until now. I just remembered it because of how we're talking about Senator Ketchum, that's what reminded me."

"My God..." says Chet. "Are you absolutely sure about this, Odell, word-for-word sure?"

"Yeah, that's pretty much what he said. I didn't take much notice at the time because it's just Dean running off at the mouth, I thought, you know how people do when they get irritable. I heard one guy one time say he'd like to kill that dog, which is the dog next door to him that was all the time howling about nothing, but the guy never did kill the dog, he was just talking, you know."

It was my old man said that about the dog but I didn't feel like admitting it to Chet, who's looking very stern and worried all of a sudden.

"You should have told someone," he says.

"Well, I forgot…"

"This means the senator is very likely a terrorist target in the lead-up to the elections. The police have to be made aware, and the FBI and Homeland Security. Is there anything more that you forgot?"

I thought hard. "I don't remember forgetting anything else."

He took out his wallet and for a second there I thought he's going to pay me for the important information I just now provided, but he takes out a little business card instead and handed it over very serious. "Odell, I want you to call me anytime if you recall any further details concerning Dean Lowry. Do you have a cell?"

"No, never did."

"Well, go directly to the nearest payphone if anything occurs to you. This is important, I want you to be aware of that."

"Okay."

"Robert Jerome Ministries and the Born Again Foundation are well connected in Washington. The reverend knows many a political entity on a personal basis, so anything you tell to me goes by way of Preacher Bob directly to some of the most important names on Capitol Hill, am I making myself clear?"

I looked at the card. There's just Chet's name and a mobile number, no job description like Manager or Sales Rep. I was expecting a little cross up in the corner maybe but there's nothing. He stood up like he's in a big hurry now. "I won't say goodbye, Odell, I'll just say so long for now."

"Okay."

"Don't get up, I know my way out."

And off he went, then the Caddie starts up outside and he's gone. I did some hard thinking and satisfied myself that my recollection about Dean saying he wanted to shoot Senator Ketchum was real and true. It was, but I should not have said it out loud like I did because it went and made Chet all excited and afraid about a terror attack on the senator that wasn't ever going to happen, not with Dean being under the ground like he is. But too late now, I guess. That mouth of mine was a wide-open hole for sure and sooner or later I'm liable to fall in it my own self from not keeping it shut like I should. This is some peculiar situation I'm in now.

I waited an hour and more for Lorraine to call but she didn't, so then I had to call her instead, which she picked up the phone after the third ring and some guy says, "Hello?" Now I was not expecting that and had no answer ready, so he says again, "Hello?"

"Who's that?"

"What number are you calling?" he said.

"Lorraine's."

"Oh, well, she's in the bathroom. You want to hold on or have her call you back?"

"I'll hold on. Who're you?"

"A friend of Lorraine's. Who're you?"

"A friend too."

"Here she comes now."

There's a double clunk as the phone gets set down then picked up again. "Hello?"

"It's Odell. Who was that?"

"Oh, that's Cole, Cole Connors from the prison. You

remember I told you about him. Cole's the one I'm talking to about maybe getting you a job interview, so I hope you were courteous and nice, Odell." She laughed and I heard the guy laugh too, only more of a snicker the way I heard it.

"Well, what's he doing there?"

"Discussing you, like I said. What's wrong, Odell, you sound real peeved about something."

"No."

"Well then, what can I do for you?"

"I'm wondering about dinner," I said.

"I'm wondering too, wondering if Cole's taking me out somewhere with table napkins that aren't made of paper or if it'll just be some greasy spoon. Cole, he's famous for being cheap."

I heard the guy laughing again and wanted to strangle him, and Lorraine too.

"How come you're going out to dinner with him?"

"I *told* you, we're discussing work-related issues, that includes you. You're on the agenda for topics of discussion. Was there anything else?"

"No, I guess."

"Well, all right then, talk to you tomorrow."

"Okay..."

And she hung up. I looked at the phone a long time without thinking anything in particular then I hung it up and went to the front door to go out on the porch for some fresh air. Stepping through the door I saw a card on the floor and figured Chet must have dropped it. But when I picked it up it says *Sharon Ziegler Channel 12 News* and underneath the two different phone numbers there she wrote *Must talk with you anytime.* I must've stepped right over it when I come in with Chet. I near almost tore it up. Fuck Channel 12, they should've been out here yesterday along with those other TV people and they weren't, so who gives a damn. Only then I had this idea – if Lorraine's out with Cole Connors at some fancy restaurant then I can have some female company also and see how she likes it.

It's way long after business hours now so I punched in the second number, the cell, and after a couple rings it got answered.

"Hello?" She has got this very sexy voice which probably got her the job on TV.

"Uh, hello, is that Sharon?"

"This is she."

"Well, you left me a card to call you anytime."

"Who is this?"

"Odell Deefus."

"I'm sorry?"

"Odell Deefus. You left me this card."

"I leave a lot of cards. What's this about?"

"I'm the one out at Dean Lowry's place looking after things here."

"Oh…" she says, sounding different now, "oh, okay…My apologies, I just didn't know your name. My colleagues said there's someone out there at the house but nobody seems to know your name. What was it again?"

"Odell Deefus."

"Got it. Were you wanting to talk with me, Odell?"

"That's why I'm calling. Got an exclusive story if you want it."

"Concerning the murder?"

"Concerning another one that might happen, only this time it's someone big."

"Who might that be, Odell?"

"I guess you better come over and find out. Or I can call those other channels if you're busy right now."

"No, no ... I'll be right there! Just give me a little extra time to pick up my cameraman and we'll be right out! This isn't some kind of joke, is it?"

"No joke. This is exclusive and you can be the first one knows about it."

Which was a lie, she'll be the second one after Chet Marchand, but she doesn't need to know that. Chet, he'll be talking to Preacher Bob not the Network News.

"Okay, don't you move."

She hung up and I felt good. Cole Connors, what was the chance he'd be on the TV news like I'm going to be? No chance at all, I bet, so now Lorraine won't be having any more dinners in fancy restaurants with that guy. Maybe they're talking about a job for me at the prison and maybe not, but there is nothing a woman likes more than to be with some guy that is famous, even ugly guys, so long as they have got money or fame or both, that's all it takes. I read somewhere that the women can't help this because back when we lived in caves it's the guy that was the best hunter got the best-looking women because they wanted a guy that can feed them. Nowadays it's not hunting it's being famous, but the same thing with regard to attractivity.

It was less than a half-hour went by till I heard them coming up the drive. It isn't a news van like I was expecting, only a private car, but that makes no difference, there's a skinny guy getting out the passenger side with a camera on his shoulder, and out from the driver's door steps a woman. Up the steps they come and the woman put out her hand very friendly with a smile and says she's Sharon and this is Huey. I took them along inside to the living room where we can be sat comfortable. Sharon is not so good-looking as I was expecting but that doesn't matter, it's me that will be on the screen telling what he knows. Me that Lorraine will be looking at.

Huey got set up for shooting and Sharon says to me, "Just so I won't be going into this cold, Odell, what kind of a story is it?"

"It's about what Dean told me before he disappeared with those Muslim brothers of his. They're not his real brothers, he's only got a sister, but that's what he called them, his brothers."

"I understand. What did he say?"

"He said he's gonna shoot Senator Ketchum."

"You're kidding."

"No, he said it loud and clear. You can give me a lie-detector test about that."

"Okay, I believe you. Just give me some background here, Odell, how you met Dean and what happened, in your own words." She turned to the camera guy. "Ready?"

"Ready."

Sharon took a breath and says to me, "Odell, tell us about how you came to meet with Dean Lowry."

And I did, I went through the whole thing, lies and truth all mixed in together the way I've been telling it to Lorraine and Andy and Chet. Sharon every now and then asked me a question to explain things better and I told her what she wants to know, until at the end she says, "And there was a specific threat made before Dean departed for places unknown?"

"There was one of those, and it's this – he said he wants to shoot Senator Ketchum because the senator is so down on those terrorists that are hiding out in America. He made no bones about it, he's wanting to shoot the senator for saying that to everyone on the TV."

"And you thought it was your duty to let the senator know about this personal danger that he faces?"

"Yeah, I did. There's too much shooting going on in the world and it all should stop right now, but I expect it won't."

"Are you aware of any weapons he might have at his disposal?"

"No, the police took away his shotgun. I don't know what else he's got hid away. For a job like that you need a high-power rifle with telescope sights."

"And did Dean Lowry give you any idea about a timetable for this assassination?"

"Probably between now and the elections would be about right," I said, borrowing from Chet but he won't mind.

"How strong is Dean's commitment to the terrorist cause?"

"It's strong. He told me the Muslims have got the answers about everything, not us, so he changed over. He had books about it. He showed me them."

"Did he try to convert you, Odell?"

"He tried, but I resisted his attempt. I don't need some book with a green cover to tell me what's right."

"Did he get angry with you?"

"No, he was only angry with Senator Ketchum."

She asked a few more things and then we're done. Huey went to another position in the room and aims the camera at

Sharon and she looks over at me again and nods her head a few times. I asked what that was for and she says, "Reaction shots, it just ties everything together. You'll see how it works when you watch the report." She looked at her watch. "Okay, if we move fast it'll make the ten o' clock slot. Let's go."

Huey folded away this little video screen on his camera and they're headed for the door. Sharon says over her shoulder, "Thanks for this, Odell. If you think of some other stuff, gimme a call."

"Okay."

And then they're gone, hauling ass out of the yard like an ambulance on its way to an accident. Now that it's all over I asked myself if I did the right thing here, getting people all agitated about something that won't ever happen, but then I got to thinking it's no harm done after all and might do me some good with Lorraine, you never know.

And I had got so distracted about all this I didn't even have dinner yet! A fast trip to the freezer and I flung another pizza in the oven. I was getting tired of pizza but there's no more of those TV dinners like Dean and me had that first night. If only I had known I was sitting down to sup with the devil as they say. Dean seemed like a good guy then, and it was a shame that he's a wolf in sheep's clothing about the whole terrorist thing, which only goes to show the truth about that old saying about the book and the book cover.

The pizza was okay, Deep Dish Meat Lover's, but I bet Lorraine and Cole had something better. That still was upsetting me even though after thinking about it I saw she was doing it for me, for that job at the prison. I was jealous I had to admit, and they do say that the green-eyed monster makes you do strange things. But talking to Sharon was not strange, it was my duty to say what I knew so nothing happens to Senator Ketchum, the man who most likely will be the next President, so I had saved the life of the President! That's what it would look like anyway, which is the same thing almost.

I fretted about nothing while I waited for ten o' clock, channel-surfing through the crap. It's an exciting thing to be on the TV news if that never happened to you before, which it had not for me. There was one time in Yoder when the county newspaper reporter asked me about a teen suicide there. What it was, I was coming home and went through this old graveyard they have got there filled with pioneers and so forth, real old tombstones leaning this way and that without hardly a name you could even read anymore on them, and then I saw this boy on the ground with a blue face. I will never forget that part. His face was blue and he was dead, I could see it straight off because he's lying so still between a couple graves. I went on home and told my mother who's still alive then and she called the police officer we had, just the one it's so small of a town. What it was all about, the story come out, this boy Anfer Sheen, that was his name, he had gone and been in a big argument with his girlfriend who dumped him for some other guy and Anfer stole his mother's prescription medicine for I don't know what and swallowed the whole bottle of pills in a private place which the cemetery was, nobody ever went there. And then the reporter come and interviewed me about all of that. I was eleven, I think. But that was not the TV news so it does not compare to this. And they never did use my name in the story that time about Anfer Sheen, just called me 'a local boy.'

At ten o' clock the announcer says stay tuned for a startling new development in the Dean Lowry murder incident. I called up Lorraine to tell her she better switch on the TV but there's no answer so she is still out with that guy talking about my job at the prison. I was expecting it to be the first big story but that was about an earthquake in China that has gone and killed thousands of Chinese people. They have usually got a flood problem over there to kill them off but tonight it's an earthquake. There was pictures of destruction and bodies, then some stories about other things that happened, then the commercial break, but they said again about the startling new development before it's all about shampoo and shit which I waited impatient for it to end. Then there's more stories about nothing to do with me. I started getting mad and wished I didn't call up Sharon after all, but then here it is, the startling new development.

I watched myself very careful to see if I made any mistakes but I didn't, not even looking away at the camera while I got interviewed like some people do and it makes them look like a real hick when that happens. But I didn't fall into that trap and come across very good, I thought, telling my story which had a few pieces missing here and there, edited out, but mainly it's all there like I told it, with Sharon nodding her head now and then while I talked, so I saw how that worked.

The phone rang and it's Lorraine, which I was not expecting.

"Odell," she says, "I just saw you on the TV."

"Yeah."

"You didn't say you were gonna be on the news."

"Well, they come over on a special trip to interview me about this new development that's happening."

"About the senator? Did he really say that, Dean, I mean?"

"He really said it."

"You didn't mention that to me before, how come?"

"It slipped my mind, then I remembered. Stuff that Dean told me is big news."

"You didn't tell them anything about that other stuff, did you?"

"What other stuff?"

"About him coming on to you, the whispering-in-the-ear thing, you didn't tell them about that, did you? Because that would be a big embarrassment, especially to Bree. She was a very old-fashioned conservative person."

"But...she can't hear about it now."

"Well, I know that, Odell, but I'm saying other people don't need to get told about that part of him, it's got nothing to do with him being a terrorist, so it's private and doesn't need to get discussed about in public. This is a favor I'm asking, okay?"

"Okay."

"So you'll keep that under your hat?"

"If I had a hat," I said, making a joke, then I remembered I have got a hat, my Hawaiian straw hat for lawnmowing. I thought about telling Lorraine that but she's already talking again.

"Hey, I talked about that job for you with Cole. He says come on out to the prison tomorrow week, that's Friday next week, and you can talk it over. I'm real hopeful about it, Odell."

"Okay, I'll be there."

"Do I get a big thank-you?"

"You sure do."

"Okay then. You think Dean'll really try to kill Senator Ketchum?"

"He might do, he's crazy enough to try."

She give out a big sigh. "That's gonna be such a blot on the family if that happens. It'll put Dean's name in the history books for everyone to hate like the guy that killed JFK and the guy that killed John Lennon. I'd have to change my name to get away from that, get married maybe, that'd solve the problem."

"That's a good idea."

"Well, anyway, I just wanted to say I saw you on the TV."

Behind her voice there's a crash as a glass or bottle breaks.

"What was that?" I asked her.

"What was what?"

"That sound, like a glass or something went and broke."

"Oh, it's that cat, it's gone and pushed something off the kitchen counter."

"I didn't know you had a cat."

"It's the neighbor's, I'm looking after it."

Behind her I could hear the cat swearing like a drunk man.

"So long, Odell," says Lorraine and hung up fast.

I set the phone down gentle so's not to smash it against the cradle. Maybe the neighbor come over to collect the cat back to his own place, and the cat didn't want to leave a nice person like Lorraine so it got skittish and bumped against something which got smashed. That was most likely what happened there, so no point in thinking more about it. Thinking about stuff is not necessarily the best thing to do, I have found, otherwise you get all tangled up thinking this and that and the other thing and you don't even know which one is true, so forget that.

Which I did. With the help of the Captain.

Then the phone rang again and I snatched it up thinking it's Lorraine and now that the neighbor has taken the cat away and the mess has been cleaned up she's lonesome and wanting company for the rest of the evening. Only it wasn't her.

"Odell?"

"Uhuh."

It's a guy.

"Andy Webb here, Odell. I just got told you were on the late news with some story about Dean Lowry getting set to kill Senator Ketchum, that right?"

"That's right."

"Well, now, I have to wonder why it is that you didn't tell me that highly important piece of information yesterday, Odell, or maybe you think the TV news is the right place to be giving out important pieces of information and not the Chief of Police that happens to be investigating the case. Is that what you thought, Odell?"

"Uh…"

"Is it even true? How come you didn't tell the TV news about it yesterday, they were out to the house, I heard."

"I forgot…then I remembered about it."

"Well, the next time you remember an important piece of information like that you call me up and give me the news, Odell, I don't want to hear it second-hand from someone that saw it on the TV. I'm the guy that's supposed to know all the angles. I could've given that information to Homeland Security yesterday, and now they'll be wanting to know why they didn't get told about this information you just now remembered and gave to the wrong people. Those Homeland folks are serious people that do not like to get fucked with, Odell, so when they get on the case you better not fuck with them the way you went and fucked with me, you got that?"

"Uhuh…"

"Damn!" he says, and slams the phone down, or maybe he just hung it up gentle, you can't tell, but I bet he slammed it down. I have gone and pissed off the Chief of Police, which is never a good thing, so then I had to turn again to my old friend the Captain for condolement about that.

EIGHT

Along about noon next day I quit for lunch and saw on a newsstand that the information has gotten around big time, on the front page with a picture of Dean and a picture of the senator which has got a circle with crosshairs put over it, and the headline reads *TARGET!* I got a copy to read while I ate my burger, and it's all pretty much how I told it to Sharon Ziegler, who had her name there in the article as well as me. That is the first time I ever saw my name in the newspaper and it brung a strange feeling to my chest that made me quit chewing till it went away. Now I am famous!

After I finished eating I went and got a couple more copies of the newspaper, six or eight, then I went back to mowing lawns, which did not feel right somehow after I'm on the front page. I guess I would have to be the most famous lawn-mower guy in the entire history of lawnmowing, and I only started the job this week, so that is Progress.

I was putting the mulching mower back on the truck after job number four when a car pulled over to the curb behind me, a beige Caddy with Chet behind the wheel. He got out and strolled over. He has got his jacket off so you can tell it's a hot day because Chet is the kind of guy keeps his jacket on till someone says okay he can take it off. He still strikes me as the businessman type and not the religious kind, but maybe that's just the suit and the Cadillac.

"How's business, Odell?"

"Business is good. That grass, it keeps right on growing."

"Barbers say pretty much the same thing when you ask them," he said, which is probably true, barbers have lawns just like other people.

"You've made the news," he says.

"Yeah."

"Becoming quite a celebrity."

"Uhuh."

"But those lawns still need mowing."

"Right."

He looked at the mowers and the truck, then he says, "So you'll be maintaining the business until further notice?"

"Until I get this other job."

"What other job, Odell?"

"At the prison. Got an appointment to talk to them next week."

"What kind of a job would they have for you there?"

"Guard. It's easy work they say."

"Are you sure that's what you want after being out in the fresh air and sunshine?"

"Well, the lawnmowing is okay, I'm making money at it,

but it isn't exactly what I had in mind for a career."

"What did you have in mind?" he wants to know.

"Well, I was thinking maybe the Army, then the lawn-mowing job kind of took over. The recruitment office in this town has got closed down so you have to go clear to Manhattan if you want to enlist. Manhattan, Kansas, not New York."

"That's a very risky profession, more risky even than being a prison guard. Are you sure that's the right job for you, Odell?"

"Well, I was going to give her a try."

"You know, Bob and I have been discussing you, kind of thinking how we might be able to help you, professionally speaking."

"Oh, that's okay, I wouldn't make a good preacher."

"We were thinking more along the lines of helping you in the lawnmowing trade."

"Oh. Yeah?"

"We think we may have pinpointed the one thing you currently are lacking for good business practice."

"A ride-on mower?"

"We were thinking a cell phone."

"Uhuh."

"You see, Odell, when new customers want to be added to your lawnmowing roster they'll call, but there's nobody at home to take that call, is there. With a cell phone and some advertising you can make bookings for new customers while you're out on the job. That'd make a significant difference, don't you think?"

"I guess."

"So Bob and I were thinking we'd like to get you a cell phone. For free."

"Free?"

"We'd pay for it, yes. Cash money. This morning I was cruising downtown and noticed they've got a cell phone special going on at The Telephone Store there on Torrence Street. You can get a pretty good deal all this week but the sale ends tomorrow, so rather than coming all the way back into town on the weekend when you want to be enjoying your hardearned rest and relaxation, it might be a good idea to go on down there right now before you start your next job and grab one of those nifty cells while they're still there for the grabbing. Are you interested, Odell?"

"I . . . sure."

He dug out his wallet and pulled out some money.

"This is four hundred dollars, enough to get you signed up on the payment schedule of your choice."

He held out the money. It would've been rude to say no, so I took it.

"Are you sure, Chet?"

"Absolutely and positively certain this is the right way for you to go, Odell." He looked at his watch. "I've got some chores to attend to, so why don't you go on down and choose a phone, they've got all different kinds, and when you've got yourself all set up I want you to make your first call on the new phone a call to me, okay? You still have my number, don't you?"

"Got it right in my wallet."

"Well, then, I won't hold you up any longer. Enjoy that phone. Believe me, it'll change your life."

He gave a chuckle and got back in his car while I'm standing there with the money still in my hand, then he waved and drove away. I put the money in my pocket thinking him and Preacher Bob are looking after me like a pair of uncles, and Lorraine is looking after me like … a sister, I guess. Well, I would not disappoint either one of them.

I did what Chet said and went direct to The Telephone Store, where inside they have got all these phones, executive desk phones that sit in a console kind of thing with buttons all over, and wall phones for hanging on the wall or you can set them down on a table if you want, which they come in all kinds of colors that I didn't know a phone could come in – red and green and yellow, even a pink one but that would be for a woman.

A young guy come over. He's got this short hair that's been filled with grease to make it stand up in little spikes and he says, "What can I do for you today?"

"I want a phone," I told him, "the carry-around kind."

"Right over here," he says. "We've got a special running all this week."

There's a counter with all kinds of cell phones under glass, dozens and dozens of them with all kinds of colors, even with pictures on them. The guy started in talking about X plan that gives you a certain number of calls per week for free, or Y plan that gives a different arrangement, or Z plan that's a different setup again. It was hard to follow what he's saying he's gabbing so fast, but while he was doing that I'm selecting the right phone for me, which is a choice between two that I liked the look of. The first one has got a picture of Bart Simpson on it with Bart's hand holding up the little screen there, and the other one was the prettiest shade of silver-green but it had no picture, just the green. I was tempted by the Bartster but knew people would think that's the kind of phone you give a kid, so I had to make myself not want it and go for the green instead.

"That one."

"The new Fumatsu nine-o-niner," he says, "good choice, and we're offering a new package – the First-Timer Streamliner, gets you mobilized pronto."

He told me all about the phone, what it does, the text messaging and so forth which I could hardly figure out what he's saying, but I bet there'll be a little book inside the packaging that'll tell me everything he's saying only slower so I can follow it. But the best thing about it, this phone has got a tiny camera inside the flipout lid that can take moving pictures and send them direct to whoever you're talking to! I have definitely made the right choice here with something like that inside of it. He took down a bunch of details about my name and address etcetera and says the number will be activated in around five to ten minutes, which will make the phone officially mine. I handed him my money and still had some change left over, so Chet had judged it all pretty close to perfect. The phone sat in my hand all smooth and sleek and I knew it was the right one for me.

Next thing the spike-haired guy did, he showed me how to choose the ring tone, how it sounds when someone calls, and you have got so much choice to choose from, all kinds of tunes and sound effects from Baytoven to a little voice that screams, "Answer the damn phone, stupid!" That one was funny but I didn't like being called stupid, so I settled for a tune that I heard plenty of times which is Greensleeves that we sang in school when I was little – Come come come away with me, Where the grass grows wild and the wind blows free, Come come come away with me, And I'll build you a home in the meadow...but no mention of anyone wearing green sleeves there, so I don't know why it's called that.

"That's nice," said the spiky-haired salesman, but I can tell he doesn't really think so. Most likely he thinks it isn't cool to have a sweet sound like that. I bet his phone tells him, "Pick it up or I'll rip your head off, moron!"

Soon as I got outside I rung up Chet. It was hard work touching those itty-bitty buttons one at a time with these big sausage fingers that I have got, but I got the hang of it and the numbers popped up on the screen while I'm pressing the buttons so I can be sure I'm doing it right. Chet answered straight off.

"Hey, Chet, this is Odell."

"Odell, that was fast."

"Well, I wanted to grab one of those phones while they're there for the grabbing. I got a green one, silver-green I guess you'd call it. These things are smaller than I thought."

"You can carry a compact model in a shirt pocket and not even feel the weight," he says. "I'm entering your number in my directory right now."

"I didn't give it to you yet."

"It's on my screen like all incoming calls," he says. "Digital technology, Odell, it's a wonderful thing."

"It sure is."

"You enjoy your new phone, Odell, and call me anytime you need to talk about anything at all."

"Will do, Chet, and thank you for the phone, I really like it. And thank Preacher Bob for me too, would you?"

"I'll do that. Bye now."

I was halfway through the job at 9846 Siefert Street, feeling very up-to-date and modern with my new phone right there in my shirt pocket, when I heard this sweet sound coming from my chest area. My new phone was ringing! It must have been Chet calling me back, he's the only one as knows my number so far. I took it out and pressed the little bar that lets you talk, but couldn't hear Chet's voice because of the racket from the mower, so I cut that off and now I can hear him.

"Odell?" he's saying.

"Yeah?"

"Odell Deefus?"

It isn't Chet's voice, it's someone else, some other guy.

"Uhuh."

"Odell, let me introduce myself. Agent Jim Ricker, Homeland Security."

"Uhuh." My heart's all of a sudden going *budumbudumbudum* because it's Homeland Security calling! But I didn't give them my number, so how come?

"How's your day going?" he wants to know.

"Okay, I guess."

"Been going through all the facts as we know them thus far on the Lowry case," he says. "Anything to add to what you told Sharon Ziegler last night, any new insights into the mind of this bozo?"

"Uh, no."

"Because we need to know before anyone else knows, Odell. From this moment on you talk to me and me only, not to TV news reporters and not to any local Chief of Police who you've already upset about the Senator Ketchum angle. You don't share information with anyone but me, got it?"

"Okay. I better get your number, I guess..."

"It's on your screen. Press hash to get the index and then enter it into your directory. That'll be the most important number there, Odell. If Dean Lowry gets in touch with you I want you to tell me about it immediately, day or night it makes no difference. Got that, Odell?"

"Uhuh."

"You haven't entered the number in your directory yet."

"I'm trying...I've got these big fingers..." It was real hard pressing the buttons and still holding the phone close enough to my face so I can still hear him. "Hash...okay, there's the directory."

"Now scroll down to Enter."

"Okay..."

"Go ahead and press it, Odell, damn thing won't bite."

"There...I've done it."

"Now type in J-I-M."

"These buttons, they're so small...Okay, I did it."

"Congratulations," he says, but it's sarcastic the way he says it.

"How come you've got my number?" I asked him. "I only just got the phone."

"A little bird on a wire somewhere must've told me," he says. "You should change your ring tone, Odell, my nine-year-old daughter's got the same taste as you. Her it fits." How the heck does he know about my ring tone? "Now remember," he says, "you do not confide in anyone but me. Are we clear on that?"

"Uhuh..."

He rang off. I stared at the phone in my hand. I was in the Big League now for sure. Homeland Security had my number and I had theirs to call direct day or night and pass on further information that come to me about Dean, which there would not be any at all on account of his untimely death that occurred. This would be a problem if Agent Jim Ricker wanted further developments to be told about.

It made me feel bad knowing about Dean being dead like I did. That was almost worse than knowing I'm the one that killed him. Jim Ricker was going to be a disappointed man, all right. The little bird on the wire was not going to be telling him anything he didn't already know, which was mostly lies anyway. This was turning out to be another one of those bad consequences that have been part of my life since forever, owing to bad planning and decisions I should maybe not have made, only it's hard to know when you decide something if you made the right decision until later when the consequences happen from it.

All across America people are talking about Dean and his terrible plot to kill the senator. Everyone is getting all worried and concerned about that, especially Senator Ketchum, I bet. His wife probably told him, 'Don't go out the door today, Dean Lowry will get you!' But he went out the door anyway because the business of the nation must go on regardless. That's what people will be thinking and most likely they'll vote for the senator because of his bravery about facing down a terrorist threat like that and going out the door every day no matter what. And there was no Dean Lowry anymore. And I'm the only one in the entire country that knows this. And if

I get found out for lying I'm in serious trouble over it, any fool could see that. So I would have to sit on the Big Secret like a hen sits on her eggs, only the hen wants them to hatch out and I'll be hoping they don't, because what comes out won't be chickens, they'll be dragons.

I put the phone back in my pocket, where it weighed heavier than before somehow. I have got to keep my mouth shut and everything will be all right, I'm thinking. If I can just do that then time will pass and Dean Lowry will be as big a threat to the nation as Jesse James and John Dillinger who they are also dead and gone. Just keep quiet and everything will blow away like autumn leaves, by which time I'll have a good job at the prison and maybe Lorraine would marry me. It's true she's an older woman but still very attractive and curvaceous that way so I wanted to marry her all right, and she'd want to marry me because of the reliability I've got with regard to a weekly paycheck coming in regular, which women are very concerned about in a man. No gottee money, no gettee datee. The prison job would pay a whole lot more dollars than the lawnmowing, I bet.

Getting back home at the end of the day on a Friday should've felt good with the weekend ahead to relax and enjoy myself. Only it didn't feel that way as I parked the truck next to my dead Monte Carlo and took out the plastic bags of lawn clippings for adding to the pile over beyond the edge of the yard. What it was, the weekend is for being with people, friends and family, and these are what I did not have currently, not there at the house anyway. The only person there was myself, and Dean, I guess, although he didn't count.

After I emptied the bags I went in the house and showered

myself clean, then sat at the kitchen table awhile wishing I smoked because that was the perfect time to smoke a cigarette and have a beer, which I had none of also, only a quarter-bottle of the Captain that I was not in the mood for. When the phone rang – the kitchen phone not my sweet new cell – it was almost a relief, I had been sat staring at the wall for a long time by then.

"Hello?"

"Odell, Chief Webb."

"Uh, hi, Chief."

I'm thinking there's bad news coming from this guy that doesn't like me.

"Got anything planned for Saturday?" he asked, which was a surprise.

I'm thinking the Chief has been feeling bad about the chewing-out he gave me this morning and has decided to be nice to me, which means inviting me over to his place for barbecued ribs with his family.

"No, Chief, I've got the whole day wide open."

"Good, because I'm sending an officer out to videotape your yard."

"Pardon?"

"He'll be dropping by around ten."

"Videotape?"

"The grave Dean dug up and filled again. There has to be a video record of that being dug out and finding nothing in there."

"But…you already did that…and there's still nothing there."

"But we didn't do the taping is what I'm saying. He'll need

to tape the layout of the house too, go from room to room with the recorder running till he's taped the entire house top to bottom."

"What for?"

"It's Homeland Security, Odell, they're insisting. They like to have video layout so if there's a siege they know where to break in and how to get from room A to room B while the air's filled with smoke from their stun grenades. It's how they get trained nowadays."

"But there won't be any siege here. Do they think Dean's gonna come on home and barricade himself in the place?"

"Who knows what they think, it's Homeland Security. I can't spare more than one man because we've got a high school baseball game Saturday that brings in folks from the whole county. Got to use my men for traffic control."

"But then... if there's just one guy with the camera, who's doing the digging?"

"That would be you, Odell. Got a problem with that?"

"Uh, no..."

"It's a whole different ball game when Homeland Security gets brung into a situation like this. If you hadn't said about Dean being a Muslim it'd just be plain old murder, but now that he's a terrorist suspect it's a whole different thing, that's the difference between getting a video record and not having to. Well, it's good to know you'll be on hand to do the spade-work, Odell. The Callisto Police Department appreciates your assistance freely offered like this. Around ten."

And he hung up, the son of a bitch. Maybe Homeland Security was on his case because of the Senator Ketchum thing, or maybe Chief Webb made it all up for revenge over the chewing-out he got from them. Either way I'm on Shit Street, Dean being where he is, and it was a real pity I went and wasted the shower I just had because now I've got to get filthy dirty all over again digging Dean out.

I do not often get to feeling slit-eyed mean, but going to fetch the gloves and shovel that is exactly how I felt about things. It was plain ridiculous to have to keep moving a dead man around like this, and undignified even if he's a murderer. Every dead man deserves to lie peaceful once he's under the soil, not disturbed over and over for no good reason. Dean's ghost would not be happy about this.

I dug like a machine I'm so steamed. It was not such hard work because the dirt is still loose from being dug out three times now already including the first time when Dean dug it. No, it was the sheer waste of time and effort had got me mad. By the time I got down to Dean I was in a fine fury about things and it may be that I treated him rough getting him hauled out into the yard. I carried him over to the grass heap breathing through my mouth because Dean stunk like nothing I smelled before, a man four days dead now and letting the world know it. I set him down and told myself not to throw up, then I opened up a big hole in the mound of grass clippings and was just about to put him inside and cover him over when it occurs to me the stink will come through something like piled grass very easy and maybe the video guy will smell it and blow the whistle.

Dean had to be stink-proofed, so I got two of the big plastic bags that had lawn clippings in them before and pulled them over him, one from the top and one from the bottom, then I got tape from Dean's workbench in the barn and taped those two bags together very careful so they're airtight like I wanted. When that was done you couldn't hardly smell him at all, and even that little bit of stench was probably coming from my shirt when I held him against me to carry him over. Putting him inside just a bedsheet had not been the smartest thing, but the problem was solved now, I'm thinking while I put him in the hole and pulled grass over him three foot thick. Then I went inside and showered again and run all my clothes through the washing machine I'm so stinking filthy dirty. Then I made pizza again, two of them seeing as they're Thin'n'Crispy not the Deep Dish kind and I'm hungry like since I don't know when. But at least the problem has been taken care of.

That's when I remembered I didn't fill in the yard hole again, which got me yelling dirty words to match my mood I'm so strung out now and mad at myself. So back out to the yard again and the hole got dirt shoveled in like before. It doesn't look like a hole that got dug out and filled two days ago, it looks like a hole that got filled in just now, but there's nothing I can do about it except hope that the video cop is not bright enough to notice that before I sink the spade in again come tomorrow. Man, was I tired.

It was coming on to night by then so I showered all over again and hung out my laundry with the last of the light bleeding away west in the sky. After that was done I went back inside and turned on the TV for the early news, which has got plenty about a manhunt across the entire Midwest now for Dean and warnings about not to approach him he's so dangerous, like he's covered in anthrax or something. They wanted him so bad there's a reward out for information concerning his whereabouts. A hundred grand, that's a bunch of cash and it's just a shame that I can't collect it without getting into deeper trouble than I'm already in. I bet Dean never figured he'd one day be worth so much.

After all that effort relocating Dean I was so tired I fell asleep in front of the tube like many people do and woke up a long time later with this voice telling me I had to change myself for the better or risk being kept from happiness, which is the natural reward for every soul that embraced the Lord as his savior. My eyes opened and there he is in front of me, Preacher Bob himself.

He's not a handsome man and he doesn't try to be, not like some of them that hurl the Book at you from TV, with their dyed hair and teeth so white they hurt your eyes. Preacher Bob looked like he slept in his suit and woke up with an empty bottle beside him, and that is the thing that makes folk love him like they do, because he's just like them, not some slick showbiz kind of preacher like you often get nowadays. To look at him you wouldn't think that he's a multimillionaire that has got his own Bible college there in Topeka that churns out preachers and whatnot to go across the globe and convert all those heathen folk to Christian ways as well as all the sinners right here in the USA. Preacher Bob, his congregation doesn't go so much for the razzle-dazzle kind of thing with lots of singing and a chapel that looks like someplace they might show the Academy Awards out of. Preacher Bob's setup is entirely different to that, just a simple stage with a little stand where he keeps his Bible to read out of. There is no choir and no second guy up there that he talks to the way some of them do, what they call Conversations about Christ. Preacher Bob does not hold a conversation, he preaches a Sermon just like they did it in olden times with no frills and mood lighting and white teeth. Not Bob, that is just not his style.

He has got these half-moon glasses that hang around his neck on a little chain till he's ready to read a passage from whichever part of the Bible he's interested in right now, Jewteronomy or Revolutions, whatever, he picks them up and perches them on the end of his nose which has got a bulb on the end of it like a red onion and he commences to read out loud. Real loud. If Preacher Bob has got a homely face he has been repaid for it with a voice that sounds like God himself, all stern and deep and serious. It gets your attention, that voice, even if you aren't the religious kind. It reaches out and takes hold of you like a big warm hand you can't stay away from, and once those fingers close around you he's got you right where he wants, listening to the Voice that's telling you where you Went Astray in life and how to fix it Like New again, which is through Jesus Christ and no other way at all.

The way he talked, you wanted to believe every part of it, he makes it all sound so simple and true. All you have to do is walk through the church door Preacher Bob is holding open special just for you and everything from then on will be fine because you're under the wing of Jesus on the one hand and the wing of Preacher Bob on the other, all safe and secure the rest of your life. Now he's talking about tithing, giving ten percent of your income to the Lord, which is every bit as important as the praying you have to do to keep tight with Jesus. It's the same old gimme-your-money message they all dish out, only with Preacher Bob it sounds so genuine and real, like every cent of the money will go to helping little starved African kids find their way to Jesus with Your Help and those generous cash donations are Tax-Deductible, folks. I could practically feel myself reach for my wallet the way he talks.

This is the guy that got a letter from someone as unimportant in the grand scheme of things like Aunt Bree was, and he didn't just ignore it like you might expect a VIP like him to do, no, he sent Chet Marchand out to Callisto to try and save Dean's soul before he went and lost it forever by going over to the Muslims. It was a surprising thing that he did that, reached out to save a single soul at risk of Eternal Damnation when he's got all this other stuff to be taking care of, so you had to admire him a little bit even if you aren't the church-going type the way I never have been.

He stopped talking half a minute or so like he does to get his wind back, just pacing back and forth a little way while he gathers his thoughts and prepares to launch into the next part while the congregation in front of him and the audience at home wait patient for him to crank it up again.

"Now what is the topic of the hour?" he asks, then he answers himself. "Terrorism. That terrible word, my friends, that we hear every time we switch on the news. Terror-ism. We have had just in my own lifetime Nazi-ism, Commun-ism and now something equally bad and terrible – Terror-ism. The dictionary defines Terror as an intense, overpowering fear, the ability to instill such fear, violence toward private citizens, public property and political enemies promoted by a group to achieve or maintain supremacy. That sums it up nicely, don't you think? But, my friends, those definitions are just not adequate to encompass the other aspect of terrorism, by which I mean the un-Christian aspect. The Christian

Church does not practice terrorism, but the Muslim religion does. It does so openly, in the name of Allah.

"Now I do not mean to imply that all Muslim people are terrorists, or the situation would be a thousand times worse than it is. But I do say that in the name of their god, certain practitioners of the Muslim faith have turned the world into a battlefield. Their aim, they openly admit this, is conversion of everyone else on the planet to their way of thinking. Imagine that. Every single man, woman and child walking the face of this earth must turn away from Jesus and accept Mohammed as the one to whom God revealed the truth. Not Jesus. Mohammed. It has been the practice of these Mohammedans to use the sword in getting their way. That was in the days when swords were the latest weapon. Now, of course, they use bombs and bullets to further their aim. According to Islam we must all do exactly as they want us to, or they will kill us. It's as simple and as terrible as that. Think like we do, pray like we do, or we will kill you, that's the message from these people."

Bob started quivering all over, you could practically feel the rage building up inside him and coming through the screen at you. "What-a-nerve," he says, then again to ram it home, "What-a-nerve! Friends, we do not tell the Muslim people of the world to think and pray as we do. We may suggest to them that our way is the true way, but we do not threaten them with loss of life if they disagree, which is their choice. Let's not forget, you *choose* to be a Christian, you cannot be coerced or threatened or bribed to be a Christian. And yet these ... *fiends* with their bombs and bullets insist that we do exactly that. In order to be *saved*, my friends! Saved from what? From the way of life you and I and countless millions of

Christians have lived and prayed for generations these last two thousand years. *Two thousand years!* Islam is not that old. Islam is centuries younger than Christianity, and yet these Johnny-come-latelies seek to tell *us* where the truth lies!"

Bob was plenty steamed about it, the situation with those terrorists. "And just in case you think that a terrorist is someone over there in the Middle East with a rag around his head, let me remind you that there are such people right here in America. Not descended from Arabian stock. Not immigrants to our fair land from their own country of scorching heat and desert sands. No, I'm referring to homegrown Americans brought up in the Christian Church and culture. How is it possible, I hear you ask, that this could happen? That an American boy from the heartland would turn away from what he knows is right, the traditions and lessons and *way of life he has been brought up in* ... turn away from those things and embrace the beliefs of Islam? How is that possible? I'll tell you how, and the answer will come as no surprise to those of you who have been listening to me these many years now. The devil is a whisperer, friends. He whispers in the ear of the weak and misguided and gets inside their head and turns their thoughts away from Jesus, yes he does. He might turn your head and make you into a drug addict. He might turn your head and make you into a child molester. He might turn your head and make you into any one of a dozen different kinds of monster, up to and including the very worst kind, my friends – the murderer."

Preacher Bob took a drink of water from the glass he keeps next to the Bible. "And not just a murderer – a special *kind* of murderer, maybe the very worst kind there is. I'm talking about the murderer who kills within his very own family. His own family. Think about that. Let's imagine there has already been tragedy in this family. A husband who abandoned his wife while she was bearing his child. A wife who abandoned her baby once he was born. Terrible burdens to begin life under, but not the worst, because that wife had a sister who was unmarried, and that sister did the Christian thing, my friends – she stepped into the breach and raised that child as her own! This happened. These are facts. It happened here in Kansas. And do you know what happened after the passing of time? Did that child thrive and become a good citizen by following the example of his aunt who took him in and devoted her life to his? He did not. The devil whispered in that young man's ear ... and he turned and *slew* that righteous woman."

A long soft whisper ran through the congregation. Bob stood there shaking his head with his lips pressed together tight, like he can't hardly bear to think about this tragedy that happened right here in Kansas. "Slew her with a shotgun, friends." The whisper ran around Bob's TV chapel again, and now I'm paying real close attention. "And put her torn and maimed body in a freezer while he contemplated how to dispose of her. This good woman who had scooped him up from disaster and held him to her bosom. What kind of a young man is this we're talking about here? I'll tell you what kind. The devil whispered in his ear not once, but twice. Twice! And what was it that the second whisper was advocating? I'll tell you that too. *Islam.* He wanted that murderous young man to convert to *Islam.*"

He said it so dramatic he had to wait for the ripple of outrage that run around the congregation to ease off, then he said, "And was the devil content to stop there? He was not.

The devil whispered a third time into the receptive ear of that young man, and bade him take up a weapon ... and gun down one of the finest men in public office this great nation has ever had the privilege of sending to Washington!"

The congregation, they got real excited and started in applauding. Bob hasn't even spoke Senator Ketchum's name out loud, but it's clear they know who he's talking about. He didn't say Dean's name either, maybe he can't on account of legal reasons, I don't know, but if folks were wondering which misguided devil-whispered young man he was referring to before, they sure as hell know it's Dean now, by God.

Bob waited for the fuss to die away a little, then he went on, "Haven't we had enough of these assassinations of our best Presidents? Lincoln, gunned down after saving the nation and freeing the slaves! Kennedy, gunned down while in his prime after staring down the Communist monster over Cuba! We will not have this happen again!"

Open cheering, even some whistling. This doesn't usually happen on a religious show. Bob is working the crowd like a man selling Youth Pills to retirees. "Now, friends," he says, "I know the man in question is not yet our President. Not yet until November 2008 rolls around ..." he says with a grin. More whistling which he bats down with his hands and goes on, "but the message is clear. The best and brightest hope that we Americans have to sustain our battle against the terrorists is being *threatened* even before assuming the highest office in the land. Threatened before he even begins his official run for that office. Threatened by the lowest of the low – an individual so blighted by lack of conscience he murdered his own aunt that raised him like her son! An individual so lacking in gratitude for having been born an American Christian he has turned away from the light and embraced the darkness! He has sworn to take the life of a man beloved by millions. Sworn to take his life! Now his target, who's known to be a man of stout heart and courage, is not going to back down from this confrontation. Not this man! He'll be there, out in the open under God's great sky, moving around our country to ask you for your vote when the time comes, and all the while this young murderer will be stalking him in the name of Allah! He will *not* succeed! Not while our prayers are with him, protecting him as if beneath the wing of the Lord our savior!"

That pretty much brung the house down, and they were still clapping their hands when the credits rolled. I have sometimes before watched these shows but never saw one that got people so excited about something that wasn't healing body pain and illness by the laying-on of hands. I wondered if the senator was watching and judging how many extra votes Preacher Bob had just now handed him.

I turned the TV off and heard a welcome sound way off in the distance, the rumbling of thunder. Why welcome? Because it means the earth filling the hole in the back yard will get good and wet and will settle some, and look like a mound that was created Wednesday not Friday, which is exactly what I needed for fooling the video cop tomorrow. It was almost like Preacher Bob had seen my difficulty and sent some rain to cover my crime. I went out on the porch to see the lightning flicker-flashing way off to the west and felt the wind in my face. The storm was coming in this direction so you could say that Salvation was heading my way. Amen to that.

NINE

Saturday morning and here comes the cop right on time, his tires splashing through the puddles. He's a rookie by the look of him, around my age with very fair hair, and he's brung his camera. He says he's there to tape the house interior and the grave hole getting emptied out, and he's not happy about it because he wasn't officially rostered for weekend work only the Chief insisted. He sounded kind of pissed about things in general, the way he talked.

I took him around back and showed him the mound, which looks like it's been there some considerable time thanks to the rain. He shot it for a few seconds to show it undisturbed, then he gave me a look that's kind of apologetic which means he's been told by Chief Webb that it's me doing the spadework today. I picked up the shovel and started in on it while he shot me doing it, then he said he may as well start in on the house while I'm busy out here. So off he went through the back door while I felt my first sweat of the day start to come through my shirt. Damn that Chief Webb!

Those first couple of feet of dirt were heavy with rain and stuck to me because of the dampness, which made progress even slower and filthier. I swore never again to pick up a shovel the rest of my life. Even my favorite dog, if I ever had one, would not get buried in the yard when he died, he'd be put up in the branches of a tree like the Indians used to do with their kin and left there to get eaten away by time and weather. The further down I got the drier the earth, so that was easier, only I'm getting tired by now so it was no picnic even then. The rookie come back out when I'm around halfway down and says he's done the entire place. I probably should've cleaned up a little before he started taping but too late now.

He lit a smoke and watched me work, which was irksome, and told me the department is so cheap it doesn't even have a DVD recorder, just this crappy old videocam that's a dinosaur, he calls it even if it is a Sony. This tape he just now shot will be going to Homeland Security for a permanent record and won't ever be taped over again. It's a special tape, he says, because it's connected to the threat against Senator Ketchum which everyone is talking about. You could tell that even though he didn't want to fritter away his Saturday like this he's kind of proud to be the one that made the tape that's so god-damn important. He stood over me smoking his cigarette while he talked, even flicked his ash down into the hole next to me, which made me want to sling a shovel of dirt up at him for payback, only you can't do stuff like that to a cop even if he's a rookie.

Finally I got to the bottom and he shot footage of me reaching it and finding nothing. The replay on this tape was going to be very exciting viewing at Homeland Security. I climbed out and he shot the empty hole, then he says he doesn't need to tape the hole getting filled in again now that it's been officially established and recorded that the hole is empty. So he can be on his way while I have to fill the damn thing back in again. I was glad about that, because I had to add a little something before shoveling the dirt back in, and I for sure did not want any cop videoing that part of the procedure for Homeland Security to look at.

I walked him back to his car and away he drove. I waited till he's out of sight then went to dig Dean out of the grass pile. The plastic bags had worked the way they should and there's very little stink coming through, even so I would not have wanted to pick him up and carry him against my chest like I ended up doing if I was not already filthy dirty. I counted it up and it's five times now that this pesky hole has been dug out – first by Dean to bury Bree, then by the cops to see what's down there, then by me to bury Dean, then by me to get him out again, then by me this morning for the fifth and final time, I hope.

I was not gentle in my treatment of Dean, had come to the end of my rope with regard to this guy that had made so much trouble and commotion for everyone. I did not get down in the hole again to lay him out careful like a fellow human being, no, I just dropped him in and didn't care that he landed all folded over and not laid out straight the respectful way. He had gone and left Bree in the freezer all folded over and undig-nified so who the heck was he to expect right and proper treatment now that he's dead. Preacher Bob had got it about right concerning Dean, that's how I was thinking as I started shoveling dirt down over him watched by curious chickens.

I showered away the dirt and had lunch, then called up Lorraine on my pretty new cell phone. Somehow I thought that if my last call to her had not met with success it was because that was done from the plain old kitchen phone. With the new cell I would very likely get satisfaction, coming at her on a different wavelength so to speak. That was my hope anyway as I pressed those dinky little buttons.

"Hello?"

"Hey, Lorraine, it's me."

"Odell, I was just about to call you."

"Yeah?"

"I'm on my way downtown to the funeral home to make arrangements for Bree. I have to be there soon because they close at twelve-thirty on a Saturday. I can't do this alone, Odell. My nerves are shot to pieces by all this. Did you see Preacher Bob's show last night?"

"Yeah, I did."

"Now it's happened like I knew it would. Dean has got to be Public Enemy Number One all over the entire country. It's a disgrace for the family name."

"Preacher Bob didn't say his name."

"But everyone knows who he's talking about! His name's in all the papers and the TV news, and his picture. You didn't tell anyone about the homo part, did you?"

"I said I wouldn't."

"Because that would be more than my nerves could stand, if people knew that about him."

"I won't ever tell, I promise."

"Thank you, Odell. You're being a true friend about all of this. So are you gonna be there at the funeral home to help me out with the arrangements?"

"I'll be there."

"It's on Fifth Street, Regis Galbally Funeral Services. I'm leaving right now."

"Okay."

She hung up. I forgot to ask her does it sound different hearing me on the new cell, but I could always ask her later. I got dressed in my best jeans and made sure there's nothing stuck to the front of my best shirt, then I headed for the truck.

All the way into town I kept thinking about Lorraine. It had been a real thrill to hear her voice again, which proves I am deeply in love, as the saying goes. She was not my ideal kind of woman which happens to be small and thin and dark, when I think about it. Lorraine is big and meaty and blonde, the exact opposite. It has always been a problem with me, this thing about the ideal woman. What does it mean, and why this particular type over some other particular type? I can't say, but my mother was small and thin and dark so maybe there is a psychological reason for it that should not be looked at too close.

I mean, until I met Lorraine, when I thought of my ideal woman, about marrying and so forth, I didn't think about my mother as such, which would be kind of sick, I think. No, I would think about Condoleezza Rice strange to say, who is older than me, even older than Lorraine is, but there it is, Condoleezza Rice was the one I thought about being married to for several years now, which I did not tell anyone about because they would not believe me, or they would have said other things that I might take offense at. Condi struck me as being about the smartest woman on the planet and the most decent also, rushing about from one country to the next in her plane fixing things between nations and doing everything she can for world peace and whatnot, all the while looking very trim and smart in her outfits with the pearls and always with a smile. I really like that little gap between her front teeth. I bet she is a very modest lady that does not bignote herself the way some of these politicians do every time they get in front of a camera, like Senator Ketchum does, for instance. No, Condi is not that kind and I respect her for that, and there is also the affection I feel that makes me think about marrying her the way other guys think about marrying some movie star or singer or whatall they never could hope even to carry her garbage out.

Of course I would do my best now that there's Lorraine not to be thinking so much about Condoleezza. I have not mentioned this till now because there was no need. This kind of thing is very private and personal, the things you think about with regard to women. But now that there's Lorraine I must not betray her in my heart or mind by allowing myself to think about Condi like I have been doing for some time now, so farewell, Condoleezza, and wish me happiness with another, meaning Lorraine.

I was downtown by then and not too far from Fifth Street when there's a flashing in my rearview mirror, red and blue so it's the police. Was I speeding? I didn't think so but you can't just keep driving when those police twinkle bars start flashing in your rearview, so I pulled over and waited for the cop to get out and come tell me what I did. When I saw who it was I felt a little chill creep over me because it's Chief Webb. He come up to my window which I rolled down nice and polite.

"Afternoon, Odell," he says, and he's right, the dashboard clock says 12.03. I have not got much time to be with Lorraine at the Gallbladder Funeral Place so this better not take too long.

"Afternoon, Chief." I gave him a big smile so he won't get mad at me about whatever it is I did wrong.

"My man come visit you this morning?"

"Yessir, he did, and shot his camera every which way, then he left."

"You and me need to talk, Odell."

"Okay."

"About Dean Lowry."

"I'd just as soon not, Chief. That's a topic that brings me a depressive feeling with all this fuss and bother going on now."

"Depressive? Maybe you think you know about depressive, only you don't. But maybe after we have a little talk you will."

"It's just I have to be at the funeral home right now with Lorraine. She's making arrangements for her aunt, the funeral and things, and she wants me there to be with her to do that."

"Is that so? Well, other matters take presidents over stuff like that. Other matters like giving false information to the police in a murder case."

"Huh?"

"Think back a little, Odell. Did you or did you not tell me you came to the Lowry place on Saturday afternoon when your car broke down? Think careful now."

That's what I told him, all right, even though it was a Sunday that I turned up for real. One thing I learned from the cop shows is they hate it when you tell them one thing and then tell them another thing that's opposite to what you said the first time. It makes them real suspicious you're lying, which I was, but not for bad reasons.

"It was Saturday," I said.

"You're absolutely sure about that."

"I sure am."

"And you'll swear to that in court?"

"Court?"

"Just in a manner of speaking."

"Okay."

"You're telling me you were at the Lowry place with Dean Lowry on Saturday night, all night."

"That's right."

"Only I've been asking around and it seems Dean was somewhere else that Saturday night."

"Really?"

"Yeah, really. There are witnesses, plenty of them."

"Witnesses about what exactly?"

"About his whereabouts."

"I don't think I know what you mean, Chief. It's only twenty-five minutes till the funeral home closes and Lorraine's expecting me..."

"Let her wait. Ever been inside the Okeydokey Karaoke Bar?"

"I never heard of it," I said.

"Well, Dean did. He went there a bunch of times including last Saturday. It's a known homo hangout. All the fruits like to get up on stage and sing their little hearts out. Last Saturday Dean, he got up on stage and sang 'Do You Know the Way to San Jose.' You know that song, Odell?"

"I might have heard it on the oldies station."

"There was a guy there at the Okeydokey Karaoke with a DVD camera. He shot the whole thing, with one of those little readout things in the corner of the screen, you know the kind, it gives the time of day or night and the date. You can't mess with those things, it's built into the computer or whatever runs those things. Dean was there, not at home with you, so now what do you have to say to me about Saturday night, Odell?"

"Well . . . it must have been Sunday, I guess."

"Sunday."

"Uhuh."

"You're changing your story, is that what you're telling me?"

"I thought it was Saturday, but if you've got this movie with him someplace else I must've been wrong about that, excuse me."

"Excuse you?" He gave me this long look through his sunglasses. "The thing I'm trying to figure out about you, Odell, is if you're the dumbest son of a bitch I ever ran across, or the smartest."

I gave him what I wanted to sound like a laugh, only it come out more like a wheeze from some old smoking guy's chest full of cancer. "I'm just forgetful, not dumb."

"Is that right."

"Me and Dean, we got drunk is what happened, so maybe that's what made me think it's Saturday and not Sunday."

"Uhuh. Anything else?"

"Well, if I was a churchgoer there wouldn't be any problem because I'd remember going to church that day, but I don't do that so that's maybe the reason I thought it's Saturday instead. Is it important?"

"Important? Did you see Preacher Bob's show last night?"

"Yeah..."

"The entire damn nation up in arms about this terrorist murderer that's threatening to assassinate a well-known public figure, and you want to know if it's important? You're just pretending to be stupid aren't you, Odell?"

"Nossir, I'm not."

"So you really are stupid."

"No, what I meant to say..."

"Were there other people out there Sunday night, Odell? People that prayed to Allah and had bomb-making equipment maybe? Are you covering up for them?"

"No way, there was just me and Dean and we got drunk on Captain Morgan. I could've sworn it was Saturday but maybe I'm wrong..."

"Damn right you're wrong." He put a finger in my face. "And don't think this won't get reported to Homeland Security. The lies you tell to me get passed along, Odell, and at Homeland they don't take kindly to liars that try and steer them away from the truth. Those Homeland people, they're like bloodhounds in pursuit of the facts. No way you're gonna tell lies and get away with it, not with those puppies on your trail."

"Okay."

"So you're officially changing your story now, is that what you're telling me? Because to change your story officially you need to come down to the station and make a statement on camera. They need everything captured onscreen at Homeland for their records."

"Could I do that after the funeral home?"

He gave me another long stare to make me afraid, which it succeeded to do that. This guy is crazy mad at me over nothing at all that I can figure out.

"Okay," he says. "You present yourself at the station two hours from now and we'll just see how you want to change the facts around."

"I don't want to change the facts, Chief, I'm just saying maybe I was mistaken."

"Two hours," he says, stabbing at me with the finger again.

He gave me this disgusted look and went on back to his cruiser which all this time has had the flashers going, so cop cars must have heavy-duty batteries to support all that extra electricity needed. It made people that are passing look across at us too with those lights flashing that way getting their attention, which would have been embarrassing if I knew anyone that's passing by, which fortunately I don't.

Chief Webb blasted past me and turned the corner. I started up and drove the rest of the way to the funeral home place feeling very bad about things. I wished Chief Webb could be swallowed by an earthquake or something so he would quit bugging me like he is, acting like he thinks I'm a criminal. That was real annoying, that part, because I didn't do anything.

It's already 12.14 when I found the place and pulled up and went inside, and there's Lorraine dressed real neat talking with a fat guy in a dark suit. She was mad at me too, I could tell, but she kept on smiling at the guy while they talked, then she come over to me and the guy went away into his office or someplace.

"What time of the afternoon do you call this?" she wants to know.

I looked at my watch to tell her but she slapped my wrist, which is peculiar behavior, I think, then she says, "I had to do it all by myself, the selections."

"Well, I'm sorry ..."

"You had plenty of time to get here. I suppose you got lost."

"No, I got pulled over."

"You mean by cops?" She looked unbelieving about that.

"Chief Webb, he thinks I'm a liar."

"What?"

I explained about what happened between Andy Webb and me, including the part about having to go down to the station and record a statement about if it's Saturday or Sunday I was with Dean because of the DVD made at the karaoke place.

Lorraine didn't like any of this. "Stick to the drunk story, it sounds better than anything else might. People always fuck things up when they're drunk, even telling time and what day it is if they're drunk enough."

"Okay."

"That's bad, though, about the Okeydokey Karaoke. That's a gay joint. I told Dean never to go there and now some gay guy has gone and DVD'd him singing some stupid song and acting gay ... Christ, think what the networks would pay for *that* to show on TV ... I think I'm going to throw up ..."

I didn't know what to do. If I had a hat I would've offered it to puke in, but in the end she didn't need a hat, kind of pulled herself together and says, "It's Andy, he's hassling you to get at me."

"Why?"

"Never mind why. There's been bad blood between us a long time now."

"But he's your old friend, you said."

"Forget it, Odell. What's gone under the bridge is long gone. Take me to lunch. No, wait, I want you to see the casket Bree picked out for herself."

"But ... how did she do that if she's dead?"

"She had a funeral plan, forty dollars a month. She had it forever."

Lorraine led me over to a display of coffins all set out in rows. Some of them were real big with gold handles and so forth and plumped-up cushioning on the inside, not that a dead person needs cushions to lie on, but I guess it helps fill out the coffin if it's one of the big ones. "That one," she said, pointing. It wasn't a big one and the polish on the wood wasn't so bright. "Five grand, including service and burial."

"Wow, that's a lot."

"Bree's policy is paying for it. Do you like it?"

"It's okay. She was only small."

"Do you want to see her? She's laid out in the other room. They fixed her up real nice."

"No."

"Why not? You're the one that found her, Odell. You're involved in this. Are you scared of dead people?"

Well, I wasn't because just this morning I manhandled a dead person and wasn't scared one bit, only disgusted and mad about all that spadework. But you can't say that to your intended, so we went in the other room and there she is all right, on a table wearing a dress, even had her shoes on which she didn't when I found her, I remember those little wrinkled old lady's feet she has got, so this way is better. "Come closer," says Lorraine so I did. Bree has got makeup on her face to make her look alive, not that cold white look she had first thing out of the freezer, so that is an improvement, only they put too much red in the cheeks, I'm thinking.

Lorraine sighed, choking back some tears. "She almost looks like she's sleeping, don't you think?"

"No."

"Of course she does. They can do miracles in this place, it's the best in town. Look at her skin, look at her hair, it's so real I could swear she's breathing."

"Uhuh."

Bree was the deadest-looking person I ever saw. She even looked deader than Anfer Sheen back in Yoder, and he had a blue face he's so dead. But Lorraine didn't want to hear that. "She looks real peaceful," I said, "like she's resting or something."

"Doesn't she. Poor Bree, she deserved better than what Dean dished out. That's just a disgrace what he did to her. Preacher Bob got that right. He'll get the death penalty when they pick him up, there'd be a public outcry if he didn't, especially if he goes ahead and kills Senator Ketchum. My own brother, and he's gone and done these terrible things…"

"It's not good," I agreed, wanting to get on the right side of her.

She put her hand on my arm and I got those electric tingles again. This woman has definitely gotten under my skin. "Thank you, Odell. I need someone to lean on a little bit right now. Ordinarily I don't, but for right now it's a burden."

"My pleasure."

"I don't think that's right, Odell. It's not a pleasure to take care of someone in their time of need, it's a duty."

"Okay."

"Especially when there's murder and terrorism all mixed up in it. Where's there any room for pleasure?"

"Excuse me, I meant duty."

"Okay, take me to lunch."

She made us go in her car even if it's so small I had a hard time squeezing inside and had to put the seat way back. She won't get in the truck because it's Dean's truck and she is very down on Dean at the moment, also she doesn't want to be seen inside of a lawnmowing truck that has still got the lawnmowers in back and Dean's evil name on the door. Lorraine drove very fast and I kept wondering if maybe Chief Webb wouldn't pick us up for speeding and spoil my day again, but we made it to the restaurant all right without getting a ticket. It's the same place she went to with Cole Connors the other night, she says, and the food here is just great.

We had to wait a little while for a table this place is so popular, Caprice, it's called, just that with no Café or Restaurant added on to explain what it is. Finally we got sat down and this girl dressed very pretty comes and handed us menus to read from. Well, I had not heard of anything they had there apart from the salad. All the other stuff might just as well have been wrote in another language, which it turns out half of it was, namely French. So this is a French Restaurant without the Restaurant part. I had heard about these places and how good the food is, but when I sneaked a peek at what folks are eating at the other tables there's nothing recognizable on their plates, but the little rolls in the little baskets were bread, I knew that much.

Lorraine asked what I liked the look of, which was a hard question. I asked her, "Have they got fries?"

"No they don't."

"But it's a French restaurant, they must have French fries."

"Well, they don't, so pick something else."

That was harder, picking out what something on the menu might be, and about then the girl comes back to take the order. Lorraine rattled off something or other, most likely the same thing she had the other night with Cole Connors so she's familiar with it, but I just couldn't make up my mind between this mystery food and that mystery food, until Lorraine got mad and tells the girl I'll have the something-or-other, which after the girl has gone she says is potatoes done different, since I wanted fries so bad. I could tell I had not handled the situation right and went quiet from that experience, which put Lorraine in a worse mood than she already is. She says, "Can't you make conversation while we wait?"

"Okay."

She waited, then rolls her eyes and asked me in this sarcastic voice if I read any good books lately. This was a big relief when she asked that, because it so happens I did read a good book lately. *"The Yearling,"* I said, "that's a real good book."

"The Yearling? That's the one about the kid and the dog?"

"No, it's a fawn. He kind of adopts it after its mother gets shot and —"

"Yeah, I remember it, we had to read it in school and do a book report. What I liked about it, it wasn't very long. I didn't say that in my report, though."

"That book they give to schoolkids," I explained, "it's not the whole book. That's a shortened book for kids. The whole book is twice as long and much better with no parts missed out. It's a Pulitzer Prize book. That's the book I read lately. Well, I'm halfway through right now. There's been a lot of distraction in my life this last week or so."

"When things calm down around here maybe you can finish it," she says, looking around at the other people eating or waiting for their food to be cooked up.

"I finished it before," I said.

"You're reading the same book twice?"

"Sixteen times."

I was proud of that. I bet nobody else ever read *The Yearling* sixteen times, that's some kind of a record, maybe one they can put in the *Guinness Book of Records*. I should ask somebody about that, then my name could be in the *Guinness Book of Records* as well as in the newspaper. That would be something to make Lorraine proud.

"Sixteen times?"

"Uhuh. It's the best book I ever read."

"Sounds like the only book you ever read."

"No, I tried two other ones but didn't like them."

She looked at me a long time then down at the tabletop another long time. "Odell," she says, "when you go out to the prison and interview with Cole, don't go telling him you read a book sixteen times, okay?"

"Why not?"

"Because it sounds peculiar. They don't want peculiar people guarding inmates, it's too important of a job. The inmates are the peculiar ones, that's the way it's always been in prisons, so don't go rocking the boat. You look exactly right for the job being tall and big like you are. You look good in that shirt by the way."

"It's my best one," I said and it was, with big curlicues stitched over the pockets fancy style. If I had worn this shirt back in Kit Carson High they would have called me a Roper for sure, so back then I only wore the checked kind, which gets you called a Roper anyway, but the curlicued kind of shirt gets you called a Roper On Saturday Night, which I did not want.

"So it might be best if you tell Cole you don't read books at all. He'll be more comfortable with that. But tell him you read magazines. To get the job you have to be able to read. They've got this test. Do you do okay with tests?"

"I passed my driver's license test on just the second try. I missed out on the question about how far do you park from the curb, plus a couple others."

"You'll do just fine. When you get the job there'll be a little bonus in it for me."

"Bonus?" I'm thinking the bonus is that Lorraine and me will work in the same place and get to see each other all day, that would be a big bonus.

"Two hundred fifty dollars, that's what they give you if you bring in someone reliable that you can vouch for and they turn out fine, after the three-month probationary period that is. I think it should be more than that, say five hundred if the guy works out. Finding the right people isn't as easy as you might think. Anyway, don't tell about the sixteen times."

"Okay, I won't."

"All right then, now what else can we talk about?"

It so happened I had a topic of conversation on my mind that I wanted to converse about so now was my chance to do that. "Is the cat okay?"

"Cat?"

"The neighbor's cat that knocked something over the other night."

"What neighbor's cat? My neighbor's got a parakeet."

"You said it was a cat."

Her face changed all of a sudden from looking annoyed to this big smile. "And a cat too, that's right, only the cat keeps trying to eat the parakeet, like Sylvester and Tweety Pie, so yeah, he asked me to look after the cat. But he'll have to take it back when I move out to Bree's place."

That made my ears prick up. "When are you gonna do that?"

"Oh, soon as the will gets probated and the place is officially mine and Dean's, only I don't think Dean'll be moving back there anytime soon."

If only she knew it, Dean has moved in permanent and forever.

"What about me?" I asked her.

"Well, what about you?"

"Do I get to stay there?"

"I already said I need someone out there taking care of the place, keeping away vandals and souvenir hunters now that Dean's got so famous. You might want to watch out for that kind sneaking around."

"I mean after you move in. I could be the lodger, kind of."

"That's weeks and weeks down the line, Odell. One thing I've learned, you take it one step at a time whatever the plan, that way you don't get all backed up with timetables and schedules and expectations that don't work out the way you intended. Easy does it and see how it goes. Just relax and enjoy being out there paying no rent and pocketing the lawn-mowing profits like I let you do, that's plenty for right now."

She made it sound like I have got it good, which I guess I have, anyway I run out of conversation momentarily and just listened while Lorraine talks about the funeral service next Monday which I'll be expected to be there with a rented suit for the right appearances and the best place for that is the prom rental store downtown, although she's wondering if they'll have something my size.

Then the food come and we ate it. She told me it's potatoes but I only believed it because I love her, anyway I ate it but will not order that dish again whatever it's called. I was not so impressed by French cooking as expected by what everyone always says, but did not say this to Lorraine who ate everything up regardless. There was wine too that I didn't like the taste of, too sharp, not mellow like beer or with a tang to it like Captain Morgan, but Lorraine says it's great so I drunk a couple glasses of it to please her. That is what being in love is all about, pleasing the one you love, so I did that. At least I was not expected to make more conversation while we ate, which Lorraine did like she has been starving herself. At the end she says to go pay the cashier while she uses the bathroom, and you would not believe how much that little bit of food and bottle of wine come to in payment for it, a very big shock to me but I paid because it's my treat. Lorraine dropped me back at the funeral place to get the truck. She said I should go to the police station and wait and she'll be there to come in with me for what she calls moral support. So I did that, drove the truck over to the police station and parked outside, and pretty soon she drove up alongside and we went in together and she says to the guy at the desk, "Where's the Chief?" which right at that exact time Andy Webb comes out of his office and looks at us.

"What are you doing here?" he says.

"You told me to," I said, but he's talking to Lorraine.

"Any reason I can't be here?" she asks, and the Chief only shrugged.

He pointed down the corridor. "Second on the left, Odell," he says, sounding friendly, not like when he pulled me over before. To Lorraine he says, "Are you his lawyer?"

"Well, I don't think so, do you?"

"Just asking. He can have his lawyer present but nobody else."

"He hasn't got one."

"That's okay, he just needs to waive that part and we can proceed."

"Odell, you don't have to do anything without a lawyer present."

"That's okay, I don't need a lawyer. I didn't do anything."

They both looked at me, then Andy says, "What's it gonna be? Getting a lawyer on a Saturday afternoon, how easy's that gonna be?"

"You don't have to, Odell," Lorraine said again.

I started walking down the corridor to show them I am a man that knows his own mind and can do without advice which I don't need anyway. That wine I drunk was making my head swirl some, so it's more strong than you might think from the taste of it. Andy come along behind me and I went in this room which has got a little table and some chairs and a video camera set up ready with the same young cop as this morning standing ready to run it.

"You already met Officer Dayton," says Andy, which I did but he never told me his name at the time. We nodded to each other and I went and sat in the chair in front of the camera. The chair had got a machine sitting next to it on a trolley cart with wires and so forth so I figured it's some kind of old-fashioned tape recorder to back up the video they're making of me. Then another guy comes in the room, an older guy with a cigarette hanging off his lip like it was superglued there. He's got his sleeves rolled up and did not look like a cop on account of no uniform. "No smoking," says Andy, and this guy gives him a look I would not call friendly and flips the butt over in the corner because there is no ashtrays in a room with a No Smoking rule. It surprised me the way he did that, though. Then he lifts up this cover on the machine and I see a roll of paper there with little metal arms coming down to touch the paper. That's when I recognized what it is – an earthquake recorder.

"What's that there for?" I asked Andy.

"Just routine," he said back to me.

"Lean forward," says the other guy, and after I did it he wrapped these elastic band things with wires around my chest, and that's when I knew this was not an earthquake machine, it's a lie-detecting machine. Andy had not said to me anything about this, only about the video statement, so now I'm confused about what's happening here.

"That's a lie-detecting machine," I said, just to let them know I was not fooled.

"Better not tell any lies then," said Andy with a little smile.

"Well, I wasn't going to."

"That's good. Truthfulness is always best, isn't it, Dannyboy.

Odell, this is Dan Oberst, kind of a specialist we brung in today just for you, so be aware you're getting special treatment here."

"Afternoon," I said to him and Dan just grunted, really pissed off about something, maybe he didn't want to work on a Saturday same as Officer Dayton said he didn't this morning out at Dean's place. I bet I was the only one in that room that isn't grumpy about this being Saturday, but sitting to get videoed is easier work than lawnmowing any day of the week. Dan Oberst put one of those blood pressure cuffs around my arm and stuck a couple little plastic gizmos on the palm of my hand.

"All set," says Dan. "I'm going to ask you a series of questions which you will answer without hesitation either Yes or No. Do not answer my question any other way, just Yes or No, you understand that?"

"Yes," I said, and laughed because it's a pretty good joke, but they didn't get it.

He switched on the machine and the paper started scrolling through real slow, then he stopped it because he's only testing that it works, which it did, so then he rolled the trolley back behind me and sits himself on a metal chair next to it.

"Face the front, Odell," Andy told me, meaning the camera, where Officer Dayton gave a nod that he's rolling too. The lie machine started up again and from behind me Dan says slow and careful, "Is your name Odell Deefus?"

It was real tempting to say No and see if the machine beeped or whatever, but everyone is so serious in there I didn't do that. "Yes," I said, very firm and serious too if that's how they want me to be.

"Your date of birth is November 21 1985?"

"Yes."

He asked other stuff with obvious answers. If the quiz shows on TV were this easy I'd be a billionaire, I'm thinking.

"You are an associate of Dean Leonard Lowry?"

"Yes."

"Do you have knowledge of his current whereabouts?"

Well, of course I did, he's buried in the back yard. I knew if I lied about that the machine will know, so I said Yes. I felt safe about that because they can't ask me where he is because that's not a Yes or No question.

Andy butted in then, saying "You know where he is?"

Dan hissed and says, "Chief, do you mind? Now we have to start over."

"Well, that question has got to be addressed directly," said Andy, getting pissed. "If he knows where the guy is, we need to know that right now. Odell, where's Dean?"

"In America," I said, which is a perfectly truthful answer.

"Where in America?"

Dan switched off the machine. "If I get any further interference I'm going to have to clear the room of anyone not directly involved in questioning or taping, do I make myself clear?"

"The question should've been put different," says Andy.

"You had the opportunity to check the list," says Dan. "Don't blame me if you didn't bother doing that beforehand. Now we have to start again."

He started in doing stuff to the lie machine. Officer Dayton asked Andy, "Should I keep shooting?"

"Keep shooting."

By now I had figured out that they were going to try and trick me into telling things I knew and they didn't, which means incriminating things like where Dean is, so it was a good thing Andy screwed up the questioning like he did because I know now what to do. I had heard that the only way to beat a lie-detecting machine is not to be yourself. What that means is you have to think about things that have got nothing to do with the questions they ask, so the answers you give will tell the machine you're lying even if the question they asked is something like Is today Saturday? Which you say Yes to, only you're thinking about the day your dog got run over or the day your daddy slapped you in front of folks for no reason because he's an asshole, stuff like that. This makes you sweat and your heartbeat goes faster, so the machine says you're a liar about something perfectly straightforward like What day is today, which means it can't be trusted to get the right reaction from all those other questions either, so the test is a washout.

But you have got to be able to concentrate to make it work, so I did that, concentrated hard on being Jody in *The Yearling* when he gets told his pet fawn has got to be shot because it keeps eating the crops Jody's family worked so hard to raise. That fawn has got to go even if Jody loved him so hard it hurts to think about shooting that pretty little creature with the long flickety ears and the little rows of spots along his back and those big brown eyes and that soft wet nose and dainty little hoofs he has got and that little white standy-up tail that gave him his name – Flag. Flag the fawn that even slept in the bed with Jody when he's little they loved each other so, and now Flag has got to be shot and killed like a bad creature, a wolf or a snake, shot down dead with a bullet in his little beating heart behind his little chest where the hair grows in these little whorls that'll be covered in blood when the bullet strikes home …

"What the hell are you doing, Odell?" Andy sounded very sore all over again.

I couldn't answer him, I'm sobbing so much, my whole body shaking in the chair with tears leaking down my face just thinking about a terrible thing like shooting your own pet fawn that you love to pieces he's so cute and loving in return, but you have to do it because your daddy told you to …

"Oh, for chrissakes … What the hell is the matter with you, Odell?"

Behind me Dan said, "I'm canceling this interview right now. The best you could hope for is Inconclusive. I have professional standards and nothing here comes up to scratch. If you want to put in a complaint, Chief, be sure and include the fact that everything right up till now has been videoed to back me up on this."

He started taking off the stickems and pressure cuff, breathing very fast through his nose so I can tell he's as pissed as Andy about the way things went, only it's not me he's pissed at, it's the Chief. "You can go," he says, and I stood up.

"He can go when I say he can go!"

Officer Dayton asked, "Should I stop shooting now?"

"Hell yes!" says Andy.

"Can I leave?" I asked, still sobbing I feel so bad.

"Get out!"

I went along the corridor to where Lorraine's waiting. She took one look at me and said, "Odell, what's wrong?"

"I didn't want to …" I said, my face still wet. What I mean is,

I didn't want to shoot Flag the fawn that I loved so, only Lorraine didn't get that, of course.

"Didn't want to what? What did they do in there?"

"They had a lie-detecting machine … The guy hooked me up …"

"What!"

Andy come along the corridor then and she says, "Lie detector? You didn't say anything about a lie detector, Andy, just a camera. What kind of a crooked setup are you running here? A *lie* detector! Exactly what kind of lies do you think he's been telling, the difference between Saturday and Sunday? He's already told you he was drunk, and now he's in there getting a polygraph without a lawyer's say-so? What the fuck, Andy …"

"Back off, Lorraine, this has got nothing to do with you."

"The hell it doesn't! It's *my* goddamn brother they're out there hunting down, *my* aunt that got murdered and *my* friend getting shafted for no good reason except he happened to walk into something weird because his fucking *car's* on the fritz! Fuck!"

"Okay, that's enough."

"You're playing this all wrong, Andy, trust me."

"Trust! You?"

They breathed hard at each other, staring daggers as the saying goes. I wasn't upset about Flag anymore, just curious about the way Andy and Lorraine are fighting over me. Lorraine called me her friend, I definitely heard her say that, and I'm hoping that before too long she'll add one little word to that word, what I mean is *boy*friend.

"Come on, Odell, we're outta here."

She grabbed my arm and yanked me towards the front

doors and was still yanking hard when we're outside. "That scheming son of a bitch," she says. "He had no right, no *right*... What did you tell them, Odell?"

"Nothing much, my name and how old I am, then Andy wanted to know where Dean is, and I told him In America and he got mad about something...then the guy said he's canceling the interview."

"And that's as far as it went?" We're standing between her car and the truck now, and Lorraine kept looking back at the station like she's expecting Andy to come out with a rocket launcher or something.

"He canceled it, and Andy got mad."

"They didn't slap you around or anything, nothing physical? Because that's against the law."

"No."

"Well, you looked almost like you were crying when you came out. They must've done something to get you upset like that."

I couldn't tell her they wanted me to shoot Flag, she wouldn't have understood, especially after she told me not to talk about that book to anyone.

I said, "What does Cole look like?"

"What?"

"Cole Connors, what does he look like?"

"Look like? Was he in there too?"

"No."

"He's around forty, losing his hair with a gut."

So there's no way she can think he's more good-looking than me, that was a big relief because I'd been wondering about that, maybe even getting a little upset.

"Why would you want to know something like that?"

"Oh … I've got this inquiring mind, I guess."

"Odell, do you have a problem concentrating on stuff? Has anyone ever said to you that you have this problem?"

Well, I don't have any such problem, I just proved that by concentrating very hard on Flag getting shot, concentrated so hard I brung the whole interview to a close, shut it down, the whole operation, so it just doesn't make sense for her to be accusing me of this.

"No."

"It's just I sometimes get the feeling you and me, we're on a different wavelength or something, you talk so weird."

"No I don't."

"Well, from now on if Chief Webb tries to make you do something, give an interview or whatever, you tell me immediately and we'll get you a lawyer."

"I don't want a lawyer, I didn't do anything."

"So what? This is America. If you haven't got a lawyer you're dead meat."

"I think I want to go home now."

"Are you sure you're okay?"

"I'm fine," I said, and I was because Lorraine is acting real concerned for me, which goes to show she cares, anyone could see that.

"Do you know the way from here?"

"I know Callisto pretty good now from the lawnmowing."

"Well, avoid taking Eagle Avenue. There's a baseball game at the high school and the traffic gets bad."

"Are you going to the game? We could go together." I was thinking how nice that'd be, her and me in the bleachers with

Cokes and hot dogs rooting for the home team, which is the Callisto Cougars – Go Cougars! – but she shook her head and says she doesn't want to bump into Cole Connors on a Saturday afternoon who'll be there because his oldest boy is on the team.

"But isn't he your friend?"

"Cole and I see plenty of each other during the week, Odell. Even friends need a break from each other." Which is a philosophy I agree with, only then she says, "Anyway, his wife'll be there and I can't stand that bitch. So listen, you go on back and maybe I'll talk to you tonight."

Away she drove very fast without waving bye-bye. I watched her little car disappear around the corner with smoke coming from the exhaust so it needs a tune-up, then I turned around and saw Chief Webb at the top of the station steps watching me and smoking a cigarette at the same time, only he wants me to think he's only out there smoking, which I knew better because I can see his eyes looking at me even if his face is turned the other way. He really did not like me, that man, and I didn't do anything.

I was about to get in the truck when my new phone rung. I took it out and keyed it and it's Agent Jim Ricker on the line. He says, "How are you, Odell?"

"Okay, I guess."

"Did you have your interview yet?"

"Interview?"

"I'm told you're scheduled for an interview today. Did you have it yet?"

"Uhuh."

"And how did that go?"

"Not very good."

"Why's that, Odell?"

"Chief Webb thinks I'm lying about everything just because I got Saturday and Sunday mixed up."

"It's Chief Webb's job to be of a suspicious nature."

"But I didn't do anything."

"A very familiar phrase, but the law requires that certain steps be taken, including interviewing innocent parties from time to time."

"He's so suspicious he's watching me right now."

"Is that right? Take his picture and send it to me, Odell, I'd like to see what this guy looks like."

"Okay! Hold on …"

I lined up Chief Webb and shot him for around five seconds till he noticed and stared directly at me, looking pissed, then I pressed the Transmit button.

Jim says to me, "Okay, there he is. He doesn't look all that bad, Odell."

"You'd have to meet him to know. And how'd you know about me getting interviewed anyway?"

"Don't go worrying yourself about that, Odell. I'm your friend and my little bird keeps an eye on all my friends, wherever and whenever."

I looked around for the little bird, kind of half expecting to see him peeking at me around a corner or something, but there's only Andy Webb over there on the station steps flicking his butt away into the car park, so how can Jim Ricker be keeping an eye on me like he says he is … unless he's watching me by spy satellite! I looked up but of course you can't see those things they're so high, especially in daytime. Homeland

Security, it's obvious now that I thought about it, they have got all this billion-dollar technology to be snooping on terrorists and Enemies of the Nation so why not use it to keep watch over a friend also which Jim told me he thinks I'm that, a friend. This has gotten very serious now with spy satellites beaming down at me protectingly this way.

"Okay," I told him, giving a wave at the sky that he'll see on his screen inside the secret Homeland Security spy station buried under a mountain somewhere that you'd think is only rocks and trees, but underneath it's like a James Bond movie with computers and blinking lights and very serious people watching bad guys from the edge of space. "I understand."

Chief Webb was watching me wave. When I did that he looked up in the sky, then stared at me very hard, not even bothering to pretend he isn't, then he shook his head and went inside the station.

"That's good, Odell," says Jim. "Now understand this, we're handling the situation by remote, you might say, which means you and me, we won't be meeting face to face, that'll be done on the ground by other agencies including the police, do you follow? You'll never see us personally. Why? Because, my friend, you are bait."

"Bait?"

"With which to trap a terrorist."

"Like Sammy bin Laden?"

"No, like Dean Lowry."

"Oh, right."

"Maybe you still think of him as your friend, I can relate to that, only sometimes our friends are something we never suspected, Odell, something that strains the friendship when finally you find out about it. That's Dean. You didn't know he's a murderer and terrorist, did you."

"No, it was a big surprise."

"Exactly. Now it could be that Dean will want to get in touch with you, Odell, if he finds himself between a rock and a hard place. Could be he'll try to exploit the friendship by asking you to help him out somehow, drive him across the border or something of that nature. What would be your reaction if that happened, if Dean Lowry approached you for assistance?"

"I'd be surprised," I said, which I would be seeing as he's dead and buried.

"Well, don't be, it might happen, and if it does, you use that new phone to call me and let me know. You're still a player in this game, Odell, maybe even an important one. Expect another interview soon, maybe even today. The Bureau has been slow to move on this, way slow. Heads will roll for that."

"Bureau?"

"FBI. That little town of yours has become a focus of attention. You still didn't change your ring tone."

"How do you know that?"

But he rung off without even a goodbye. Agent Jim Ricker had got the strangest way of talking but he's likely a very busy man with no time for chit-chat so it's understandable. He seemed like a nice person so in a way it's a shame about us not meeting face to face. Or maybe not, seeing as I would have to lie direct into his face about things if we did. That made me sad for a minute, thinking about that, but I have got no choice now except keep on lying about Dean or be in Very Big Trouble about everything.

TEN

It sure had been a long day and I wanted to go home, but before I did that I went to the liquor store for more beer and another big bottle of the Captain. They had a special on for Carlsberg so I got that, plus Cheetos and Doritos for food variation which is necessary for good health, also beer nuts that have got nourishment in them, that's why monkeys and elephants eat them.

Then I went on home but forgot about Eagle Avenue and got stuck there for a little while in the traffic for the big game, but then I'm through and on my way again, feeling good about things mostly which has always been my way. There are people that are forever thinking dark thoughts and frowning hard about this and that but I am not that kind, no, I don't see the point in that. When things were bad for me in Yoder with my old man I didn't get to brooding and moping the way some might have. Corky Busch, for instance, who had this big problem with his old man that wanted him to be in the hardware store that he owned and take over one day, a family business since way back when, only Corky wanted to be a gangster instead and talked like a black kid, Yo muthafuckuh etcetera and wore the baggy clothes like a Skater only no skateboard. Corky was the only Gangsta in town, which made him lonely, I guess, with no gang to help him kill people and do drug deals and so forth. His old man went on and on at Corky about the hardware store until the time Corky got his gun to complete the costume and used it to shut his old man up and fled the scene. Corky went down to Colorado and shot someone else in a convenience store and ended up in prison where he got to join a gang after all, the Aryan Brotherhood, so I bet he quit talking like a black kid. This is what happens when you think dark thoughts, and you are better off not doing that.

The afternoon was half gone when I put the beer in the fridge and turned on the TV for company. There's no news at this early hour except on the news channel so I watched that thinking maybe there'll be something about Dean I didn't already see, but mainly it's about some war going on in Africa where there is always some war going on there. I can't see why because they have got nothing over there except AIDS and starving people, so why fight over that? Pretty soon there'll be no Africans left to fight each other, they will all be dead from disease and bullets and the animals will take over again, lions and zebras and so forth for the tourists from over here. Well, there was nothing I could do about that situation but it dented my mood some seeing all these little kids with just rags on their little bodies and maybe an AK-47 in their hands if they didn't have AIDS yet.

While I'm waiting for something about Dean I heard this car coming up the drive and got up fast thinking it's Lorraine come over to be with me, but when I looked it isn't her car it's someone else, maybe the FBI come to interview me like Jim Ricker said they would. But it turned out to be Officer Dayton when he gets out of the car. I felt something like fingers close around my heart then, thinking maybe he needs to get more video of the grave, but then I saw he hasn't got his camera so that's okay, only why the heck is he here?

He come up on the porch and said, "Hello," very friendly, not grumpy like he was this morning over Saturday duty and again this afternoon at the police station. And he isn't wearing his cop uniform so this is not police business he's here about. I opened the door and we went on through to the living room.

"Want a beer?"

"I could go for that."

"Are you all done with police work for today?"

"All over and done with."

I got him a cold one and he popped it. "Not watching the Red Sox game?"

Well, I wasn't, he could see that, but I can take a hint and surfed around till I found it to keep him happy because a happy cop will do you no harm, I'm thinking. We watched it for a few minutes and he whooped when someone hit a home run, then he kind of looked over at me like he just now noticed I'm there and he's not at home watching his own TV.

"So," he says, "pretty intense day for you. Can I call you Odell?"

"Okay."

"I'm Larry. That was one messed-up interview Chief Webb tried to give you."

"It was okay."

"Okay for you, you walked. Not so okay for the Chief. He wanted to get something on you, implicate you in this murder somehow. Plus the terrorist thing if he could. You're not really mixed up in any of this are you, Odell?"

"I just had my car break down and walked in here looking for a glass of water."

"That just goes to show anything can happen to anyone, anytime. Coincidence. Wrong place, wrong time and you're in the frame. That's a bad place to be if you're innocent of wrongdoing."

"Well, I am. I didn't do anything."

"I know that. When you're a cop you get to where you can tell the wrong guys from the right ones. Chief Webb, he's losing that."

"I think he just doesn't like me."

"Could be, he's the kind to take a dislike to someone for no reason, I've noticed that about him."

We watched some more of the game, then Larry says, "You know, what he did to you today, that's legally actionable in my opinion."

"Yeah?"

"Oh yeah. The way he broke you down and still got nothing, that makes him look real bad, professionally speaking."

"He didn't break me down."

"You were tearful there in the end. I talked about it with Dan Oberst later and he says he never attended a worse conducted interview and polygraph. Dan's very much a professional guy and he hates it when people butt in like the

Chief did, that was inexcusable and he wrapped it up right then. He told me he never saw the like of your emotional reaction and you aren't a good type for polygraphing in the first place, he didn't say why exactly, but you can take Dan Oberst's opinion to the bank."

"Well, I was just pretending."

"Uhuh, listen, you get many reporter types out here?"

"Not now, but earlier. It's all about Dean now, not me."

"Right. Dean, he's hot news. News about Dean, that'd be worth plenty to the networks. They'd come up with the big bucks for news about Dean. New news, not the old stuff. How're those lawnmowing bucks, Odell?"

"They're okay."

"Just okay? That's too bad."

I saw now what he wants. He wants to dig something out of me about Dean and sell it to the TV news, only there's nothing to dig out that I didn't already say, plus a little more that didn't really happen, so I'm already overextended with news about Dean so he's out of luck. And why would I want to share any TV news money with Larry Dayton anyway? What's it got to do with him?

"It's just I thought you might want a copy of the so-called interview and polygraph, you know, to keep for yourself, for your records or whatever. Maybe for your lawyer."

"I don't have a lawyer, I didn't do anything."

"I know that, only I'm thinking ahead to future times when a lawyer might do you a world of good."

"How?"

"By asserting in court that you've been subjected to official harassment not to mention incompetence at the hands of

Chief Webb, who deserves to get his ass kicked for conducting matters that way. Satisfy my curiosity, you weren't expecting a polygraph when you walked in there, were you?"

"I sure wasn't. That was a big surprise."

"I could tell just by looking, Dan Oberst too, I bet. He'd be the kind of guy to get on your team to make the charge stick, as backup for the taped evidence, I mean. Oberst, he'd come across very cool and clean, totally professional, the kind of guy you want in your tent, not the other guy's. You'd have a real tight case for prosecution right there."

"Prosecution? I didn't *do* anything..."

"No, what I'm saying, you'd be the one doing the prosecuting, I mean, your lawyer would. Against Chief Webb."

"Chief Webb?"

"Right, because he abused your legal rights setting you up like he did, which is an offense big time, and then he went and screwed up the whole process anyway by not keeping his mouth shut. He really thought you knew where Dean is, that's what made him blow it." He took a swallow of beer. "But it wouldn't even get to court."

"It wouldn't?"

"No way. The Police Department would have to spring for a lawyer to defend Webb because the offense took place on police property while police business was being conducted. The Department wouldn't want to risk any of that bad shit getting out to the media, not after they see the tape they won't. They'll settle big just to keep your mouth shut and the tape away from those newshounds. You might get a hundred grand, maybe two, three times that, depending on how good of a lawyer you get. Get a shark is my advice. Only there's no case without the tape. Your lawyer could litigate to get that tape from the Department and we'd have to provide it by law, only there's a good chance that tape'll disappear in the next twenty-four hours. Webb, he can go everywhere in the building, including Records. Two minutes in there and that tape's gone, Odell. That tape is history, burned or dumped off a bridge, buried way out somewhere nobody'll ever find it. No tape, no case. No case, no settlement. No settlement, you keep right on mowing lawns."

"Maybe he already did it," I said, thinking out loud.

"Maybe he did, which is why it's a good thing I moved fast and made a copy."

"You made a copy?"

"Yes I did. Would you be interested in owning that?"

"I guess."

"I thought you might. That'd be a sure thing, that settlement. You might get a half mil, maybe more, and all because I had the foresight to do what I did, which will wreck my career with the PD when it comes out I made that copy. They'll know it was me, probably subpoena me to say so outright, and there goes my job down the toilet, all because I wanted to help out a fellow human being."

"Thank you."

"So bearing that in mind, the wrecking of my career, I'd have to have compensation for that risk."

"Money?"

"Or gold bullion if you got it," he said, then laughed real loud.

"How much?"

"Well, now, wait a minute. I'm gonna presume you don't have

a whole lot of cash lying around the place or you wouldn't be doing lawnmowing for a living, am I right?"

"I've got another job lined up."

"That's fine, but it isn't running the Bank of America, is it."

"No, it's out at the prison."

"The prison? You're kidding me. What, in the kitchen? I think the trusties do that, don't they?"

"Prison guard."

He laughed again like that's so funny, then he stopped but he's still got a big grin on his face. "Look, Odell, you don't want a job out at that place. It's the lowest kind of work you can get. Forget that, they wouldn't hire you anyway."

"Why not?"

Larry sighed like he's running out of patience, and not smiling anymore. "You're not the right type. They need tough nuts to run a dump like that. You aren't tough, Odell."

"I'm big."

"Right, but that doesn't mean tough. What I'm offering is more than you could make in a lifetime as a guard, provided you get the right lawyer. The tape will provide a bright new future for you, guaranteed."

"I don't have any money, not a whole lot."

"And knowing that, I've come up with another arrange-ment – a percentage of the take, which is what your lawyer will be taking his cut from too, so there's his motive to go in hard and win big, the high six figures at least. Interested?"

"Yeah, I guess."

"You guess. Okay, this would involve drawing up a legal contract for the sale of the tape to you or your representative for a certain percentage of whatever your legal counsel can get for you from the PD. Which will be plenty, believe me, more than enough to make everyone happy."

"It wouldn't matter to you if you lost your job and they didn't like you anymore, the other cops?"

He set his can down, serious again. "Are you kidding? It's only a job that I got to put me through school. This way I can trim years off my courses by doing them full-time, and the tuition's all taken care of."

"What kind of school?"

"The best, dude – Law School."

"Uhuh."

He got up. "So do we have an agreement?"

"I guess."

"Get yourself some legal counsel and get back to me, I'm in the book."

The phone started ringing, the kitchen phone.

"No need to see me out," says Larry, heading for the door. I went to the kitchen.

"Hello?"

"Odell, it's Lorraine. They were just here and now they're headed out to you." She was all excited and breathless.

"Who is?"

"The F-B-I, Odell. They just got done grilling me about Dean and now they're gonna do the same to you, so get yourself ready."

"Oh, okay, I was expecting them."

"Expecting them?"

"I got told they might be doing interviews today. That should've happened sooner. The Bureau has been slow on this, way slow. Heads will roll for that."

"What are you talking about?"

"A little bird told me."

"Odell, have you been drinking?"

"Yeah, just a beer."

"Well, quit right now, you've got to be sober when they come and start asking questions. You know what not to talk about, don't you?"

"Uh…"

"About him being gay, we went over this."

"Yeah…but now somebody has got a movie of Dean in that Okeydokey place."

"Which does not mean he's gay, doesn't prove it. It doesn't prove anything except where he was on Saturday night, which you've got to say you were confused about that, Odell, Sunday not Saturday, that's when you met him, okay, or they'll get suspicious of you like Andy Webb. And you know what other thing to say nothing about, right?"

"Uh…"

"The package, Odell, the freaking package that never got delivered and there'll be no further packages on a Tuesday because those packages Do Not Exist. Got it?"

"Okay."

"Go rinse your mouth out and put that beer away. Do it now."

"Are you coming over later?"

"I'll give you a call. No, you call me after they've gone and we can compare notes."

"I have to take notes? They're gonna think that's weird."

"Mental notes, Odell. Call me when it's over, and don't mess this up or they'll keep coming back and poking their noses in."

She hung up. I went and brushed my teeth and combed my hair which was a waste of time because it's so short it doesn't need combing, but now I felt like I'm ready for the FBI. I went to the front door to wait for them. Larry Dayton had already driven away so the yard was empty. I waited a long time before they arrived in a big blue Ford.

There was two of them in neat suits, one with glasses. They come up the steps and said they're Agent Kraus and Agent Deedle, he's the one had the glasses. I brung them in and sat them down and they started in to interview me, which I will not go into detail here because I told them everything the same way I already told the police which is boring to say it all again. Only I made sure I said this time it must have been Sunday the Monte Carlo broke down, not Saturday. They asked all the same questions the cops did and I took them to the back yard so they can see the dirt mound, which I made sure they know all about how the cops have had it dug out twice now to show there's nothing there, and Agent Kraus said they know that, it's in the report. They stayed an hour maybe and then they thanked me for my cooperation and drove away, which was a big relief that it's all over now at last, so I called Lorraine's number on the new cell.

"How did it go?" she wants to know.

"It went fine. They just now left."

"And you didn't talk about things you shouldn't talk about?"

"Nope."

"That's good. My god, this has been an exhausting day, and it's the weekend. I'm supposed to relax on the weekend, not get into arguments with the Chief of Police and give interviews to the FBI and go to funeral homes to make arrangements for my aunt that got murdered. This is so stressful I'm falling apart here."

"Want me to come over?" I'm thinking maybe she could use a back rub that'll lead to other things.

"No, I need to take a long hot bath and try to relax about all this."

"I could maybe scrub your back."

"I've got a loofah for that, genuine sponge. You take a long bath too, Odell, you've had it hard today like I have. You know, this kind of pressure is gonna keep up until they catch Dean, I know it is. I bet *60 Minutes* calls me for an interview about what it's like growing up with a terrorist for a brother. Only I don't think they pay for interviews."

"Some of those other TV people do. I got offered fifty bucks."

"The other shows don't have the prestige, Odell. It isn't just about money, it's about setting the record straight about Dean."

"Except about the gay part."

"Right. Andy Webb better not splash that Okeydokey thing around. I guess he won't, I mean, it's official police property, he can't just sell it to the highest bidder. It's got nothing to do with Dean being a terrorist anyway, and it doesn't prove a thing about his sexuality in any case. The Muslims, they're very down on gays. Shit, they don't even like drinkers, which Dean is a big fan of along with dope and you name it, so he'd make a lousy Muslim. But that's nobody's damn business. The terrorism thing alone is gonna get him locked away forever when they catch him. Are you listening to me, Odell?"

"Uhuh. Do you know any lawyers?"

"A couple, but they're no good. Dean's gonna need someone high-powered to try and get him off, that is, if he gets caught before he kills Ketchum. If he gets caught afterwards it won't make any difference who his lawyer is, he'll get the needle."

"No, I mean for me."

"What do you want a lawyer for, in case Chief Webb drags you down to the station again?"

"Kind of."

"Wait and see if he does that. Maybe all the interviewing is over and done with now that the FBI talked to us."

"It's just...I don't know, maybe I'm not right for being a prison guard."

"Sure you are, I told you, and the word is in with Cole so all you need to do is show up for the interview Friday and prove to him you can tie your own shoelaces and the job's yours. Don't let me down on this, Odell."

"Only I'm thinking I might not be...you know, tough enough."

"What are you talking about, a guy as big as you? Don't start doubting yourself. Self-doubting is a negative force that eats away at you from the inside, I read a book about that and it made a lot of sense, so you quit that right now."

She hung up. I forgot again to tell her I'm using my new phone. Next time. One thing I kept thinking about is how she thinks official police property like the Okeydokey DVD can't get sold. My interview tape is official police property and it's already on the market. But Lorraine has got enough to worry about without that on top of all the rest.

That French food was not enough to satisfy the inner man, so I went down to the freezer for something real to eat for a late afternoon snack or maybe early dinner, and made a selection of Tater Tots and corn on the cob plus Sara Lee cheesecake, only I'll have to let the cheesecake thaw in its own sweet time before eating, so that will be a late dessert to be having. Then I settled down to do some thinking about what Larry Dayton has told me, his offer about the tape. I turned it over and over for a long time while the Tater Tots and corn were cooking, and by the time they're ready to eat I still couldn't make up my mind about that, so I decided to sleep on it as the saying goes and maybe make a decision tomorrow. It was good American food I dished up for myself and it went down easy, after which I napped awhile in front of the TV with the sound off, very comfortable there on the sofa. I had been sleeping in Dean's room after spending that one night in Bree's. I had expected nightmares in both rooms, but that didn't happen, so I have not got a guilty conscience or anything like that, this is the proof.

But now on the sofa I did have a nightmare that happened this way – I'm in my car which is running smooth and strong for once and Dean is next to me toking on a joint and watching the world speed by, only I can't really see the landscape so it could be anywhere. Dean looked exactly like I remembered him except he's wearing this bright orange jumpsuit like prisoners wear, only he's not in prison he's in my car.

He turns to me and says, "I only did it to piss her off, you know, for a joke."

"Piss who off?"

"Bree, who else. She's been beating me up over not going to

church since forever, and I got so sick and tired about the way she's shoving Jesus down my throat I got hold of some Muslim books and said to her I'm gonna go to the mosque, not to church. And I would've done if we had one around here but we don't. Man, did she have a shitfit about that, got real upset and says my soul's in danger. Well, I was only kidding, but I started reading those books and it seemed to me like there's truth in there, you know, wisdom. I needed some of that, everyone does. So I'm thinking okay, I'll quit drinking which I know is a bad thing, and quit with the pigmeat and see how I go with that, baby steps, see what I mean? Starting to be a Muslim but only a little bit, like I'm still not sure but I'll go along with it awhile and see what happens, you know?"

"And what happened?"

"You killed me, man, so now I'll never know if I had it in me to be a good Muslim. That might've been all I needed to turn my life around, only you went and fucked it up for me, Odell, you son of a bitch prick-eating fuck!"

He reached across and grabbed the steering wheel and we went over a cliff that I didn't even know was there, and on the way down he starts singing at the top of his crazy voice, "I'm a little teapot short and stout, Here is my handle, Here is my spout…" That cliff was a long, long drop. When we hit the ground it woke me up so sudden I flew up from the sofa like it's a bed of red-hot nails. I fell on the floor with my throat all closed off and struggling to breathe, then it opened up and I pulled in air like a pump, with sweat rolling off me like I just got out of a pool or something and my heart racing *budumbudumbudum.*

I stunk like a dead fish I sweated so bad. After a shower I

felt better, but not much. By then the cheesecake was thawed and I ate half to calm myself down and put the rest in the fridge for tomorrow. After that I was okay, it was only a dream after all and nothing to get weird about.

It was sundown by then. I went out to the back yard and stared at the mound, telling Dean to back off, it wasn't my fault and he never should've woke me up with a whisper in my ear about some bullshit intruder he thought he heard, especially not with a shotgun in his hand even if it had no shells. It was Dean's fault what happened, not mine, him and his fucked-up personality! I felt like I didn't have a friend in the world.

But I did have a friend. Agent Jim Ricker was my friend, he told me so himself. His little bird kept an eye on all his friends which I am one of, he said. So I took out my little phone and keyed the index and up popped Jim's number. I pressed the call bar. You don't even have to dial the number, the phone does that all by itself, which is digital technology which I am now a big fan of.

"Hello, Odell."

He said that without me saying who I am because the caller ID number is flashing on his screen. Digital technology!

"Hey, Jim."

"What's on your mind?"

"Oh, nothing much. The FBI come and talked to me about everything."

"Uhuh, and how did that go?"

"Oh, fine, I guess. They were nicer than Chief Webb."

"Professional courtesy, Odell, it goes a long way."

"Yeah."

"Anything else?"

"Well...I'm in the back yard and the sun's going down. Wait...I'll show you."

I sent him a little movie, sweeping the phone around so he can see the mound in the yard and the sunset happening behind it.

"Is that the so-called empty grave I'm seeing there, Odell?"

"Uhuh, with nothing in there but dirt, they checked it twice, the police."

"Good to know they're being thorough."

"Yeah, but I had to do the digging-out the second time."

He laughed. "Is that why you're sore at Chief Webb?"

"No...well, maybe. Hey, Jim, can you see me?"

"Why do you ask that, Odell?"

"I'm just wondering. If those satellites are always going around and around the earth there must be times when yours is on the other side of the world, so then you can't see me."

He chuckled very friendly then says, "Any system worthy of the name has got more than one arrow in its quiver, Odell. There are hundreds of satellites up there, so just as one is passing below the horizon another one is coming up over the opposite horizon, and chances are there's one in between that's pretty much over your head as we speak."

"So you *can* see me?"

"The answer to your question is classified, Odell. You wouldn't want me to break the rules now, would you?"

"I guess not." I had a great idea then and raised my left arm. "Just tell me which arm is lifted up right now."

He laughed again. "The left," he said, and my mouth dropped open. He really *can* see me! "Wow!"

He laughed again. "You're right-handed aren't you, Odell."

"Uhuh."

"Then that's the hand your phone is in, which means you raised your left arm, right?"

"Uh…yeah. So you can't see me?"

"I told you, that's classified. You have a pleasant Saturday night, Odell."

He rung off. It was a disappointment about him not being able to see me after all. It made me feel good for a moment there knowing he's watching over me like a big brother. But maybe he *could* see me and just can't say so outright because that's classified.

I went inside and poured myself a shot of the Captain and drunk it down, then poured another. There is nothing like the Captain to settle me calm and peaceful. I surfed the channels and found one of those Nature shows about wolves in Canada or somewhere. All the wolves have gone from America except some they brung back into the national parks to cull the buffalo which we have not got very many of these left either, so why bring the wolves back to kill some more? Anyway these were not wolves from around here, about six of them living in a pack, but then tragedy strikes when one of the wolves goes blind with cataracts in his eyes.

This poor wolf, he blundered around not seeing anything and acting weird because he's blind, and the other wolves they couldn't understand why he's acting that way because they're only animals so they don't know about blindness, they only know this wolf is acting weird. And here's the sad part, it pisses them off to have him hanging around and acting weird like he is. They have got no sympathy for this poor wolf and just snap at him when he comes blundering along to be close to them. They don't want him around so they bite him to make him go away, and the poor fucking wolf he gets lonelier and lonelier and hardly ever gets anything to eat because he can't hunt and only feeds on leftovers now and then that he finds with his nose. So after awhile he died and the other wolves wouldn't go near him even then to give him a farewell sniff or something. It was just the saddest thing to see. Going blind was not the wolf's fault but he got punished anyway, not just by being blind, the worst thing was how the other wolves turned on him and run him off just because he's different to them, that was the saddest part about this, and it made me start crying like a baby, it's so sad. Ordinarily I don't do that, cry, I mean, but I felt so sorry for that poor creature that didn't do anything wrong but got punished anyway and then died never knowing why any of it happened. I was glad when it ended and I could watch something else.

No matter how much I flicked from one channel to the next there's all these political commercials even if the election is still a year and more away. They always do this, start telling you which way to vote a long ways before you need to be choosing. You just can't get away from it even by hitting the mute button. Those flags just keep right on waving and those people keep right on smiling and looking proud to be American, especially the cute little girl waving this tiny Stars'n'Stripes, about four years old with a big grin and underneath it says *Do It For Her*.

Senator Ketchum is in most of the Republican ads looking stern and wise and proud, saying things like, "America was built on hard work and the promise of Justice for All. That same promise works in other nations too if they're given the chance. That's why we're there. Americans will never cut and run when called upon to help. That's what makes us Americans." The other team is saying stuff like, "When it's broke – fix it. Let's not go any further down the Wrong Road." And they've got their own cute little kid waving a flag and saying, "Bring my Daddy home, we miss him so bad."

Whichever ad was on, that's the one I liked, the party I intended voting for. But then the other team comes on saying the opposite thing and it seems like they're the ones talking sense and I should go vote for them instead. Only then the first bunch come on strong about Holding the Line and Not Backing Down and I think they're the ones have got the right message now, so I seesawed back and forth between them till I wished I could go hibernate like a bear and not hear another word about voting and let someone smarter than me decide which one should be in the White House.

Now, my personal opinion, it should be Condoleezza Rice running for President and not Senator Ketchum. I would give my vote to her whichever party she was with regardless, I like her so much. And what most people don't know, Condi is a very good piano player, not just political but artistic, and how many of that kind do you get in Washington? Not too damn many that's for sure. If it was Condi got elected President the first thing she'd do, she'd tell the park rangers to bring in any blind wolf they saw out there in the wilderness and give him a cataract operation so he will not die lonely and not understanding why. Condi would do that because being a woman she is sensitive to the needs of others, which I am not so sure about Senator Ketchum.

ELEVEN

Sunday back in Yoder, Wyoming, was the dismalest day of the week bar none, I am not kidding. Sunday in Yoder is good for preparing you to be anything at all in any other place in the world, because you don't want to be someone in Yoder on a Sunday anymore. This is true for everyone that lived there even if they tell you different. Feenie Myers one time told me nine out of ten Yoderites say outright they can't stand the place and the tenth one is just a liar.

But Sunday in Callisto was okay by me. I woke up on the sofa where I fell asleep drunk out of my mind with the TV hissing at me. I worked my way through to the kitchen and drunk some water then followed with aspirin for a breakfast appetizer then went back and lay on the sofa again.

I napped awhile waiting for my head to quit thumping like that, then got up a second time and made myself waffles and hash browns brung up from the freezer which has still got plenty of food in there. It's surprising how much is left after a body has been removed from a freezer, but she was not a big woman.

Along about lunchtime I'm feeling better and thinking maybe I should call up Lorraine and see if there's anything I can do for her, maybe take a sixpack over to her place for lunch or something. She has never invited me over to see if it's a house or an apartment or whatever, and you don't truly know a person good enough to be called a friend without you have been invited over to see what kind of place, so this is not a good sign and I'm beginning to wonder about that, if she cares for me at all or what.

Then I heard a car coming up to the house, but I knew even before I got to the door it isn't her because of the engine sound, too big so I'm not surprised to see it's Chet come back to visit. I was happy to see him because it's Chet and Preacher Bob had the goodness of their heart to buy me that cell I am so crazy about. He waved at me and come up on the porch where I invited him in but he said it's so nice of a day why don't we sit on the rocker, so we did. I didn't wait, I brung the new phone out right there to show him and explain all the things it can do.

"That's a nice one, Odell. I'm pleased for you. Now you have to advertise the number so new customers can call you up and get their lawn mowed."

"I'll take care of that Monday," I said. "No, wait ... I have to cut into my lawn schedule Monday to go to the funeral service for Aunt Bree. I don't even know what time yet. So I'll take care of it Tuesday."

"It's a nice gesture," he says, "you going along for the service.

Miss Lowry must be appreciative of that. You and she have gotten to be fairly close because of all this."

"It's a terrible way to be introduced to someone, but there you go. Lorraine's needing someone to lean on about all this."

"And you're providing a sturdy shoulder. That's good, Odell. That's a Christian thing to do. You're a fine example of the faith."

He must have seen me looking uncomfortable about a compliment like that which I don't deserve, because then he says, "You *are* a Christian aren't you?"

Well, it would not have been a good thing to lie to him, a man that gave me cash money to buy a phone that I really like, but at the same time I hated to disappoint a churchgoing type like Chet by telling him I don't believe all that about God watching over us like they say. If God was watching over us, all those little kids in Africa with raggedy clothes would not be carrying around AK-47s and dying from AIDS, if you want my opinion. So I wriggled around trying to think what to say, and Chet being a smart man saw what kind of trouble I'm in and says, "Just speak your natural mind, Odell. The truth is what the truth is according to the mind that gives it voice."

So I gave it to him in a plain brown wrapper. "Not really."

Chet patted me on the arm like some old uncle setting my mind at ease. "No need to sound that way about it, Odell. Not everyone chooses to let the light shine upon them, and there are those who come to the light later than others. It's never too late to open your eyes to the special radiance that comes from the presence of the Lord."

"Okay."

We both sat quiet for a little while, then he says, "Odell,

would you say that, taking everything into consideration, you might one day become a Christian?"

Chet was worried about my soul, which was very decent and caring of him but a waste of time frankly, because there's no way I would ever change my mind about what I think in regard to this hard question about Believing or Not Believing. I wanted to tell him I would, just to make him feel better about things, but then he might want us to get down on our knees and pray together to make that happen sooner, which I did not want anything so embarrassing to happen so I told him, "Not really."

I felt ashamed to give him that answer, and Chet, he just nodded slow and careful, not looking at me, then he said, "Things are the way they are for a reason, we sometimes just can't see what that reason might be."

That sounded very wise so I agreed with him to smooth things over.

He says, "I believe I need a glass of water, Odell, would you mind?"

"With ice?"

"Just as it comes from the tap. The prophets of old didn't have any ice water to cool their thirst out there in the desert."

I got him the prophet kind of water and he drunk it down, then he stood up and shook my hand. "I'm going back to Topeka tomorrow, so this will be goodbye, Odell. It's a shame about Dean being the way he is, but that's no fault of yours, you didn't know."

"I sure didn't."

"Life is a mystery," he says, "or it appears so to mortal eyes."

"Uhuh."

He gave my hand one last firm Christian shake and then went down the steps to his car. He got in and started driving away, leaving me with a sad feeling. He was a good man that saw things different to me so there could not be that special connection which is friendship. Watching his Cadillac drive away slow I asked myself who I ever had the special friendship connection with, and after kind of running everyone I ever knew through my head I had to admit it never really happened yet, I don't know why, but then I'm young still and so have got plenty of time. I had high hopes for Lorraine regarding this. Maybe tomorrow at the funeral I'd get the chance to tell her what's on my mind. Then again, a funeral day is something sad that you shouldn't talk about your own problems in, just the relatives of the dead person, their problems are up for discussing instead, so maybe all of that about telling her how I feel will have to wait awhile yet.

Looking out from the porch at all that Kansas emptiness made me anxious to be doing something, only I couldn't figure out what that certain thing might be, which I know sounds peculiar but that's how it was, kind of like having a plan and then getting knocked on the head and you lose your memory of the plan, but you remember that there *was* a plan, which now is running around in circles like a record inside your head wanting to get made into reality, only you can't do it because you forgot what it is. It made me restive and unhappy to be that way, but what can you do about that – nothing.

And then I knew what it was I wanted to do. It was just as plain as plain can be. I wanted to tell someone I killed Dean accidental and he won't be sneaking up on Senator Ketchum with a gun to kill him like everyone expects. The whole country is in an uproar about Dean because I have not told what I know, and the Big Secret is weighing me down like a hundred pound sack of flour set across my shoulders. I wanted to tell Condoleezza Rice the whole truth. I would not want to tell anyone else. I only trust my friend Condi to understand what happened and be forgiving about it, knowing none of it was intended to happen that way. And now that I knew what it was that I'd been wanting to do all along, nothing could stop me now from going ahead and doing it.

I went through the house till I found a pen and some paper and a box of envelopes that had one of those little rolls of stamps inside of it, then I sat down at the kitchen table with a shot glass of the Captain to steady me I'm so excited about this. And I wrote her a letter, which this is it here.

Dear Condoleezza Rice,

You do not know me but maybe have seen me on the news about Dean Lowry after he murdered his Aunt Bree last week. Dean has been in the news about that, also his connection to Muslim Terrorists that he knows. Only here is the actual fact about that – He does not know any Terrorists, only thought about being a Muslim to make his aunt mad at him, nothing serious, but she must have yelled at him too loud about this and drove him over the edge as they say. And that is where he killed her, in the state of madness not like his Regular Self at all. But yes he did that terrible thing. But now everyone is thinking all this about Dean killing Senator Ketchum, which he did say but was not serious. And even if he was serious, nothing could happen about that because Dean is gone from Among Us. I have killed him with a baseball bat but I swear it's accidental what happened. He woke me up with a gun in his hand and I panicked I think and hit him with the bat before even thinking if I should do that. He was okay until next day when he died, but at first I thought he's sleeping. Then I found out he is dead. I have got him buried in the back yard here, so you can tell Senator Ketchum from me there is no danger about this, Dean is gone now. I swear to you I did not mean this to happen. And now I confessed to it I am hopeful you can forgive me the lying which was something I had to do, I'm sure you can see why. So that is why I have sent this to you dear Miss Condoleezza Rice.

Yours truly,

Odell Deefus

I checked it two times looking for mistakes but there aren't any, so I put it in the envelope and sealed her down with a lick, then the same for a postage stamp up in the corner and Condi's name, *The White House, Washington DC*. I left off the zip-code not knowing it, but the Post Office knows where Washington DC is, they are not idiots. Then I put the envelope all stiff and flat up on the mantelshelf between the brass Indian chief head and the seashell ashtray Souvenir of Florida. Then I sat on the sofa and stared at the letter like it's a famous picture hung on the wall. I wanted to mail it right away, but it's Sunday so there's no point, it wouldn't get emptied out of the mailbox until Monday anyway. What I would do, I would mail it after I went to the funeral.

It was so much of a relief knowing I have done the right thing at last. I think one reason I didn't do it yet is because I would have to get interviewed by Chief Webb who I do not like and he doesn't like me, which would be a bad experience to happen. This way it's Condi Rice who gets told the truth and she is a gentle person even if sometimes she has got to be very firm with those leaders of other countries that don't think like we do, but very fair-minded above all so I have done the smart thing here telling her and not Chief Webb. Condi will invite the top guys from the FBI and Homeland Security and Senator Ketchum around to her place for coffee and cake and explain to them that I did not mean it about Dean and not to throw me in jail. I felt like crying I am so happy about this relief I gave myself.

The kitchen phone rang and it's Lorraine! This shows how today was a day different to all the rest with so many good things happening. The first thing she says to me, "The service is at eleven, so you need to be at the suit rental place at nine to get rigged out. It's at 2389 Kerwin Street, that's downtown. It's called Tux deLuxe and they've got suits for big guys, it's in their ad in the phone book. But they don't rent shirts and shoes and neckties. Have you got that stuff? It has to be suitable."

"Uh, no, only some boots and sneakers."

"Are the boots okay, I mean, are they black?"

"Uhuh."

"And not all wore down at the heels?"

"No, they're in good shape."

"Okay, just polish them up so they look respectable, and get yourself down to Target first thing to get a shirt and tie, no stripes and no patterns, nothing bright, okay?"

"Okay."

"And while you're at Target get yourself some slacks and a few polo shirts, neat casual wear for your interview with

Cole, plus a sport jacket. When you don't look like a lawn-mower guy you look like a cowboy, which is not the right look for success, okay?"

"Okay."

"Got enough money for all that?"

"Yeah."

She gave a big sigh then said, "I'll be so glad when this is all over, I don't just mean about Bree, I mean about Dean. He hasn't called you, has he?"

"No."

"Well, if he does, you tell him to give himself up but to keep his mouth shut about the deal with the Tuesday package. There's no point in him telling about that, it just gets me in trouble and doesn't help him out with his own situation at all, you make sure he understands that. In fact, if he calls, tell him to call me and I'll give him the message. I'd be the one he calls anyway, being his sister."

"Uhuh."

"I just want this to be over and done with, one way or another. It's eating me up with nervousness this business, the waiting, wondering if Dean's gonna spill the beans about Donnie D and all of that. You do understand you're part of it now, just passing the package along, so if I go down, you go down. Dean has got us both in the palm of his hand about this."

"Right."

"You don't sound like you give a shit. This is serious, Odell. The Tuesday arrangement will get us serious cell time if Dean blabs his mouth. I just hope he's gone so far underground with those terrorists he won't ever show up again except in the headlines, you know, Suicide Bomber Explodes Himself, that kind of a deal."

"You want Dean to explode himself?"

"Hey, that way he'd die happy like these fanatical religious freaks like to do. Dean was never happy his whole life, so I'd like to think at least he died happy, that'd be something at least. You're not saying much today, Odell."

"No, but I've been thinking plenty."

She laughed. "Yeah? About what, deep shit?"

"I'm not in deep shit."

"No, I mean deep thinking. If I meant big trouble I'd say deep doo-doo, there's a difference."

"Oh."

"So what kinda deep shit have you been thinking?"

"About doing the right thing, that kind."

"The right thing? Haven't we just been talking about that? The right thing to do is make sure Dean understands he has to keep his goddamn mouth shut and not get his sister and his friend in deep doo-doo like he's already got himself in with no help from us, right? That's the right thing to do, only Dean has never in his life done the right thing, up to and including what he did to Bree. Relying on Dean to do the right thing is like relying on fartpower to keep a hot air balloon in the air – sooner or later you run out."

"I guess."

"So I just want to be sure you understand what the stakes are here, Odell, for you and me both."

"I understand."

"Well, you sound so calm and peaceful about it all I have to wonder. Have you had some beer today?"

"No beer."

"Anything else?"

"Nope."

"Well, aren't you Mister On-Top-Of-It-All."

"Yeah."

I listened awhile to her breathing at the end of the line, then she says, "Maybe I've got you all wrong. You come across a certain way that makes me nervous, you act so dumb sometimes, then other times, like now, I think maybe the dumb act is just that, an act, and you really do know what's going on."

"I know what's going on, all right."

"Well, good, that's good, Odell, you keep that up and the sun'll keep on shining."

"Do you live in a house or apartment?"

"Why?"

"I just was wondering. You didn't ask me over there yet."

"Well, it's an apartment, way small but that's okay, soon as the probate gets taken care of I'll be moving out there and take over Bree's room. I hope it's not haunted."

"I didn't see any ghosts."

"Well, you have to have a special kind of sensitivity to be aware of the spirits. Most guys, they don't have that, only women. That's why most of the psychics are female."

"I could come over if you haven't got anything to do."

"Didn't I say I'm turning into a nervous wreck? That's a full-time job that takes up all day. You go ahead and think some more of your deep-shit thoughts, okay?"

"Okay."

She rung off and I hung up the phone. Lorraine is hard to figure sometimes but I think there is progress getting made in the relationship, she just has to quit worrying so much about Dean and be able to concentrate on me more, and I had taken steps to make that happen with the confession for Condi that's sitting right there on the mantel. When all of that problem has been cleared up Lorraine wouldn't need to be worrying anymore and could spend the time to get to know me better, which is what successful relationships are all about, everyone says this.

So I just had to be patient about that and wait for Condi to get me off the hook, which she will make happen soon as she gets the letter. With a bit of good luck and speedy post it will all be taken care of by the end of the week and I can go interview with Cole Connors for the prison job with a clear conscience. Except if I decide to take Chief Webb to court about that dumb interview he gave me with the stolen tape for evidence and get a million dollar settlement from the Police Department. That way I would not need the prison job and could marry Lorraine and she wouldn't need to be a drug smuggler anymore, which they call a win-win situation. I had forgot about Larry Dayton all day today until just now. But I had all of Sunday afternoon to be thinking about this, so no problem. That and getting my boots polished.

After awhile I got bored and started snooping around in Dean's room looking for more Muslim books or I don't know what, just snooping to pass the time, I guess, but there's nothing there. Since I was already snooping I snooped through every part of Bree's room as well. But all there is is this old Bible very dogeared and a book called *The Way of the Nun* also very beat-up, which goes to show how religious the old lady was.

I opened the book up and started reading page 36 just to see what ways they were talking about and was very surprised to find that nuns have got many ways, with each other and some sacred candles and then a bunch of priests that drop by the nunnery for some praying.

I took it away downstairs to read on the sofa and spent a restful hour or so absorbing knowledge about the religious life as seen and experienced by the writer, Sister Volupta, which I think is Latin. After that I took a nap, then read some more about how to exorcise a demon from the vagina area, which turns out to be a lot harder than you might think and needed a bunch of exorcists to take over till it's done. After which I napped again and before you know it the whole day's gone, just slid by like a quiet river and now it's getting dark outside and I'm hungry like a starving animal after all that reading.

Tonight it's meat patties and Oriental Stir-Fry followed by Sara Lee cheesecake, the other half. Man, was all of that gooooood. This had been one of the best days of my life even if I didn't get to spend it with Lorraine the way I wanted, so even for second best it was pretty damn good. Then I switched on the TV and heard the lady say, "Next up on Fox News – is this the face of terror, or is someone just murdering a song?" I looked at the screen and there's Dean singing very loud for a few seconds, then it's commercial time. I think my jaw must've dropped about a mile because I know what this is, it's the DVD someone made at the Okeydokey Karaoke that got me in trouble with Chief Webb about the Saturday or Sunday problem. And here it is on TV already!

Now, as already stated before, I am no genius, but it only

took me a couple seconds after I saw that to know what has happened here and who did it, which is Larry Dayton. He told me he has got his own DVD that he offered to use at the house yesterday only Andy Webb told him No, use the crappy old videocam. So now it's obvious that Larry was at the Okeydokey Karaoke last Saturday night and is the one that aimed his camera at Dean while Dean's onstage, not thinking how later on this would be very important after Dean got famous. He showed it to Chief Webb yesterday and got me in trouble, and in the afternoon come over and offered me that other tape of the interview, that's how I know it's him that is behind this now, with his wanting fast money that he can walk away from the PD with and be a lawyer instead.

I got the phone book and looked him up. I used the kitchen phone because the phone book was right next to it and I think I left my cell out on the rocker after I showed it to Chet.

The phone got picked up on the seventh ring. "Hello?"

"Is that Officer Dayton?"

"Speaking."

"This is Odell Deefus."

"Hey, Odell, did you get a lawyer?"

"No. Did you make a DVD at the Okeydokey Karaoke place last Saturday? Not last night, the one before."

"That would be Friday."

"No, I mean the Saturday night before."

"I'm just funning with you, Odell. Sure, I make DVDs at the Okeydokey on a regular basis. The patrons pay to have their performances immortalized, usually the really drunk ones, and I'm the guy there to do that. It brings home a buck. Were you wanting to organize a shoot, Odell? I can see you doing something by Johnny Cash, how about 'I Walk The Line.'"

"Did you DVD Dean Lowry and then sell it to Fox News?"

"Why would you make that assumption?"

"Because you wanted to sell me that videotape of me getting lie-detected."

"And so you extrapolated from that?"

Well, I didn't know what that meant, so I kind of growled at him, "Could be."

"I wouldn't have any comment to make about such a baseless accusation."

"But did you?"

"Email is a wonderful thing, don't you think? It's speeded up every part of life including making deals and transmitting digital data and getting paid via online banking. Hey presto! Instant swelling of the bank account."

"So you did do it."

"No comment on that, and no comment on the size of the payment ... Hold on, I'm watching something here."

I know what it is he's watching because I can hear it on my own TV. I set the phone down and sprinted to the living room.

"Top item this hour, the release of surprising DVD material of America's Most Wanted Man, Dean Lowry. Fox News received this from a wellwisher this last hour and we warn you, what you're about to watch is ... criminal."

And there he is, Dean singing "Do You Know the Way to San Jose" and doing a very bad job, I mean he has got no voice at all worth listening to, so bad I'm embarrassed for him even if he's dead and beyond the reach of the critics, to put it that way. After about thirty seconds they stopped it and the good-looking presenter has got this pained expression on her face. "Ouch!" she says, "that makes a bin Laden tape look and sound like an Emmy winner. Dean Lowry was caught recently demonstrating that he does indeed lead a double life, not lawnmower man and terrorist so much as lawnmower man and karaoke king. If any agents are watching, here's more..."

And there was, so bad I started reaching for the mute button, then they stopped again. "Kidding aside, Lowry is still very much on the mind of Homeland Security following his avowed intention to assassinate Republican presidential contender Senator Leighton Ketchum. This is the only live footage of Lowry available to the public and security services, and Fox News is happy to present it for the public good. Be warned, do not approach this man with a loaded mike."

That was the end of it and she moved on to something else. I went back to the kitchen but Larry Dayton has hung up the phone. So now everyone is going to be laughing at Dean instead of being scared of him, which in a way is better, kind of. After Condi gets my letter everyone will see that the karaoke guy is realer than the assassin guy, which will make Lorraine feel better, especially since they didn't say the DVD was shot in a gay bar. The phone rang, so maybe Larry has just remembered I didn't tell him yet if I got a lawyer for the video interview deal.

"Yeah?"

"Odell, are you watching the early news?"

It's her, Lorraine, sounding very upset about you know what.

"Yeah, I saw it, about Dean."

"How the *fuck* could that happen?"

"Uh, I don't know."

I didn't want her to know I know the guy that did it, I don't know why, maybe to sidestep more complication than I've already got with Lorraine.

"Why the *fuck* would anyone want to do this?"

"I guess to make money off of Dean being a famous guy."

"That doesn't make it right!"

"I know…"

"It makes me sick! What kind of a shitty person could go out and do this?"

"A bad person?"

"Bad just doesn't cover it, Odell. I'm gonna make inquiries and find out who this prick is that did this."

"Uh, how would you find out?"

"Andy Webb, he's the one got given that karaoke DVD so he knows who shot it. If he doesn't tell me, I'll sue him. I'll sue the whole fucking Police Department! And then when I get told who did it I'll sue that guy too for invasion of privacy! Dean's privacy!"

"Well… but how about the fact that this makes Dean look like not so much of a terrorist. That's a good thing, to have people laughing at him instead of being scared of him, isn't it?"

"Listen, Odell, Sammy bin Laden used to like disco, that's how much that means. Right now they're laughing at Dean but he'll wipe the smile off their faces when he finds out. A terrorist doesn't change his spots overnight."

"Okay."

"Andy did this deliberately, let it leak out to get at me, I know he did, the prick."

"Why would he do that?"

"Because ... none of your business, Odell. He tried getting at you for the same reason, because you're a friend of mine. He's the kind of guy that uses his power to fuck people over just because he can, that's Andy Webb. He's running for County Sheriff later this year, that's his lust for power going crazy. Well, I won't let that happen. I'll make such a shitstorm about this he'll think twice before throwing his fucking hat in the ring. You should sue him too, Odell, about that stupidass interview that he didn't even let you know beforehand there's a polygraph involved and no lawyer present for any of it. That'd fuck him up good, a scandal like that ... Get a copy of the tape they made! There was a camera there, right, recording everything? Get a lawyer and have him issue a subpoena for that tape and Andy's head is in the shitter for sure. Between the two of us we'll make him holler, Odell. You want to do that, don't you, make him pay for what he did in that interview? You came out of there looking like shit, remember?"

"Uhuh."

"Okay, listen, we'll talk about this tomorrow at the funeral. Something good is gonna come out of this, Odell. We'll get a lawyer and sue Andy's ass together. No way am I letting that prick get to be Sheriff, not after this. He's allowed Dean's image to be tarnished and it was deliberate. Okay, funeral's at eleven, don't forget. Bye."

I went out on the porch and picked up my phone from the rocker. Then I sat down and started swinging. There is too much happening now and it's getting harder for me to keep track of this and that. What I want is the simple life, just me and Lorraine and a couple of kids in this house right here which is fine for raising kids with hardly any traffic on the road out there so it's safe for kids. A lawsuit against Andy Webb might get me that. Lorraine and me could get by easy on a million dollar settlement or whatever if we're careful and don't go buying brand new Lincoln Continentals or something. Her plan about getting a lawyer was pretty much what Larry Dayton told me to do, so it must be a good plan, I'm thinking. And once I mail the letter to Condi Rice and get that part cleared up there's nothing to stop me starting up a whole new way of life. And to think that just a week ago I intended joining the Army for a plan! This is way better than that.

TWELVE

Driving into town Monday morning I felt good. I already rung up my customers and told them I'll have to switch them around because I'm going to a funeral. They were very sympathetic about that and said I'm in their prayers which was very nice of them seeing as we are not related. I had my phone in my pocket and my letter to Condi on the dashboard so I don't forget to mail it. Today was shaping up to be a Real Important Day.

First I went to Tux deLuxe and had them outfit me with a suit which the guy recommended dark blue or gray for a funeral, so I picked the gray and paid for it, forty dollars and back by five o' clock or it's extra, plus cleaning costs if required. Then off to Target for the shirt and tie, which it's easy to pick the right ones of, plain white for the shirt and a gray tie to go with the suit. So now I'm all set. I drove to the Gallbladder funeral place and got there way early, Lorraine's

car isn't there yet, so I parked and waited, and while I'm waiting the phone tinkles Greensleeves at me and I opened it up.

"Hello?"

"Odell, how are you today?"

"I'm fine, thank you, Chet."

"I thought I'd wish you and Miss Lowry all the best on this
difficult day. How is she holding up?"

"Lorraine's okay, only mad as hell ... heck about what's on
the TV last night."

"I saw it. That must have been distressing for her."

"She says she'll sue because of it."

"Well, she may change her mind when it blows over. A silly
development like that, it's nothing in the long run, and it may
be that Lorraine is inflating it out of proportion given her
state of mind over all the other developments."

"Could be."

"Are you with her now, Odell?"

"Just waiting at the funeral place."

"The thoughts and prayers of myself and Bob Jerome will
be with you and Lorraine today."

"Thank you."

"Don't forget to leave the phone in your truck so it doesn't
ring during the service. I've seen that happen and it's a big
embarrassment to all concerned."

"Okay."

"Goodbye, Odell."

"Bye, Chet, and thank you for calling."

"My pleasure."

Just then Lorraine's car come into the parking lot and
pulled up next to me. I set the phone down and got out to say

hi. Lorraine, her mood was not good, I could see that straight off with her lips all tight like that and a frown also, meaning she has not gotten over the TV news, not yet.

"Was that the best one they had?" she asked me, looking at my suit.

"I don't know," I said, because I didn't.

"Well, it'll have to do. The tie shouldn't be the same color as the suit, it should be a color that goes with it. Oh, forget it."

I felt like some kind of turd when she said that, and only a minute ago I'm thinking I looked pretty sharp with the suit and tie etcetera, but I put it down to her temperament that was all out of whack on a day like today with all of the big problems Lorraine has got. Now she's looking at my boots. "You said they'd be okay," she says.

I looked down. "I polished them twice," I said, which was no lie.

"But they're all wore out in the toes."

"I covered that with polish."

She sighed another one of those big sighs I am getting used to with her, then she starts walking towards the funeral place with her heels going *clickclickclick*. I forgot to mention she has got this very nice suit on like a businesswoman wears, nice and tight around the waist to show up everything above and below if you know what I mean. I followed along behind her wondering if I'll ever do or say something to Lorraine that'll make her see the real me and not this bozo she thinks I am, which I am definitely not that kind.

We went inside the place and the same fat guy she was talking to on Saturday come over with a sad look on his face

and said some stuff to her but I'm not listening, I'm somewhere else thinking about how pretty soon things are going
to be so different to now that I'll look back and think to
myself, That was a whole other life I was living back then, not
like now. Lorraine and the fat guy went away into his office
and I sat on a plush chair so soft it felt like I'm sinking into
quicksand, but comfy when you got used to it so I started
falling asleep, then they come out of the office and Lorraine
tells me everything is all set and we can go to the cemetery
now.

Back out to the parking lot and she says I'm coming with
her, not in the lawnmowing truck, so I went around to the
passenger side of her little car and she says, "No, we're going
in the limo. You think I want to be seen today in my shitbox
of a car?"

"I guess not."

"You guess not. Well, you guessed right."

She is in some kind of a temper, all right. Then this long
dark limo comes out from behind the place, only it isn't ours
it's Bree's, with long windows so you can see the coffin inside
all covered in flowers, so really it's a hearse and not a limo.
Then behind that comes another car the same color, only the
regular limo kind with four doors, which we got in the back
of and drove away very silent. There was a sheet of glass
between us and the two guys sat up front so they can't over-
hear us, privacy for the bereaved people, I guess that's for.

All the way across town Lorraine never said a word she's so
mad about everything, just looked out the window. I reached
across to hold her hand for comfort but she didn't want that
and snatched it away. Well, that made me about as mad as her,

that was so rude and I'm only trying to be friendly in her hour of need, that's what friends are for. So she must've picked up on that because she says, "There'll be some mourners when we get there, friends of Bree from church most of them. Just be nice if they talk to you even if it's about God, okay?"

"Okay."

"You're going to be one of the casket bearers. Cole Connors will be there too, so it's a nice way for the two of you to meet before the interview Friday. Galbally are providing the other four. All Bree's friends are too old for carrying a casket."

"Okay."

"I'm sorry I got mad at you before, I'm on a knife edge today. I'm expecting the media to be there and you know how that goes. Don't say anything to them, not a single word after the way they've treated Dean lately. Just be big and strong, and if I lean on you for support like I'm about to fall down from emotion, you be sure and support me. That's the picture I want to see tonight on the news."

She put a pair of sunglasses on that made her look like a movie star wanting not to be recognized. I had gone and left my own sunglasses in the truck and it's a bright day out there, so that was a mistake but too late now to be fixed, we're already there. The limos went through some tall gates made from fancy iron and slid along an avenue of trees very quiet to where there's a bunch of cars all parked. The limos pulled over and stopped.

We got out and I saw there's quite a gathering there including guys with TV cameras that got aimed at us just as soon as we're out of the limo. I watched the back of the hearse get opened up and the coffin got slid out easy on these little rollers, then two guys from the hearse and two guys from our limo took hold of the corners and hefted it up onto their shoulders. That's when Lorraine give me a nudge to go help, so I did, taking hold of the handle halfway along, and another guy stepped up and took the one on the other side, so that must be Cole Connors there but I can't see him with the coffin between us.

Then we started walking. The two guys up front knew which way to go. I had to concentrate hard keeping the coffin level because I'm bigger than the other five guys so I had to stoop a little, which made walking harder. But I did see out of the corner of my eye all these guys with cameras aimed at us while we carried Bree along between rows of gravestones. The crowd moved right along with us, talking soft among theirselves, dozens and dozens of them and not all of them the media kind, so I'm thinking these must be Bree's churchy friends come to pay their respects.

Finally we're at the place, this long narrow hole in the ground with little brass rails all around so nobody falls in and a canvas party awning set up next to it to keep the sun off of folks mourning, blue and white striped with plastic chairs under it in rows. The coffin got walked over to the hole and then set down easy on this canvas cradle thing to hold it up till she's ready for lowering.

Once it got set down the guy standing opposite me says very soft, "Hey there, Odell, I'm Cole."

"Hey, Cole."

He's not bald and fat the way Lorraine talked about him, just losing a little at the temples and getting a little chunky around the middle there, basically handsomer than I'm expecting so Lorraine is not so good at describing people.

"We have to sit over there, buddy."

He means on the chairs under the awning, so we did, alongside Lorraine, me on one side and Cole on the other, which made me mad, she didn't tell me we'd be sat like this with him right next to her same as me. It's clear Lorraine has been withholding information but there's nothing I can do about it now with cameras aimed at me, like sock Cole Connors on the nose for being younger and better looking than she made him out to be, and is there a reason for this, I'm asking myself? At least he's not so tall as me, not by a long ways and can never catch up there.

A preacher come out of nowhere and starts talking about how life is sometimes filled with sorrow and so forth, with stuff from the Bible mixed in there to give it the right kind of tone, only I'm not listening, I'm looking at Chief Webb who surprising enough is there too, watching me through his sunglasses and looking very evil. Or he might've been watching Lorraine, it's hard to say.

I snuck a look across Lorraine at Cole Connors but he didn't look back. He looks better from the side too than I was expecting, so now I'm thinking Cole means more to Lorraine than she is giving out. Man, did I get jealous about that. All through the preacher's sermon about this and that all I can think about is if she prefers him over me, which she has never really said outright how she feels about me so it's hard to say, but I'll ask her soon as all this is over and we're alone. But I couldn't act like I'm jealous, that only makes a woman harder to get if they know you feel that way, just to make you squirm and look dumb. That happened to me two times in Kit Carson High, these two girls that I liked, I asked them out but they said they were with some other guy. This is two different times I'm talking about here, not together, maybe a year apart. But it was the same both times with me getting jealous about those other guys that these girls liked better than me, and I let it show how I'm jealous and they got a real good laugh out of that. One of them, she starts calling me Doofus not Deefus to let me know she thinks I'm some kind of idiot. Man, did that make me mad, but what can you do? So this time I would not let the jealousy show like before. That is what they call Learning from Life, from your mistakes so you don't do it again is what it means.

Finally the preacher quit and the coffin starts going down out of sight, lowered down by this little electric gizmo attached to the sling thing, then the bunches of flowers along the top sunk down below the ground and the whole thing is gone but still heading down because I can hear the motor whirring, then it stopped so Bree has reached the bottom of the hole. Two of the funeral guys stepped up and unhooked the sling and brung it up so it doesn't get buried along with the coffin, then the preacher comes over and gives Lorraine this little spade. She got up and went to the hole and stooped to dig up a little of the dirt piled beside it and tossed it down onto the coffin. It wasn't much dirt but I could hear it hit, kind of a spattering sound. That's all she had to do. It would've taken all day to shovel all that dirt into the hole with that little spade, more like a garden trowel.

Then Lorraine is looking at me like she doesn't know what to do next, and Cole whispers, "Get up, Odell, it's your turn." Well, someone should've told me ahead of time about this, but I got up and went over and took the spade that she's holding out to me and I flung some dirt down there into the hole alongside hers, then the preacher took the spade out of my hand. All of a sudden there's a long line of folks stretched out from under the awning, old people wanting to throw some dirt down onto their churchgoing friend Bree. Some of them were in tears about this and some not, but they all took their turn tossing dirt. One old girl, she almost fell over stooping to dig out a scoop from the pile, so after that the preacher did the stooping and scooping for them and had a little load of dirt all ready for the ones that come next, so accidents were avoided that way. Pretty soon everyone had had their turn, including Cole last of all, which I got steamed about because I bet he didn't go to Bree's church but he got to throw dirt on her anyway, probably Lorraine told him he could do this, which she has got the right to do, I guess, but should've told me about it ahead of time.

There was cameras shooting all of this so it's a good thing nobody took a dive into the dirt or fell in the hole or anything, then last of all Lorraine got given a bunch of flowers by the preacher and she flung that down onto Bree too, kind of a farewell posy, after which the preacher said some more and then the show is over, with the crowd breaking up slow and starting to drift back towards where all the cars are parked. Lorraine started jawing with the preacher so I went over to the hole and looked down at Bree's coffin one last time. I guess you are supposed to be thinking thoughts about the dear departed and what it all means about dying after being alive so long, but all I could think about was how that nice shiny coffin that cost thousands of dollars was going to get covered in dirt and left to rot under the soil after only getting admired and used for just one morning, which is kind of a waste if you think about it, which is the kind of thinking I'm doing there as I said. Then there's someone stood next to me and it's Cole, putting sunglasses on and he's saying, "Don't do it, Odell, you're too young."

"Huh?"

"You look like you're about to throw yourself down there with her."

"No."

"Well, good, we're needing new men out at the correctional facility. Lorraine tell you it's Friday?"

"Uhuh."

"Make it around ten-thirty." He looks me up and down. "Might have to get a uniform made special for a big dude like you. Ever been in charge of recalcitrants before?"

Now I didn't know what he meant by that so I just stared at him, and he gets this grin on his face and says, "Okay, you're right, this is not the time and place for the interview, but hey, you do a mean stare real good, Odell, that'll come in handy more than you might think." I kept looking at him, not knowing what to say, wanting to pick him up and throw him down in the hole with Bree, and he says, "Okay then, see you Friday."

"Okay."

He went away and Lorraine had a few words with him as she's coming over to me only I couldn't hear what it is they're saying. Then she's next to me and takes my arm, kind of leaning into me like she needs support. "Walk me back," she says, "and go slow so we look sad."

"They haven't filled in the hole yet."

"That happens after everyone's gone."

"Oh."

"Start walking."

So we walked slow and steady back to the limo and hearse with cameras aimed at us along the way but I didn't look at them because this makes you look like a fool when that happens. Lorraine leaned on me all the way like she's about to collapse in a heap from sadness which I know she isn't feeling, but it's for the TV news so it has to look good. Back at the cars I saw Chief Webb getting in his cruiser and driving away, then we got in our limo and soon we're going out through the fancy gates and on our way back to the funeral place, with Lorraine in a much better mood.

"I think that went fine," she says.

"Uhuh."

"Did you see Andy Webb there? That's intimidation. He's got himself a big shock coming, that guy."

"He does?"

"When we sue his ass. We talked about this."

"Right."

"Sometimes I think you're off in a world of your own, Odell."

"Could be."

"Well, come back to this one and concentrate. I saw you talking with Cole, how'd that go?"

"Okay."

"He's one of the good guys, Cole. You two'll get along okay so long as you don't go zoning out around him like you do around me."

"You're better looking is why."

It's not often I come up with something funny on the spur

of the moment like that, so Lorraine was not ready for it. She looks at me then says, "Oh, I get it." Then she punched me on the shoulder and says, "You dog, you," and laughed, but not very much. The punch felt good, though.

We didn't talk for awhile, then she says, "Poor Bree…" and started crying, then followed up with, "Poor Dean…" I scooted across and put my arm around her shoulder and she leaned against me, sniffling and so on, and let me keep my arm there all the way back to the funeral place, then she sat up straight again like she's back to her old self and no more comforting is required, thank you.

Out of the limo Lorraine said to wait while she went inside and had a few words with the fat guy, so I waited in the parking lot, but something was wrong there. I looked over at her car and there's something wrong that I couldn't put my finger on at first, but then I did – the truck was gone! It was right next to her car when we got in the limo to go to the funeral and now it isn't there anymore! Now, how could that happen when this isn't even a public street with No Parking signs and it isn't a Tow-away Zone either, so how come the truck isn't there? The lawnmowers were in back of it so how can I mow to schedule with the truck and mowers gone? I went over and stood there where the truck used to be with my head whirling. I just can't believe it. Someone has stole my truck and my customers are gonna be plenty mad when I don't come to mow their lawn like they're expecting. Of course I knew straight off who did this.

Lorraine come outside and walked over to me. "What's wrong?" she says.

"The truck's gone…"

She looked where the truck was before and says, "Shit."

"I know who did it."

"Yeah? Who?"

"Chief Webb."

"He couldn't have, he was at the funeral."

"Well, he had one of his cops do it."

"Why would he do that?"

"Because we're gonna sue his ass."

"He doesn't know about that yet. And stealing your truck would be dumb, and Andy's not dumb even if he is an asshole sometimes."

"Then who took it?"

"Jesus, I don't know. You better report it."

I reached for my phone, then remembered it's in the truck. Along with my letter to Condi Rice, so it's a double blow as they say.

"Fuck!"

"It's okay, Odell. A truck like that, it's easy to spot with the mowers and the name on the door...Hey, maybe this has got something to do with it being Dean's truck...you know, souvenir hunters wanting the actual vehicle of America's Most Wanted Man."

"But...they can't drive a famous truck around without someone'll report it when they see it, so why...why *would* they?"

"They might just take off the doors where the name is and leave the rest."

"But that's...so dumb!"

"Yeah, well, it's a dumb world." She looked at her watch. "I've got to get back to work. How about I drop you off at Tux deLuxe and then at the police station so you can report it."

"Then how am I gonna mow my lawns?"

"Tell your customers what happened and they'll understand. Everyone gets their car stolen sometime or other. It's okay, Odell, don't get all panicked."

"But...all the phone numbers for the people were there in the schedule, which was in the truck...And my clothes to switch back into after the suit gets taken back, so what am I gonna wear?"

"Jesus, Odell, just relax and we'll work it out, okay? I've never seen you like this before. It's not like it's even your truck or your customers, it all belongs to Dean."

"No it doesn't!"

"Don't go all weird on me now, I've had all the stress I can handle for today, so just *calm down*."

Well, that was hard, calming down. I couldn't think straight with all this loss and stealing going on. What happened in the end was, Lorraine drove me to Target and I bought a new checked shirt and jeans which I changed into at Tux deLuxe when I took the suit back, then she dropped me off outside the police station to report the truck getting stole, then she drove away to work. I went inside and talked to the guy at the front desk, and while I'm doing that who should come strolling by but Andy Webb.

"Hey there, Odell," he says, grinning this big shit-eating grin. "Didn't recognize you there for a second without your businessman's outfit on."

"I took it back."

"Good for you, otherwise they would've reported you for stealing."

"It's his truck got stole," says the desk guy.

"Yeah? When'd that happen?"

"While I'm at the funeral," I said, watching his face for clues that he is one lying son of a bitch when he says it had nothing to do with him.

"Is that right? Well, that is peculiar, a truck with lawn-mowers on board getting stolen in broad daylight like that. Maybe they only wanted the mowers and they'll dump the truck someplace. Those were pretty good mowers, weren't they."

"Uhuh."

"He doesn't remember the license plate," said the desk guy, like I'm some kind of moron.

"Well, he wouldn't, would he," says Andy, "seeing as it's not even his truck, it's Dean Lowry's. Not a problem, Odell, it'll be in the Vehicle Registration records. Did you iron those jeans special for today?"

"They're brand new, that's why there's a crease. I had my other clothes in the truck too."

"So it's theft of clothing as well," says Andy to the desk guy, just barely keeping his face straight. "Make a note of that."

"Doin' it," says the guy, also with a grin now so I knew they were not serious about this, which only made me madder but not showing it, I would not give them that satisfaction.

"Don't you worry, Odell," Andy said, "we'll get your truck back...sometime."

I didn't speak a word, not wanting to say something as might get me into Trouble with the Law, only give them both a steady stream of eye-daggers to let them know I have smelled the rat here and am not fooled one little bit. The funny thing is, it calmed me down knowing the cops stole the truck for harassment because I most likely will get it back when they figure they've had all the fun to be got out of this situation and bring it back, most likely saying they found it parked somewhere. I didn't think they would wreck it or any extreme behavior like that.

"How about I give you a lift home," offered Andy, still smiling like this isn't a total setup with me the dumbass at the center of it all. But I did have to get home somehow.

"Okay."

We went out to his cruiser and got rolling. He says, "That was a pretty nice funeral. Lorraine looked real good, don't you think?"

"Uhuh."

"She always did look good in a suit or uniform. Not every woman does."

I didn't say anything, still mad at him about his stupid truck-stealing trick.

"Say, Odell, did you watch the news last night, Fox News?"

"Uhuh."

"That was the DVD at Okeydokey Karaoke I was telling you about, the one that shows you weren't exactly telling the truth about being with Dean at his place Saturday night."

"I told you I made a mistake about that. I even said so to the FBI that come around asking, so you can't get me into trouble about that."

"Who's trying to get anyone in trouble here? Not me. Course, there is *one* double-dealing shithead who's gonna find himself in big trouble about revealing secret police evidence to the media, but that's okay, I know who he is – an ex-cop, or pretty soon will be. You can't trust anybody these days.

Everybody just wants to make a buck and say Screw you to his friends and colleagues and the reputation of the department. But he'll get his, oh yeah."

And you'll get yours is what I'm thinking but I didn't say it, let him get a big surprise about this when the lawsuit hits him in the face, the smartass. Andy gave out this little chuckle, like he's thinking about dipping Officer Larry Dayton into boiling oil nice and slow from the toes on up, then he turned to me very serious and said, "Odell, if there's anything at all you feel like telling me, anything at all, in strictest confidence, just between you and me and the dashboard, I want you to feel free to do that without fear of retaliation. Anything you told me that might be useful enough information to get passed along to Homeland, I'd treat that as confidential, you know? From an Unknown Source. No blowback to you, see what I mean?"

"It's just souvenir hunters, I expect."

"Huh? No, not the goddamn truck, the *real* case, the Dean Lowry situation. Any information I can provide to Homeland will be received with thanks, maybe even reward money. Course, as an officer of the law I'm not entitled to any kind of a reward, I'm just doing my job, but the one that told me the information, he'd be entitled to whatever they're offering. It's a hundred grand for Dean right now, but I heard along the grapevine that's gonna get upped to a cool half mil. Know why? Because Senator Fucking Ketchum got pissed when he saw how low the reward is for this guy that's out to kill him. Makes him look less important, like he's just a bank president or something, you know, not the guy that'll most likely end up *the* next President of the United States. It's all about status and who swings the biggest dick in Washington. What a shit-hole that place must be, all that corruption and brown-nosing they do there. Would you want to live in Washington, Odell?"

"Nope."

"Me neither. Where would you like to live? Now me, I'd choose Hawaii if I was the one got that half mil reward money. But that's just me. Where would you choose, Odell?"

"Hawaii."

"See? You and me have got more in common than you might think. Maybe if you took the time to consider the situation you might remember things better and have that nice chunk of change made available to you for getting a whole new lifestyle over there with the palm trees and hula girls. They're cute, those brownskin girls. Ever had one of those, Odell?"

"No."

"Me neither, but I've been told. What's your preferred type of woman?"

"Condoleezza Rice."

He laughed about that like I'm kidding, which offended me and would've offended Condi if she's sitting in the back seat listening to all this. But at least she'd know the level of respect I have got for her, which will go in my favor when she gets the confession letter ... which she won't be getting now because it got stole along with the truck and phone and mowers and lawnmowing schedule and all the mess that's littering the floor of Dean's Dodge, they stole everything. But then I started worrying what happens if before they give the truck back to me the cops decide to open up that letter?

Chief Webb will get the very thing he needs to make a big impression on the guys at Homeland and maybe get on the news and use the publicity to run for Sheriff...

Shit!

Maybe they would've thought it's just a joke letter and left it alone, but now that I said Condi's name out loud it'll make Chief Webb get curious to know what's inside the envelope. Which he'll report and then come directly out to the house and dig up Dean and claim the glory, which will be better than the reward money for him because it's his reputation he's wanting to show off to people so's he'll get their vote. The first thing I'd do when I got home is dig Dean up again and hide him someplace else until Condi gets the letter and she'll be the one gets the glory for finding out Mad Muslim Dean is no threat at all. No way was I gonna let Chief Webb steal the glory from Condi Rice! It's a matter of personal honor, the way I see it.

"Me," he says, "I could go for Oprah."

I kept my mouth shut. He says, "Think there's a chance Lorraine'll move back out to Dean's place now that Bree's gone and Dean's on the run?"

"Maybe."

"Nice big old house like that, all it needs is a new coat of paint. I guess you'll be moving out when that happens."

"Maybe."

"That is unless you and her have come to some kind of a personal arrangement."

"I'd be happy to pay rent."

He snorted like a horse that's got chaff up its nose. "Sure, Odell, you play it cool if you want, only don't forget any of this that I'm telling you. You can do yourself a power of good with half a mil. Maybe Lorraine'd want a share in that. Nothing makes a woman more pleased with a man than he delivers the bucks and plenty of it. That's the real secret of happiness between the sexes, Odell, only nobody wants to talk about it because it doesn't put women in a nice light where the libbers have put them, all superior to men. Show 'em the money and they'll call you Honey."

"Not all of them."

"Right, there's a ninety-seven-year-old widow in Poughkeepsie thinks different."

"I just want my truck back."

"*Your* truck? Seems to me you're kinda taking over there, Odell. Not that I can't see your point of view. Dean won't be coming back to mow lawns anymore, that's for damn sure, and like I said it's a pretty nice place out there, and then there's Lorraine to consider, the way she'll need comforting over all this loss and publicity. The house'll be hers once Dean gets put away or shot down like a dog, either one. That's a real nice package for any man to be dealing with, especially if it comes with a half-mil bonus prize. Course, you'll be wanting to spend that in Hawaii, not on Lorraine."

"I don't *know* anything and I didn't *do* anything."

"Sure, I hear that. Only think about it."

We didn't talk again till we're at the house and he's pulling into the yard. "Odell," he says, "this business won't be over until Dean is caught or buried." That's what *he* thinks. "Until that happens there's all kinds of ways the situation can develop. You need to be thinking about what's best for you. That's good advice for free I'm giving you."

"Thank you."

"No charge."

I got out and he drove away. When his cruiser's out of sight I went and got the shovel and started in digging up that god-damn fucking mound of dirt. This is the sixth time it's been dug out now and I'm the digger four of those times, so I felt like if those times were strung end to end I could just about have dug my way down to Hell. This time I didn't have my lawnmowing gloves so my palms started to smart after awhile and I got a couple of dishrags and wrapped them around to stop any blistering that might be used for evidence against me when Chief Webb and the cops open that letter and come screaming out here with lights flashing to dig up Dean and get their glory. No way is that gonna happen. I didn't know yet where I'll stash him this time, I'd think about that when he's out of the hole.

I dug like a machine and pretty soon there he is in his plas-tic bag outfit. The problem now was where to put him. If my Monte Carlo was running good I could just drive him away someplace and hide him under a bridge on some lonely stretch of highway, but it isn't, so that idea is a nonstarter just like my car. I went in the barn and found an old rusted-out wheelbarrow that I can use to trundle Dean around instead of lifting and carrying him in my arms, which I'm grateful for because even if he's wrapped up good in plastic the smell is coming through pretty strong. This way I can take him a little way away without getting myself stinking like a dead man, but only as far as the wheelbarrow will go without breaking my arms or falling to pieces it's so old and rusted. So where would be a good place?

I did some thinking and walking at the same time around

the property and saw that way out beyond the back yard there is this little stand of cottonwoods, some of them fairly old because they are a good size. I went over and found there's kind of a dried-up wash close by that would likely be running with water in springtime but now in midsummer it's bone dry, and it has ate away the soil there, kind of undercutting the bank and leaving a gap just about big enough to cram a dead man inside of it. So there was my hideyhole for Dean, provided by Nature. I put him in the wheelbarrow and trundled him over some fairly rough ground to the dry wash and down into it to the crevice there and shoved him inside.

Anyone standing above would not have been able to see him there, but anyone stood on the other side of the wash or down in it like I am could see him easy, so what I did was get up on top of the bank and jumped up and down hard as I can until the bank finally gave way and collapsed down over him like I wanted. I went down with the earthslide but it's only a little way so no harm done only I'm twice as dirty now than before. But Dean has been hid away very nice for the time being so I'm satisfied. So long as nobody comes back here and sees that the soil has slid down just recent I'm okay.

I wheeled the barrow back to the barn and then filled in the hole. Again. Then I took a shower and run my brand new but very filthy shirt and jeans through the washing machine to get that fresh dirt out of them, disposing of the evidence, they call this. Now if Andy Webb wanted to come out here ready to dig up Dean he would be a disappointed man. If he waved the Condoleezza letter in my face and says he can prove it's mine by a handwriting expert I'll just say it was a joke letter and not really true, hah!

I fixed myself something to eat and wolfed it down fast after all that physical exercise hiding Dean, expecting any moment to hear sirens coming my way but that didn't happen, so after awhile I started to relax a little and watch TV with a beer or two. They are still running the Okeydokey stuff making Dean look like an idiot and barely mentioned the manhunt for him that's still ongoing, so it looks like the story is losing its legs they call that, which is okay by me, I want it all to go away.

I was hoping Lorraine might call me tonight but that didn't happen. I would've called Agent Jim Ricker to ask him to tell Chief Webb to give my truck back, but Jim's number is in the phone that's in the truck. All in all I felt kind of steamed about things being the way they are, but I told myself I had gone and done everything I could to make things turn out right and that's all you can do. So with the help of a couple more beers and a shot or three of the Captain inside me matters were not so bad that I couldn't find sleep, or maybe sleep found me.

Hello, Odell.

Hello, Sleep.

THIRTEEN

They do say that there is no rest for the Wicked, and the fact that I was woke up from a deep sleep there in front of the TV might prove that's true if you have it in mind that I had done some wrong things so far. I don't know how long the phone had been ringing by the time I got up from the sofa and blundered into the kitchen to pick it up.

"Who's that?" says the voice at the other end.

"Odell…"

"You sure?"

I thought about it. "Yeah."

"You sound different."

It's a guy I'm talking to and the voice is familiar, only I can't recall who.

"I just now woke up," I said. "Who's this?"

"I'm not saying my name, not over the phone, man, it's too risky with all this about Dean."

The nickel dropped. "Donnie?"

"No, man, don't say that. No names, okay? Maybe the line's bugged."

"I don't think so."

"You haven't been hearing, like, clicks and stuff on the line?"

"No."

"Well, that don't mean squat, it could be bugged anyway. I won't talk business on a line that's maybe bugged. We need to meet someplace."

"I can't, I'm stuck here. Someone stole the truck."

"Stole the truck?"

"I know who did it. He'll give it back but not just yet."

"You got no wheels at all?"

"No."

He's quiet for a little while, thinking, I guess. I heard him squeeze out a fart but not a loud one. "Okay," he says, "this is how we'll do it. No way am I coming near the place. They've probably got it under observation looking for Dean to come back, so no way. If you can't drive someplace and talk to me, what you gotta do is this, you go down to the road and start walking in the direction of Callisto, and I'll come along there and stop when I see you, okay?"

"I'm pretty tired right now. You woke me up..."

"Hey! I don't give a rat's ass how fucking tired you are, man! We have got business to discuss and that's just how it's gotta be! You do this my way or you can forget about doing business with me anymore, okay? Okay?"

"Okay."

"Start walking," he says, then he hung up.

Well, I could not ignore him because that would mean

getting in trouble with Lorraine who would be expecting the Tuesday package as per usual tomorrow night for delivery Wednesday to the prison, and trouble with Lorraine I did not want. So I started walking, stopping to take a long leak between the house and the road, then when I got to the road I did what Donnie said and started walking towards town, asking myself if Donnie was smart to be so careful about not coming to the house or just nervous.

I walked and walked, smelling the night air and admiring the moon, still kind of drunk after all that beer and rum. Around fifteen minutes after I started, here comes a set of headlights, the first I saw since I started walking, this is a real back road with very little traffic as I have said before, so I'm expecting this is Donnie. He pulled up a little ways off and turned off his engine, then his lights. I kept walking and saw it's the green Pontiac all right. I saw a cigarette lighter flame and then the little red dot of a smoke, then he got out of the car and leaned against the door, waiting for me.

"Lonely road," he said when I reached him.

"Yeah."

"You probably think I'm paranoid, but being careful has kept me out of prison."

"Okay."

"Now what we need to discuss here is the delivery date. No way am I doing things the way we did it before. I was okay with the regular Tuesday run even after Dean was on the news for murder, but now this other thing, this terrorism thing, that's got me spooked. No way can we continue on as before under circumstances like that, it's way too risky now with federal agents and whatnot hunting him down. Dean's place is too hot for comfort from here on in, so we need to be doing things different. With me so far?"

"Uhuh."

"Now I've spoke to my people about this and we think the deal should be as follows. Number one, I won't be coming to the place anymore, ever, so a different place has got to be arranged for the handover. And number two, from now on, to cover the extra risk we're taking in dealing with the sister and associate of a known terrorist, the price has gone up. From now on it's two and a half, not two. Same package as before but the price has gone up, that's just how it has to be with all this new dangerous element. Oh, and number three, the delivery day is Monday from now on, not Tuesday, just to make me feel safer, beginning tonight."

"Tonight?"

"Yeah, so have you got the extra five hundred? I know it's short notice but that's the decision taken by me and my associates about this."

"I haven't got anything."

"Nothing?"

"It wasn't supposed to be until tomorrow."

"Yeah, well, I explained about that, about the risk, so now it's tonight. The sister, she's the one supplies the cash, so give her a call."

"I haven't got a phone."

He pulled a cell from his pocket and handed it to me. "Feel free."

I had to think awhile before I remembered Lorraine's number, then I called. She answered before the second ring. "I told you to stop calling me! So stop calling me!"

"I didn't," I said.

Silence, then, "Odell?"

"Yeah, it's me."

"What do you want?"

"Well, I've got Donnie with me and there's been some changes."

"Changes?"

"To the way things are getting done from now on."

"About what?"

"You know...the package."

"Package?"

Donnie snatched the phone right out of my hand and started yelling into it. "No names. From now on it's Monday, not at the house and it's two-five not two!"

Lorraine must have yelled something back at him because they started arguing. I went over to the side of the road and pissed again. I had certainly had my share of beer earlier, but then I'm under a lot of stress these days. I let them keep on arguing back and forth, just glad it isn't me having to do it, then finally Donnie smacked his phone shut and says, "Bitch..."

He turns to me. "Here's the deal. We're going over to her place and she'll be waiting outside with the two grand which she already got together for tomorrow, then we go to a cash machine and she gets the extra five hundred. Then you get your package. Get in."

He turned his car around and we headed for Callisto. He says, "She's some piece of work, that Lorraine. Dean used to say what a hardass bitch she is, that's why I was happy to deal with Dean and not her, Dean was mellow. But she's the one takes it behind prison bars for distribution, so it's not like I can cut her out of the loop. Like to but no can do, uh-uh, so we're stuck together like the shit and the shoe. I'm the shoe." He laughed about that.

He hadn't been to Lorraine's place before and neither had I, so Donnie had to stop at a late-night convenience store with a gas station out front and look up her address in the phone book dangling all battered on a chain from the public phone in the forecourt. He come back to the car and started it up, saying, "Got it committed to memory. If I never went there again for twenty years I could find it, I've got a photographic memory. I could've joined a college program where they study brains, live brains in people not dead brains in jars. This university back east offered me a room and all I could eat for a month while they studied my brainwaves, me and some others with a mental gift, only I quit after the second day, too fucking annoying having them ask you questions all the freaking time and having these little wires stuck all over your goddamn head. Fuck that. I walked out. But I can remember stuff like you wouldn't believe."

"Uhuh."

"Okay now...it's next left, then three blocks and turn right, then left again."

Lorraine was waiting for us at the curb in front of this apartment block. They looked like pretty nice apartments. Donnie pulled over and she got in. "Turn right at the next street then keep going straight," she said. No Good evening or anything. No Hi, Odell. Lorraine was pissed about all this on top of everything else she has had to deal with lately, which is understandable, so I didn't take offense that she didn't even look at me the whole time we're in the car till we got to her bank and she tells Donnie to pull over.

"You two are coming with me," she says. "It's too risky, a woman alone at night in front of an ATM."

We all got out and went across the sidewalk to the ATM. Lorraine punched buttons there for a half-minute with Donnie and me standing right behind her on the lookout for thieves and bandits. The machine poked out some money like a long green tongue and Lorraine took it, then we got back in the car and drove away.

Donnie says, "I'm gonna drop you both off at the movie theater downtown while I get the package from a certain place, then I'll be back to make the exchange, okay?"

"Fine," said Lorraine, very grumpy.

He stopped in the parking lot of the Metrolux and says he'll be ten minutes, fifteen at the outside, then away he went. Lorraine dug a pack of cigarettes out of her purse and lit one up with a Bic.

"I didn't know you smoked."

"I quit last year, it's just very nerve-wracking at the moment. Want one?"

"No thank you."

She looked over at the theater standing all lit up in the middle of the parking lot.

"I haven't been to the movies in a long time."

"Me neither."

"I couldn't even tell you what's playing nowadays. Couldn't even tell you who the big stars are. I used to be right on top of the movies, now I don't give a shit."

"Who was calling you up?"

"Huh?"

"Who were you yelling at on the phone when I called?"

"None of your business, Odell."

"You sounded really mad, so I wondered."

"Well, stop wondering and mind your business. That Donnie, what a prick, him and his fucking associates. This is a complete ripoff. They're just taking advantage, you know that. I can't afford to break off with them, though, it's an established pipeline and it works. I couldn't put that together with anyone else and have it go so smooth. It was Dean got it all started and I don't have Dean anymore. You could say we're lucky they accepted you as a substitute. But it's a fucking ripoff anyway."

"Was it Cole?"

"What? What are you saying? No it was not Cole. Why would I be yelling at Cole? Cole's a friend."

"Well, then, who?"

She flicked ash from her cigarette and blew smoke over me which I pretended she hadn't. I'm not looking for a fight, just information.

"Why would I tell you anything private? Why do you think I should do that?"

"Uh, because we're ... partners."

"Partners in crime, you mean."

"Uhuh."

"That's got nothing to do ... Oh shit, I guess it has, once we get the lawsuit started."

"Against Chief Webb?"

"That's who it was. I made a big mistake and called him up to let him know what I think about him, maybe I was a little drunk, anyway I gave him an earful, especially about the truck, which he denies he's got anything to do with that, by the way, I mean really denies it."

"Did you believe him?"

"Yeah, pretty much, only too late to keep from telling him we're planning on getting a lawyer to get him back for it. That and the fucked-up interview."

"You told him?"

"Didn't I just tell you I told him? Yeah, I told him. It won't make any difference, it just means he'll respond quicker with his own lawyer when ours does a dump on him. It makes no difference at all hardly, anyway it's done. He kept calling back to abuse me over the phone after that, the prick."

"That's not how a Chief of Police is supposed to act," I said.

She blew more smoke, then says, "Odell, sometimes I think you fell out of the sky the day before yesterday. *Nobody* acts like they're supposed to act. Not the politicians getting fat on lobbyist money, not the woman-chasing TV preachers, not the cops and not me neither, that's why I don't complain like I should. Only someone that fell out of the sky and didn't know shit about how the real world operates would even bother complaining about how things are."

"Well, then...so why did he keep abusing you on the phone?"

"It's personal," she says. "Andy and me have known each other a long time now. People that know each other a long time, every once in a while they fall out and have a big argument about something, so that's what happened, okay?"

"But what was it about if it wasn't about the lawsuit?"

"Didn't I just now say it's personal? That means between him and me. Not you, get it?"

"Okay."

She says, "Andy just has got into this habit of treating

people like they're suspects at a crime scene, like they did something wrong so he can lord it over them."

"You're not doing anything wrong, Lorraine."

"What? Jesus, Odell, you think running drugs into a state correctional facility is work for angels? You think Donnie's an angel? Is Dean? It's a dirty world with not enough cash to go round, so you have to do some grabbing and stabbing just to get by without falling under the wheels, that's how it is on God's green earth, okay? Come Friday you'll be doing it too if Cole takes you on."

"Is Cole part of it?"

She flipped her cigarette away. "You know too much already. Wait and see. Maybe Cole won't take you on if he sees what a starry-eyed baby bird that just fell out of the nest you are. You've got to grow up, Odell, and stop acting so weird. Has anyone ever told you you're weird?"

"A couple times."

"Well, they did it for a reason. So stop being that way and get with the program."

Now this was harsh critical talk from a woman I had strong feelings for, so it hurt to hear her calling me this baby bird out of the nest thing, trying to make me feel small. If she only knew all the trouble I have gone to about Dean, digging him up and putting him here and there without letting on to a soul, she'd be impressed about that and have to quit saying I'm weird. It takes concentration and smart thinking to do what I have done this past week without getting caught, and if she thinks I'm all innocent and dumb like a baby bird she'll have to change her mind when Condoleezza tells the cops to back off from me because she understands how Dean was killed accidental so they should go easy on me. That will be some kind of a big surprise to Lorraine, all about how I killed her brother and hid him away all this time without spilling the secret like most guys would. If Lorraine wants the strong silent type that knows how to make all the right moves she'll have to admit this is what kind I am, not some baby fucking bird.

"You're not such a dingaling as you look, Odell," says Lorraine, "it's just this impression you give, okay? Ditch the dingaling and show me the real man, okay?"

"Okay."

"I'm not so much mad at you as I'm mad at myself. I never should've called Andy and told him. Now he's prepared. I should've waited, but I had a few drinks and got mad and called him at home. He hates to be called at home, especially by a woman. It's his wife always picks up the phone and she gets real suspicious when there's a woman asking for Andy. He told me this a long time ago. So that's where I went wrong, calling him at home. I know that's what made him madder than he ought to be about the lawsuit thing, it's because now he's gonna catch hell from his wife about who that woman is that called. That's why I wouldn't want to get married, all that shit that goes on between husband and wife, the suspicion."

"It's not always that way."

"Sure it is. What, your mom and dad got along great?"

"No."

"There you go, it's all bullshit."

She got out another cigarette and fired it up, like she needs to be doing something with her hands to keep her from pulling her hair out or whatever. I never saw her so nervous and distracted by everything as this. Usually Lorraine was on top of things and giving orders like she knows exactly what she's doing and everyone better jump, but tonight she's somebody else, just barely keeping it together with the help of a Marlboro.

I said to her, "How would you feel if you found out Dean isn't running from the law like everyone thinks he is?"

"That'd be just fine, only that's not how it is. See, this is what I mean about you being weird."

"No, I mean if he's dead, not running."

"Well, that'd be a different thing if he's dead. That'd be the end of all this shit flying around, all this crap about the karaoke thing. Fox News practically put a laugh track to that, making him look stupid... They'd all quit laughing if he's dead. Only he isn't."

"But what if he was?"

"Odell, you're pissing me off again. Dean is my brother and I don't want you jinxing things by talking about him that way. Every time I turn on the news I'm expecting to hear he's been gunned down somewhere in a shootout with the FBI or someone... Don't talk that way, please, I don't want to hear it."

"So you're saying it'd be a relief if you found out he's dead."

"No I did not say that! Christ! I hope he gets across the border to Mexico and starts a new life down in South America or someplace, even if I never get to see him again."

"So you don't want to get told he's dead."

"That's right, Odell, you're getting the picture at last. Thank you for being so upbeat. I really go for that kind of optimistic talk at a time like this."

"Okay."

"Let's just wait for Donnie Dickhead and not talk anymore."

"Right."

So that's what we did. She smoked three cigarettes before Donnie got back and pulls up next to us. He didn't get out of the car or even turn off the engine, just shoved a package all taped up exactly like the other package last Tuesday out the window and wiggled it, then pulls it in again while Lorraine digs in her purse for the cash, which then they exchanged these two things.

"I need a lift home," she says.

"Get in."

Lorraine and me both got in and Donnie drove away directly to her place and stops again with the engine running while Lorraine got out. I started to get out behind her but she says for Donnie to take me home too.

"I'm not running a taxi service," he says.

"You brought him here so you can take him home again."

I was halfway out the door and she pushed me back inside again and shuts it.

"Go on," she says, and Donnie kind of hissed but he puts the Pontiac in gear and away we went back across town again.

"Some kinda bitch, all right," he says. "How do you tolerate it, man?"

"Lorraine's okay, just under pressure right now."

"Hey, we're all under pressure all the time. You and me, we're not losing our cool, right? Some can handle it better than others. So who stole your truck?"

"I don't know."

"You said before you knew."

"Well, now I don't."

"That's Dean's truck. Maybe Dean come back and took what's his, you think?"

"No."

"Nah, he wouldn't be dumb enough to come back here and go driving around in a truck with his name on the door, that'd be too stupid. They got the mowers too?"

"Everything."

"The world is full of thieves, from the White House on down. That's why it's a waste of time trying to earn an honest living, those thieves just take it all back in taxes. All those big-time CEOs, they're thieves too, ripping off their own people and their own stockholders, they don't care, so why should I? The cops do shakedowns and lawyers are so crooked you could open a bottle of wine with one of those bastards. Now dealing, that's different. That's providing a resource people want and you provide it for them at a reasonable cost with just enough markup so you can make an honest buck and feed your family, no bullshit and fake promises. I can go to sleep at night knowing I did nobody no harm, just provided a service people genuinely want and need. If I was doing something bad I wouldn't feel that way, now would I?"

"No."

"Damn right I wouldn't. You and her fucking?"

"No."

"But you'd like to, right? She may be bitchy but she also witchy, you know? What's wrong with you, she seeing some other guy?"

"No."

"So get in there, my man. That's a fine-looking lady going to waste. You're really not poling her?"

"No."

He shook his head and sighed like it's something he'll never understand. "You are one strange bird, Odell. There's something about you just don't add up. You're the kinda guy has secrets, I can tell."

"Secrets?"

"Uhuh, the deep and dark kind, I'm betting. The thing about secrets, they eat away at a man till he's just a hollowed-out guy, what they call a husk."

"A husk."

"Right. You got any secrets to share, Odell? Or maybe you wanna be a husk."

"I don't have any secrets."

"You sure? I'm good at character judgment, and my mind is telling me you're a secret-keeper."

"Well, your mind would be wrong about that."

He kind of snickered and kept looking across at me, which a driver shouldn't do, he should keep his eyes on the road. We're getting to the edge of town about then, where the streetlighting ends and the night takes over. Donnie turned on the radio and music blasted out over us, so no more talking. We turned off the main highway onto the road that goes past Dean's place, and he slowed down a little because this is a dirt road and not so smooth riding. A car passed us going the other way, just a pair of blazing headlights set on high beam that got Donnie swearing and he flashed his own at them but they didn't turn theirs off, real selfish behavior in my opinion, but then they're past us and we're driving through the dust they kicked up. "Asshole," says Donnie. After another ten or so minutes driving along the road he pulls over and turns the music down.

"Okay, I'm gonna drop you off here. Near as I can guess it's about where I picked you up. No way I'm going anywhere near that house again."

I got out and he did a U-turn, throwing up dust that hung in the headlights, then he's gone back down the road, which I was not sorry to see him go, that is not the kind of guy I can get comfortable with. I started walking, thinking about everything and trying to untangle what I think about all of it, not so easy because the letter has gone missing and I don't know who has got this. Maybe I should not have wrote it after all, but I was feeling bad and the letter made me feel good for a little while anyway, but now I'm not so sure.

It was a nice feeling walking along the road under moonlight, swinging my arms and whistling, which I do not do so good but nobody's around to say so. All in all I would be feeling good except for all this stuff about Dean plugging up my Happy Valve, this thing everyone has inside them that opens up every now and then for no particular reason and lets loose a blast of Happy Feelings. I have got one and I am no freak so everybody has got one of these, a good thing to have but you can't turn it on or off, it does that itself whenever it wants, generally not too often.

I could see the house because I left a light on inside plus the porch light, not too far away now so I slowed down a little to make the walk last. Maybe I should do more moonlight walking. Then I got to the end of the driveway and turned in toward the house, which is when I stopped because there is someone parked right there in the driveway, maybe twenty yards in from the road. At first I thought it's a federal servaylance team watching the house like Donnie thinks they are, but this is no government sedan, it's a truck. I got closer and it's Dean's truck!

I got closer still and found out there's nobody inside, just an empty cab, and the mowers are still in back there like they should be. The hood was warm so it was returned just recent by Andy Webb after Lorraine yelled at him over the phone, this is so obvious. They didn't take it all the way up to the house because the porch light and front room lights are on and they figured someone must be home, so they drove it partway along the drive, most likely with the headlights off, and left it there and fled the scene in a backup car, which I bet was the one and only car that passed me and Donnie coming back here.

I had left the keys in the house, but the truck door was not locked so I opened it up and checked out the cab by the overhead light. Well, it looked no different than before, still with all that trash covering the floor, only the ignition wires are dangling down under the dash so they hotwired it to drive it away and return it. Well, no harm done there, but the letter to Condoleezza was gone, and my sweet little phone. I scratched around among the fast food trays and candy wrappers and kingsize Coke containers including lids and straws but could not find neither one of these Important Items, so they have been stolen even if the Dodge got brung back. I looked at the odometer and it says they have not been driving it around very much, probably just to the police garage where it got stashed for twelve hours or so and then it got returned. I only lost one day's mowing after all and the schedule is still there with all the customer phone numbers so I can call around and explain things to them tomorrow, no problem. But I was mad about that phone.

I got out and started walking up to the house to get the truck keys, thinking to myself Andy Webb has got that letter after all, so why isn't he out here digging up the hole in the yard where the letter says I buried Dean, so now I'm worried all over again. When I got to the porch I heard the kitchen phone start to ring and hustled out my door key to get inside fast because I'm thinking it's Lorraine calling to apologize for acting cranky tonight and she'll say next time I'm over at her place I can stay the night and not get sent home with Donnie Darko. Or maybe it's Chief Webb making a prank call and he's going to say to me something like, "We brung your truck back, but next time we won't."

I sprinted along the hall to the kitchen and lifted the phone. "Hello?"

"Odell? This is Chet Marchand."

"Oh … Chet. Hi."

"Sorry to call you up so late, Odell, but I've been trying to reach you all afternoon and evening. Your new phone seems to have the ring tone turned way down."

"No, it's been stolen."

"Stolen?"

"Along with my truck … Dean's truck. They just now brung it back."

"Your truck was stolen? This is the lawnmowing truck, you mean?"

"That's the one, stolen this morning while I'm at the funeral, only now they brung it back okay, safe and sound. But they took the phone."

"Oh no, your brand-new phone …"

"Yeah, they took it, all right, I looked for it but it's gone."

"Well, that is a shame I have to say. It's a world of thieves out there."

I'm thinking that must be true because Donnie D said the same thing not twenty minutes ago, but of course I can't talk about that with someone like Chet Marchand, he'd be disappointed to hear I'm not only not a Christian, I hang out with drug dealers.

"The reason I've been calling, Odell, is on the way back to Topeka I got to thinking, and I made a call to Reverend Jerome concerning you."

"Me?"

"That's right, Odell. What the idea was, is how would you feel about coming to Topeka for Preacher Bob's Fourth of July Revival?"

"Fourth of July?"

"That's right. This is an important time for America, Odell, with this election coming up on us next year, a time for doing what's right, for holding firm and not giving way to weakness and compromise. Those two things are just another way of saying Defeat. Bob and I are very much aware of the public mood and Bob wants to serve up his followers with a real American celebration on the fourth, something special that'll lift our hearts and get the political blood racing. Guess who the celebrity guest will be, Odell. He'll be giving a speech that we know will be a great speech, a stirring speech."

"Uh, the President?"

"Close but no cigar. Try the *next* President."

"Senator Ketchum?"

"God willing, and we want you to be there as well, Odell."

"Well, I…I don't know. I don't think I could give a very good speech, Chet, not even if it was wrote out for me by a speechwriting guy…"

"Odell, sorry, I seem to have miscommunicated here. We don't want you to give a speech, that'll be Senator Ketchum's role, plus an introductory speech by Bob, of course. No, we're inviting you to attend as a guest, a special attendee behind the scenes, as it were. You'll get to meet the senator and Preacher Bob too, but you don't have to worry about publicity, I know you've had it rough about your association with Dean Lowry. No, you'd be there as kind of a special secret guest, that's all, away from the cameras so you won't get any unwelcome attention from the media. You're probably asking yourself why Bob is doing this, aren't you, Odell."

"Kind of."

"Because Preacher Bob is that kind of guy. There it is."

"Uhuh."

"Tell me you're interested, Odell. Tell me you'll be there. I want you to know I am not proselytizing, merely extending an invitation to someone I'd like to call a friend."

"Well…okay, sure."

"It'll be a huge crowd. We've made arrangements to take over one of Topeka's biggest parks, so it'll be an open-air gathering with a stage and lots of free food for everyone. We're expecting in excess of ten thousand souls."

"Wow, that's big, all right."

"Big and special. You won't regret this, Odell. And your truck has been brought back, you say?"

"Parked out there along the driveway."

"That's good, that's your transport taken care of. We'll

compensate you for your gas consumption on the trip, Odell, a big truck like that will burn a hole in your pocket the way those OPEC countries have got us paying a fortune at the gas pump nowadays. But then again, bigger is safer, they say. Big American cars and trucks are what all of us should be driving, but people are turning away from them for smaller imports. That's a bad thing, Odell, an unpatriotic thing...But don't get me started on that subject. And, Odell? As a special reward for your attendance, I think I can guarantee Preacher Bob and I will provide you with another cell phone at no charge. In fact, you can count on it."

"That's real...that's a very generous thing, Chet, thank you."

"No thanks required, Odell. Just you be there on the fourth, and make sure nobody steals your truck again in the meantime, okay?"

"Okay."

"Well, I'll let you enjoy the rest of your evening."

"Okay then."

"Bye, Odell."

"Bye, Chet."

We hung up and I had to shake my head this is so surprising, getting invited to a big show like this will be with Preacher Bob and Senator Ketchum and who knows who-all else besides. And another good thing about this – when Chief Webb starts waving my letter around that says I killed Dean I can say I have got friends in High Places as the saying goes, being backstage with Preacher Bob and Senator Ketchum like Chet wants. It was Chet talking to me on Sunday that made me write the letter that will get me in trouble anytime now, and Chet calling me just now that will get me out of that self-same trouble, so this is just perfect!

Of course it would be better if I didn't ever have wrote that letter, especially seeing as I don't know where it is right now, maybe still in the truck, lost in all that crap on the floor, maybe the phone too, I just couldn't see them with only that tiny little overhead light to see by. Maybe I should go out there with a flashlight and give the cab floor a real good going-over to be sure about this and not worry anymore about who has got that letter. Then I had a better idea. I'm still standing next to the phone, thinking hard, and it struck me all I have to do is call my cell number and if the phone is still someplace in the truck it'll ring and I'll find it easy by following the sound. That was a good plan, so I concentrated, remembering the number, and then I called it up.

It rung once, then all of a sudden I got picked up by an invisible hand and flung against the kitchen wall, which give way when that happened and the wall and me and the refrigerator and some other household items were moving along together through the air it seemed like, and I'm thinking this must be some kind of crazy dream that's happening, did I fall asleep with the phone in my hand? Then the wall slowed down a little so I caught up and was flung hard against it while the refrigerator went on by, still going fast. Then me and the wall begun falling down, it felt like, but I can't hear a thing, a deaf man's dream. This is all going on around me very slow and quiet. Now I'm dreaming about the house all shattered to smithereens somehow and flying through the air alongside me and the wall I'm bumping up against. Then it's the grandaddy clock comes sailing by, turning slow and stately in the air with the pendulum sticking out at a crazy angle and the dial separating from the rest and showing the curly springs and gadgets behind. Here comes the front porch rocker turning over and over very slow with the cushions like fat wingless birds flying alongside looking for someplace to land. I wanted to reach out and grab one of them but I can't seem to move, the way you get in dreams, and so those cushions kept on going past me because I'm slowing down, pushing harder against the kitchen wall which is leaning over now and turning in a slow circle under the moon, so I have gone and dreamed myself outside, one of those flying dreams you hear about, only I'm spinning too so the moon keeps going in silent circles up there.

Then there's this big eclipse that happened and everything went dark very fast.

FOURTEEN

Now, you will have read in the newspapers about those people that wake up in bed and there has gotten to be some aliens in the room all standing around looking strange and communicating telepathically, this has been on TV also. That's how I knew something very unusual had happened to me, drugs or something to make me think I'm surrounded by aliens that are giving me commands I don't understand. Maybe Donnie D spiked my drink, he's a drug dealer, only we did not have any drinks. And this is not my room anyway, Dean's room, that is, and this is not my bed. One of the tall thin aliens was disguised like a nurse, all in white and blue, and another one has got a special probe device around his neck to insert the locator bug up my nose so they can always find me even if I run to the ends of the earth, only it looks like a regular stethoscope so I don't get alarmed and fight back when the bug goes in.

"Can you hear me?" he says.

He almost looked human, but you can always tell if it's an alien by the way the edges of the face have got makeup to hide where the mask ends, the mask that hides the lizard face underneath, so I was not going to be fooled into talking when I'm not ready for alien interrogation and a nasal implant. Or else this is still a dream I'm having, only now it hurts. My hand hurts and my head hurts and my shoulder, also one knee. I have got bandages around my head and my right hand which is kind of throbbing.

"Mr Deefus, can you hear me?"

"Uh…"

"Can you tell me how many fingers I'm holding up?"

He gave himself away there because he forgot to hide those extra alien fingers for a total of seven. These aliens are not so clever as you might think, only technogistically more advanced than we are just yet. But I was ready now to fool him into thinking I don't know what's going on. This is a white room inside the mother ship for sure.

"Five…" I croaked, and he looked pleased.

"Good. Do you know what happened to you?"

"I saw the moon…"

That wasn't the right answer. He leaned in closer till his humanoid mask was long as a cartoon face. "There was an explosion," he says. "The house was destroyed. You're very lucky to be alive."

So now I'm thinking did the propane tank explode or what? And maybe these people are not aliens, just people, hospital people. In which case something real has happened, not a dream after all. That propane tank had not looked like it was in good shape but the propane delivery company is supposed to tell you if it needs fixing, so obviously Dean had ignored the warning is what I thought.

"A bomb," says the doctor, which I can see now he's a real doctor and the nurse is a real nurse, and those two over there in the suits watching me close look like cops. I had heard that word before – bomb – but couldn't think what one of those was. It sounded like something round and full – bommmmmm – kind of like a propane tank, but that wasn't it.

"A truck bomb," he says.

I thought about trucks and come up with Dean's truck, the old Dodge with the lawnmowers in back of it, but it wasn't in such bad shape you could call it a bomb, not even a junker like my Monte Carlo, so there is still confusion in my mind about this.

"Can we talk to him?" asks one of the suits.

The doctor looked into my eyes like he's trying to make up his mind. He has got a small mole on his cheek. "Are you able to talk for a little while, Mr Deefus?"

"Uhuh…"

The two cops come closer and the doctor and nurse slid away out of sight with the doc saying over his shoulder, "Not for too long."

Then they're hovering close beside the bed, both of them. "How are you today, Mr Deefus?" says the one without the glasses. "Agent Kraus and Agent Deedle, do you remember us from last week?" So they aren't cops, they're FBI, now I remember.

"Uhuh."

They dragged over some plastic chairs and sat down.

"Are you in much pain, Mr Deefus?"

"Uhuh."

"Well, we'll go as fast as we can so you don't get inconvenienced. There's some questions need answering about this incident. We've been told the truck was stolen, is that right?"

"Uhuh, yesterday."

The agents exchanged a look, then Deedle says, "You mean the day before yesterday, I think. This is Wednesday now."

"Wednesday …"

"You had a blow to the head, Odell. Can we call you Odell?"

"Uhuh."

"And it was returned to you late Monday night?"

"They left it in the driveway."

"They. Do you know who?"

"Chief Webb, I think, but he was only fooling around. He brung it back. Was it the propane tank exploded?"

"No, it was the truck. We found one of the doors a half-mile away with *Dean Lowry Lawnmowing* on it. It was a truck bomb, Odell."

"Truck bomb …"

"What time did they bring it back?"

"I … don't know." I didn't want to tell them about being out with Donnie and Lorraine collecting cash for her drug package. "I found it in the driveway … it was after ten o' clock."

"And what happened then?"

"I … went back inside to get the keys and drive it up to the house."

"And did you do that?"

"No, I … I lost my cell phone inside the truck and I rung the number from the house to make it ring so I can find it …"

Kraus nodded like this is something he can use. "Was the phone in the truck when it was stolen, Odell?"

"Uhuh. I thought maybe it's still in there, the floor's kind of messy."

"So you called your own cell and the truck exploded. That's how it's done nowadays, using a phone call to activate the detonator. What happened then?"

"I don't know. I saw the fridge and the rocker sailing past me like it's a dream..."

"Now, think hard, Odell. Could this be the work of Dean Lowry?"

"Dean? No, he's...he wouldn't blow up his own truck."

"It isn't about the truck, it's about what was done to the truck. They must have crammed every body panel in the vehicle with high explosive. That was one hell of a bang out there, Odell. You can't remember that part?"

"No, it was real quiet, so I thought I'm dreaming. Is the house wrecked?"

"Completely demolished. It's a miracle you're still alive and with so few injuries. The emergency team found you way over in back of the house near some cottonwoods. Those trees had every leaf stripped off them, and they had the house in between the bomb and them, so that gives you some indication of how powerful this blast was. We're still doing the analysis but it looks like this was intended to take out a city block, more or less."

Deedle says, "Why do you think it was Chief Webb?"

"Oh...he just doesn't like me, I guess."

"That's an extreme reaction to not liking someone, turning their truck into a bomb. Why doesn't he like you?"

"He...I made a mistake about Saturday and Sunday, if I met Dean this day or that day, and it's like he thinks I'm lying. I told him later I got drunk with Dean so I got that part wrong."

"We remember you telling us about that, Odell. It still seems a bit of a stretch to think the Chief of Police would steal someone's truck and jam it full of explosives just because of something like you described, don't you think? There'd have to be a better reason that that."

"Maybe..." was all I could say. To myself I'm thinking it most likely wasn't Andy Webb after all, only who *was* it? Who could hate my guts so much they wanted to blow me into a million pieces? This was not making any kind of sense. And I bet Lorraine was mad as hell about the house that she was just about to inherit, but most likely Aunt Bree kept up those insurance payments. But would the policy include terrorist bomb destruction? There are some policies that don't include flood damage and unless you ask special for it you don't get it, and if you get flooded out, tough tit, you weren't covered for that, so was Bree covered for bomb destruction? I would need to ask Lorraine about this.

"Has she been in to see me?"

"Who's that, Odell?"

"Lorraine."

"No," says Deedle. "You're restricted."

"Huh?"

"Nobody gets to see you except us. She's been told you're okay."

"Don't worry about that, Odell," says Kraus. "The important thing is to figure out who took the truck and converted it into a bomb. We suspect there was a team behind it. Rigging a truck to explode on that scale doesn't get done like having the oil changed. We think three or four guys arranged this in the ten to twelve hours the truck was missing."

"The second big question, " says Deedle, "is whether you were the intended target. Have you got enemies, Odell?"

"No."

"Nobody at all? Think back. Has there been anyone you got into an argument with lately?"

"Only Chief Webb."

"Forget Webb, we know he's not a player in this. Think some more."

"Okay," I said, and I did, I did think some more till it hurt, but nothing come of it.

"Did you and Dean have an argument?"

"No, we got along great. I only knew him a couple days, then he went away. There wasn't time to be getting into arguments. He didn't do this."

"But maybe a terrorist cell he's involved with did," says Kraus, with this look on his face that says he thinks I'm hiding something.

"Well, I wouldn't know about that. I never met a terrorist."

"They look like you and me, Odell. Maybe you met a terrorist and didn't see that he's a terrorist. That's no crime. They make themselves invisible in society, that's how they do the terrible things they do without anybody suspecting the plans they're making for mass destruction and terror."

"Well, then, maybe I did, but I wouldn't know which one it was."

They looked at me like they're disappointed somehow, but

there's nothing I can tell them about this bomb that I know because I don't know anything. I don't *know* anything and I didn't *do* anything.

"I want to see Lorraine."

"Would that revive your memory, seeing her?"

"Maybe."

"You and her an item, Odell?"

"She's my fiancée … pretty soon."

"Is that right?" Deedle looked over at Kraus. "The sister of a terrorist and the victim of a terrorist bomb are going out together. That sounds like a movie plot."

"Maybe you should get an agent," says Kraus, smiling a little.

"You guys are agents," I said. They looked at me a long while, then at each other, then Kraus says, "We know about the drugs, Odell."

"Drugs?"

"Your girlfriend's phone has been bugged this last week, just in case her brother called. We know where you and her and Donald Hubert Youngman, aka Donnie Darko, went Monday evening."

"Huh?"

Deedle reached in his pocket and brung out a picture he handed to me, and there we are together, me and Lorraine and Donnie. "That was taken at the Fifteenth Street ATM. Those pinhole cameras keep getting better and better."

"Nice tone," says Kraus. "Nice clarity. That's evidence of intent to parlay money into drugs, Odell, and there you are, right in the middle."

"Mmmm …"

"We know about Lorraine's sideline in delivery of narcotics

to the state pen and her relationship with the guy on the inside that passes it on."

"Relationship?"

"That'd be a sexual relationship," says Deedle.

"It starts with two people working in the same place," says Kraus, "and develops over coffee in the cafeteria to a mutual interest in making untaxed money on the side, and before you know it the whole enterprise ends up getting those concerned ten to fifteen. That's a fairly young woman there, Odell. You wouldn't see each other for a long time."

"Relationship with who?"

"Mean to say you didn't know about that, Odell? She's your fiancée, after all. She didn't tell you about the guy she's been humping, her boss?"

"Cole?"

"That's the guy. He'll get a longer term than her, being her superior. You don't look good, Odell."

"I didn't do anything..."

"Right, you're an innocent bystander. Got your picture right here, standing by innocently while your girl the mule takes out more cash for the new inflated price to pay her supplier. It looks bad, Odell. At the very least I'd say this leaves you wide open for a charge of conspiracy, trafficking, aiding and abetting, take your pick."

"Three to five if the judge doesn't like you," says Deedle. "Maybe you can all wave to each other through the bars."

Kraus gave the picture back to Deedle then leaned close to me. "This can all go away if you'll cooperate. We want the big fish. You're a minnow, we know that, only it looks bad the way you've been associating with criminals this past week, beginning

with Dean. Either you're part of it, Odell, or you're the unlucki-
est son of a bitch I ever met."

"I'm unlucky," I told him.

"That's what I'd say too," says Deedle.

I didn't know what to think. Lorraine has been humping
Cole Connors, and I just told these guys she's my fiancée.
They were right – it looked real bad, like I'm some kind of
idiot blinded by love as they say. "I'm unlucky in love," I told
them.

"That's just the beginning of your bad luck, Odell."

"It could get a whole lot worse," says Kraus.

They both of them were looking very grim now, like I
handed in a lousy report card and have to take some bad consequences on account of it. I needed a friend, but who was
there I could call and have him help me out here? Then it
come to me who.

"I want to talk to Agent Jim Ricker."

"Pardon?"

"Agent Jim Ricker from Homeland Security."

"The folks at Homeland don't generally refer to themselves
as agents."

"Well that's what he said, he's Agent Jim Ricker."

"And how do you happen to know Agent Ricker?"

"He called me on the phone a few times, and I called him
once."

"We don't have any record of those conversations, Odell.
We bugged your phone too and that name does not feature in
our recordings."

"Well, then, you must not have been listening close
enough. Pretty soon after I got my phone he called me up and

says he's Agent Jim Ricker and I have to tell him everything about what's happening."

"This is your new cell phone you're talking about."

"Uhuh."

"And this Agent Jim Ricker has held conversations with you on that cell?"

"Two or three times now."

Kraus gave a nod to Deedle, who got up and strolled over to the window which has got the blinds drawn against the bright sun out there. He took out a phone and starts talking to someone while Kraus keeps looking at me like the report card has gone from D to F minus. "See, Odell, when you got that cell last week, the minute your name and number were registered it prompted an alert, a red flag, you might say, given that you're a person of interest to us. Your conversations on that phone, as well as on the landline out at Dean Lowry's place, have all been monitored, and I have to tell you now, Odell, there's no record of conversations with a Jim Ricker. We'd know if any such thing happened. That's our job."

"Well...he called me, I'm not lying. You can hook me up to a lie detector. It was Agent Jim Ricker. He calls me up once in a while to let me know he's keeping an eye on me with the satellite."

"The satellite."

"Uhuh, up there in the sky, a whole bunch of them watching over me."

"Like guardian angels, Odell?"

"Kinda, yeah, maybe."

Deedle come back over and says, "Just been talking to Homeland Security, Odell. They don't have any Agent

Jim Ricker, definitely no such person working there."

"Sure there is. I talked to him two, three times."

Kraus says to Deedle, "Odell has just been telling me that Agent Ricker keeps a watchful eye on him by way of spy satellites, a whole bunch of them, isn't that right, Odell?"

"That's right, that's what he told me."

"Even though our intercept failed to monitor any such conversations with any such person. We have the best equipment in the world, Odell, your taxpayer dollar at work."

"Well, it isn't working right," I told them, getting kind of steamed about how they aren't believing me concerning this important person.

"What's his number?" asks Kraus.

"Uh, I forget. I had it entered in the phone like you can do nowadays, but the phone's gone and I can't remember the number."

"The number we'd have a record of if calls ever came through on your phone."

"The calls did come through ... Give me a lie-detector test." Then I thought how they could ask me about did I know where Dean is, like Chief Webb asked me, so maybe I better not get lie-detected after all. "Only you can just ask me that one question, not any others."

"Hardly seems worthwhile setting up a polygraph for just one question, Odell. We heard you had one of those and burst out crying. We wouldn't want to upset you all over again for one piddling question that we already know the answer to."

"You do?"

"We do. You're bullshitting us, Odell, and we don't like that."

"I'm not lying! He really called me ... Maybe he's got one of those ... those machines that make you not be able to understand what he's saying ..."

"A scrambler?"

"A scrambler, yeah, he must have one of those."

"Odell, our ability to suck it up on landline and cell and satellite calls is unparalleled. We can listen in on any conversation, anytime, anywhere in the world. You did not receive calls from any Jim Ricker. You received calls on Lowry's phone and your cell from Donnie D, Chief Webb, Lorraine Lowry and Chet Marchand and that's all. We've looked into Chet Marchand and he's told us he came out to talk with Dean about his conversion to Islam. He came out again when he learned you'd been impersonating Dean, and he took pity on you because he thinks you're a disturbed person, Odell, so he gave you a cell phone to help you build up your customer base and mow more lawns. If there's anyone watching over you like a guardian angel, Odell, it's Chet Marchand and his boss, Bob Jerome. Those two have got an interest in you based on their religious faith and belief in good works. We know Mr Marchand invited you to attend a big revival meeting in Topeka on July Fourth, that's an invitation that isn't extended to just anybody."

All of a sudden I understood! It was so clear it's like a light turned on inside my head. "I'm bait ..." I said.

"Excuse me?"

"Jim Ricker told me I'm bait for flushing out Dean ... That's why they want me at the big Topeka meeting, because Senator Ketchum is gonna be there to make a speech ... and Dean wants to kill him ... so maybe you think I'm gonna help Dean do that ...?"

Kraus was looking kind of pissed now. "Nobody told you you're bait. Dean wouldn't come within a mile of you, Odell, not unless he's retarded, which clearly he isn't. Messed up, maybe, but not retarded. Jim Ricker told you nothing because Jim Ricker doesn't exist. Most people, Odell, they give up their imaginary friends by the time they're six or eight."

"He's not my imaginary friend. He's got a daughter, a nine-year-old daughter that's got the same ring tone on her phone as I picked for mine, he told me – Greensleeves."

"Greensleeves?"

I started whistling it for them but quit when they gave each other this long look that says I don't whistle so good.

"Odell, listen up. Your friend Jim would need to have equipment of incredible sophistication to evade our scanners. No such conversation about his daughter took place because we have no record of it. This man does not exist, so let's move on."

"He *has* got incredible equipment, or how else could he know what kind of ring tone I had on my phone?"

"That'd have to be something pretty new on the market," says Deedle, "and we know about everything that's out there, all the gadgets. Odell, we *invent* most of whatever is the latest and greatest, and what you're describing is something out of a James Bond movie. Don't tell us about equipment, we *know*."

"You guys invent stuff?"

"Not us directly, the National Security Agency, they're the backroom boys that come up with all the sniffers and scoopers, all the filters and fine-tuners. Nothing gets by their equipment, Odell, so don't try and bluff us into thinking someone can. No more bullshitting."

"Well, I wasn't."

"Sure you were," says Kraus. "No more fairy tales, Odell. You're holding something back and we want to know what it is. Nobody walks into the life of a terrorist with car trouble and gets to be such an instant friend he gets roped in to take care of business while the terrorist goes off somewhere with his cell buddies to plot against a high-level member of the United States government. That just doesn't happen in the real world, Odell, so start telling us the real story. You are in a world of shit, son, only you don't seem to realize it."

"Am not."

They looked at me like two judges at a dog show, only the dog has gone and peed on their shoes so now he has got no chance for a blue ribbon at all. The truth is, I was real upset about how they are not believing me even though I didn't tell them a single lie so far. And I'm not the only one in trouble here – Lorraine has gone and been found out about the drugs and this will finish her career as a prison guard. Cole Connors I didn't care about, or Donnie D, they knew what they're doing, but now Lorraine will hate my guts. But then she must not have cared about my guts anyway because she's been humping Cole all along ...

I felt very bad about that. I had gone and let myself fall for an unsuitable person. Again. Why am I like this? And now everyone will know about my stupidass ways and how dumb I have been regarding all this that has happened here. A giant ear has been listening to every dumb thing I said, practically listening in to my brain thinking stuff, so now the only secret I have got left is about Dean being dead and where he's buried, which is another big worry on top of all the rest. If I got blown out of the house as far as the cottonwoods, that means there must have been cops and rescue workers all around those trees, right where Dean got covered over. But that was two days ago now, and Kraus and Deedle are not acting like they know where Dean is, so maybe nobody noticed that fresh soil that slid down into the wash. So I have still got this one ace up my sleeve.

Kraus's phone rung in his pocket. He has got a very ordinary ring tone. He brung it out and listens, then he closed it and says to Deedle, "Go down to the front desk, there's a fax coming through for us. Our eyes only."

"Got it."

Deedle got up and left the room. Kraus says, "I'm waiting, Odell."

"I expect he'll be back soon."

"I'm waiting for *you* to tell me something I need to hear."

"Well, I don't know what that might be. And anyway, you wouldn't believe me even if I told you something, so why bother?"

"That's not the right attitude, Odell. That kind of an attitude is only going to sink you deeper in the poop than you already are. You're running out of friends fast. Agent Deedle and I came here prepared to be your friends, but you've treated us like enemies, told us untrue things and got us thinking you're deliberately withholding important information. This is something serious you've gotten yourself involved in here. Now, look, I can understand how you might've gone over to these people because you fell for Lorraine, but that's no excuse in the eyes of the law. You don't strike me as the lawbreaking type, Odell, so I'm prepared to give you the benefit of the doubt, but you've got to deliver something we can use. Will you do that?"

Well, I wanted to, but then I'd be confessing to murder, which I was prepared to do last Sunday because Chet made me feel bad about not being a decent Christian and so forth, so I wrote that letter to Condi, only now I don't want anybody knowing about that so it's a good thing I didn't mail the letter because I see everything different now. Maybe it was still in among the floor mess in the truck and got blown to smithereens like the phone, so I'm safe about that so long as I keep my mouth shut. Being a murderer and body hider as well as being mixed up in drugs is not what I need right now to improve my situation. And why did Agent Jim Ricker tell me lies?

"So, got anything you want to say to me?" asks Kraus.

I didn't have one single thing, so I crossed my arms over my chest, which hurt the hand that's bandaged but I kept it there so he knows I have got nothing to say about what he wants to know. That's how things stayed till Agent Deedle come back in with a sheet of paper which he showed to Kraus, who reads it twice then looks up at me very sharp around the eyes.

"Odell, are you a letter-writing kind of guy?"

"No."

"Only I've got a letter here with your name on it."

"Well, I don't see how."

He showed it to me. It's a fax copy of the letter to Condi.

"I didn't write that."

"You haven't read it yet."

I pretended to read it then gave it back to him.

"I didn't write that."

"A handwriting expert will find out just by comparing this with an example of your own handwriting."

I held up my bandaged hand. "Got a problem."

"That'll mend. You aren't going anywhere, Odell."

"Why would I write a letter like that to Condoleezza Rice that says I killed someone. I'd have to be totally crazy to do that."

"Uhuh. Did you expect a reply by return mail?"

"No."

"Maybe later in the month?"

"I didn't expect any kind of a reply because I didn't write it."

Kraus gave me this look says he's disappointed in what I'm saying. "Odell, when you got pulled out of the wreckage there your clothes got cut away at the hospital they're so torn up and filthy, and we took a peek inside your wallet, that's our job, and guess what we found. Well, you wouldn't need to guess, would you. A picture of Condoleezza Rice. Now that is an unusual thing to carry around, wouldn't you say? What's your interest in the Secretary of State, Odell? Is she a target in some assassination plot, or maybe she's the object of your affection, which is it?"

"I don't know how that got there. Maybe you put it there."

"You're accusing us of fabricating evidence against you?"

I didn't say anything. Kraus put the fax away in his jacket and says, "There's a forensics team still going over the Lowry place. We'll have them dig up that so-called empty grave again. That'd be smart, to stash him in a hole that's already been opened up twice and videoed as being empty. Maybe you're smarter than you look, Odell."

"No I am not."

They both got up. Kraus says, "You think things over. Think hard and you might just see where your safest course lies. It's not just dope now, Odell, it's murder, even if the victim was a terrorist."

I asked him, "Where did that letter come from?"

"Head office in Washington."

"No, I mean how did they get it?"

"That would be classified information. Admit you wrote it and maybe I could give you some background. Just to help you do the right kind of thinking, I'll tell you this much – the informant who handed this in says he got it from inside the cab of a Dodge truck with lawnmowers in the back. He's after that Lowry reward money. Think hard, Odell."

They went away then. Things did not look good for yours truly, I had to admit. So how come the ones that stole the truck and set the bomb are now trying to get reward money from the letter? Wouldn't they be admitting they did the deed and get in trouble over it? There has gotten to be way too much confusion here since I woke up with a sore head and sore hand.

Then the nurse comes back in and asks is there anything she can get me. Well, a helicopter would be nice, only I can't fly one, so I asked for lemonade. She says they don't have that but will get me some apple juice, which I don't like but I didn't want to offend her by saying so.

In the movies the guy in the hospital that wants to leave just gets up and goes to the closet and puts his clothes on and walks out, so I gave that a try. Only there's no clothes in the closet, too messed up to keep after going through a bomb blast like they did, and when I went over to the door in my hospital gown with the peekaboo slit up the back there's a cop sitting in a chair right next to the door. "Forget it," he says, so I got back in bed and drunk my juice when that got brung to me. Even if it was liquid sunshine it would've tasted like piss, the situation I'm in.

I think I slept for awhile after that. You might think that sleeping all day Tuesday would be enough but no. Then I got woken up by the door opening and closing, and here's Lorraine coming over to sit beside me looking real concerned for my health.

"Listen," she says, "don't be such a selfish prick. *Tell* them."

Well, that was not what I'm wanting to hear from her, which got my back up so to speak. She's glaring at me like I'm someone did something wrong to her, which I never did, I didn't do anything.

"Well?"

"Huh?"

"Odell, I'm in big trouble about this. They tapped my phone and have got me and Cole discussing the operation openly and —"

"You had an operation?"

She has done me wrong but I still cared, how about that for dumb.

Lorraine rolled her eyes and says, "The *drug* operation. They played it back for me and now me and Cole are toast because of it. That wire tap wouldn't have been put in place if you hadn't done what you did, Odell. You *owe* me."

"What did I do?"

"Jesus... okay, they just now showed me this letter you wrote to that woman, that Condi Rice, where you say you killed Dean and buried him in the yard. Is that true?"

"No."

I made a decision on the spot about that. From now on I'm denying everything till I get a lawyer. I am not a liar by nature but I am between that rock and that hard place we have all heard about.

"Odell, they showed me the letter. It says you did."

"It's a forgery they made to trap me."

She squirmed around in her chair some, then she says, "Now, you listen to me, you big idiot, Cole and me are look-ing at serious prison time because of you. Those agents, they told me confidentially they can help if they get what they want, which is the terrorists, not Cole and me, we're little fish. They say you know something, so why don't you tell them and then they'd go easy on Cole and me. You don't want us to get thrown in prison, do you?"

"I don't know anything. And I didn't *do* anything."

"Oh, jeez, Odell, can't you think about other people for once in your life? Look what I did for you, offered you a steady job with perks over the moon, let you keep all the lawnmowing money for yourself and sleep in my house… that isn't even *there* anymore! What did you do to make some-one want to blow you up like that?"

"I don't know…"

"Like hell you don't! You're hiding something, Odell. You put on this big dumb ox routine but I can see through it now. Too late I see it, this other side of you, the terrorist connection. You've got to tell them what they want to know, Odell. They're digging up the yard out there where you buried Dean, so when they find him they'll know it's true you killed him… Why the *fuck* did you put it in a letter? You aren't dumb, I know that now, so why did you do that, Odell? What's the hidden agenda here?"

While she yelled at me I felt a very sad thing. I felt my affection for Lorraine seeping out of me like steam from a leaky boiler, all those fine feelings about love and getting married blowing away in little wisps of vapor. I can't stop it, can't plug it up, it just has to leak away now that I know the truth about her and Cole. It only took a little while, maybe less than a minute for all that love steam to drift away on the breeze and get replaced by ordinary air. Having that steam inside of me made me feel good for a week now, and feeling it ease out of me like a silent fart left me empty and alone, not a good feeling.

"Well? Say something."

"I don't *know* anything and I didn't *do* anything."

"Selfish," she says, slitting her eyes at me. "Selfish and mean and unbelievably vicious, to let two people that offered the hand of friendship and employment and got smacked down for it, to let them get burned this way ... Christ, Odell, just tell the feds what they want to know and they'll go a whole lot easier on all of us ... Can't you see what it is you're doing? Odell?"

"I'll think about it," I said. What else could I say? She didn't love me and never had, it was all in the mind as the saying goes, and it made my mind a happier place for a week but it isn't like that anymore. My mind is a cold place now with snowflakes and icicles. I could tell them where Dean is really buried and do Lorraine a favor even if it makes more trouble for me, but the fact is I wanted to punish her a little for letting me fall in love like that, cupid's dart, and not returning the feeling one little bit, I could see that now.

"Think about it? You better do more than that, Odell."

"I need to get out of here."

"No shit."

"You have to get me out."

"Yeah, how?"

"I don't know. You get me out and I'll sign a legal paper that says where Dean is buried."

That brung her up short. She looks at me then says, "So he *is* dead?"

"I won't answer that question without a lawyer right here says I can."

"You ... you aren't a normal person."

"Am too."

"No normal person could refuse to tell a sister if her own brother's dead or not."

She did have a point there even if I don't care for her anymore, so I told her, kind of a teaser to keep her going, I told her, "He didn't suffocate from the burying."

"Meaning he was already dead."

"My lips are sealed about that. It was an accident but I'm real sorry."

"Sorry doesn't cut it, Odell. What can I tell them?"

"Tell 'em ... I'm thinking about it. Meantime, I want you to get me out of here."

"That's just ridiculous. There's an armed cop outside the door and those FBI guys are hanging around this place like it's their headquarters. Cole and me are both under the hammer for smuggling drugs into a state penitentiary. We're looking at hard time here, Odell, and it's your fault for telling the world Dean's a terrorist! If you had've kept your mouth shut about that and finding Bree in the freezer none of this would've happened, he'd just be another missing person like all those hundreds of others that take a hike every year. But because of you we're all under the spotlight now. For fuck's *sake*, Odell . . . do the right thing . . ."

Lorraine was real upset now, with tears etcetera, not faking it. This made me feel bad all over again and wanting to tell her the truth that will get passed on to Kraus and Deedle, only I could feel myself holding back just like they all told me I am, so that part is true.

"Lorraine?"

"What!"

"You don't need to shout at me."

"I can't help it, Odell, you make me so mad."

"I'm sorry. Do you watch *CSI*?"

"What's that got to do with anything?"

"But do you?"

"Yeah, not every week, so what?"

"Well, is it true what they can do, examining dead people and finding out stuff, how it happened and so forth? Is that part true?"

"I guess. What's your point?"

"What I'm thinking, if they brung in the CSI team to look at Dean, for example, which I'm not saying it *is* Dean, I'm just saying some dead person, brung the team in to do an examination, would they find out the exact truth of how that person died?"

"Probably. Is that what you want, to get Dean examined? Did you kill him, Odell? If you did I forgive you, he was asking for trouble all his life . . . only now it's important to say what happened and let other people off the hook. It's not just about you, Odell, other people are involved here. Do you want me to tell those agents to bring in a CSI team and find out what happened to Dean?"

"If it *was* Dean, which I'm not saying it was."

"Is that what you want, Odell?"

"I . . . okay."

There, I had gone and done it, said what I was scared to say. But the CSI team would be able to see that I didn't hit him hard with that baseball bat and it was accidental that he died that way. They would see this with their special examinations that they do and maybe charge me with accidental manslaughter instead of murder, that's what I'm hoping here, plus it was a first offense and I feel real bad about it and told the truth at last so maybe they won't go so hard on me as I've been thinking, death penalty and so forth for premedicated murder, that's the worst. So now I'm hopeful for something not so bad as that and it's a big weight off of my shoulders all of a sudden.

"I'll tell them, Odell, but they're going to want to know where Dean is. Are you saying he's not in the back yard like you wrote?"

"He's over by the cottonwoods in this little dry wash where the stream kind of cut away the bank. He's under there, they'll see the new dirt I brung down to cover him up."

She looked at me a long time with this expression which I don't know how to say what it means, like she can't believe me or she hates me, I just can't say. Then she says very slow, "When did it happen?"

"Monday night. He come downstairs and says he can hear a prowler or something, whispers it in my ear . . ."

"I know, you told me that part about the whispering. Then what happened?"

"Well, he had this shotgun in his hand…and I already saw the hole in back of the house and I figured it's for me…and when I saw that shotgun I guess I thought…He's come to murder me. Which he would not have whispered me awake if that's what he wants to do, just shot me while I'm sleeping… but I didn't think of that fast enough and just kind of…hit him with the bat to save my life, I guess…"

"With a bat? A baseball bat?"

"Uhuh, had it right there beside me for protection. On account of the hole."

She looked down at her lap, gone all quiet now, then she got up and looks at me again with the strangest expression. I'm thinking this is where she says it's okay, I didn't mean to do what I did and she can understand how it happened the way I told her and it's okay about all of this. What she says is, "You lame-ass idiot son of a bitch. I hope they burn you good for all this trouble you caused." Then out she goes, leaving me feeling very confused over what she said, that last part.

In a little while Kraus and Deedle come back in with this little laptop computer. They said to tell the whole thing again about how I killed Dean accidental and where he's buried etcetera. Deedle types up the whole story while I'm telling it, real fast with his fingers, then this little scroll of paper comes winding out of the computer and Kraus gave me a pen to sign at the bottom, which I did. He says to me, "You did the right thing owning up to all this, Odell."

"I know it. I feel better now."

"That's good. We've told the forensics team to check out

the cottonwoods. They already found the backyard hole is empty an hour ago."

"Did you call the CSI team yet? If they look at his skull they'll see I didn't hit him hard. I think maybe Dean had one of those thin skulls you hear about that break real easy."

"They're on their way."

"But it won't be the TV team, will it. It'll be some other bunch."

"That's right, Odell, it won't be the TV team. They're busy today solving other crimes."

"Well, I didn't expect it would be them. Uh, can you tell the nurse or someone I'm real hungry now?"

"Sure. You take it easy."

Out they went. I felt good after all that confessing and signing, plus real hungry like I said. And my head and my hand didn't hurt so bad anymore, which is a sign that confession is good for the body as well as the soul. After awhile the nurse come in and asks what I feel like eating, which I told her a Whopper, but they don't have those on the menu but she'll see what she can do. Then later she come back with food on a tray for me, good and hot the way I like it, beef and potatoes and corn. I ate it all and wished there was a second helping, but when she come to take the tray away I got told I'll have to wait for the regular evening mealtime which is still a couple hours away yet so I'll just have to be patient. I told her I would be and she went away again. Then I had to use the bathroom, this little room opens up from mine, a special bathroom just for me, not down the corridor someplace so this is a private room they have got me in and I appreciate that.

Then Kraus and Deedle come back and they did not look

happy. Kraus says, "Odell, do you stand by the statement you gave to us earlier?"

"Uhuh."

"You're sure? Think carefully."

"I'm sure."

"Because we've looked where you told us, in the dry wash right beside the cottonwoods. And he isn't there."

"Huh?"

"Dean isn't there, Odell."

"But ... that's where I put him ..."

"Well, he isn't there, so now what do you have to say for yourself?"

"I ..."

But there was nothing *to* say. It was like the bed under me vanished and I'm falling through space. Dean not there? How could that be?

"You've let us down, Odell. We thought we were making progress with you, but now we see it was all a waste of time. Are you happy that you made us dig out a second gravesite that's as empty as the first? Is this some kind of weird game for you, Odell? Because we don't like it."

"I ... that's where I put him, honest! Someone must've come and took him away again ..."

"Yeah? Like who?"

I thought hard. Only one name sprung to mind.

"Agent Jim Ricker," I told them, but they did not look like they believed this.

FIFTEEN

Now you can imagine what kind of confusion I had inside my head as night come down. When the evening meal come along I did not eat it, that's how messed up I was by this big surprise about Dean not being there. How could that have happened? I turned it this way and that and could not come up with any kind of an answer to the situation. My head started to hurt again I'm so messed up, and the nurse brung me a little glass of something for the pain which tasted awful but I drunk it anyway.

There's a TV in the room so I watched the news and there's the house, totally flattened by the Dodge bomb, so it's a real miracle I come out of that alive. They had this helicopter camera to show what it looks like from the air and the crater in the driveway is like something where a meteor hit the earth it's so damn big. The driveway isn't even there anymore, just this giant hole from the road clear to where the house used to be, only now it's all blown away like a twister come through and sucked it up, every piece of timber and shingle, and then spit it all out again every whichway. It was a nice old house and did not deserve this that happened to it. The barn is gone too, with my Monte Carlo way over yonder on its back like a dead bug with its wheels in the air.

So I have got these Three Big Questions. Who turned the truck into a bomb and why? Who is Jim Ricker and why won't he step forward now to explain himself? And who the hell took Dean's body away? Plus other questions not so big, like who is it found the letter in the truck and turned it in for reward money? And why didn't Lorraine tell me about this big affair she's having with Cole Connors? And what is this big argument going on between her and Chief Webb that got them screaming at each other over the phone Monday night? I didn't have the answer to a single one of these, and the painkiller drug wouldn't let me think anything through so I could maybe come up with the facts to explain even a little bit of it all. I did know one thing, though – I was in deep doo-doo as the saying goes.

I watched TV on and off, not really following anything I'm feeling so weird and confused. One time when I went to the bathroom again I went to the wrong door and there's another cop out there in the corridor snoozing on a chair. I thought about sneaking past him while his eyes are closed but there was still this problem of no clothes and no money and no car and nowhere to run to anyway, so I closed the door again and went to the right one this time, feeling very sorry about everything and not knowing what to do about any of it.

I fell asleep later on but then got woke up again by

someone coming in the room. My eyes come open and there's a nurse standing there with a wheelchair next to her.

"Get up," she says, and the voice give her away even if the lights are low. It's Lorraine, only how come she's wearing a nurse's uniform? "Get up, Odell, we don't have a lot of time." I couldn't do or say anything for a moment and she says, "Will you please get the fuck out of that bed?"

I did it and she shoved me down into the wheelchair. "Sit tight and don't wriggle around," she tells me, then pulls the chair back and rolls it to the door. Lorraine is helping me escape! She spoke strong and hurtful words to me before but now she's come around in her thinking and is helping me escape! So right then I fell back in love with her, which it was hard to fall out of in the first place so I'm glad to be back there in love again. This has got to be the riskiest thing, getting me away like this in disguise like nurse and patient this way, and what about the cop outside the door?

Well, I needn't have worried about that because the cop outside the door is Larry Dayton who I thought must've been fired by now because he copied that interview tape and also sold the Okeydokey DVD to Fox News so his ass should be in a sling about these things. But there he is, tipping me a wink as Lorraine trundled me past him and away down the corridor, so now this is a conspiracy to get me away from the FBI with two people not just one, which makes sense for the *Mission Impossible* adventure caper this is turning out to be.

She wheeled me to the elevators and pressed the button. There is no one else around it's so late at night, and the elevator when it hisses open is empty too, like it was all arranged that way special by Fate to make the plan succeed. In we went and she presses the bottom button. The doors closed with a whisper and we started sinking.

"Lorraine…"

I could barely talk my body is so slowed down by drugs.

"Shut up and listen. I'm doing this to get back at Andy Webb. I want him in trouble over putting a man who's about to get fired from the Police Department in charge of guarding your door, and I want him fired about what happened a long time ago between him and me."

"Uh…"

"Shut up. You asked me about that, so here's the answer – Andy and me had a fling I guess you could call it when I'm underage for sex, and there was photos we took when we're drunk that I kept all this time, so there's nothing he can do to me when he gets fired over this without getting into deeper shit about that, so he can kiss his campaign for Sheriff good-bye and good riddance, I've had about enough of that guy trying to run my life. Did you follow all that, Odell?"

"Uhuh…"

"Officer Dayton, he plans on selling his story to Hollywood so he wanted in at the last scene helping get you away. He wants Ashton Kutcher to play him, but that's a stretch, Dayton isn't that good-looking. Anyway, he's helping out. Are you drugged right now?"

"Uhuh…"

"Well, that's okay, we've got someone else that can't stand Andy waiting for you in the carpark to drive you away, so just sit tight and soon this'll be all over with."

We slowed down and the doors hissed open. We're a little way down from Reception it looks like but there's nobody around, just these shining corridors spotless clean with the rubber wheels making a squeaking sound as Lorraine spins me around and heads away from the front desk, back the other way to an emergency exit that we go through and then we're outside where the air smells different and the stars are blazing. She wheeled me very rapid along a path with bushes either side.

Lorraine says, "You're probably asking yourself why I'm doing this. Well, the answer is, I don't want to see you take the fall for someone as fucked-up as Dean. I don't know what went on between you, but I don't want the responsibility of knowing you went to prison for a long time over getting involved with Dean like you did. He just isn't worth that on my conscience. And I'm sorry I spoke those harsh words to you earlier, I was just so upset about everything. But nobody should take the blame for Dean, that's my point, so once you're away from here I want you to go wherever it is that you feel safest, Odell. Go to people you can trust and keep your head down for a long long time is my advice to you. I know you like me, and if things had been different who knows, maybe you and me could've moved the relationship up another notch. But happiness just isn't in the cards for us, Odell, we have to face up to that and move on with our lives. Dean went and messed up those lives for us but there's no use crying over it now. The important thing is for you to get away and go to those people I mentioned, those people you know you can trust because they think the same way you do. Those are the ones to go to, Odell, do you understand what I'm saying or are you too doped up?"

"Mmmmm…"

She wheeled me to the end of the path and then across to the carpark where there is a big car waiting with a guy opening the door. I know I've seen him before but can't remember the name or where.

"Any problems?" he asks.

"Like clockwork," says Lorraine, helping him get me out of the wheelchair and into the car, then she says, "Odell, this is Detective Sergeant Vine. You met him when they came out to take Bree away in the coroner's ambulance, remember?"

"Uhuh…"

"Detective Sergeant Vine wants Andy's job once they get rid of him, so he's motivated by that, okay."

"Uhuh…"

It was just incredible the way these three have got together to screw Andy Webb and help me escape this way, and my heart was just filled to overflowing with gratefulness about what they're doing, the risks they're taking to do this for me. They say a man doesn't know who his friends are till the chips are down and now I know this is true because these three have gone and done this against the odds and very risky for all concerned. And now I am free!

"Take care," says Lorraine and turns away with the wheelchair before I can say Thank you, then Vine gets behind the wheel and starts the engine. What a wonderful sound the getaway car makes when you know it's all going to work, the planning and the risk and now someone that shouldn't be held in custody against his will is out of confinement and making his escape in the middle of the night to freedom!

"Buckle up, Odell," he says as we left the carpark and turned onto the road. I fumbled the seatbelt into place and noticed the dashboard clock says 2.37 so they have done this at the right time when most folk are sleeping. How did these guys get together so fast to do this? I am so impressed about how smooth it has gone so far, and what could go wrong now?

Vine turned sideways to look at me, then he passes me something in his hand, three little pills. "Take those, two caffeine pills and one speed, that'll wake you up out of the narcotic haze you're in right now. Here, use this." He hands me a plastic squeeze bottle of Gatorade to wash them down. I wrestled the pills into my mouth and washed them down okay even if I spilled a little Gatorade down my chin.

"I've got some clothes and sneakers your size in the back seat. We'll get you changed into them when we get to where we're going. This'll work, Odell. You're gonna get away with this."

"Uhuh…"

"I can't wait to see Old Andy's face when the shit hits the fan. That guy is a goner, trust me. And I want to thank you, Odell, for making it possible for me to get rid of someone that outlived his usefulness. The whole Department thanks you. You have got no idea how low morale has sunk around here with Webb at the wheel. But that'll be changing real soon, and you played a part in it."

"Uhuh…"

I think I dozed off even with all this excitement going on, but then woke up again when Vine stopped the car. He reached over into the back seat then put a bunch of clothes into my lap. "Get out of that gown and into these, Odell. Now listen, see that car over there, the little white one? That car belongs to a girlfriend of my niece. She's always leaving the damn thing unlocked and the keys under the mat because she's always losing them, which is a dumb thing to do but very useful for our needs. That's your escape vehicle, Odell. You aren't getting out of the gown. You've got to do that before you can change into the clothes."

I started wrestling my way out of the gown and he goes on, "I'm going to give you five hundred dollars, Odell, to help you get to wherever it is you're going. My niece's friend is out of town for a whole week with her parents checking out colleges in the east, so the alarm won't be raised on that car for awhile, plenty of time for you to get there. Will you be going interstate, Odell?"

"Mmmmm..."

"Need a hand with the shirt?"

"Uhuh."

He reached behind me and helped out getting my arm into the second sleeve. I had to lift my butt to get the pants on but managed that part okay, only it feels peculiar to have pants on but no underpants, Vine has forgot about those but I guess it isn't all that important. I fumbled the zipper closed and tied the sneakers which have got no socks, and then I'm ready. He says to take off the bandage from around my head because it'll make me stand out, so I unwound it with a little help and now I'm really ready.

"The money is in your pocket, Odell. Try not to do anything to attract the attention of the law. Don't exceed the speed limit or drive erratically. I'd advise you to go directly to the people who can help you get even further away, whoever those people happen to be. Don't waste any time, because the more time you waste the more opportunity for things to go wrong, so just go directly to them and your chances for success are multiplied accordingly, okay?" He put out his hand. "Good luck, Odell."

"Thank you...and thank Lorraine for me, will you? She went away too fast."

"I'll do that. Go on now before someone at the hospital realizes you've gone."

I got out of the car and went across the street to this little white Honda and opened the door, so he's right, the girl that owns it is real careless. Then I went back to Vine's car. "Where did you say the keys are?"

"Under the driver's mat, Odell. Good luck."

I went back and he's right, the keys are right there where he said. I squeezed myself inside the car and put the seat way back as far as it'll go, then fumbled the ignition key into the dash. The engine come to life sounding good. I put her in gear and away I drove. The needle says the gas tank is totally full which is a good thing, I won't have to stop anytime soon so I can just keep going and going like the Energizer Bunny.

Only where?

Where am I supposed to go? The first place it occurred to me to go was back home to Yoder, Wyoming, but then what? My old man, he'd tell me to give myself up all over again, I know he would, so forget that, I didn't want to see his face or hear his voice anyway, so that's that plan gone out the window. I didn't even know what part of Callisto I'm in, never mind knowing where the hell I'm supposed to go now. Then I saw a sign that says this way to I-70 so I went that way and got out of town after a little while and then onto the interstate heading west. Why west and not east? That's just the way back towards some places I know, I guess. Callisto is the furthest east I ever went. Manhattan is further east but I don't think I can go back to my original plan of going there and signing up for the Army, not with my face going to be on the TV news again when they find out I escaped like I did.

My brain was starting to come alive with the new drugs Vine gave me, humming and buzzing instead of wanting to snooze, and as I drove along at a steady seventy-five miles per hour I got to thinking about how Lorraine and Larry and Detective Sergeant Vine had got together to save my ass. I thought about the different reasons they said they're doing it, well, okay, Lorraine kind of spoke on behalf of Larry Dayton, but what she said made sense, kind of, and Vine would get to have Andy Webb's job when Andy got fired because I escaped from under the nose of one of his cops that's already in trouble, so that was his reason. Then I got to thinking about how Lorraine was very up and down in regard to her feelings for me in the hospital and I wondered how she got in touch with those other two to set up the escape plan. It must not have been very long, maybe five or six hours. And how would she have known they'd do what she wanted ahead of time to approach them like that? That was way risky, to approach two cops and ask them if maybe they'd like to help her get a suspect in a federal case busted out of custody like she did.

This question about how she did all that in so short of a time went around and around inside my head like a dog chasing its own tail. I tried to think about other things, like where should I go from here, but that other question kept whirling back into my thoughts, it just would not go away. I was thirsty now and wished I had kept the bottle of Gatorade but I left that in Vine's car. He was certainly very well prepared to help me escape, with the clothes and the wakeup pills and the friend of his niece's car with the keys right there and the door unlocked. And the hospital was very empty even for a hospital at night, I mean not a soul around to stop Lorraine from wheelchairing me away. And how did she get hold of that nurse's uniform anyway? Now that I thought about it, the whole caper had gone about as smooth as a TV show adventure with nothing getting in the way to mess things up.

Like a TV show. A TV show is how it went. A TV show has got a script that gets wrote out on paper and they rehearse it and then do it with the cameras rolling. My getaway was a TV show. I started to sweat big time, could not stop my heart going *budumbudumbudum* as that one thought kept on spinning around until the dog caught hold of his tail and tasted it. It tasted like dog tail, the only real thing going on tonight, I could see it now. They had got together, those three, Lorraine and Larry and Vine, and put together a script to fool me. Or more likely it was Kraus and Deedle come up with the idea and roped Lorraine in first because they know I have got this sweet spot for her like I do, or did anyway, and she said the best way to fool me is to use the fact that I don't like Andy Webb, who was most likely the next one brung into the plan and Andy brung in Larry Dayton because he already told me Larry is in big trouble about what he did . . . and they brung in Vine next with his bullshit story about wanting to take over Andy's job when he gets fired for letting me escape . . . And there isn't a single speck of anything real in the entire thing, it's just a TV script they put together and worked out all the bugs till it's a smooth story like on TV, and then they sprung it on me while my head was ripped with painkiller drugs so I can't see how stupid it all is. How could they have expected me to fall for it once I got to thinking about it all? Did they think I was stupid or something?

Well, there it was, the one thing that made it all hang together, the one thing nobody likes to admit about how people think about him. They thought I was stupid, every single one of them. They thought I'm so fucking stupid all they have to do is put together a bullshit TV script and spring me from the hospital ward like in *Mission Impossible* and set me up with a car nobody'll miss for a week with a full gas tank ... and let's not forget the way Lorraine and Vine both told me more than once to go find my friends to be with in safety so the get-away succeeds in its mission ... which is not to let me get away, it's to follow me and find out where my terrorist buddies are holed up, most likely with Dean running the show ... because why would they believe Dean is dead when I told them two different places he's buried and he's not in either one, so they figured that's all bluff on my part to buy myself time in which to plan my big escape ... but they know I'm not smart enough to get away on my own so they put their heads together and helped me out, knowing I'm too dumb to see how it's all been arranged like a TV show ...

Except I did notice. And now, believe it or not, I started to cry about how dumb they think I am. This is a hard thing to say about the crying, but that is what I did, started crying because all those people think I'm so dumb. And what made it worse, I had to admit they're right, I am dumb. I am a big dumb stupid idiot, that's me, for covering up the way I killed Dean accidental, then for pretending to be him, then for getting sucked into the drug-pushing thing with Lorraine because I liked her and thought maybe she liked me, which I see now was the biggest dumb thing I thought, she always looked on me as a fool...and then for writing that dumb letter to Condi Rice, and letting them – whoever they are – steal the truck and turn it into a bomb...and last of all, being dumb enough not to see how they let me escape like putting a rat into a maze and watching him from above as he scuttles this way and that, up one skinny corridor and down another searching for the cheese, which is this terrorist cell they all think I belong to.

Watching from above. They have got a tracking bug somewhere inside the car and are following me along I-70 in a FBI car with this little screen inside going *blipblipblip* as the little glowing dot gives out its signal. Or maybe overhead in a chopper. Or way overhead with spy satellites tracking me like Jim Ricker kidded me about. Maybe Jim Ricker is the real terrorist here, I don't know because I am a big dumb idiot that should've kept going and not stayed one minute in Callisto, kept going to Manhattan, Kansas, and enlisted in the Army like I planned. But I walked through the wrong door when my car broke down and got swept up in Something Big that I still don't understand how big it really is, and all those people tracking me and trying to fool me, they don't know either, so there is plenty of ignorance to go round, which made me feel a little better and I quit crying and started to think like a normal man, which it is high time I got to be one of those.

So I am being tracked. Going nowhere. In the movies the guy in the car with the bug finds it and puts it on another car that goes in a different direction and fools the bad guys following the bug with their blipscreen. Maybe the bug is tucked away in a wheel well nice and convenient, or it could be stuck anywhere inside the car where I can't find it even if I pulled the whole thing apart, those things are small. The speed and caffeine had took hold very nicely and my brain fizzed with all kinds of things I might do to get out of this Bad Situation, but as soon as one of these popped into my skull it got smacked down again for being totally stupid and unworkable. And I was hungry again too, seeing as I was too upset to eat that evening meal on account of the big surprise about Dean not being buried near the cottonwoods anymore. So now I'm starving hungry on top of everything else, but this was a problem easy to take care of at the next big gas station and truck stop which is only another ten miles to go this sign tells me – *Brubaker's All-Niter, We Never Close.*

I pulled off the interstate and parked with all the other cars, a fair number even at this hour of the morning. Over on the other side of the gas station/diner with the big neon Brubaker's sign there's a dozen or so eighteen-wheelers lined up neat in rows with their diesels grumbling while the drivers are inside chowing down or even taking a shower, Brubaker's has got this service also a sign tells me, but I'm only interested in food right now.

I went in and the bright lights hurt my eyes for a moment then I got used to it. I went and found a booth to sit in alone and private, orange vinyl, then a waitress come along looking perky even if it's way past 3 am now and asks what I want. I ordered a double cheeseburger plus fries and a large Coke, plus coffee to keep my mind working overtime on a way out of this situation I am in. Only a smart plan is going to save me now, and I'm not exactly sure how smart I am even if I figured out I'm a runaway rat with a bug up my ass. But I had made up my mind on one thing – I would never again shed a tear for how dumb I am, this is not my fault, just the way I was born and nothing to do with me you might say, and anyway I'm not so dumb as everyone thinks, so there you go. From now on I would use every bit of smart in me to figure out a way to stay free.

The food got brung out and I ate like a starving man, which I am, but not anymore after I got through eating everything and was drinking down the last of the Coke. I used the bathroom and had them give me another tall coffee to go, which I carried out to the car and already I'm asking myself if I should keep going west or maybe go north, not that it made any difference to me.

I'm standing there with the key in my hand asking myself this when I noticed a guy over by the exit with a piece of cardboard in his hand wanting to be given a lift. I went on over and the cardboard has got *DENVER* wrote on it in big letters. It is just a young guy, maybe eighteen, and my mind with the new smart part took over my mouth.

"Hi."

"Hi," he says back.

"I can get you to Denver."

"Okay, great." He looked real pleased, probably not hopeful of getting a ride until I come along. He was dressed kind of shabby which most people will not allow in their car, but I would, even if it's not my car.

"This way," I said, and we started walking over to the Honda. "You'll have to do all the driving, is that okay?"

"Sure, I'm a good driver."

"Can I see your license just to be sure?"

He dug it out of his jeans and showed me. Wendell Richard Aymes dob 23-6-89.

"Okay," I said, "this is the situation. This is not my car, it belongs to a friend, uh, Feenie Myers." I used Feenie's name because it's hard to make up a name on the spot that sounds real, otherwise I would've come up with something like Susan Smith or whatever. "Feenie goes to college in Durango, so this is her parents' address I'm giving you, okay? Uh, 1286 Newton Drive in Lakewood, that's in Denver."

"I know, I'm a Denverite."

"Well, good. Now Feenie is expecting this car back tomorrow, only I've got this situation here with one of the lady cooks over there in Brubaker's. She wants me to stay over, you know, and she's real pretty, but then I've got to get Feenie's car back to her like I promised, which I'm a man of my word about stuff like that."

"You want me to drive the car to Denver?"

"That's it."

"Without you in it?"

"That's it exactly. I'll hitch a ride maybe tomorrow or the day after, depending, but meantime Feenie gets her car back and I didn't break my promise, that's important."

"You'd trust me to do that?"

"Sure, because if you steal the car or crash it or whatever, I've got your name and driver's license number. You got a pen I can write it down?"

He dug in his rucksack and brung out pen and paper which I wrote down the details of his license and also Feenie's parents' fake address for him, then I give him the keys and a hundred dollars for his trouble. Wendell was so excited about driving himself all the way home to Denver he's grinning like a game show winner.

"Hey, thanks, man. I'm a responsible driver, I won't wreck it. Good luck with your girlfriend."

"Thanks. Now don't go over the speed limit, okay? The Highway Patrol, they won't believe I handed you the keys like this and then we're both in trouble."

"I'll keep it under the limit, depend on that. Hey, thanks again, this is the best thing that happened in a long time."

"Okay then."

He got in and started her up, then headed for the exit with a wave through the window. When he got out of the parking lot he aimed for the interstate ramp and then he's gone from sight, *blipblipbliping* his way across Kansas and Colorado with the trackers following along behind like fish on a line. It felt good to know I fooled them with the smart intelligence they don't know I have got, which I used to think up the next part of the plan, which is go over to the truck parking area and wait for a driver to come out.

That part only took ten minutes or so in which I drunk down my coffee, and here comes a trucker with a beard halfway to his waist which has got this fat gut hanging over a rodeo belt and a big cowboy hat with a bunch of fancy feathers in front of it. I kind of stood up straight to let him know I want to talk to him but soon as he's in talking distance he says, "I don't take no riders ever, my policy."

"Okay," I said, because what else could I say.

He marched on past me in these high-heeled cowboy boots and goes to a big rig, orange I think but it's hard to say what's a real color under the sodium lamps they have got on poles out there. He opens it up and sets his boot on the first step, then he turned back to me and says, "Okay, get in."

I went around to the other door and climbed up into that cab like a mountaineer and got settled in this big captain's chair with armrests. The driver is sat way over there on the other side of the cab getting comfy, then he puts her in gear and we started rolling slow across the asphalt to the exit which he eased us through and then across to the interstate ramp. The truck climbed up onto the highway and he run up through the gears like a piano player, real sure of what he's doing, and pretty soon we're going back east toward Callisto, which give me a nervous feeling but you know, they would not think I'm doing this so maybe it's for the best. He might take me as far east as St Louis, which is about as far as my plan was planned for the moment. I was hoping the next stage would come to me around daybreak.

"What's your story?" the driver asks me.

"I'm going home to St Louis," I said. "Then I'm joining the Army."

"Why?"

"They need men. They're begging for men, even paying a bonus."

"Better be a big one," he says.

"Big enough."

"What part of St Louis?"

I thought about that for two seconds. "East St Louis."

"Man, now I know why you want into the Army. That's a hole."

"Uhuh."

"That place has got a reputation. Drugs, domestic violence, crime, gangbangers, you name it they got it."

"Yeah."

"Someone should drop a bomb on East St Louis."

"That might work."

He laughed and told me his name is Gene. I told him I'm Wendell. It rolled right off of my tongue, a fib on wheels. I didn't care that I'm lying, so this must be the New Me coming out, so there's no arguing about it inside me, Truth versus Lies, I just didn't care about that anymore, only about getting away.

"That's a dangerous job, the Army."

"Someone's got to do it."

"My daughter, she rides around on planes with a gun in her armpit."

"She's a hijacker?"

He snorted. "She's there to stop hijackers. Federal Air Marshal. Those terrorists don't expect a woman to be packing, so that's her advantage. The money's real good but I worry about her. My boy too, he's working in freelance security over there in Iraq, goes to sleep with a machine gun under the pillow. Great wages, though."

"The world is a bad place."

"Got that right. Hear about that bomb close to here, that huge fucker that's big enough to take out a city block?"

"I heard about that."

"Some stupid terrorist bomber probably blew himself up, they do that sometimes. They should do it more often."

"Uhuh."

"You can't reason with some religious nut thinks he's doing it for Allah."

"Nope."

"Can't stop 'em either, just gotta kill 'em off one by one till the problem goes away and we can get back to normal."

"Right."

"You don't get Americans flying planes into skyscrapers and planting bombs to kill innocent people, that's strictly a Muslim thing, crazy fuckers."

"Yeah."

"Happened just a little ways down the road here, Callisto. They still can't find that ringleader, though, that Dean Lowry guy. What kind of an American does he think he is, doing shit like that? When they catch him they should waste him right there in whatever hole in the ground he lives, save the tax-payer some money for a trial. Shoulda done the same for Saddam. Everyone knows who's guilty and who's not. Trials, they just drag it out and make folks feel bad watching some asshole in a nice clean jail cell when he oughta be burning in Hell."

"I guess you'll be voting for Senator Ketchum then."

"Ordinarily I don't discuss politics, can't stand those guys, but the senator, he's got a hard line I can relate to. The other bunch, they talk the talk but they don't walk the walk, you know, like their heart isn't really in it and they'd prefer to pussyfoot around the problem, bring in the fucking UN and talk some more. Screw that. If someone shoots at me I shoot right back, never mind no asking why he did that and what's it all about. Ketchum, he'll blow them terrorist bastards back to Arabia where they belong. You know what I think every time I fill up the tanks on my baby here? I think how I'd be paying half as much if those terrorist assholes didn't exist.

Don't get me started on that subject. My daughter, I put her through college, she's real smart, and the job with the best pay she can find is packing a gun on airplanes, just flying around waiting for some shithead to start waving a knife and screaming about how he's gonna kill everyone for the glory of fucking Allah. You know what I'm talking about or you wouldn't be going in the Army."

"I sure do."

"I'd join up myself if I was twenty years younger. The Army, they shouldn't have to be offering bonuses just to join. Young guys should be trampling on each other to join up and do some good in the world. I wouldn't have thought that way five, six years ago, but it's a different world nowadays. Your folks backing you on this?"

"Yeah."

"Good people."

"Uhuh, my dad especially. He wanted me to get into professional football but when I said I'm joining the Army he said he's proud."

"Well, he should be. My kids, they make me proud. Their mother run off a long time ago."

I tried to think of something I could say about that, but nothing come to me and Gene seemed like he talked enough anyway, there was just some things he wanted off his chest and after he did that he's happy just to drive. Time rolled along and sooner than I expected here comes the sign that says *Callisto Next Two Exits*.

"There's some guy in hospital here," says Gene, talkative again. "The one that got blown up in that big blast. There's speculation I heard he's one of them himself, maybe a bombmaker went and got his wires crossed, something like that. They'll squeeze that sucker till he talks."

"Maybe he was just there accidental."

"Sure, and maybe I could teach my dog to drive a truck. They'll get it out of him all right, only when they do they won't broadcast it around for fear of scaring off the rest of them. I bet they're already building a new bomb. They don't ever give up, that kind."

Hearing him talk that way made me realize how it's going to be impossible to prove I had nothing to do with any terrorists, or that Dean had nothing to do with that kind either, only regular drug pushers, nothing religious with bombs and so forth. Kraus and Deedle, they didn't believe me, and Lorraine didn't at the end there, even helped them set me up for a big escape that'll lead them to the terrorists that don't even exist. Except who made Dean's truck into a bomb if they weren't terrorists? If it was a rival drug gang or whatever they would've taken out Dean nice and quiet with a gun, not gone and planted a bomb that made the news nationwide and around the world. It just does not make sense, and I could see why the FBI thinks there's something terroristic going on in Kansas, and maybe there is, but I would not have Clue Number One about any of that, I'm just a guy that his car broke down on the wrong road, only now nobody will believe me so I am fresh out of luck with regard to this.

Gene kept on driving east a couple hours or so and here come sunup all pink and beautiful across the entire sky ahead of us.

"Now that's a picture," says Gene. "I don't ever get tired of that, same with sundown, both ends of the day are just the prettiest things."

I watched the new day come up in front of me like watching a giant movie screen, not sitting in the cab of a truck with Thursday coming at me from the eastern horizon like this, and it made me wonder what kind of scenery I'll be looking at this time Friday.

It turned out Gene wasn't going as far as St Louis, he's dropping his load in Kansas City, so that's where he set me down. I told him Thank you and he told me Good luck and I strolled away wondering what to do next. It was around noon by then so I'm hungry again. I ate lunch at Denny's then found a Wal-Mart and got some socks and underwear which I changed into these in a gas station toilet and come out again feeling more comfortable but still no plan. Even if I got another ride and made it as far as St Louis, then what? What am I doing except enjoying a little freedom before they nab me again, which I know they will even if I sent them on a wild goose chase to Denver. When they figure that out they'll put my picture on the news and tell everyone to watch out for the six foot three terrorist that organized the Callisto bomb, a big lie but they won't care so long as it gets me captured again, and this time they won't bother with tricksy stuff like fake getaways, they'll just hammer me until I tell them what they want to hear, namely where is Dean Lowry, which is just one question of which I don't know the answer.

I found a little park and sat down to think about things next to this little pond with ducks, but instead of thinking I found myself just watching those ducks, even getting a kick out of the way they waggle their tail ends when they get out of the water, which they all did hoping I'll feed them, but I didn't have anything so they wandered off again quacking at each other, maybe saying what a cheap human I am. A movie hero would be thinking hard and teaming up with a good-looking woman who'll fall for him in around three seconds and agree to help him get past the cops or whoever, and then there'll be exciting moments with car chases and so forth while the hero works out who framed him or whatever and goes after him with the cops hot on his trail, but he gets to the bad guy and tricks a confession out of him that the cops will get to hear on an open phone line or it gets tape-recorded or whatever and now the hero isn't a Wanted Man anymore, plus he's got this gorgeous woman hanging around his neck as the credits roll. Me, I get to watch ducks walk away from me. I just did not know what to do. I didn't have a plan anymore. My brain had kind of shut down. I couldn't plan a damn thing beyond lunchtime. It was nice and shady by that duck pond and I didn't want to move.

The speed and caffeine Vine had given me was all wore off by then and I wanted to sleep real bad now, so I dragged myself off of that park bench and walked a few blocks till I come to a Motel 6 and got myself a room. I'm thinking if I can just sleep awhile maybe my brain will shake the cobwebs off and I can think of something smart that'll help me get away some more. I took my key with the room number tag along to door 8 and let myself in. The curtains were pulled shut against the sun and I sat on the bed asking myself if there was anything I should do before going to sleep. Well, I couldn't think of a single thing, so I stripped off and got between those nice fresh sheets naked and fell asleep, how about that.

It's night when I woke up. I took a shower but before I got in I took the bandage from around my hand. The wound there is scabbed over around the stitches and the bandage wasn't so clean anymore so it went in the trash bin. I used the little bar of soap that's always in these places and the little plastic bag of shampoo and dried myself off feeling good and rested and clean, plus I'm hungry again, so the next part of the plan is to eat supper and maybe do some more thinking about all this. I wondered what Wendell Richard Aymes did after he got to Denver and found out the Lakewood address is bogus. Most likely he parked the Honda someplace and walked away, which the FBI tracker team will wonder why the bug quit moving and investigate, maybe watching whatever house the car got dumped in front of. That made me laugh to think about them wasting their time like that.

I went out and ate a big meal, then on my way back to the motel I stopped at a liquor store and got myself a big old bottle of Captain Morgan and a sixpack of Bud to chase it down with and a couple bags of Doritos for a snack and settled myself down in front of the TV. They still did not know I fooled them because my face is not on the news yet, so I have got time still to come up with an escape plan. I watched two Cop shows and a Lawyer show then a Doctor show. All those people spoke very fast and never once stared at the wall or the sky trying to think what to say or what to do, all of them clever and handsome and knowing which way to turn to keep the story rolling along. Then I switched over to the inhouse movie and I had to laugh – it's *Donnie Darko*. I watched it from the beginning to the end, this story about a weird kid and jet plane engines falling out of the sky and this guy in a creepy rabbit suit and could not make head nor tail out of it, but maybe that's the Captain and Bud confusing me. The actor playing Donnie Darko looked nothing like Donnie D so I don't know why he calls himself that.

It was late by the time the movie ended and I'm ready for bed again. But then while I'm undressing a sad thing happened. I'm taking off my shirt that Detective Sergeant Vine gave me and I felt these little buttons on the inside of the shirt down near the bottom at the front. You have seen these, they're spare buttons for when you lose one, but generally there are just two of these, and this shirt had three, only the third one was not like the other two, a little bigger and sewed on a different way.

I studied that third button a long time, feeling this sad feeling about it. I had told myself they put a bug in the Honda and I sent that away west thinking I'm so smart, but this button here in my shirt they gave me for the getaway, it does not belong there. I told myself what it truly was but didn't want to believe it, so then I told myself again and this time I accepted that they are smarter than me after all except for the fact that they believe I'm leading them in the direction of a terrorist cell with Dean as the chief terrorist, which is wrong of them to believe that. I wasn't leading them anywhere, and did not know which way to go next, so this has got to stop right now.

I ripped the button off my shirt and hammered it with the sole of my sneaker but that was just rubber so no good. I could have taken it outside and found a rock or brick or something and smashed it, but that seemed like a waste of energy, so in the end I flushed it down the john. Then I sat and waited.

They talked about it for six or seven minutes, then knocked on the door. I was expecting them to blow it off the hinges and come storming in, a SWAT team in black with machine guns and goggles and so forth, but it was just Kraus and Deedle with a few uniformed cops standing behind them, no guns drawn or anything

"Hello, Odell," says Kraus.

"Hi."

"I guess you found it."

"Yeah."

"Did you smash it?"

"Flushed it."

"Why did you do that? Those things cost about five hundred bucks."

"I'm sorry."

"Sorry won't cut it anymore," says Deedle.

SIXTEEN

I had to sit between them in the back seat of a big SUV that took us away from Motel 6. They didn't talk much. I felt like I had let them down. Maybe I should have thrown the shirt on the back of a moving truck and run the other way, but with less than $400 where could I go? I couldn't be bothered anymore playing the fugitive game. They all think I'm some big-deal terrorist but I didn't do anything, so I will sit down and explain all this to them as many times as they want until they understand. This has all been a big misunderstanding and I want it to stop, and I told that to Kraus.

"It's out of our hands now, Odell," he tells me.

"We're handing you over," says Deedle, kind of smirking. Kraus just looked tired.

"Over to who?"

"Some other people in a different line of work."

"They don't do terrorism stuff?"

"They do terrorism stuff, they just do it different."

"Different how?" I wanted to know.

"You'll find out," says Deedle, still with the smirk. He really did not like me.

I was expecting a long drive back across Kansas, but they took me to some airport instead and I got put inside this small type of jet that Donald Trump flies around in with a special fitting on the chair arms for handcuffs. I forgot to say I have got handcuffs on now but not too tight, not hurting or anything, just there, and these got fastened to the arms of this chair they sat me in. It was a comfortable chair apart from not being able to move my hands. The engines got switched on, this high-pitched whine.

"See you around, Odell," Kraus told me, but I could tell he doesn't think that will really happen, he's just being polite. I kind of liked Kraus but not Deedle, who did not say Goodbye or anything else, just give me this look that says I don't matter anymore. Then they both left and another guy with a crewcut comes along and closed the door, which cut down a lot on the engine whine outside.

"All set?" he asked me.

"Sure. I was never on a plane before."

"Is that right. Well, this'll be a whole new experience for you, what we've got in store. If you get airsick let me know and I'll hold a puke bag under your face."

"Okay, thank you."

"Don't mention it."

He took a seat facing me but without the special handcuff fasteners and right away we started rolling. I could see other planes and buildings out the window but nothing big, no jumbo jets so this is just a small airport.

"How long will it take to get back to Callisto?" I asked him. "Not long, I bet."

"Callisto? Forget it."

"Are we going somewhere else?"

"Yeah, somewhere else."

"Where?"

"That's a big surprise, son. If I tell you ahead of time it'll spoil your enjoyment."

"Okay."

"You just relax and think nice thoughts, then hang onto those thoughts."

"Okay."

He looked at me as we rolled along slow past all those other small planes out there, but his face said nothing at all. He wasn't wearing a suit like the FBI, just a casual polo shirt and slacks and comfy-looking shoes. He's almost as big across the shoulders as me but not so tall, and he has got these little pits in his face make him look tough and hard, also his eyes never blinked no matter how long I looked at him, so after awhile I quit that and looked out the window, a little round window like a ship porthole. Now there aren't any buildings, just grass with little lamps along the edge of the asphalt.

Then the plane swung around sharp and stopped. I said to the guy, "Have you flown in a plane lots of times?" He nodded once but didn't say anything. He never took his eyes off me, like I'm real interesting to look at or something. The engines all of a sudden started screaming and we got rolling again only a lot faster, so fast the little lights outside went by *flickflickflick* and the vibration went all through me although nothing like a vibration bed I tried one time, this is different. Then the vibration stopped and my guts sunk inside me as we lifted off. It was the most exciting thing ever happened to me except for sex, which I have had three times now but not recently.

"Wow!" I said to the guy. He just smiled this very small smile.

The ground fell away and tipped sideways. It was like being on a slow roller-coaster and worth getting captured to experience this particular thrill of flying, which I would like to do again. The plane leveled off and all the lights of Kansas City were spread out below, but before long it's just clouds down there as we flew higher, and stars above, very nice but after awhile I got a sore neck from looking sideways out the window all the time, so I decided to make conversation with the guy instead.

"I expect it's Washington," I said. "Where we're going."

"You do."

"And then to the FBI headquarters."

"Son," he said, "you're big, so I have to assume you've got a brain somewhere inside that body. You left the FBI behind when our wheels left the ground."

"I did?"

"Now you're with us."

"Who's 'us'?"

"We are."

"Huh?"

"Stop talking," he said. "Just sit."

"Okay."

It was hard to read the look on his face, somewhere between

feeling sorry for me and wanting to scrape me off his boot. That was when I got this feeling that everything had gotten much worse for me than before, just that look on his face and him not wanting me to talk. So I looked at the clouds instead, and fell asleep that way. I had a lot of booze in me after all.

When the plane slowed down for landing it was still dark but dawn was coming up along the horizon. It was strange to think that just twenty-four hours ago I was in Gene's truck watching the sun come up and now I'm somewhere else entirely. I could see water below, then land with some palm trees, then an airstrip with a long chain-link fence, but that's all I could make out before the pilot set us down. I was busting for a piss by then but the guy said I had to wait till we quit rolling, which happened pretty soon and he opened the door. When that happened I felt all this heat and humidity come blasting through into the plane, so we are somewhere tropical, but not Florida, it wouldn't have taken so long to get there.

He unfastened me from the chair but kept the handcuffs on. I went down these little pop-out steps onto the ground and there's two soldiers in a Humvee waiting next to a small tin building. The guy in the polo shirt handed them a clipboard and one of them signed it. The guy got back in the plane but didn't close the door, so I guess they'll be refueling before taking off again. There was more light in the sky now but everything around the airstrip was dark, so this is not a town or city they have brung me to.

"Excuse me," I said, "I have to pee."

"So pee," said one of the soldiers.

I looked around but the tin building didn't look like a toilet block or anything, plus the only window in it was dark.

"Where?"

"Two places. On the ground or in your pants."

Well, that was an easy one. My wrists were handcuffed in front of me so I could open my zipper okay. I pissed on the ground while they watched me with hands resting on their pistol belts. When I was done they told me to get in the Humvee. My handcuffs got handcuffed to a metal bar in there so I can't get out again until they let me out. One of them sat beside me while the other one drove with the headlights on, it's still that dark.

"Where's this place?" I asked.

"Guess."

"Hawaii?"

They both laughed, then the one next to me says, "This is a special holiday camp."

"Yeah?"

"Yeah, Camp Winalottawakkin."

The one behind the wheel laughed his head off. These are two happy soldiers, not like the polo shirt guy. Along the road I could see more palm trees in the headlight beams. I asked them, "Have you got canoes?" That was even funnier, I guess, because they just laughed and laughed. The one next to me smelled of pot, so I asked him, "Have you been smoking wackyweed?" I only asked to be friendly, but should not have done that because they both got upset, even stopped the Humvee but kept the engine running.

The one in front leans back and says to me, "You say that to anyone and your days are numbered, and the number is less than two, get me?"

The other one punched me in the side of the head, which

was a big surprise because I did not do anything to him. It didn't hurt much, was just surprising.

"Answer the man!" he screams at me.

"Uh, okay," I said. That was all I could think to say. These guys were not so funny anymore.

"It fuckin' better be okay, shitwipe!" he yells.

It was clear to me they were not so playful as I thought, and I decided not to say anything else unless they asked me. They were big guys but not so big as I am. If they didn't have me handcuffed like I am I could've swung their heads together to settle this but I have got this disadvantage handicap situation so the best thing is to shut up and just sit, which was good advice from the plane guy so I did that.

We were driving along a chain-link fence, then the Humvee comes to this one-story building made from cinder blocks and stops and I got brung out of it.

The first soldier says, "This is your new home, asshole."

"It's special for enemies of the United States," says the second one.

"I'm not that," I told him. Big mistake. He slapped me hard across the face. Well, that was too much for me to take. My leg come up like when the doctor taps your knee with his little rubber hammer and my foot went between that soldier's knees and up into his crotch hard as I can kick it. He screamed out loud and fell over and the other one pulls his pistol and aims it at my head yelling at the top of his voice, "Freeze! Freeze! Move a motherfuckin' muscle and your brains are on the ground!"

The ruckus brought more soldiers out of the building and they pulled their pistols too, standing around me in a circle aiming at me. The soldier on the ground was curled in a ball, moaning a little. Then an officer come out and wants to know what's happening here, which the Humvee driver says to him, "Sir, the prisoner attempted to escape!" which is a big lie. The officer looked at me and then at the guy on the ground.

"Mulholland," he says to him, "get up and bring this dickwad inside without getting hurt again, think you can do that?"

The guy on the ground got up okay and I got brung inside by all of them. There is this desk and some filing cabinets and a Coke machine in a long room with two electric fans pushing the air around. "Number three," says the officer, and they hustled me along a corridor to a cell with one wall made of bars just like in the Westerns. There was a bunk bed and a basin and a toilet with a plastic bag underneath, a chemical toilet which I can smell the chemicals in it. They took off the handcuffs and pushed me inside and closed the door.

"Beat it," says the officer, which is not the way officers are supposed to talk to soldiers, not in the movies they don't. They went away and he stayed behind, just staring at me like I'm an animal at the zoo, and not the kind you admire like a tiger maybe, more like a fleabitten chimp or something. He was in his thirties with a crewcut like they all have got or else shaved completely, and a mustache.

"So you're the one," he says.

"What one?"

"The one that set off that bomb in Kansas."

"No, I got blown up by it."

"Yeah? I see a little cut on your head. That was a big bomb, big as the Oklahoma one. I had a cousin died in that blast. She died in the childminding center they had there. One minute

357

it was a childminding center and the next minute it's a graveyard with small bodies blown to pieces by a coward with a
grudge. What was your intended target, some government
building?"

"It wasn't my bomb…"

"Right, you were minding it for someone."

"No, it was put in my truck."

"So it's your truck bomb."

"No, it was Dean's truck."

"Your buddy Dean Lowry who wants to kill Senator
Ketchum."

"No…Dean's dead."

"Not according to my information. What happened, he
leave you stranded when the bomb went off by accident?"

"No, nothing like that…"

"The reason you're here is to get information from you the
system stateside ordinarily isn't able to extract. Ordinarily
you'd be dispatched to an unnamed foreign country for interrogation, but that system got blown out of all proportion by
the media, so now we do what we should've done from the
start with terrorists – handle it ourselves below the radar.
That's why you're here. Do you understand?"

"It's a mistake…"

"The security services of the United States do not make
mistakes. Is your name Odell Deefus or is that a cell name?"

"That's my name. What's a cell name?"

"Odell Deefus is a nigger name. Are you a nigger?"

I did not like this man. He had it all wrong about me and
didn't want to listen. He could see I'm not black but he asked
the question like it's serious, so I know this is some kind of act

he's putting on to make me afraid. Since I got off the plane they all wanted me to be afraid and I was, kind of, but then I decided to show him I'm not.

"I repeat," he says, "are you a nigger?"

"Yes I am."

"What kind of a nigger are you, Deefus? Are you a light-skinned nigger or a brown nigger or a nigger black as the inside of your own asshole?"

"That's a dumb question," I said. I hated him now for play-acting so dumb.

"Excuse me?"

"You can see what color I am just by looking."

"That is an incorrect statement. The color you are has got nothing to do with race. The color you are is determined by what kind of asshole you are. Do you want me to tell you what kind of asshole you are, Deefus? You are the worst kind of ass-hole. You are the kind of asshole that blows away women and kids and old people in wheelchairs because they don't wor-ship the same god you do, which is your miserable cunthole excuse for killing them, isn't that so, Deefus."

"No."

"I'm surprised to hear this. Please explain to me the reason why you like to kill women and kids and old people in wheelchairs."

"I don't do that."

"Because you made a faulty bomb that went off prema-turely and was a wasted bomb, isn't that so, Deefus."

"No…"

"And isn't it a fact that only lies and Muslim propaganda spill from that ugly mouth of yours."

"No."

"You are two kinds of color, Deefus. You are Muslim green and coward yellow. Do you know what color gets made when Muslim green and coward yellow are mixed together, Deefus?"

"I don't know ... Orange?"

"When Muslim green and coward yellow are mixed together the resulting color is blue. That's the color a white face goes when deprived of oxygen. It doesn't get so blue unless close to death. This is the shade of face you would see in a mirror if a mirror was provided to you. This is the color face you will have soon because I intend depriving you of oxygen. Your face will get bluer and bluer until it reaches a very deep shade of blue that I like to call nigger blue. You were funning with me, Deefus, when you told me you're a nigger, but believe me I am not funning with you that you will indeed reach that shade of nigger blue before you are much older than today."

The words come spilling from him at a regular rate like a news ribbon at the bottom of a TV screen, all the same speed and tone like he's reading from an invisible book. "This is my solemn promise to you. I swear by the faith of our founding fathers I will have the truth out of you or humble myself before God and tell him out loud I have failed in my mission, and if there's one thing I hate to do, Deefus, it's fail in my mission and have to humble myself before God and admit that failure. Failure before God is unforgivable and will be passed on to you, Deefus. Your denial will fail and then your spirit will fail, and then your lungs and heart will begin to fail until you become a complete failure. I, Lieutenant William Harding, faithful servant of the United States and God Almighty, do promise this."

He didn't wait to hear anything back at him from me, just turned away and walked off down the corridor with the heels of those officer shoes hitting the concrete floor hard and crisp, like something being smacked over and over again, trailing off into the distance. After the place was quiet a thought come tiptoeing into my head very meek and mild, almost like it didn't want to be there, and the thought was this – I am in the hands of a crazy person that wants to kill me dead. The thought spoke its words again in my head and I began to understand them better, like it's an important lesson I'm teaching myself, one side of my brain talking to the other side, getting it to understand this simple fact about the crazy person wanting to kill me. And then I was afraid.

A soldier come back with a one-piece orange jumpsuit. He told me to get naked and hand over my clothes, then put on the jumpsuit, also he had these little black slipper things for my feet because my new sneakers and socks got handed over too, which he carried these away. The jumpsuit has got no pockets at all. Then another soldier come along and stares at me awhile. There were no windows in my cell and none along the corridor that leads there, but it had to be broad daylight outside by now, so I asked him, "What time is it?"

"You don't need to know."

"I'm just asking."

"Time has got no meaning for you no more. That light up there, that's the sun far as you're concerned, only it's a special sun that don't ever rise or set or go nowhere at all. Only time you're gonna get away from that sun is when you go to the romper room."

"What's that?"

"Kind of a exercise room playroom kinda thing, you'll see."

"Is the food here okay?" I asked him, wanting to maybe make a friend.

"Most of the time it's okay, but that's our food I'm talking about, not yours. Your food is shit. I hope you like to eat shit 'cos we got all the shit food you can handle."

This guy was not suitable for a friend, but I had seen at least a dozen soldiers around the place since I got there so maybe one of them is not a complete asshole like the rest of them and their officer. What I would have to do is be friendly even if they didn't treat me the same way in reverse, and not get them riled about things that they have got wrong. If I did this they would sooner or later come around to seeing the true way things are regarding me and terrorism, what I mean is, no connection there at all, but I saw it would take awhile to convince them about this. If only Dean's body had not been taken away from where I left it there would not be this problem about disbelieving me, and I still could not figure out who did this and why. They have got me in the biggest kind of trouble because of it whoever they are.

"Thank you," I said to the soldier. This was my first move in the official policy of friendliness.

"Fuck you," he says.

He went away then and I lay on the bunk, which was hard but not like a rock. I just had to wait out this bad situation and they would set me free. It was not like I did anything so very bad I could get myself executed over it. This was all just a mistake that should not have got made but it did.

The light in the ceiling hurt my eyes it's so bright, two hundred fifty watts easy, so I flung an arm over my eyes to shut it out. That worked for a minute or so then this same soldier comes back and tells me I have to take my arm away from my face or else put myself in deep shit. "Why?" I asked him and he says it's the rules.

"We can see you all the time," he says, pointing up in the corner of my cell, where I saw this tiny camera up there like a spider on the wall. "That thing is never shut off," he says. "We watch you day and night, eating your shit food and shitting it back out again, sleeping and not sleeping, beating your meat, walking around, whatever, we're watching you. We see you try to damage the light or the camera and we're on you so fast you won't believe it. You won't like it, what we do to prisoners that don't take the rules serious. When you lie on the bed you keep your arms at your sides or across your chest if you want, but not over your face like you did just now. That's a bright light there, makes a big electric bill, so we want you to appreciate how bright it is all the time, see?"

"I see."

"Hell you do, you're just pretending, but you'll see."

He went away again. I closed my eyes but the light come through my eyelids like sunshine through a cheap window shade. I turned on my side away from the light, half expecting the soldier to come back and say that's against the rules too, but he didn't, and so despite everything that happened and all the crap surging through my brain like shit through a sewer pipe I fell asleep.

They brung me breakfast later on after I woke up. It isn't shit like that soldier said, just Corn Flakes and milk, nothing wrong with that, and while I'm eating it here comes another soldier looks just like the rest only it isn't, he's a chaplain, you can tell the difference by the little chrome crosses on his lapels there. He says he's Chaplain Turner and can he get me a Bible or do I want a Koran, he can get either one, which is the rules here, freedom of religion. He says the Koran comes with a little cloth sling that you can hang it up with so it doesn't touch the ground, which is against the Muslim religion for that to happen, a big insult to the words of Mohammed. "But I'm sure you know that already," he ends up saying, which I didn't, how could I?

"I'll take a Bible," I told him, to be friendly as per The Plan. It felt like I'm ordering the Big Mac instead of the Whopper, that's about all it means to me, but I wanted the chaplain to think I'm a real Christian so they quit thinking I'm a terrorist.

"I'll bring it tomorrow," he says, then, "Are you really a Christian?"

"I pretty soon will be."

"So you're converting?"

"Just catching up on what I've been missing, I guess."

"A latecomer to the fold," he says, looking suspicious but trying not to.

"That's me, always late and never at the right place neither."

I laughed but the chaplain didn't. He says, "Is there anyone on the outside who you'd like to send a message to?"

"A message? Like to a lawyer?"

I'm thinking if Johnnie Cochran got OJ Simpson off a murder rap he's definitely the guy for me, but then I recalled hearing he died a few years back, so that won't work, but there was another lawyer on that case that's still alive, I think.

"Effley Bailey," I said. "Send him a message, please, that says I need him pretty bad because I'm innocent, that should make it easier. Effley Bailey, he's my man."

"I meant to a family member or associate, a personal message."

"Oh. Well, now, I don't get along with my old man so that'd be a waste. Can't seem to think of nobody else ... Maybe if you ask me tomorrow I'll know."

"There are no associates you'd like to contact?"

Now I saw what he's doing. He wants me to give him the names of all those crazy Muslim terrorists I'm supposed to hang with, like I'm some kind of idiot fool that doesn't know he'll take those names directly to the FBI, but there's one person, or two really, that maybe can help me here.

"Okay, tell my associates Preacher Bob and his number one guy Chet Marchand that I can use a little help here, so maybe they could put in a good word for me, okay?"

That made him blink. He says, "Preacher Bob? Robert Jerome of the Born Again Foundation? *The* Preacher Bob?"

I held up two fingers twisted together like pretzels. "Him and me are like that. He even got me my own little cell phone because he likes me so much, just you ask him about that. Yeah, Bob and Chet even invited me to the big meeting in Topeka July Fourth, kind of a special guest, you might say. That's not long now, too bad I'll probably be stuck here for something that's all a big mistake anyway. Bob'll be kind of pissed about it, me not showing up, I mean, but when you tell him how I got sidetracked I guess he'll understand okay."

He looked at me like I'm making a joke, so I said, "No kidding, I'm their buddy. Just you ask the FBI if they didn't tap my calls back and forth to those two, well, mainly to Chet, calls I made on that phone they gave me for a gift and issued the invite to Topeka on. Talk to Agent Kraus and Agent Deedle, they'll tell you, okay?"

"Okay," he says, but like you'd accept street directions from a totally drunk man.

"Maybe they can spring me outta here," I said.

"You'll get that Bible tomorrow," he says. "Are there any other works of a religious nature you might like?"

"Well, there was one religious book I read all the way through, it's called *The Way of the Nun*, but I don't think it's so famous as the Bible is. Or you could get me my favorite reading book which is *The Yearling*. Did you ever read that? It won the Pulitzer Prize. But not the short version for kids to read, the long one with everything in it the way the writer wrote it in the first place, that's the one I want."

"I don't run a lending library," he says.

"Okay then, just the Bible."

He went away and I did some walking around in the cell, thinking this is the most exercise I'll get, walking circles in the cell, until I get to see the romper room that is, which is for exercising in, that soldier said. And while I'm thinking about him along he comes, and this time I read the name tag on his shirt, hard to read because it's black on brown, but this guy's name is Fogler, and he did not look happy, kind of chewing his own lips he's so mad about something.

"Quit that!" he barks at me.

"Huh?"

"Quit walking in a circle that way! You can walk back and forth or back, along the wall there, then come up to the front again, but no going circular. It's directly back and forth or in a square kinda, but circularizing is out, you got that!"

"Okay. I didn't know."

"Learn!" he says and stomps away down the corridor again.

He must keep his eyes glued to the TV screen out there every second in every minute. This would be a big embarrassment the first time I had to take a dump with him or someone else watching. There is something not decent about that, I think.

Lunch was beef patties and fries, not bad at all. Fogler was just fooling with me about the shit food here. Then I got another visitor, this one is bald, also with glasses. He said his name is Lieutenant Beamis and he's there to ask me some questions, get-to-know-me kind of stuff he says, but what it is is these sheets of cardboard he starts holding up with splatters of black ink across them.

"You've probably seen this in the movies," he says. "Just give me your first impression of these as I hold them up."

"It's to show what kind of guy I am, I've seen it."

"You could put it that way. What's this one suggest to you, straight off the top of your head without thinking about it?"

"Someone dropped the paint pot."

"And this one?"

"Damn, he did it again."

"This?"

"That is one clumsy son of a gun you've got making these."

He let the sheets down. "I'd advise you to take this seriously, Deefus. You don't seem to realize you're in the worst kind of trouble. I'm actually here to help you, to customize our approach to your problem so we can resolve this."

"I'm sorry, I thought you just wanted information, like where Dean Lowry has got his hideout."

"Revealing that kind of thing could be useful in this instance, yes, but bear with me a little while and I'll just run

through these. It's the way we do this." He held up those cardboard sheets again.

"Okay, that one is two zebras with football helmets.

"A butterfly that has got tattered wings.

"A face with eyes but no nose. That could be a mouth there.

"Elephants walking away from each other. Maybe they had
a fight.

"A jungle plant with flowers, also beetles all around.

"Now this one...I don't know...a feathery ladies' hat?
Exploding?"

He set the inkblot sheets down and opened up a notebook
and clicks his pen, then starts asking questions about my life
so far, childhood memories and so forth, so I was happy to do
that, then after awhile he wants to know, "Where and when
did you begin to feel that society failed you?"

"Failed me? How?"

"Failed to measure up. Failed to provide what you need.
Failed to provide for others in need?"

"I've got no fight with society. Society is fine by me."

"But there are things you'd like to see changed?"

"Sure, everyone wants to change this or that."

"What kind of changes would you institute if you were
President, let's say."

"Well, first thing, I'd organize to get me set free."

"And after that?"

"Go on TV and tell everyone exactly how it happened, this
big mixup."

"What about other issues? Issues of faith, issues of social
justice, that kind of thing."

"Okay, I'd make it against the law to have commercials on

TV. There'd be this one channel, the commercial channel, where you go if you want to see commercials. People would like that, I think."

"Anything else?"

"Uhuh, I'd make it so the TV companies can't put a laugh track on any comedy show. No more canned laughter, I hate that. And I'd like to see those Hollywood movie stars get paid less. I heard the big ones get fifty million dollars just to make a single movie. That's too damn much."

"What about religion in the schools? Any opinion on that?"

I was getting suspicious of this guy. The inkblots meant he's a shrink, but his questions were not very shrinky. He's supposed to be asking me about personal stuff, like what happened when I lost my mom, stuff like that, and did I get over it and so forth, but he isn't doing that, he's asking all this other stuff, so maybe he's just another FBI in disguise. I decided I would test him about that, so I said, "How's Kraus and Deedle?"

"Pardon?"

"Agent Kraus and Agent Deedle. They're the ones brung me in."

"That doesn't concern me. Were you happy in school?"

"Uhuh, a very popular student, always getting elected for this and that, kind of a nuisance all those positions on councils and committees and so forth, but hey, when the public wants you that bad you just have to go along."

"My information is that you were a very withdrawn student, the opposite of what you're telling me."

"Well, you have got the wrong information. See, that's what landed me in here, wrong information, which just goes to show you can't trust that stuff to be reliable."

"I'll take that on board," he says. "Now, how about your sexual relationships?"

"What about them?"

"Hetero or homosexual, for the most part?"

"I'm not gay. Dean was gay, his sister said, but I didn't get to know him all that well myself."

"You didn't form a homosexual union with Dean Lowry?"

"No, he's not my type."

"And what type is your type?"

"I generally prefer them female."

"Generally?"

"Well, all the time. I'm not gay."

"Did you have a sexual relationship with Fenella Myers?"

"Who?"

"A school companion. You gave her name when you told the hitchhiker you wanted a car delivered to Denver."

"Oh, you mean Feenie. That name just sprung into my head when I did that. She doesn't even live in Denver, she goes to college in Durango."

"We're aware of that. No sexual or close personal relationship with Miss Myers?"

"No, but I liked her. She was smart."

"You're attracted to smart women?"

"I don't know. Maybe."

"Is that why you carry a picture of the Secretary of State in your wallet?"

"I think Condi's cute. I like her style of dressing too. You do hear some people say she's way conservative the way she dresses, but I think that goes with the job, don't you? I never once saw someone with a political job wearing Spandex or something."

"So Doctor Rice is your ideal woman?"

"She's a doctor too? I knew she was a piano player as well as a political person, but I didn't know she's a doctor on top of that. How long did she go to medical school?"

"She's not that kind of doctor. You wrote her a letter of confession, but that confession contained incorrect information. What do you think would be her reaction to being lied to by someone who says he's an admirer?"

"I didn't lie, only Dean isn't where I buried him, that's the reason for all this mixup. I would not lie to Condi. And what you said about my wallet? I had pretty near four hundred bucks in there that got taken away from me. I'd like to have that back."

"Have you written letters to public figures before?"

"Just to Condi. And once to Marjorie Kinnan Rawlings."

"Who's that?"

"She's the one wrote *The Yearling*. That's my favorite book. I read it sixteen times now. I wrote her how good her book is."

"Any reply?"

"I got this letter back from the book publisher says she's dead."

"Nobody else? No political or religious figures?"

"No, but I'll be writing to Preacher Bob about all this."

"Preacher Bob the televangelist?"

"He's a friend of mine. He should know what happened here. It was Preacher Bob's phone that set off the bomb, so he'll want to know about that. Can I have some paper and a pen?"

"You can request those items from Lieutenant Harding. How often have you voted?"

"Never have done. If Condi runs, though, I'll vote for her."

He shut his notebook and clicked his pen. "That's it for now. I may ask you some more questions at a later time. Thank you for your cooperation."

"No charge. You're a shrink, aren't you."

"That's right."

"I knew from the style of sexual questions."

"That was very observant of you," he says, and away he went. It was nice having company that didn't yell at me, but maybe he'll be back like he said.

Lieutenant Beamis must have said something to Lieutenant Harding because a minute later he's stood at the bars. "You have a request, Deefus?"

"Hi there, Lieutenant. Yeah, I'd like my four hundred bucks, maybe it's closer to three-fifty. And some paper and a pen to write Preacher Bob about all this."

"You don't need money in here, we provide all essential needs. Pen and paper are provided only for a full and frank confession."

"But I didn't do anything."

"Then you don't need them."

"Well...but I'd like to tell my side of the story."

"Will that include the whereabouts of Dean Lowry and his cohorts?"

"What's a co-hort?" It sounded to me like some kind of girl-friend, which Dean would not have had any of those.

"Would that information be included in your written con-fession?" he wants to know, glaring at me all bug-eyed. This guy really is a crazy person.

"No..."

"Next time you bring me to your cell on a wasted mission,

Deefus, you'll be punished. I'm not a man that likes to have his time wasted."

And he marched away down the corridor. So no letter to Preacher Bob, that was a disappointment. And that money is good as stole from me the way he talks.

I did some more walking back and forth for awhile but nothing circular, then Fogler comes back and I'm thinking I must not have been concentrating and walked in a curve or something, but he's not mad at me, he's smiling very friendly, so maybe I had this guy all wrong.

"Okay, Doofus," he says, "exercise time."

"My name is Deefus with two ees."

"You don't tell me how to spell, dirtbag, you just do what I say. Turn around and put your hands together."

I did it and he reached through the bars to put handcuffs on, then he opened the door. "Step out and proceed along the hallway till I say stop."

I come out and started walking but then he screams at me. "Stop! Did I say that way? The other way, shitwipe!"

So I went along the corridor the other way, still with no windows, and when we come to a door that's open he says, "Left turn!"

I went in and it's a room with a metal table and chairs, the spindly kind, and a heavier chair off by itself. "Get seated," barks Fogler, so I went to the table, only he screams, "Not there, dickwad! That chair there!"

He means the other chair, so I sat on that one, thinking to myself how I'd like to get ahold of his neck and squeeze it for a good long time, I would really like that, but I kept up the conversation just to be friendly.

"Is this for exercise?" I asked him. "The romper room?"

"This here is it."

"So I'm gonna get some exercise."

"For sure, bro."

Then two other guys come in wearing just T-shirts and camouflage pants with boxing gloves on, so these must be sparring partners, but where's the ring? Then in comes the pitfaced guy from the plane, so he didn't go back with the plane after all, or maybe the plane is still here. I nodded at him because we're acquainted, you might say, but he didn't nod back. I had got to notice even so soon as this that everyone here is rude, which I didn't think was the way military guys should be. I had wanted to be in the Army and now I'm thinking maybe I wouldn't like it. In the commercials they show you these handsome young guys jumping out of choppers and saluting the flag etcetera but nobody being rude.

"Allrighty, then," says Fogler with this big grin, "Doofus, do you know why you're here?"

"Boxing match?"

"That's exactly right! You're smarter than you look, Doofus. Lyden and Croft here are gonna demonstrate a display of boxing just for you, how about that."

"Okay."

"The man says okay! That chair under your ass, that's the spectator chair where the special sporting guest gets to sit and watch what goes on. Pass your hands back here."

I did it and he locked my handcuffs to the chair frame somehow, so they must be thinking I'll try to escape while everyone is distracted by the boxing match, but I'm not so dumb I couldn't see that was an impossible thing. So now

Lyden and Croft come over and stood in front of me like those gladiators who had to kind of stand and present themselves in front of Caesar before they start killing each other. "We who are about to die salute you," that's what they say. It was like they're waiting for me to say something before they can start boxing, like I'm Caesar, which I'm not expecting, so I said, "Okay, let's go."

"You heard the man," says Fogler.

I knew there's been a mistake when the first blow got flung at me, not at one of the guys with the boxing gloves. It hit me along the jaw and just about sent me out of the chair, which two legs left the floor, no kidding, then back again, just in time to get hit the other way so the same thing happened. When the third punch hit me at the top of the gut and made all my air rush out and none can get back in again that's when I knew this is no boxing match, this is a setup with me as the patsy. That was some nice trick Fogler played. This is the scene where the Nazis try to beat out of the hero the plans for the D-Day invasion, only he won't give them nothing but his name and rank and serial number, so they keep on beating him. This means I am the hero, but I was not happy to be this.

They smacked me around the head and guts mostly but no kidney punches because the chair is in the way. There's a roaring in my ears that won't quit and it gets louder every time they hit me again, like I'm tumbling along underwater in a fast stream and every few seconds I run into another boulder. Then they quit and when I opened my eyes Pitface is standing in front of me with a cigarette in his hands. He taps the ash onto the floor because there's no ashtray on the table, then he says, "Where is Dean Lowry and who are his friends?"

"Dean's dead...I killed him...I didn't mean to..."

My own voice sounded weird to me, like hearing it on a tape and you never heard it before and you can't believe this is how people hear you.

"And where's the body?"

"I don't know...I buried him but someone dug him up..."

"That's no different to the story you've been telling all along."

"I know..."

He turned away and they flung me into that fast stream again. I went tumbling along there a good long while and then they let me surface again with my ears still filled by roaring blood. There he is again, Pitface, asking me about Dean exactly like before, so I answered him the same way again, what else can I do? He's asking me and I'm telling him, but it isn't what he wants to hear, so now I'm back in the stream getting pummeled this way and that and thinking maybe soon I'll drown if they don't quit. Which they did, like they heard me say this. And here he is again with a fresh cigarette spilling ash all over the concrete floor.

"Deefus, can you hear me?"

"Uhuh..."

"Tell me what I want to know and this will stop, you've got my word."

Well, I did not trust this man's word, but I wanted not to get punched around anymore with my hands tied behind my back like this, so I told him, "Okay..." I was ready to give him the plans for the D-Day invasion, but only because they're old now so what harm is there.

"Where is Dean Lowry and who are his friends?"

"Dean…" I gulped some air awhile.

"Yes?"

"Dean…"

"What about him?"

"He's dead…"

"Don't fuck with me, Deefus."

"And I put him in a drainpipe under I-70…"

"Okay, that's good, but that's a long highway."

"Just the other side of…Ogallah…the west side. A drain-pipe there. He's all wrapped up in plastic bags for lawn grass…"

"Is this true? If it isn't, you'll regret it."

"It's true."

He took out his phone and started telling someone what I just told him. I knew then I had made a big mistake and would pay big time for that when they didn't find Dean, but it felt so good not to be punched around. Pitface snapped his phone shut and gave a nod to Fogler. I got set free from the chair, then they tipped me out of it onto the floor.

"Get up!" yells Fogler. "Get up off that fuckin' floor!"

So I did and got taken back to my cell. Taking off my hand-cuffs Fogler says to me, "I knew it wouldn't take much to bust your balls, man. Soon as I saw you I knew you're a pussy that's gonna rat out his friends the first time he gets pushed around a little. A few taps with the gloves and you started to cry. That's so pathetic. I got no respect for a man does that."

To be honest about this, neither did I. I did break easy, just to make them quit punching me, but there'll be a bigger test of toughness when they find out I lied. And when I told them the truth again they would believe it even less than before, which will make them beat me all the harder for that first lie they believed. Punishment was waiting for me around the corner like a big dark monster just waiting for orders to rip my head off. I had done a dumb thing and would pay for that. And knowing this would happen made me afraid. Some hero.

Well, when it happened I would just have to be stronger than today, that's what I told myself. Fogler was still right in front of me on the other side of the bars, still grinning and sneering at me like I'm a piece of shit. I could've reached through and grabbed him and pulled him into those bars to show him I'm not who he thinks I am, but that would mean I got no recovery time between now and when they find out I lied, and I wanted that time to make myself strong. So what I did instead, I winked at him, one slow wink, then a little smile. It made him mad because he doesn't know what it means.

"You like me, Doofus, huh? You wanna buttfuck me? That what you want?"

I just kept smiling until he went away, then I lay on my bunk and wondered how many hours I had left until the big dark monster would be let into my cell for a meal. My head and upper body ached and throbbed from all those punches, but at least it hadn't been iron bars they hit me with. That most likely would come later, and I would have to be ready this time for pain and suffering to make today's little sparring match seem like a hug and a kiss. I had stopped fooling myself I was in America anymore. This was some other place where life the way they showed it in the movies, with good guys that always win and bad guys that always lose, that life was a joke. By lying to them I had made an appointment with Real Life. I closed my eyes and wished like never before that there really was a God who could give me strength, but knowing I would have to do this all by myself. It was so awful to think about this that I fell asleep, which is something I do when I'm afraid, how about that.

SEVENTEEN

Those Kansas cops worked fast looking for Dean, or maybe there aren't any drainpipes under the interstate just west of Ogallah, because even before suppertime I had Pitface come visit me. He stood by the bars and just looked at me for the longest time. I looked back at him wondering if his face ever looked different, like if he'd smile at a kid's birthday party or whatever. This guy has got a face carved from rock.

"Deefus," he says, "you made me look bad. You told me a lie and I passed it on as truth. This goes into my record. My record is a precious thing to me and you have gone and Fucked It Up."

I almost felt sorry about that, then I told myself this is not a good person that does good things, so why should I care about his record? I said to him, "You wouldn't believe me when I told you the truth, so I told you a lie."

"Yes, you did."

"If I tell you anything else apart from what I told you in the first place, it's a lie. I just want you to know that. You're gonna have me beat so bad I'll say whatever you want to hear, but it's all gonna be a lie because I already told you the truth and you had me beat up for it. Everything I know I already told it to you and Kraus and Deedle, only none of you want to hear it, you want to hear something else, something like I told you today. You can beat me up all you want, it doesn't change anything. This is the truth about the truth I'm telling you."

He looked at me a long time, so long I'm thinking he's turning it over in his mind and slowly accepting it because for me to be saying this now doesn't make any kind of sense unless it's true, which it is. Then he says, "You worked all that out, did you? Made a little speech about truth, very sincere, very direct. You want me to believe you because you're actually telling me the actual truth, is that the message here?"

"Yes."

He smiled at me. So his carved rock face can change after all. It was a terrible smile, like when a crocodile opens its jaws. "I don't buy it," he said, and that's when I knew Pitface is another crazy person like Lieutenant Harding. And I knew that everything I was not looking forward to, the big dark monster, it would be worse even than I figured it will be. That was a bad feeling when I knew that. But I didn't let him see, because what would be the point? I already let him see me tell him the absolute truth and he let it bounce off his rock face like a blind man. My truth was not his truth. You would think that the truth is the truth, like a broom is a broom. Two men could stand either side of a broom and agree it's a broom because there it is – a broom. But the broom I'm looking at isn't what Pitface sees. He sees a garbage can instead. And there is nothing I can do about this, which is the really bad part.

He says, "I'll be waiting for you."

He went away down the corridor towards the romper room. I had to take a bunch of deep breaths then because I knew in a few minutes I will have pain shoved down my throat like a fist and I better be ready, which I was not, even if I had been trying real hard all afternoon. When Fogler come along with the handcuffs and two soldiers with sidearms it was almost a relief to have the waiting over with and the pain get started.

This time the two boxers are already waiting in the room along with Pitface. I didn't see them walk past my cell so this place is bigger than I thought, with other entrances than the one I saw when I got delivered. It makes no difference to me how big. There are only two rooms in this entire building that matter – my cell and the romper room. I was expecting to be sat on the chair again but Fogler says, "This time it's more interesting than before. This time you get to move around and defend yourself. You know how to do that, Doofus?"

What he said made me feel a little better. This time I could fight back, I thought, and even if I'm not much of a fighter I'm big and can maybe land a few lucky punches before Lyden and Croft tear me apart between them. But that was not what Fogler meant. This is what happened. He left me with my wrists handcuffed behind me, then he put a black bag over my head. I hated that, hated that black bag the second it cut me off from the room, from everything. There is nothing worse than a black bag over your head.

Then they started punching me. They could punch me wherever they wanted, whenever they liked. They liked the kidney punches they couldn't do this morning, but they also liked a head punch or a belly punch in between. I staggered around the romper room, not knowing what kind of punch was coming at me next, or from what direction, only knowing there's plenty more on the way. Sometimes I hit the wall with my shoulder I'm lurching around so bad, and one time with the side of my head, which I fell down when that happened and they backed off until I'm on my feet again. I was grateful to them for backing off and not kicking me when I'm down, isn't that strange, really grateful for that little piece of mercy before they started in again.

They were not pulling their punches because I can hear them puffing and panting through the bag, in between my own puffing and panting. It's hard to breathe inside a bag, and I passed out once I think from lack of oxygen inside there. They backed off like the last time until I can get on my feet again, only this time I'm not feeling grateful about that. I'm not feeling anything that you could call an emotion or whatever, just concentrating now on getting enough air into my mouth inside that bag to keep on going in circles like a punching bag on legs. That's what I am now, not a man anymore, not to them, just a thing to be hit over and over till I break.

When I went down the third time it felt like I'm drowning because I just cannot get enough air inside of me to keep alive. Then this voice says in my ear, so he's bending over me on the floor there, he says to me, "All this can stop. Tell me the truth. Make it stop." His cigarette breath come to me even through the bag, that's how bad it is. There's nothing I can say to him because I already said everything there is to say about what he wants to know. I just sucked air inside myself while I'm in between punches on the floor, taking advantage you might say, but pretending to be thinking about his offer, which is no kind of offer at all on account of his craziness.

I didn't want to get up again and be punched some more so I laid there long as I could until Pitface saw what I'm doing and had them haul me up onto my feet again, and now the real beating started. Lyden and Croft, they got their second wind while I'm on the floor and now they're mad at me because I won't talk. I could tell they're mad because the punches were harder than before, I mean they really put theirselfs behind every punch, put all their strength into it now to make me speak the truth, and there is nothing I can do except take it because I already know the truth will never save me from a damn thing.

The one thought running through my mind is this – sooner or later this will end. I just had to keep on getting punched until Lyden and Croft got all punched out and hope there isn't a second punching team waiting outside all fresh and vigorated and ready to hammer me into the ground then stomp on me awhile. If a second team come in I knew I would come real close to wanting to die, that's how bad I'm feeling by then.

Finally I slammed into the wall spinning away from a punch to the neck, slammed into it hard with my forehead and like they say, I saw stars for a second, then I'm on the floor again, only this time I would not get up. If they picked me up like before I would pretend to be unconscious and crumple down again. I have just had enough, enough, *enough* of this now. "Put him to bed," says Pitface, and again, that strange gratefulness come over me. I should hate him for causing me all this pain, but what I really am is grateful that he's ending it. That is so fucked up I can hardly believe myself.

I got picked up and carried to my cell. They dropped me on the bunk, took off the handcuffs and left. When their footsteps went away I lifted my hands to my head, which is still inside the bag, and felt my face, all swole up and in a few hours it'll be even bigger, that's how it goes with bruising like I have got. Then I pulled the bag off real slow because it hurts to move at all, even for something so simple as pulling the bag off. The air felt cool and good. I let the bag fall on the floor and stared a long while at the ceiling which is painted white. Then I moved my head a little and saw that Pitface is standing by the bars. He's been standing there all the time since they brung me back in here, just watching me.

"I knew you were playing possum," he tells me. "I gave you a break."

It's like he wants to hear me say Thank you or something. I stared at him then turned away because I can't stand to look at this man.

"You think I'm a prick," he says, "but I have to do this. People need to be protected from your kind. That's my job – protection. I do my job and people don't get blown away by crazies. You have to know that I'll keep on doing my job until you crack. You were a pussy the first time, not so bad the second. You're learning to tough it out. That makes me sad, because no matter how tough you are, I'll break you. I've been through this plenty of times, here and other places. The end result is always the same – the guy breaks and tells us what we need to know. And if he doesn't know anything, which isn't the case here, he breaks anyway, and he stays broken. I know this. A broken man, that's a sad sight, especially if he didn't know anything. But we have to do this regardless, to be sure. When we're sure, whichever way it's gone, we stop. But the guy is broken anyway and stays that way. He stays that way forever. He's not himself anymore, he's some broken guy that just wants to find a hole in the ground and crawl inside and die. That's what happens. You can't change it. I can't change it. Nobody can change it. Tomorrow we'll start again. You rest up and eat your dinner, it'll be along pretty soon. There's pie for dessert, with cream. I like that. Everyone likes that. But tomorrow you won't want the pie, only the cream, because tomorrow you won't have teeth."

He went away but his words rolled around the cell a few times before trickling into my ear like drops of ice water. I believed him. I believed every word.

They brung me the dinner which is pizza from the commissary at the "main camp over the hill", that's how the guard explains it, and pie like Pitface said from the same place, so there has got to be a big camp over there for this to happen. Pizza in prison, hooda thunkit. There's even a cardboard box to keep it warm like back home, only no Pizza Hut or Domino's on it. Plenty of meat, plenty of cheese. Prison Pizza, that's what should be on the box, delivered to your cell in five minutes or your money back. There was Coke too, and the pie was apple with cream like I was expecting. Eating all this slow because of my aching face I wondered how I'll feel looking at the same stuff tomorrow with no teeth. Maybe Pitface just wanted to make me afraid. Well, it worked. I am afraid.

After I'm finished I sat on my bunk feeling all the bruises everywhere, too sore to get up and walk around in straight lines, I would've wobbled and gone curvaceous and got in trouble about that, so I just sat and tasted that last bit of pie taste in my mouth.

Then they come for me again and I got hauled to the romper room, feeling very bad because Pitface told me we'll start again tomorrow, not tonight, so that was a lie to get me feeling like I've got time to get prepared for pain, which now I have not got, the lying shithead. I hate that guy. He was in there smoking another cigarette with no ashtray like before, and I only saw him for a second or two before they put my black bag on again and here comes the punching all over again, *thump thump thumpthumpthump* . . .

Then one of them punched me real hard in the guts, and all that good food come up again and I barfed inside the bag, the entire meal. The smell was so bad it made me puke again till there's nothing more to come up. They kept on hitting me all through this, so finally I went down on my knees and doubled over to make them quit for just a minute so I can get some air. But they were not inclined to give me that minute, not even five seconds. Soon as I'm down they started hammering at my back and kidneys hard as they can. The inside of the bag was coated with stinking puke that made me ashamed it come from inside of me, almost as bad as shit.

They hammered and hammered and all I can think about is breathing through my mouth so I don't smell that awful smell, then I fell over completely and they backed off. Pitface come over and squats next to me. He says, "Where is Dean Lowry and who are his friends?" I couldn't say anything, I already told him that, so maybe he wasn't really expecting an answer, I don't know. Then all of a sudden they're going at me again on the ground, only now it's boots not gloves, combat boots so these are not ballet shoes that keep thumping into my ribs and back and legs and arms. "Not the head," Pitface tells them, and again I feel this awful gratefulness to him about that, which knowing this is not right to feel that way made me feel even badder than before.

Just for something to do, and maybe take my mind off of things, I started counting those kicks, for distraction you might say. When the number climbed past twenty, thirty, forty, I felt a kind of amazement that they could do that, kick a handcuffed and headbagged man forty-three, forty-four, forty-five times without stopping. These guys are dedicated to getting the truth out of me, all right. At kick number fifty-six Pitface says, "Enough," only this time I'm so fazed by everything I can't even feel grateful. I can't hardly feel nothing at all.

They picked me up and carried me back to the cell and dumped me there, but this time they left the bag over my head and the handcuffs on so's I can't reach up and take it off. That awful puke stink got sucked into me every time I took a breath, which I took plenty because getting beat up like that leaves you exhausted. I bet Pitface knows this. I bet he knows every single way to make someone feel bad and he uses one way, then he uses another way, then another, kind of like choosing which gadget to put on your handydandy all-purpose kitchen power tool – the cutter, grinder, chopper or blender. Pitface is the Celebrity Chef of Pain. He is Dr Feelbad.

Before they left me alone Pitface says to me, "I can tell

you're depressed, Deefus, so I've arranged a little phone conversation for later. You'd like to hear the voice of your fiancée, wouldn't you? I'm setting this up as a favor. Do you love her very much? Sure you do, so hearing her voice will cheer you up, I guarantee it." I heard his footsteps go away and the cell door closed. I thought about talking to Lorraine and didn't know what I could say to her, or her to me, not after she set me up with that phony breakout and was all along humping Cole Connors. If it's true and we can talk on the phone like Pitface says, I'll give her a piece of my mind about all of that. She needed talking to, that woman.

Maybe an hour went by with me breathing in the stink of my puke, then someone come in the cell and took off my handcuffs. I pulled off the bag and sucked in fresh air a minute or two. Out in the corridor they were setting something up on a little table but I didn't want to know about that until I need to know, because I bet it's something to make me feel like shit. Finally I looked over and what they have done is set up this laptop computer and right next to it a tape recorder, which did not make sense. How can they make me feel bad with these things?

Well, they showed me how after it all got switched on. The screen on the laptop has got me right there in a chair with some stuff tied around my chest and one of those blood pressure cuffs around my arm and some wires taped to my palm. It's me in the police station in Callisto getting lie detected! I wondered if somehow Officer Larry Dayton has sold the tape to the government like he wanted to sell it to me. It isn't the whole tape, they left out the part where Andy Webb screwed up the interview by butting in. This is just the part where I made myself mess up their lie-detector readout by thinking about Jody having to shoot his lovely pet yearling. They had it arranged in a loop, so all you see over and over is me blubbering like a big idiot, that's how I looked even to myself.

But it got worse when they turned on the tape recorder. What come out of that is some pieces of conversation from the FBI bug they put in Lorraine's phone. She wasn't talking to me, she's talking to Cole Connors about me. This is very painful, this part, because she's telling him what a dumb bastard I am but okay to use for a prison guard. Then they started talking dirty, describing things they did last time and what they'll do next time, including the Dark Deed whatever that is, but Cole knows what it is and he must like it because he goes, "Whooooohoooo, show me that thing!" This tape was looped also, playing over and over. What's interesting is the way it seems like I'm listening to the tape on the computer screen and crying about it, blubbering away like a baby while Lorraine says that dirty stuff. I know Pitface set this up to make me feel bad, but he fucked up this time because watching myself cry about Lorraine did not hurt half so much as getting kicked and punched. It did hurt, but in a different way. I think this is supposed to be mental torture, not the physical kind, and I will take this any day of the week over what happens in the romper room, so this did not work like Pitface wanted, which made me feel good. Hah!

After awhile I didn't hear the crying or the dirty talk anymore, just stared at the camera way up there on the wall and kind of drifted away inside my head, thinking about how I come to be here and how bad my luck is for that to happen without I intended it to, and how there's more bad stuff waiting for me tomorrow, things like that. Then Fogler come along with this police type baton that he bangs on the bars real loud and says, "Doofus, you're pissing me off. Every time I look at my monitor back there I see you looking straight at me. I don't want to see you looking at me like that. It's bad enough I got to look at you at all, I for sure don't want you looking back at me that way. Take your eyes off the fuckin' camera, okay? Do it now. You got your own TV entertainment center here so why keep looking at the camera. Doofus!"

I just plain ignored him and kept on looking at the camera. Well, that got Fogler mad. He says, "If you don't quit looking at that camera I'm coming in there and I'm gonna fuck you over real good. Doofus, I mean it!"

I kept on staring at the camera, kind of enjoying it that I've made him mad. He won't come in here, I'm thinking, he's all talk. But then he's opening the door and coming at me with that baton swinging back to take a crack at me. It seemed like it's happening real slow, but my mind was working fast. Fogler, he must've forgot I don't have the handcuffs on now, so when he got close enough I jumped up and grabbed his baton arm and twisted it back hard as I can till he dropped it. He sure was surprised about that. His face went all red and he opened his mouth to yell but I didn't want that, didn't want soldiers running in there to beat me up some more just because this asshole wanted to give me more pain outside of business hours to make himself feel good. So I socked him hard in the chin and his teeth clicked together, then while he's still being surprised about everything I socked him again hard in the guts and the wind come out of him in a big *whoosh*.

I loved that sound, I really did. If I didn't know he's been emptied out I would've hit him again the same way to hear that sound again. But instead I pulled both his arms behind him and marched him over to the chemical toilet which I crapped in one time already plus a couple pisses since I got here and I forced his head down into that thing till he's in up to his fucking neck and starting to kick and struggle to get free, but I'm in no mood now to let this prick out of my hands, nossir, I held his face in the shit another half-minute maybe then brung him out and run him across the cell and straight into the wall before he can even get his breath back. He hit hard and fell down like a sack of cement. That felt great, seeing him go down like that. I wanted to kill him. I wanted to kick him and punch him and gouge his eyes out, I am not kidding. I know this is mental behavior but that is what happens when you get pushed too far like I have been today. But I had to smash something to stop myself killing Fogler, so what I did, I went out in the corridor and picked up that laptop computer and flung it the entire length of the corridor, which it fetched up against the door there and come apart very satisfying in a dozen pieces. No more crybaby Deefus. Then I picked up the tape recorder and smashed it hard on the floor. No more dirty-talking Lorraine.

The door down there with the smashed computer in front of it opened and here comes three soldiers with pistols in their hands. I jumped back in the cell and slammed the door, then went over to Fogler and scooped up his baton. By the time those soldiers got to my door I had got that baton tucked up real tight under Fogler's neck, holding him in front of me like a shield. They stopped when they saw that. I told them, "If you come in here I'll pull his goddamn head off!"

"Just let him go and that'll be fine …" says one of them.

"No it won't," I said, "it won't be fine. I let him go and you'll beat the shit out of me. Well, I already had enough shit beat out of me, so fuck you!"

"Listen, buddy, you're making it worse for yourself …"

"I know! I know I am! I don't care!"

I hitched the baton up tighter and Fogler made this gurgling sound. Those soldiers didn't know what to do about this, no more than I did. We just looked at each other and wondered what next? Fogler's head smelled like shit and chemicals right under my nose.

Next thing Lieutenant Harding comes along and he can't believe what he's seeing. "Release that man!" he yells at me, but I didn't. He yelled it again, then he yells at the soldiers to get in and take me down, but they didn't want to, they can see I'm crazy and willing to hurt them all, even hurt myself maybe.

Harding, he tried it another way then. I watched him rearrange his face and voice and say to me all wheedling and fake-friendly, "Now, listen to me, Deefus, you can't treat my men like that. Let him go and we'll just back off, okay?"

"You're lying!"

"No I'm not. Now, listen, you have my word on this. Let him go and there'll be no retribution, I mean it …"

"I don't know anything and I didn't do anything!"

"Right, I understand that. Those aren't my men, the ones asking you questions, that's another outfit entirely. That man there, he's one of mine, so I'm asking you to let him go and I can promise you he won't come near you again. Think about it. You have my word as an officer. If that means anything to you at all you'll see this is the way for you to go, the sensible way. Just let him go and we'll get him out of your life, okay?"

"And no retribution."

"And no retribution."

"And no more phone calls."

"No more phone calls."

"And a TV."

"What?"

"I want a TV. I like to watch TV."

"Okay, a TV, but that's it. You let him go and none of this happened, plus you get a TV right here in your cell."

"And some hot water and soap and another set of clothes. This stinks!"

"A trip to the shower unit and a fresh outfit, fine. Anything else?"

"Another dinner. I puked up that one before."

"Another dinner, no problem. Is that it?"

"You give me your word as an officer?"

"I've already done that. Let's not waste any more time, that man looks unwell."

"Okay then. Your word as an officer."

"You're doing the sensible thing, Deefus."

"Do you get cable and dish here?"

"We get everything they get stateside."

I let Fogler go and he slumped onto the floor, coughing and gasping very hard. That sounded good. He started crawling away from me towards the door. I waited for them to rush me when he passed through to the corridor, but that didn't happen. They helped Fogler get on his feet and two of them went away with him. The rest closed the door and stayed where they are.

"The baton," says Harding.

I took a chance and walked over to him and passed it through the bars.

"Thank you," he says, then they all left.

I waited. They hadn't locked the door, which means they're coming back with the TV like Harding promised. Maybe it means that. Maybe it means they'll be back with something else. He gave me his word but that didn't mean squat. Everyone here is a lying son of a bitch that I can't trust. I only let Fogler go because how long could I have held them off that way without them bringing in tear gas or whatever, so I let him go and now I'm waiting to see if they are good as their word or not. I am expecting Not.

Here they come back along the corridor, a bunch of them with Harding. They stood outside the cell and they weren't carrying their pistols, which is a good sign. One of them is carrying a portable TV, which is another good sign, so maybe I'm wrong. They put the TV on the little table that the computer had stood on. It must be the battery kind because there's no electric outlet I can see. Then one of them puts his hand through the bars with something in it, something like a big old electric shaver, like he's offering it to me, but then he presses a button and something shot out from that thing and stuck me in the side like two little knife points. There was two wires stretching from the gadget to my ribs and I'm wondering what that is ... and then someone turned off my switch. That's what it felt like. I fell down twitching and could not control any part of me. They did it again, sending a shock through me, so this is one of those police Taser guns to knock out guys that are fighting drunk and don't want to get arrested. This second shock, it made me quit twitching, took hold of me all over so I'm lying like a dead man.

I'm on the floor again, no part of me moving now except my brain. They come inside the cell and stood over me. I looked up at them, hating them because now they can do anything they want, even kill me. I couldn't see batons or boxing gloves but they all have got boots on for kicking.

Harding, he kneeled down next to me and says, "This is what happens when you don't give us what we want. These are important matters you're expected to help us out with, but you're not cooperating at all." He pulled out the Taser barbs and stood up. "Hose him down," he told the soldiers. I could not see any hosepipe so this was strange, then they took out their dicks and pissed all over me, three of them but not Harding because I guess officers don't do stuff like that. Worst of all was the one guy that made sure he pissed in my face. Him I wanted to kill for the extra insult. They run out of piss and Harding told them to go away, which they did.

He says, looking down at me, "You think this is no way to behave, I know, but the thing you have to bear in mind is this —you are not a human being. You are a terrorist, which is a thing shaped like a human being but is not a human being. You don't think like we do. That's why you do the things you do. These are bad things and you have to be stopped. I'm here to stop you. We all are. There is absolutely and positively no chance you'll get what you want. You want to see America on her knees, but that can never happen. If you weren't completely crazy you could see this. America is the greatest nation the world has ever known and ever will know. Nothing will stop America. You're like an ant raising its fist to an elephant.

If I didn't hate you I'd feel sorry for you. The worst thing is, you were born American. If you were some kind of towelhead I could feel sorry for you because you come from a part of the world where everything is shit. But you don't come from there. You come from Wyoming. They must hate you there, Deefus. You can never go home again. Even after you break you'll be held in some federal prison for your own protection. Even there you'll need to be kept in solitary confinement because the other prisoners will be Americans, real Americans, and they'll hate you enough to kill you. Me, I'd release you into the general prison population and watch you die in twenty-four hours, but we Americans are too softhearted so you'll live. If you can call it living. Give us what we want, Deefus, and you can leave here to begin again in some other cell stateside where the climate is kinder and the treatment is gentler. Cooperation would be your best option, believe me." He stood up. "I'm a man of my word, so you get your TV."

He left me soaked in piss and not able to move a muscle. I heard him close and lock the door. He switched on the TV out there in the corridor and walked away. I heard a voice talking about something but could not take it in. This had got to be the worst single moment in my life, lying in the piss of three men and staring at the ceiling. No shower and change of outfit and no meal too, but I only half expected these things. I did not expect to get pissed on like this. The shame of it was terrible, enough to make me cry if I was not so strung out about all the other things they did to me. They had done so much I could not cry about it, only lie there feeling like this is all a nightmare happening while I'm asleep or something. But it is not.

After awhile I could move again and sit up, then a little while later I could stand up. I took off the stinking orange jumpsuit and flung it in the corner, then I sat there naked and watched some sitcom rerun with my eyes but not with my brain, if you know what I mean. Then it was over and here's the late news. About three items in there's something about me, with pictures taken from that interview with Sharon Ziegler for Channel 12, only it's not really about me, it's about Feenie Myers. When the FBI set up the fake breakout they must've followed the car all the way to Denver as well as following me to Kansas City, because they interviewed Feenie after they caught up with the hitchhiker guy, Wendell Aymes, and he told them who he's supposed to deliver the car to, which is Feenie. So here's Feenie now getting interviewed, and she's saying that she remembers me from Kit Carson High but we were never friends and "Odell Deefus couldn't even *spell* terrorist, let alone *be* one, it's just ridiculous," which is a pretty nice thing to say, so thank you, Feenie. She looked a lot different to when I remember her back in school, with this wild hair and nose-ring now, a real college student type. They went on to say that I'm helping the FBI with its investigation, which is not true, the FBI got left behind when I got on the plane with Pitface, but I guess nobody told the news people about this.

Then I got a real shock because there's my old man walking fast away from the cameras with reporters asking him to comment about his terrorist son, only he doesn't want to and all he'll say over his shoulder is, "I don't know anything about him, I don't know anything about him," which was probably a true statement that could've been made years ago. And that's all there was about me, not much more than a minute and most of it bullshit.

I kind of drifted off again for the rest of the news, then perked up again when Preacher Bob come on with his Friday night show. He's pretty damn agitated tonight, jerking his glasses around and he kicked the little Bible platform one time by accident he's so upset, and here's the reason why. "My friends," he says, "those of you who tuned in last week would have heard me say some words of praise for Senator Leighton Ketchum, words that most of you out there would have been in agreement with. His suitability for the post of President is what I'm talking about here. That's my opinion on the matter and I make no pretense of not feeling that way. That's free speech the last I heard, something we're all entitled to in this great land of ours. Free speech, it's in the Bill of Rights. But you know what I discovered, friends? I discovered there are forces at work within our society to curtail that right. You've no doubt heard that odious phrase, 'separation of Church and State,' and thought, like I did, that this doesn't mean I can't express my opinion inside my own house of worship. But that's exactly what these malign forces are suggesting to me through my lawyer. Oh yes, I have a lawyer. I have Jesus Christ beside me at all times, but for certain earthly matters it's best to rely on your attorney."

That got him a good laugh from the congregation. He twirled his glasses and let them fall against his chest on their little chain and gripped his Bible hard. "Every law worth listening to and obeying is found within these covers! There are other laws we must respect, of course, as well as those laws handed down to us from God by way of Moses. Good laws, fine laws, sensible laws for the most part. But, my friends, all of these man-made laws are open to ... *interpretation*. Yes they are. And one man will interpret them thisaway and another man will interpret that very same law thataway. And there you have the seeds of discord nicely planted among us."

He walked around a little while, thinking hard. Preacher Bob does this real good, you can almost see the thoughts pouring through his brain just from that crease he gets down his forehead. He looks up all of a sudden and says, "Secular law says I can't say that about Senator Ketchum because it's a political opinion, and political opinions have no place in the house of God. You know what, folks? I take exception to that interpretation, I surely do. I take *ex-ception* to that because I know in my heart – which belongs to the Lord my God – that some political matters *transcend* the label 'political' and are the very *essence* of God's work. We are surrounded by enemies of the state, my friends, and at their mercy when they explode bombs among us without warning. Those bombs are *political statements* in the mind of a terrorist, but the evil behind them is *religious* in nature, being as it were *inspired* by a certain *religion* that is not our own. But, of course, I can't say what that particular religion calls itself. I spoke its name last week and have got myself into hot water over that also. Tonight I'll be *diplomatic* and not speak its name. I can't state plainly and openly its name because if I did so, folks, there would be blood-letting across the world. You know what I'm talking about, yes you do. Everyone knows what I'm talking about ... but we *can't talk about it!* How about that for a conundrum, my friends. We know something bad is smelling up the planet but we dare not speak its name because to do so will create riots and revenge attacks and outrage that will spill innocent blood. Because evil does not like to hear itself spoken of with disdain. Evil is offended by that. *Evil*, the practitioners of that other religion would have us believe, is *sensitive*, and will have its finer feelings *offended* by a bald statement of truth!"

They all agreed with that and give Preacher Bob a fine hand of applause to keep him going. He waited till they're all calmed down again, then he says, "So the forces at large in the world, both here and abroad, my friends, are telling me – telling *you* – that we must not speak our minds for fear of a bloody result, an incident – many incidents – of carnage that would be avoided by keeping our mouths shut. I ask you this – is there any real difference between those voices overseas telling me to keep my mouth shut and those voices here at home telling me the same thing? Can you see any difference?" The congregation could not, no way, and Bob goes on. "So this thing that we call free speech, this thing *sanctified* in the Bill of Rights, is in fact a will-o'-the-wisp, a thing that isn't really there, or there part of the time but not there all of the time, according to your politics. This very day, my friends, *this very day* I have been informed by certain members of Congress that what I did last week was not allowable under the law of this land. That I cannot and must not endorse a political candidate for the highest office over the airwaves because this violates the *separation* of Church and State. I have been warned, my friends, that if I persist in doing this I will be audited by the Internal Revenue! They say I'll have the tax-exempt status of my business – which I remind you is also *God's* business – removed! *Removed!* They think they can dictate to a man of principle simply by way of the office they were elected to by the good people of America. Well, I have got news for them. The good people of America will not take kindly to having their churches messed with by the Internal Revenue! Remove our tax-exempt status? I'd like to see 'em try!

"Americans are not cowed by threats, not even by explosions in our midst as happened in Kansas just four days ago. That was a bomb went off by mistake, I think that's plain. Who knows what its intended target might have been. I do know this much, friends. If that bomb had gone off as planned right next to the target of choice, Americans would have died by the hundreds, if not the thousands. They are not done with us yet, those terrorists. That bomb in Kansas proves it. That bomb, my friends, was our latest wakeup call. And I make the following statement to our elected representatives in Washington as *their* wakeup call. I say to them – we will not defeat this implacable foe by dividing our house! We will only survive this onslaught from within and without by electing men of purpose and will and grit! We will not survive by endlessly talking and accommodating and backing down before our enemies! America must realize, once and for all, where its destiny lies!"

They just loved Preacher Bob for what he says, and it sounded good to me too, only I didn't get to hear more because one of the soldiers comes along then and switches off the TV and picks it up to take away. I told him, "The Lieutenant said I could have that," and he says back at me, "Lieutenant Harding just now said Go get that TV, you've had enough." And away he went with it. That's all I got, less than an hour. Listening to Preacher Bob, I felt like joining the

Army all over again to defend America against all those crazies that want to kill us and change us into Islamites, but now with the TV gone it made me think how shitty it'd be to serve under someone like Harding. Playtime is over and I'm a prisoner again.

I didn't know what time it was, but Preacher Bob's show comes on late so it's getting near midnight now. I got to this place before dawn and went through a whole lot of bad shit already. I did not earn any of this except by being dumb, not mean, but nobody will believe this. Getting punished for being dumb is not fair, but so what, it's happening anyhow so I have just got to tough this situation out and hope someone gets through to Preacher Bob and Chet about me. Those two will get me out of here even if nobody else gives a damn. If I was the praying kind I would send a prayer asking them to hurry up and spring me before I get stomped down into a greasy spot on the floor here. I bet Bob would tell me I had to have faith, and I do, I have got faith in Bob and Chet. They are real men that know who I am and have been friendly. I could not send a prayer to God instead of them, because if he's there, God is too busy with the big jobs like keeping all those planets and stars and so forth from bumping into each other out in space. So I have just got these two on my team, but it's enough to let me lay down all stinking and naked and turn my face away from the light and slide away into sleep at last.

EIGHTEEN

Lieutenant Harding woke me up so I guessed it's morning now. He says, "Today we've got outdoor activity scheduled, Deefus. How do you feel about getting out of this place for awhile?"

"That'll be good," I said.

"Don't make predictions," he says, but he's smiling, so maybe it will be okay, you can't tell with someone like this that thinks I'm his enemy.

He handed me a fresh jumpsuit and I put it on, then he had me handcuffed and blackbagged and taken along the corridor by two soldiers holding onto my arms. I heard a door open and the heat outside hit me like I walked into an oven. I had not been given breakfast but it must be way past early morning for the day to be this hot already, so this is punishment after all, this outdoor activity with no food inside me. But I expected that so it's not so bad. If I had believed

Harding's smile I would be feeling twice as bad.

I could feel rough ground through the soles of my slippers which are real thin. The soldiers guided me to a spot and told me to get down on my knees, which I did and felt gravel digging into my knees through the jumpsuit. My hands are behind me and all I can see is blackness from the black bag, but I can feel the ground beneath me and the sun overhead. That is some powerful object they have got overhead in the tropics, not like the sun at home. This is like a sledgehammer that someone heated up in a forge before they hung it in the sky for those rays to come down hot and hard on my back and shoulders and head which has got no hat on it, just the black bag, but maybe this is giving me protection. Already my toes are cramping from being folded like they are in those thin slippers, and my knees are telling me to get up off that hard gravel.

"This is rest period," one of the soldiers says to me, "so you just rest there awhile. If you move, that means you're not resting, and that's against the rules, so don't do that."

"Okay," I said.

He give me a kick. "You don't speak unless we ask a question, asshole."

"Okay."

He kicked me again and the other one says, "This guy's a fuckwit."

"Ain't he, though. Hey, fuckwit, where's it say in the Koran about how it's okay to blow up women and babies? Go ahead and answer."

"I never read it."

"No? Maybe you can't read."

"I've read *The Yearling* sixteen times..."

He kicked me again. "I didn't ask you a question!"

"Here's a question," says the other one. "How come an American turns into a Muslim? How come you did that, you and Dean Lowry?"

"I didn't, and Dean didn't either, not really, he just acted like he was to make his aunt mad at him."

"That is one bucket-of-shit answer. You think you'd be here now if you weren't a terrorist for Allah? What the fuck for if you're not? And Lowry, how come he's in the news for wanting to kill that senator if he's not a Muslim?"

"I don't know."

"You don't know? Fuck, man, you'd be about the dumbest terrorist we got here."

"How many have you got?"

The other one kicked me. "We didn't ask you a question!"

I put a lock on my lip and kept on kneeling there, wishing I'd had a good long drink of water from my basin before they brung me out here because that sun is strong, but they didn't tell me I'd be kneeling under this kind of heat so I didn't. They should have told me but they don't care, I'm just this crazy Muslim bomber that's threatening to blow up women and children.

"Hey, Deefus, that chick on the news, she acts like you don't impress her at all."

I didn't say anything.

"Deefus, you fuckin' deaf?"

"No, you didn't ask me a question."

"I just asked if you're fuckin' deaf, dumbo. You didn't hear me ask that?"

"The time before..."

"The fuckin' time before I asked...whatever I asked. Now I wanna know how come that chick on the TV news says you can't even spell but you told us you can read, huh? How come?"

The second one says, "Did you fuck her in school, Deefus? She looks like she'd take on a pile of shit like you. So did you?"

I didn't like it that they're badmouthing Feenie that way. Feenie told the whole world she doesn't think I'm a terrorist, so it isn't right to be talking about her like this.

The first one shouts in my ear, "Hey, Deefus! You go deaf on me again?"

"No."

"So how about this chick? Was she a dirty-talker on the phone like your 'fiancée,' huh? She make you come on the phone, huh? How come your 'fiancée' talks dirty to other men, Deefus? She don't get enough real dick from you, huh? Huh? Answer me, you fuckin' freak!"

"Go fuck yourself."

Well, that was not the right answer. They kicked me down from my knees onto my side and kept on kicking, but it seemed to me like they're not putting much effort into it. Maybe I'm getting used to punishment so it doesn't seem so bad, or maybe it's just so hot out here they haven't got the strength. After a dozen or so kicks each they quit.

"Gimme a smoke," says one.

"Filter tip or plain?" says the other, and they both yukked and yukked, then the first one says, "Just regular, bro."

I heard them both light up and blow smoke. Me, I'm happy lying on the ground sideways and getting the pressure off my knees and toes. These bozos have done me a favor but they're too dumb to know it.

"Jeez, I hate this fuckin' place."

"Yeah, rotate me, baby."

"We should just kill 'em all and go home."

"Put me down for that."

They smoked awhile, then one says, "Okay, Deefus, on your feet."

I stood up and the other one says, "Rest period's over, now you got to get some exercise. What kind we want you to do is the song and dance kind. You know how to sing and dance, Deefus?"

"No."

"Well, you better fuckin' learn real fast, my friend. We don't care what kinda song and dance, but you gotta do it, do it now, my man."

"Do it," says the other one, "or we'll make you kneel on hot asphalt all fuckin' day while we stand over in the shade and have us a nice cold beer."

"Start now," says the first one.

I did not want to kneel on hot asphalt all day, so I started shuffling around and singing, kind of. What I sang was, "I'm a little teapot short and stout, Here is my handle, Here is my spout..." I couldn't do the handle and spout part with my arms because I'm handcuffed, so I just sung those same words over and over and shuffled around. They laughed their heads off and told me I'm a fucking great dancer and singer too and keep it up or else, so I did, singing it over and over till I tripped over my own feet and fell down. That got them laughing again and they lit more smokes, letting me lie there like before, which was better than the singing and dancing.

Then one of them says, "Shit, here comes the dork."

I heard footsteps coming closer, then Lieutenant Harding's voice says, "That man is supposed to be on his knees, not resting on his side."

"He just now fell over, sir."

"Deefus, stand up, you've got a phone call."

I'm thinking to myself, Sure I have, maybe more dirty talk on tape from Lorraine.

"Get up and take this call!"

I got up and he tells them to uncuff me, which they did, then this little phone with the lid open gets put in my hand. So this is real, I'm thinking. Who the hell is calling me here? I put it up to my head inside the bag.

"Hello?"

"Odell, this is Agent Kraus. How you doing there?"

"Okay. It's hot."

"No kidding. Well, the heat's off you here. We've located Dean's body."

"Where I said he was?"

"No, in Hays City."

"How'd he get there?"

"Your house was being closely watched, Odell. That same afternoon you dug up Dean and relocated him you were under observation through binoculars by Donnie D and his drug-pushing buddy Marcus Andrew Markham – aka, Marky Mark. Ever heard of him?"

"No."

"They were intrigued by what they saw, so that night when you were out with Donnie and Lorraine getting cash from the ATM in town, Markham dug Dean up and drove him away.

They thought you murdered Dean and were going to turn you in for the reward while denying any involvement with Dean themselves. Donnie broke after we showed him that ATM photo. You'll be brought back here for further questioning about the murder. You still maintain that you killed Dean and buried him?"

"By accident."

"Forensics have confirmed he died from a blow to the head, but his skull is abnormally thin."

"Told you. Hey, did this Marky guy see who put the truck in the driveway? That would've been happening around the same time as he's digging up Dean."

"No, he drove up to the house, went around back to get the body and drove out the same way. The truck was delivered later, maybe just minutes later. There's something else. These calls you claimed to have received from so-called Agent Jim Ricker, do you stick by that story?"

"He called me, like I said."

"We've re-examined our recordings and discovered several anomalies. You know what that means?"

"It's … a sea creature with lots of little wavy arms. But not a fish."

"Traces of interference we didn't notice before, like someone had a new kind of scrambler. We'll need to talk to you about that as well. How are they treating you there?"

"Okay, I guess."

"Good. Well, I just wanted to let you know your story is now more or less accepted and you'll be booked for homicide, not terrorism. Congratulations."

"Thank you."

"Put the officer back on."

"Agent Kraus? Did Lorraine get her dope-trafficking charges dropped for going along with that phony breakout? I think it's good if she did. I don't bear her any grudge. And is it true about her doing certain things with Chief Webb when she's, uh, too young? She told me that's why she's busting me out, to get back at him about that, but maybe it was a lie to make everything seem more real. It's none of my business, I'd just like to know."

"Those allegations are part of an ongoing investigation, so I can't discuss them. Put the officer back on."

"I don't bear a grudge against Donnie D neither. He was just concerned about Dean, I guess."

"Odell, put the officer on right now."

"Okay, bye." I held out the phone. "For you, Lieutenant."

He took it off me and listened, then he says, "Right away."

I heard the phone snap shut. Harding says, "Take him inside."

Which they did, and when I'm in my cell and the black bag was took off they told me I can have a shower, which I did and it felt great. Then they give me back my clothes that I come in and my sneakers, even give me back the money I had. Then they brung in breakfast, eggs, bacon, raisin toast and waffles, plus coffee. It's like I've gone from being a piece of shit to a VIP all of a sudden, which I know I have got Agent Kraus to thank for this.

Midmorning along comes Chaplain Turner with my Bible. He looked real surprised to see me wearing regular clothing and not the orange jumpsuit. He says, "The Lieutenant told me you wouldn't be needing this, but he didn't say why. Has something changed here?"

"I'm going home."

"Really, and why is that?"

"They swapped the charge from terrorism to homicide."

"Oh."

"But I expect that'll get changed again to manslaughter because it was accidental. I just need to explain to them about that."

"I see. So you won't be needing this?" He held up the Bible. It looked new.

"Not now. They won't think I'm a Muslim now that I'm not a terrorist anymore."

"Is that the only reason you wanted it, to look less like a Muslim?"

"Uhuh."

He looked disappointed. "You told me you were a lapsed Christian."

"What kind is that? I think I'm supposed to be a Pisscapalian. That's what my mom was when she's little, but my dad talked her out of it."

"It's never too late," he says, and put the Bible through the bars, which I took it out of politeness and took a peek inside to see if it's the kind with pictures. I recall seeing one of those with pictures of Jesus with long gold hair and eyes blue as the sky. He looked like a Viking in a bathrobe. But this one has not got the pictures.

"Thank you," I told him. He's looking at my face all swole up like it is, and I know he wants to ask about that, but he doesn't. I said, "Did you talk to Preacher Bob about me?"

"Preacher Bob? No, I thought you were joking."

"Well, it doesn't matter now, I'm going home. That means I

can still go to the big show he's got planned in Topeka for July Fourth."

"I've heard about that. It should be quite spectacular. Well, take care, and study that book, it'll make a huge difference in your life."

He's probably right about that. Dean's Koran made a big difference in my life and I didn't even read a single word from it, just picked it up a couple times, so these religion books are dynamite. Chaplain Turner shook my hand very friendly and I said, "Can you ask the Lieutenant or someone on the way out if I can get let out of this cell now that I'm not a terrorist? They didn't say yet how long till I'm outta here."

"I'll ask," he says, and away he goes.

Ten minutes later Harding comes to visit. He says, "You won't be permitted out of that cell until it's time to leave. There's a flight stateside this evening. Until then you have to remain where you are. This is a military facility, strictly off limits if you aren't one of us."

"Just a couple weeks ago I was thinking about joining up."

"Is that right. I'd forget that idea if I were you, Deefus, you're not suitable."

"Uh, why not?"

He studied me awhile then says, "You're too peculiar. We get peculiar types once in a while and we iron out their wrinkles, but with you...I don't know, there's just something not right. Forget the military, get a job with some city council emptying trash cans, that's my recommendation to you."

"Thank you, I'll think about that."

"And stay away from Muslims. That's what got you into trouble."

"I will, definitely."

"Would you like the TV again? That'll help pass the time till your release."

"Okay."

He went away. He was a lot nicer to me now after Agent Kraus's phone call. That was like a phone call from those people that tell you you just won the lottery or whatever. It changed everything, and I intended saying a big Thank you to Kraus next time I get to see him. You might say I have won the lottery, getting out of here and not having people think I'm a terrorist now, just a criminal.

The TV got brung back by Fogler, who has got this red welt across his throat from the baton. He unlocked the door and shoved it at me. I took it and he says, "You ain't left yet, not till tonight."

"I know."

"So there's still time," he says.

"To do what?"

"Be afraid," he says.

He means afraid of him, it's there in his face. I didn't like to hear that kind of talk from someone obnoxious as Fogler so I told him, "Okay then," and give him a slit-eyed mean look to follow up. He give something similar back to me and went away.

I switched on the TV but it's all soaps and stuff this time of day, so I switched it off again and thought maybe the time has come to dip into the Bible like everyone says you ought to for the good of your soul. I opened it up just anywhere and started to read. Only I didn't get far. This has got to be a book for geniuses, because I can't seem to follow more than a few words at a time without getting lost and thinking, What does that mean? I tried for ten minutes to make sense of this one little section and had to give it up. That made me feel like I must be an idiot like some people have said now and then about me, which made me sad, but this is not my fault, just the way I am, which I did not choose to be this way.

I thought about emptying trash cans and felt sad again. Maybe I should go back to the grain silo when all this other stuff is fixed up and they let me go. Or maybe they won't, and my next job will be in prison sewing mailbags or making license plates, that's what I heard they do in there. That made me even sadder thinking about it. I could always get a job as a dishwasher, anyone with two arms can. There would be something I can do, but not in Callisto. I don't ever want to go back there. That has been a bad luck place for me. Most of all I didn't want to bump into Lorraine again after what I learned about her and Cole, and her and Chief Webb if that part is true, but mainly her and Cole. I have gone and closed my heart against Lorraine after that, not that she would give a damn what I'm feeling anyway. That woman was a fake friend for sure.

Lunch was chicken in a basket, very tasty and plenty of it. I felt better about things after that, and started wondering if I'll still be here for supper or maybe they'll feed me on the plane. I wanted to be back in America. I didn't like this place. They have hit me too much here for me ever to like it even if the food is good. After I'm done eating I had myself a good long nap to make up for yesterday when they're too busy torturing me. That's what that was, those things that happened. I always thought torture is some guy in a long black robe with a pointy

hat shoving irons into a fire till they're red hot and then poking them in your eyes, or getting pulled apart by horses or
whatever. But that's just the old-fashioned way, I guess.
Nowadays they don't want to go to all that trouble of heating
up coals in a climate like this, that would be too sweaty and
would leave marks. Punching the shit out of a guy with the
gloves, that's the way to go. Lots of pain and swelling but nothing that'll show after a few days, so that was smart.

That was some nap I had because next thing here comes
dinner – steak! Maybe this was done special for me to say
Sorry About The Torture, or maybe the soldiers get this regular. I ate it down whichever, then watched some TV news but
there's nothing about me or Dean's body getting discovered at
last but plenty about the election, with both sides sniping at
each other like always. Me, I never once voted, but if Preacher
Bob says Senator Ketchum is the one to go with, I figure I owe
it to Bob for his kindness etcetera to do that if he says to.
Preacher Bob would know more about politics than me.
Come to think of it, anyone would. Sometimes you just have
to trust the brain of somebody smarter than you, which that
is the case here, I think, so most likely I'll do that and be taking part in politics the first time ever, which everyone should
do this that can vote. There are countries where you can't vote
and are stuck with the same evil bozos forever, so our way is
better.

Around eight-thirty two soldiers and Lieutenant Harding
come to escort me out of there. Harding says to me, "Deefus,
we've never before had someone stay with us so short a time.
Just to make sure there's been no misunderstanding, I'd like
your signature on this." He hands me a piece of paper which it

says very simple that I did not suffer any ill treatment while in the custody of the United States of America and do so hereby declare same.

"You guys punched the shit out of me," I said.

"That was a mistake based on an erroneous communication. We were told you're a terrorist. I think you'd agree that if you *were* a terrorist you deserved what you got and much more besides. As an American, don't you want your armed forces to protect you?"

"Uhuh."

"That's what we were doing. It was a miscommunication. Sign there."

He handed me a pen. I looked at it and I looked at the paper, then at Harding.

"But I'm not a terrorist, I'm an accidental murderer."

"Then consider yourself lucky you didn't get what those others are getting, or for anywhere near as long. Count your blessings, Deefus. A foreign government acting on the mistaken belief that you're a terrorist would have done terrible things to extract a confession. Fortunately you came to us. Sign right there and you're on your way."

I took the pen but still didn't sign. It didn't seem right somehow.

"There's a plane waiting, Deefus, a plane laid on especially for you. Do you know the cost of a run between here and Miami? Thousands of taxpayers' dollars are being spent to get you back where you belong. We've wasted time and effort on you that should have been spent on other individuals that *are* terrorists. Don't waste any more of our valuable time, Deefus – sign."

So I did. I signed at the bottom of the paper very scrawly so it's hard to read. I signed it Odouell Derfuse so it isn't legal. Harding gave it a glance and he's satisfied.

"Blindfold," he says.

One of the soldiers blindfolded me and I got led away outside and put in the back seat of a Humvee alongside of another soldier and we drove away from there, which made me happy even if I can't see a thing. We drove a longer time than when we come here, so they must have taken me another way than before, and then I can smell that airport smell of aviation gas and hear a chopper coming in to land. The Humvee stops.

They brung me out and marched me across some smooth asphalt and a soldier says, "There's a ramp coming up." My foot touched the edge of something hard and sloping upwards, so this is the ramp. The other soldier says in my ear, "So long, Doofus," and punched me so hard in the gut I folded over. I knew that voice, it's Fogler.

"What's going on down there?" another voice calls out.

"Prisoner stumbled, sir."

"Get him up here."

They marched me up this metal ramp, not steps like you'd expect to get into a plane, and I got sat onto this chair still with the blindfold on and they buckled some kind of hard leather cuffs around my wrists and ankles. "Safety measure," says another voice to me. "Got to make sure you arrive at the other end safe and sound. Can't have you bouncing around in here. The blindfold comes off when we're airborne."

"Okay."

I could hear more voices around me, then there's the

sound of hydraulic pressure lines as the ramp comes up and the airport sounds outside were cut off as it closed, so I'm guessing I'm inside a big C-130 transporter. All the noises I can hear now are inside, and they sound hollow, like there's a lot of empty space around me. Then the engines start up, four of them, and they were loud! They built up to a kind of whistling roar and we started moving. I could hear voices talking but only just, it's so loud in there. We got to rolling a whole lot faster, then stopped and swung around, I could feel that, then the engines got cranked up even more and we started moving fast with all the vibration coming to me through the seat I'm buckled into. This was a whole different experience to my other plane ride in the little jet but kind of fun too same as that one. Then the plane lifted off and everything got smooth again. We climbed higher for maybe ten minutes then leveled out with the engines throttled back.

Someone come up to me and took off the blindfold. It's a guy in a one-piece flying suit with a helmet. He says to me, shouting above the engine noise, "No in-flight movie! No meal!"

"Okay!"

"Enjoy the ride!"

"Can you take these off?" I'm talking about the restrainer cuffs.

"No can do!" he says. "Regulations!"

He went away. There's no one else aboard, it looks like, just me inside this big huge space with lights here and there glowing very dim, so it's like being inside a metal cave with this droning roaring sound everywhere. There's no windows to look out of so nothing to do, just sit there and feel everything shudder and shake. I could hear voices way off in the front where the pilots are, so they don't sit behind closed doors like pilots in an airliner do, but no one come near me after the blindfold got took off. I'm going to Miami, Harding said. That's somewhere I never went before, so this is good.

I bet Kraus and Deedle are waiting there to take me into custody. I have still got this problem about killing Dean, so that is not so good, but now they know Dean had got this thin skull that broke easy. That's what they call extenderating circumstances, which is a fancy name for something that shouldn't have happened and was never meant deliberate. Maybe this will mean they go easy on me with the man-slaughter charge, I hope so. Maybe I can call Feenie Myers to be my character witness seeing as she already said on the news she doesn't think I'm a terrorist. If she takes her nose-ring out and combs her hair nice the court will most likely believe her. I couldn't think who else will speak up for me. Not having friends is a big problem sometimes.

I can't say how long we're in the air when the same guy come back to me with a headset and plug-in jack in his hand.

"Call for you," he says, and put the headset over my ears and plugged the wire into something in the wall behind me, then he goes away. There's a little mike on a rod curving in front of my face to speak into, but so far nothing in my ears except static.

"Hello?"

I'm expecting it'll be Agent Kraus same as this morning, checking up to see that I'm okay and maybe he'll have more news about developments behind the scenes, as they say.

"Hello?"

The static cleared and a voice come through very clear, only it isn't Kraus.

"Odell?"

"Uhuh…"

"Jim Ricker. Can you hear me okay?"

"Uhuh…"

"Heard they put you through the wringer down there. Did they make you sign a paper says they didn't lay a finger on you?"

"Uhuh…"

"That's their style. Don't worry about that. You're off the hook, my friend."

"The hook?"

"Free and clear. This is a private conversation, Odell. Even the guys up in the cockpit can't hear this, okay? This is strictly between you and me and the bird on the wire. All charges against you have been dropped. Not just the terrorism and conspiracy charge, not just the involvement in drugs, I'm talking about murder or manslaughter charges pertaining to the death of Dean Lowry. That's all gone away. I just found out myself."

"But…how come?"

"Let's go back a little way. That letter you wrote to Condi Rice, it came into the possession of the FBI thanks to the guy who stole Dean's truck on behalf of a third party. He took the letter out of curiosity when he saw who it's addressed to. This guy, you don't need to know his name, he's a professional car thief. When he delivered the vehicle to the party paying him to steal it, he kept that letter. When he read it he offered it to the Bureau for a reward because your name and Dean's name were in the news. That started wheels turning. Are you following this, Odell?"

"Uhuh."

"When Dean's body wasn't where you said in the letter the federal boys were very annoyed with you. Everything you told them was suspect after that. They staged a breakout for you but you figured that out and went the other way, only they had you covered for separation from the getaway vehicle and followed along. By then they're figuring you had no idea where to go, no terrorist buddies to turn to, just a scared rabbit going this way and that. So they picked you up again for some hard grilling to make you fess up, which you and I know was a pure waste of time. Still with me?"

"Uhuh."

"Meantime, heads are being scratched when the guy with the letter got brought in for interrogation. He broke down and put investigators on the trail of his employer, the one who had him steal the truck. Guess who that was?"

"I...don't know."

"Ask yourself this. Why did Chet Marchand tell you to leave your phone in the truck the day of the funeral?"

"To...not to have it ring while the funeral's happening."

"Odell, all you need to do to avoid that is switch the damn thing off. He wanted you to leave the phone in the truck so they could use it to trigger the bomb their people planted. If bits of the phone survived the blast it'd lead to you, the friend of a Muslim terrorist, Dean Lowry. That's what they thought he was then. No one in law enforcement thinks that about him now. Dean Lowry the dope pusher and all-round idiot, that's the thinking now."

"But...why would Chet want to blow me up?"

"Chet went to Callisto looking for a patsy, someone to

blame for a terror attack. He knew Dean Lowry was messing with Islam because his aunt wrote a letter to Preacher Bob about him. Dean was the target, the one to befriend so his truck could be used as a terror bomb. Only trouble was, Dean was already dead, thanks to you, but Chet didn't know this and started making himself your buddy. When he found out Dean's disappeared and you're available instead, he passed on Dean's role as patsy to you, thinking you're a nobody that no one's going to miss."

"Chet...?"

"Yeah, Chet, mister nice guy churchgoing friend of Preacher Bob. Put it together, Odell. Bob Jerome wanted Leighton Ketchum in the White House, but enthusiasm for the mess in Iraq has divided the nation. What does Bob need to increase the senator's chances for election? He needs another 9-11 to make the people mad, to make them vote for the guy who's a hardliner on terrorism. Remember the invitation to Bob's big meeting in Topeka on July Fourth? That's when the bomb was supposed to go off. Too bad you got the bright idea of calling your own phone to see if it's still in the truck. Kaboom! End of Bob's homegrown terror attack plan. I'm thinking the phone was supposed to be switched off until you got to Topeka, then someone would've snuck under your truck to activate it for the big rally. They fucked up and left it switched on. You saved hundreds, maybe thousands of lives by detonating that bomb ahead of schedule, Odell."

"I did?"

"You're the invisible hero, my man. Preacher Bob and Chet Marchand have denied any knowledge of this, and there's no way they can be indicted because the evidence against them is purely circumstantial. If Senator Ketchum was in on the scheme, and his phone records between Washington and Topeka indicate he was, there's nothing he can do now except run with no terrorist attack to boost his chances. He knows we know and he's running scared. You did that, Odell, thwarted a plot that would have made the Oklahoma City bombing look like a rehearsal for the real thing. Take a bow."

"I..."

"Now, listen up. All of this is strictly confidential, not for public consumption. I'm not even supposed to tell *you*, but I'm going out on a limb because I don't like to see a decent guy left in the dark. This call is not happening. It's not happening because nobody on the entire planet can intercept and record these words you're hearing. I want you to make me a promise, Odell. I want you to promise me never to speak of this to anyone. Nothing about Preacher Bob or Chet Marchand or Senator Ketchum. Ever. To anyone. Make that promise to me, Odell. Make it now."

"I...promise."

"Speaking out would only fuck you up at this stage. You're no longer being charged in the death of Dean Lowry because Dean Lowry has officially been declared missing, not dead. He's still a hunted man even though his body has already been destroyed. Donnie D and Marky Mark have been given some dough and told to leave Kansas. If they talk about what they know – and they don't know even a fraction of what I'm telling you now, Odell – they'll be eliminated. They know this and believe it. Your girlfriend and her prison guard back-door man have been let off the charges pending against them just to keep every aspect of the story quiet. Don't go near either one again. This is the compromise my bosses worked out. Preacher Bob has ducked for cover big time. If Dean is thought to be still out there, a homegrown Muslim terrorist boogeyman, Ketchum still has a chance, maybe. Me, I think he's already toast. A big plot has been reduced to a small plot. That's the way it goes. You're in the clear. None of this ever happened. All you need to do now is go far away and keep your head down. Find a small job in a small town and zip that lip. We'll be watching, wherever you go. There were those that proposed eliminating you, Odell, but I spoke out against that, I want you to know. Don't disappoint me."

"I ... I won't."

"That's good. That's the sensible thing to do. Any questions?"

"Uh, no ..."

"There'll be one final message from your government to you, then it's all over."

"Message?"

"So long, Odell. You made your mark. Too bad no one'll ever know."

"Uh ... Jim?"

"What?"

"Uh ... who do you work for? Agent Deedle said to me you're not with Homeland Security. Was he lying?"

"Odell, have you ever heard the expression 'wheels within wheels?'"

"No."

"Well, one day you will, and then you'll understand, maybe."

"But ... who do you work for?"

"The good guys," he says.

There's a click and my ears filled with static again. The guy in the helmet come along a minute later and took off the headset. "Did the call get through?" he asks. "We couldn't hear jack shit up front."

"No, it . . . all I could hear was buzzing."

"Maybe they'll try again."

He took the headset away. I sat looking at the opposite wall, thinking about everything Jim Ricker told me, trying to believe it. If Jim Ricker was speaking the truth then everything that happened to me made sense, kind of. I had been in the middle of Something Big and Bad and never knew it. A long time ago I saw this old silent movie on TV with this guy walking through a town being blown apart by a windstorm, but no matter how many buildings fell down right next to him or even on top of him, he never got touched out of sheer dumb luck. It was real funny. I am that guy, lucky and dumb. I didn't know what to think about all of this, still trying to swallow it down, all those things Jim Ricker told me. And what was this final message from my government to me? The guy in the helmet didn't bring the headset back, so maybe the message would be waiting for me in Miami.

I'm still considering all this when two guys in flying suits and helmets come along from the front of the plane and started unbolting my seat from the wall with a couple big wrenches. They didn't say anything, just worked at those bolts. Finally I asked them, "What are you doing?"

"Orders," says one of them.

They lifted my seat away from the wall and carried it to the back of the plane where the loading ramp is and set me down, then did something behind the seat, I couldn't see what. They passed a wide belt around my waist from behind and cinched it tight. Then they started checking the wrist and ankle cuffs. "What are you doing?" I asked them again, but they didn't say anything this time.

They went either side of the ramp and put on harnesses like you see on a parachutist, with cables attaching them to the walls, then one of them goes to a control box on the wall and does something there. Even over the roar of the engines I could hear the sound of hydraulic lines as the ramp started lowering itself. I knew the ramp could do this even in flight because I saw a movie about a Navy SEAL team on a secret mission that parachuted out of a C-130 from the open ramp.

It took maybe a minute to be lowered all the way, and the wind coming through from the outside got stronger and louder the lower the ramp got, until you could've screamed in there and nobody would've heard a thing, there's so much noise coming from outside, the engines roaring and the wind howling past like it is. My hair is real short but I could feel it twisting around on my head as I looked out at the night sky, very bright with stars and moonlight all around, even beautiful.

The two guys come back and steadied my seat, which was wobbling crazy from all that wind whipping around in there. One of them puts his mouth close to my ear and yells, "We have to do this! Nothing personal intended! Okay?"

I didn't know what he meant. They took hold of my seat, one on each side, and lifted it, not so easy with all that buffeting and blowing going on, then they carried me closer to the edge of the ramp, like they want me to see the view even better than before, which was considerate of them but kind of scary too, because now we're on the ramp itself and there's sky either side of us and the wind and noise is terrible. I appreciated that they're giving me the kind of thrill you get on a real fast switchback roller-coaster, but my heart is hammering very hard which means I'm scared too, because the only thing keeping my seat from flying away into the sky is these two guys holding onto it with their safety harnesses connected to the walls.

"Okay!" I yelled. "Take me back!"

But they didn't take me back inside the plane. They took me further out along the ramp! All the way to the trailing edge! Down below I can see the ocean all crinkled and silver like tinfoil, and now my heart's galloping like a herd of wild horses. I felt like someone that got captured by pirates and now they're making me walk the plank, only they're doing the walking for me because I'm tied to a chair. When pirates do that there's always sharks waiting below ... And then I saw that they're not treating me to a special once-in-a-lifetime experience ... they're gonna throw me overboard, only I don't need to be worrying about sharks because the fall from this high up means I'll die when I hit that water down there ... A mile or more to gather speed and I'll hit the ocean like a melon hitting the sidewalk from the top of a skyscraper ... This is the message from my government to me ... and the message is – Fuck you, buddy, you know too much!

And then they threw me out ...

They threw me out of the plane ...

The sound of the engines got suddenly louder, then started getting quieter as I fell away from the plane, this black shape against the stars. I tumbled end over end with sky and ocean whirling all around me and one awful thought scampering around in my head like a cornered rat – I'm gonna die now, I'm gonna die…

Then there's a godawful jerk that almost yanked me out of the seat. I kept on spinning but wasn't falling anymore. Every couple of seconds I could see something snaking between me and the plane, a long way off now, and what it is is a cable. They don't want to kill me by impact with the ocean, they want to kill me with fright, or maybe they're just spinning out the suspense and after a few minutes of this they'll release the cable's other end and down I'll go again, this time all the way. I was never so scared in my life. My mouth opened and vomit flew out in a wide arc. My ass opened and filled my pants with shit. I pissed myself. I screamed like a girl. I begged them to reel me in, save me from death and I'd never ever say anything to anyone about anything, only save me, please save me save me save me…

I can't say how long I dangled in the sky, twisting and turning, but after awhile I noticed the plane is getting bigger again. I'm so dizzy by then all I can do is close my eyes to shut out the ocean and stars circling around and around that way and try to ignore the blood thundering in my ears. The plane come closer and closer as they winched me in, a spinning black cross dancing with a whirling crescent moon. By the time I could see the open ramp jutting out I'm so grateful they didn't cut the cable I'm crying and sobbing like a little kid that lost his mommy and here she is again, big and warm and rescuing me from everything dark and evil.

My seat was hit by the slipstream and twisted like a crazy thing before they could haul me in over the lip of the ramp and grab the armrests to steady me. When the seat hit the floor it was the most welcome feeling in the world. They yanked me further inside and set me down, then the ramp got raised and slowly the sky outside was shut away as it closed. My seat was picked up and taken over to the wall, where they rebolted it in place, all of this without those guys saying a word, just doing their job like it's a regular part of their duty as aircrew. I wanted to hate them but couldn't. I could only sit there in my own shit and be grateful I'm alive.

I have heard my government's message loud and clear and will not complain about bad treatment, ever. I have not been a prisoner, I have been a guest in my own room with onsweet. Thank you. I was not tortured, I was closely questioned. Thank you. I was never a suspect, only a person of interest. Thank you again. My government has taken me to a foreign shore all expenses paid, and given me a thrilling ride home again, no charge. Thank you thank you thank you.

I sat like a zombie in my special chair, my skychair, and did like Lieutenant Harding said and counted my blessings, then counted them again, and again and again till the engines were throttled back and the plane tilted sideways, lining up for an airport approach. My nose is filled with the smell of shit and piss. My mind is filled with gratitude and fear. I am very very sorry and promise I'll never ever do it again. I want all this to be over and done with. Finished. Gone.

The wheels hit the runway and we slowed way down. I'm thinking now that I'm back in the USA things will start going right for me again if I only keep my nose clean. I can't wait for us to stop rolling so I can get out of this plane, this time through a side door, I hope, and onto solid ground. But then

while we're still rolling this guy comes up to me with no helmet on, and he rolls up my shirtsleeve. He has got this little
medical kit and he swabs my arm and jabs a needle in there.

"What's this for?" I asked him.

He says, "Inoculation against tropical disease."

I should've known it's a lie because you get those shots
before you go away to those dangerous tropical-disease
places, not when you come home. I'm still thinking this when
it felt like someone pulled that black bag over my head again.

NINETEEN

It was church bells woke me. I lay there wondering if I'm in heaven I feel so calm and cozy. After awhile I sat up to see what heaven looks like. It looks like a room in a Motel 6. I looked down and I'm naked. Someone has cleaned me up so the sheets aren't stained. Over there on the stand is a brand-new suitcase I never saw before with clothes in it.

I got out of bed. Those bells were still ringing, a very restful sound. I went to the window and peeked out through the closed curtains. There's a concrete forecourt with a driveway to the street. Anywhere USA. Who brung me here? I went to the suitcase and grabbed the clothes on top. The pants felt kind of bulky so I checked out the pockets. There's a big wad of folding cash in both. I counted it out for a total of ten grand, all in crisp new hundreds. My hush money. I pulled on a shirt and reached for the brand-new sneakers beside the bed. Everything fit just right.

There's a knock at the door and a woman's voice says, "Sir, are you staying beyond noon? You need to register again if you are. Sir?"

"No!"

She went away. I closed the suitcase and went to the door. Some kind of instinct made me open it slowly, like I'm expecting a surprise party or something out there waiting to explode in my face, but there's nothing, just an empty corridor painted pink. Those church bells have stopped. I stepped out and closed the door behind me. I feel guilty, I don't know why, like I'm leaving without paying what I owe.

I walked across the forecourt, almost blinded by sunlight, and went into the Office. A lady about fifty looked up at me. She has got purple hair all piled in a heap on top of her head.

"Change your mind?" she asks.

"No. Where am I?"

"You're right here, hon."

"I mean what town."

"Your friends must've got you real merry last night. Did they run out and leave you?"

"Yep."

"Well, this here is Vero Beach."

"Florida?"

"My, you must've been having fun. Florida."

"Is there a bus station?"

"Right down the street. Your friends aren't coming back for you?"

"I hope not."

"Come stay with us again, and tell your friends. Not the bunch that left you. Other friends, okay?"

"Okay."

I walked out and hit the street, squinting hard. The first thing I'll do to break a hundred is get a bus ticket, then I'll buy some sunglasses. I followed the sidewalk with my new suitcase, every now and then looking behind me to see if I'm being followed, which I am not. There's the bus depot, which in a town this size is not large. I went inside and got a ticket to Atlanta. The guy tells me the bus will get here in around thirty minutes.

Across the street there's a gas station and convenience store. I went in and got myself a tall Coke with ice and a giant pretzel nice and hot plus shades and a baseball cap to hide my face. I also got a bunch of school notebooks with cartoon characters on the covers, and a couple ballpoint pens. They have got a newspaper stand in there too, and the headline jumped out and smacked me in the eyeball – *SENATOR KETCHUM QUITS RACE*. I read what it says underneath and it's this – the senator has decided to spend more time with his family for personal reasons which the item never did say what they are, but it's got nothing to do with the threats made by Dean Lowry, which the search for Dean goes on regardless, it says. So there you go.

I went back across the street to sit on the bench there and wait for the bus. I have never been to Atlanta, but I know I won't be stopping there to see the sights. Ten thousand dollars will get me a lot of bus tickets until I get to where I feel safe, wherever that might be. I ate that pretzel and drunk my Coke and felt better than before.

There's one question running around in my mind like a headless chicken and this is it – was Jim Ricker telling me the

truth? I just could not believe all that about Preacher Bob and
Chet. They would not do that, blow up a bunch of folks from
Preacher Bob's own flock at his own tent meeting in Topeka.
That would not happen in America except done by some
crazy person like that guy set off a bomb in Oklahoma when
I was a kid. I remember that and how nobody could believe
an American would do that. But that guy had a big chip on his
shoulder everyone said later, so that explained it. But
Preacher Bob is not that kind, so now I'm thinking Jim Ricker
got told by someone, maybe the President, to tell me lies. But
I'll never know. I tried to settle it in my mind but that headless chicken kept right on running in circles till I started
getting a headache so I quit thinking about it entirely, which
was a good thing because it made me feel better about everything. If you can't break a big rock in your path, step around it
and move on.

Here comes the bus.

Now if you have read my story this far you will have figured
out I didn't write all these words on just one bus ride. That
would be a bus ride to the moon and back. No, I begun the
writing there in Florida and kept it up through to Georgia,
then across to Mississippi, then up to Illinois. From there I
went west and kept on going till I fetched up in Oregon and
still only wrote out three and a bit chapters. I'm tired of trav-
eling by then and got myself a little room in this boarding
house in a small town that I won't say its name out of wanting
privacy for myself, you know the reason why.

So I kept up the writing, but coming near the end I asked

myself Now what? It's too long for the *New York Times* after all, much longer than I intended for it to be. So maybe I'll send it to a book publisher, or maybe just sit on it awhile and think it through, because nobody will believe this and Jim Ricker told me not to talk about what happened or else I'm in Big Trouble, and I believe him. So maybe after all my hard work setting it all down the story will just get put in the closet forever, or at least until I'm dead. Anyway, there is now other things in my life besides what happened to me before.

What happened is, I went in this barber shop for a trim and the guy there, he tells me he can't find nobody to take over his shop because all the young guys leave here for the Big Smoke and don't ever come back. Meantime, the population hereabouts keeps growing their hair so he feels like he can't quit, he's a public service now. I asked him how hard is it to be a barber and he figures he can teach someone inside of two weeks, three tops. So I said to him Okay, teach me. He says For real? I told him Yes and that's how it got started.

I learned fast and he says I'm a natural even with my big fingers. I was thinking I'd have a problem with talking to all those customers the way barbers are supposed to, and me being not much of a talker like I am, but Guido, that's the guy, he says don't worry, just let the customer do the talking if he wants to, all you have got to do is agree with whatever he's saying and everyone goes away happy. I tried this and it works! From trimming lawns I am now trimming hair, which both of these things just keep on growing so there is a lifetime of work ahead of me. Maybe I'll drop with the scissors in my hand.

Also there is this girl works in the Morning Glory Café just down the street. I get my morning cup of coffee there and she has got into the habit of talking to me. I might be wrong but I think there is interest on her side as well as mine, so Wish Me Luck, as the saying goes.

But there is one thing bothers me. Most evenings after I'm done eating I take a stroll through town for exercise. It only takes fifteen minutes to walk across town, that's how small this place is. And sometimes while I'm strolling past the one and only phone booth outside the post office the phone will ring. I know it can't be for me, even though it happens at the exact moment I'm walking by. This has happened maybe a dozen times now so this is no coincidence. I know who I don't want it to be on the other end of the line. Maybe this is his way of letting me know I have not gotten as lost as I wanted and they are watching me still, I don't know, and I'm not going to pick up that phone and find out. I figure as long as I don't touch that phone I'll be okay. I don't know why I think that way but I do.

Tonight it happened again while I'm walking over to Donna's house, that's the girl in the coffee shop. I stopped and let it ring, then I walked on. I have got better things to think about now than mysterious telephones because I am In Love.

The End